Judgment Call

THE EXONERATED

A Suspense Thriller

Book 1

By JC Ryan

This is the first book in The Exonerated Thriller Series.

Want to hear about special offers and new releases?

Sign up for my confidential mailing list www.jcryanbooks.com

Copyright 2016 by J C Ryan

This book is protected under the copyright laws of the United States of America. Any reproduction or other unauthorized use of the material or artwork herein is prohibited.

This book is a work of fiction. Names, characters, places, brands, media, and incidents are either the product of the author's imagination or are used fictitiously.

All rights reserved.

ISBN-13: 978-1532951565

ISBN-10: 1532951566

Contents

Prologue 6
Chapter 1 - To make a difference 10
Chapter 2 - There's nothing you can do 16
Chapter 3 - Looking for a good time 29
Chapter 4 - Which one was more stubborn 43
Chapter 5 - If he isn't all of those things 58
Chapter 6 - A few words with Mr. De Wit 62
Chapter 7 - Interesting 65
Chapter 8 - Going to have to wait 69
Chapter 9 - Solid facts and data 78
Chapter 10 - Young and stupid 91
Chapter 11 - Underground taxi service 101
Chapter 12 - I know a guy 107
Chapter 13 - I'm willing to accept that this is serious 117
Chapter 14 - Trembling with dread 125
Chapter 15 - It'll get worse before it gets better 131
Chapter 16 - This was serious 147
Chapter 17 - It's a long story 155
Chapter 18 - Too good of a distraction 164
Chapter 19 - The damned thing was locked 170

Chapter 20 - Following a suspect 177

Chapter 21 - This is what it must feel like 185

Chapter 22 - Two seconds away from an explosion 192

Chapter 23 - You don't gossip 198

Chapter 24 - It was a promising night 203

Chapter 25 - She didn't remember anything 207

Chapter 26 - I have already made my decision.................... 214

Chapter 27 - Poisoned?... 224

Chapter 28 - The enemy wasn't as clearly defined.............. 234

Chapter 29 - Justice by PowerPoint...................................... 237

Chapter 30 - The Honorable Judge John St. Clair................ 257

Chapter 31 - Mr. X... 272

Chapter 32 - I Know Him 288

Chapter 33 - Play stupid.. 296

Chapter 34 - I'll send you a Christmas card 305

Chapter 35 - You're quitting too 315

Chapter 36 - Forget I said anything 329

Chapter 37 - It was what'd both expected 335

Chapter 38 - It's called plausible deniability........................ 343

Chapter 39 - Have they now become our problem? 353

Chapter 40 - This was the nice meeting 362

Chapter 41 - Confessing 370

Chapter 42 - Licorice cats and bees in the snow 378
Chapter 43 - She sketched out her plan 394
Chapter 44 - And then they would all be safe 400
Chapter 45 - Abandoned 407
Chapter 46 - Staying calm 415
Chapter 47 - Keep my little girl safe 421
Chapter 48 - The sound of a lock 431
Chapter 49 - Almost family 438
Chapter 50 - If he didn't answer 441
Chapter 51 - Begun his move 447
Chapter 52 - The wall disappeared 455
Chapter 53 - If not you, then... 460
Chapter 54 - Don't let him in 466
Chapter 55 - Who is he? 471
Chapter 56 - But her mind was racing 474
Chapter 57 - Now that's a checkmate 484
Chapter 58 - Yes 491
Other books by JC Ryan 499

Prologue

Jamie Gibbons didn't turn on the lights, she just set her purse down by the front door and took off her coat. The wooden door was mottled with clumps of old paint, and it didn't want to close. She lifted and leaned on it, and it settled into the frame, protesting the whole way. She locked it.

The clothesline strung across the living room was hung with damp clothes that weren't going to be dry by the morning, but, at least, they were clean. James' school books were scattered all over the place. She'd have to get up early and nag him to get them all picked up before he left for school. That boy. He was the smarter of her two sons, but he had the worse grades. Tyrone squeezed every point he could out of his schoolwork, turned it in on time, did all the extra credit he could get, and took care of the house and his brother while he did it. James seemed to think he could coast through life on his wits. She was just lucky Tyrone was the older of the two. She couldn't have done it otherwise.

She peeked through the doorway into the larger of the two bedrooms, too small for a pair of growing boys, but the best she had to give them.

They were asleep, or, at least, James was, snoring away. Tyrone had the covers pulled up over his head, and she thought she saw the wink of a flashlight under them. It wasn't too late yet. She'd let him read for a while. Her feet hurt, and she wanted to sit down for a minute anyway.

As soon as she wrote one more letter, she'd look in on them one more time, then go to bed.

There wasn't a door to the kitchen, just an old curtain. She pulled it shut and turned on the overhead light. It flickered and went out. She'd have to call the landlord in the morning. She turned on the tiny lamp she had on the kitchen table for writing. It turned the room soft and yellow.

The dishes were done and drying in the plastic rack, and a note on the table said James needed more lunch money by Tuesday. She didn't have any on her, and the next check was all spoken for. Time to dig around under the couch cushions — as if she hadn't done that a hundred times already this year.

Jamie didn't have to look inside the refrigerator to know it was empty. She'd wait until work tomorrow to eat. The boys would have a few days' grace until the school cut off their lunches.

When her check came in, well, a couple of bills would just have to wait.

She sat down on the cracked vinyl chair and opened up her letter-box from under the table, a printer paper box she'd picked up from work. It held handwritten copies of all the letters she'd sent out, the few responses she'd received, and the last packet of information she'd copied at the library. The originals were in her closet, along with the lease and her tax forms from work.

The packet had come from the detective working the case, telling her he was sorry but her husband was guilty, and here was the proof. She'd picked through the documents and put together another story. She didn't have the legal know-how to prove Andy's innocence, but some of the 'facts', as they called them in court, didn't add up — and some critical pieces of information that she knew they had were missing.

She knew she wasn't any great writer, but the fact was she'd written over two dozen of these letters asking for someone to help her with Andy's case, and she was starting to get good at it — or at least, less bad. Not less desperate, though. At this point, she'd be happy if a janitor would pick one of her letters out of the trash, read it, and hand it around like a piece of interesting gossip.

She had already sent letters to the detective, lawyers, and the judge involved in Andy's case. She hadn't given them any attitude about it. Even from her bench in the public gallery of the courtroom during the trial, she could see how it looked like Andy could be guilty. But, she also had enough common sense to know that the jury hadn't heard all the facts. Just because it looked bad didn't mean Andy was guilty of murder.

It most certainly didn't mean that he deserved to rot in prison, not with two kids growing up fast. Tyrone was in eighth grade now, fourteen years old and about to start high school. James was ten. They were good kids, but the Lord knew all kinds of things could go wrong, growing up with their father in prison and their mother working two and sometimes three jobs, struggling to feed them, pay bills, and keep them in cheap shoes.

She wasn't around enough to keep them out of trouble, and that meant they were going to fall into it sooner or later.

While she understood how Andy had gotten dragged into all this by taking too many chances and getting too close to some evil men, her boys were losing out on the lives they should've had if their father hadn't gone to prison to pay for someone else's crime. And, that was something she could not abide.

The next letter and packet, along with the last of her stamps, was going to the Honorable Regan St. Clair, a county judge up in White Plains, a lovely blonde woman who didn't have kids. Her father had been a judge in Brooklyn back in the day and then moved north with his family. She vaguely remembered voting for the Honorable St. Clair once or twice when she first got out of high school and Mamma was still telling her who to vote for — not that Jamie often listened. Then suddenly he'd gone north and disappeared, leaving behind a series of cold-hearted men who were only interested in keeping people in line.

Andy had been kept in line. She'd always wondered if old St. Clair had been driven out somehow, gone running with his tail between his honorable legs.

Andy wasn't in the same jurisdictional district as Regan St. Clair; he wasn't her problem. As it stood, he wasn't anybody's problem but hers and the boys'. No reason for St. Clair to open the letter at all.

Well, couldn't hurt to ask. As Mamma always said, 'If you don't ask, the answer's always no.'

Chapter 1 - To make a difference

A long white puff of steam hung in the air over a manufacturing plant off in the distance. It was bunched up at the top, looking like a high-altitude weather balloon, white against the flat, low ceiling of clouds. It remained fixed in place, neither rising nor falling.

If only the breeze would push it away, then maybe Regan could get something done with her morning. Watching the steam struggle to get any further past the horizon always stirred up feelings of melancholy.

But the steam lingered in the air. Every couple of minutes, the plant would send up another puff to join the first. The puff never got any bigger — just stayed there, hanging in the air, refusing to disappear ... just like the letter on her desk.

The leaves had fallen, and downtown White Plains looked dull and ugly. Except for a few skyscrapers that reflected the clouds as they went past — and that could be utterly gorgeous in a daytime thunderstorm — the area was a collection of gray, prisonlike buildings of a brutal modern style that seemed ready to topple over and crush the nearby traffic. Going out for a walk at lunch in the shadows of the buildings always made her feel less than human.

She'd been thinking a lot lately — about getting out.

It wasn't much of a life. If she wasn't looking up from legal documents at the huge gray buildings outside her window, she was inside one of the courtrooms in her robes with her hair pulled severely away from her face, looking down at the people in the courtroom. She sometimes felt like a childless mother, threatening to ground an entire courtroom full of unruly lawyers and citizens if they didn't behave. When she wasn't providing an example of seriousness and probity to the court, she was at home, staying in one of three rooms in her enormous, echoing house: her bedroom, the library, or the bathroom. She ate takeout at her library desk and watched television from her bed as though she lived in a motel room. A maid came in once a week to clean, wash, and iron.

She didn't need this job. She'd been to the Taconic Correctional Facility to see her friend Jessie last Saturday, and it had reminded her all over again that nobody in her family needed the money - or the justice. They'd always had more than their fair share of both, thanks to her father's best friend who'd struck it rich investing in foreign stocks after Vietnam, and had paid for both her father's and her education.

If she didn't still believe that she could make a difference, it would be easy to walk away. She still did — although her ability to believe had been rapidly diminishing lately. And if she hadn't been popular, it would've been easy to drift away. But, she was popular. She was one of the most respected judges in the Ninth District, even if the local attorneys did call her the Ice Queen, and worse behind her back.

She had a reputation for honesty and insight, fair-mindedness and integrity, and was considered competent always, and brilliant most of the time. If she'd still had the passion for justice that she'd once had in law school, she could have been on the state Supreme Court by now, maybe being groomed for an even higher office.

But she didn't have the passion anymore. Otherwise, she wouldn't be wasting time holding a cold cup of coffee in both hands like it was supposed to warm her in front of a window full of gray skies and gray buildings, whose most impressive feature was a puff of steam that lingered too long. And...

The letter on the desk in front of her was from a woman whose husband was in prison for a murder she claimed he didn't commit. The front page was a handwritten plea with a drop of coffee smeared across it. The rest of the pages had been pulled out of a packet of evidence that someone had given her. Regan could read between the lines as well as the woman. Something fishy had gone down. Criminal cases were sometimes like Mount Everest — they made their own weather. This one was starting to look like a real blizzard.

If only, the letter on her desk would go away.

If only she didn't have to decide what to do about it. Naturally, she couldn't just leave it there.

It wasn't like she didn't have the money. She could give the family something to live on. She could sell a few stocks and set up a trust fund for the wife and kids as a gesture of her pity.

It hadn't been her case; she'd had nothing to do with the situation. The woman lived in Brooklyn. It should never have come to Regan's attention, let alone become her problem.

The pettiness of her thoughts appalled her. She was becoming institutionalized.

Once upon a time, she'd dreamed of changing the world, of making it a more just, fair, reasonable place to live. Now she just had nightmares of paperwork.

She dreaded the thought of what her father might say if she told him how she really felt about her job lately. She wasn't looking forward to the holidays. He always seemed to be able to get a confession out of her even before the turkey was cooked.

She put the coffee mug on top of the blotter, already splotched with brown rings from the other cups of coffee that had gone cold this morning. Her admin, Gary, was probably sick of listening to her sigh from the other side of the hollow door between her office and his. He'd probably written her a dozen sarcastic sticky notes and added items to her email calendar like, "To do today: put your big-girl panties on," and "You are not living in a chick flick! Stop waiting around for your life to happen."

He knew she hated that kind of cheery sentimentalism. So of course, he used it on her every chance he could get.

She gave out one more big Gary-annoying sigh, then got up, brushed her hair away from her face, and walked out of the office.

Gary looked up at her over the top of his little librarian glasses. His eyebrows twitched. If he gave her any attitude, she was going to tell him he was going bald again.

"Going somewhere?" he asked.

She ignored him and went into the hallway, where she ignored two of her colleagues with a thin smile, reached the break room, and dumped the cold coffee from her mug down the small aluminum sink. Then she poured herself another cup of coffee from the pump-driven air pot, which spluttered as she emptied the last of it.

The break room was empty The only signs of any previous inhabitation were damp coffee rings on the white counter, and plastic chairs pulled away from the small circular gray tables. A muted TV on the wall played CNN. Her eyes swam; she couldn't read the ticker at the bottom. Just as well. Two men in suits talked to each other on the screen, tilting their heads conspiratorially.

She yawned so hard her jaw cracked and then turned to leave, but she couldn't make herself go through the doorway.

It was stupid. The empty coffee pot bothered her.

It was someone else's job to fill it. At what she made an hour, the county of Westchester could afford to hire five or six people to take care of the coffee pot. She could have afforded to hire at least a dozen employees to refill it just based just on what she was making on her investments today. The break room wasn't even occupied. No one would ever know that it was her who had left an empty coffee pot behind.

But that wasn't the point.

She turned back to the coffee pot, tipped the last dregs into the sink, and then manhandled the pot under the coffee maker. The lid didn't want to behave; it kept getting in the way. She knocked the grounds into the trash, then added a new filter from the top of the coffee maker, where one of the admins had left a stack of six filters already prefilled with fresh coffee grounds. *Thoughtful*. She brushed the grounds off the bottom of the filter, slammed everything together, and pressed the start button.

The coffee maker started to rumble.

Undoubtedly helping Andy Gibbons and his family would be the same. She was making a mountain out of a molehill. The wheels of justice had skipped a cog; that was all. She'd look over the evidence, see what she could do with it, and call someone at the King's County Clerk's office.

It'd probably only take a couple of hours' work to get the ball rolling. And she'd feel better, too. Make her father proud over some sliced turkey.

And who knew? It might just make a difference.

Chapter 2 - There's nothing you can do

Regan threw on her blinker at the last second and swerved into the gravel parking lot of the Musgrove Ale House. The green banner on the front of the building in a Celtic font was unmistakable, confirmed by a bright yellow neon harp in the window: Guinness was served there.

It was a small, ugly bar in a tiny strip mall next to a dark field on a narrow highway edged with plowed snow — and it was a godsend. Regan must have passed it at least half a dozen times, driving back and forth to Green Haven to speak with Andy Gibbons. She didn't usually stop at places like this, but she couldn't go another hour without food, not without breaking into some form of road rage.

She pulled in alongside a Chrysler minivan with chipped paint. Her hands were shaking with shock and hunger. Next door was a pizza place with a red sign, but their only beer sign in the window was Budweiser. Being a wealthy judge and the daughter of a wealthy judge father, she'd never picked up that particular taste.

She could probably order a pizza and have it delivered next door, or fill up on a burger and fries. As she opened the door of her Lexus she smelled the hot fryer oil, and her stomach growled.

She did the things single women do when getting out of a car in a strange neighborhood: check for anyone watching the car, make sure keys are in hand, and lock the doors. After the first couple of times she'd visited Andy, she'd abandoned her heels in the car. The warden was shorter than she was, and their conversations went much more smoothly once she switched to flats.

Her breath steamed in the cold air, rising and disappearing quickly.

The bar thumped with music — something that sounded amateurish and out of key. At least, it wasn't live; her body didn't care about the music. It was in survival mode. It needed to be fed.

As she came up to the door, it opened, and the music doubled in volume. For a split-second she almost turned around to go to the pizza place. Then a pair of big buff guys wearing matching, wrinkle-free navy sweatshirts and sunglasses stepped out, holding the door for her.

They straightened up as they saw her. The three of them all paused, staring at each other for a second. Then her stomach growled another warning, and she went in.

A big, doughy-looking bouncer near the door reached out and grabbed her wrist as she stepped into the bar. "ID?"

She flashed some at him, and he stamped the back of her hand. She checked her phone: it was seven o'clock. A dais had been cleared of tables up front, and a technician was setting up equipment under bright white lighting. Great. She'd have to eat fast and get out before whatever no-name garage band hit the stage. The band couldn't be very good; the place was almost empty.

A blond guy looked up from the pool table in the back when she came in. Otherwise, none of the few other patrons seemed to notice her entrance. Blondie lined up a shot and made it, knocking a couple of stripes into side pockets, staring at her the whole time. He smiled at h.r, flashing blue eyes and dimples.

She tore her eyes away before the guy could take her glance as an invitation. She was hungry, and she was upset. She didn't need to get hit on — not tonight — no matter how handsome the guy was… and this one was.

She grabbed a seat at the bar. The goateed bartender floated from the other side of the bar toward her.

"Guinness, hamburger, fries," she said, raising her voice over the music. "Well done on the hamburger, extra crispy on the fries."

He nodded and floated toward the kitchen, sliding sideways through the double swing doors. He returned in a second, and she watched his feet: he was moonwalking. He caught her looking and smiled. A glass and coaster appeared, and ten seconds later she was sucking the creamy, rich, foam head from the Guinness. Her shoulders relaxed an inch.

Pool balls cracked behind her. Blondie must be a decent player; he was sinking them fast enough.

She hadn't played since law school. She wondered if she could take him, then blew the thought aside.

She pulled her phone out and started scrolling through the news. The music had to be deliberately bad. Whenever she caught a snatch of lyrics they sounded like the out-of-key epitome of misery — but, at least they were on par with her mood.

Andy Gibbons had told her to give it up; he wouldn't be talking to her anymore.

Go home, Miss St. Clair. There's nothing you can do. This place will be my home for the rest of my life. I have made peace with that. I thank you for your sympathy, but it ain't doing me any good. You neither.

It made her feel sick to remember the look of calm acceptance on his face. It was like looking at someone and knowing that they thought of themselves as a piece of trash that had to be tossed out with the rest of the garbage.

The beer was gone. The bartender glided by with his eyebrows up; she nodded. The glass disappeared and was quickly replaced.

Her phone buzzed, and she checked her email. It was from Gorman, an ex-cop turned PI, who she'd hired to help her with gathering evidence. He'd come up dry again. And moreover, he had to step away from the case as a personal matter had come up.

She jabbed out a quick response, thanking him and asking him for his final bill, then flicked the phone off and shoved it in her jacket pocket.

A red basket mounded with fries appeared in front of her. The hamburger's greasy bun glistened underneath. The bartender stood in front of her, his fingers hovering in the air for a moment, then snatched a bottle of malt vinegar and a white plastic bottle of mayo from under the counter. She raised her fingers in thanks, and he floated away again.

She ate the fries first — a sprinkle of malt vinegar and then dipped in mayo. They were good, extra crispy, almost burnt in spots, extra thin. The hamburger was nearly as good — mediocre beef that had been treated well, with onions and worcestershire mixed into the patty.

She drank her second beer more slowly. She didn't want to have to hang around while she sobered up enough to drive. Getting pulled over for DUI was not a pleasant prospect for a judge, let alone a judge in her emotional state.

Tomorrow she'd have to call Jamie Gibbons and tell her the news. Andy had told her to give up, and the private investigator had quit. What she wouldn't tell Mrs. Gibbons was that when she'd come out of the facility at five, she'd found one of her tires slashed and the words 'go home bitch' written in the dust on her back windshield.

She'd changed the tire herself, feeling eyes on her every second, too proud to ask for help.

It made Andy's words hurt worse, knowing that she'd stepped on someone's toes like that. It meant she must be coming too close to the truth for someone's comfort. She could almost smell the blood in the water.

Jamie Gibbons would look up at her with her dark, full eyes, and blink her long lashes in slow motion, and it would be perfectly clear that Regan had failed to bring her boys' father home. Had failed, in fact, to make any progress whatsoever, other than to invoke a couple of low-level threats.

She didn't give a damn about anything else; she wanted her husband home and free. The word justice would have no meaning for her unless her innocent husband were let out of jail.

Regan started counting the actual financial cost of her failure: trust funds for the boys, a stipend, getting Mrs. Gibbons into nursing school — if that was what she wanted — get some workmen in to repair the boarding house, at least the inside, or try to get her to move out of the neighborhood altogether.

She could afford it, but it still felt like a red line on her internal ledgers.

She took another sip of her beer. The mirror behind the bar showed Blondie still shooting pool by himself. He racked and broke them, dropping the stripes first, then working through the solids as methodical as a clerk filing a stack of paperwork.

She let her attention slide back to the case and the many holes in it.

On the afternoon of April 7th, 2003, the body of a blond Caucasian woman, Angela Ligotti, was found under a bunch of old newspapers near a busy highway. She had been stabbed to death. Detective Peter Marando had led the investigation.

An eyewitness out cycling on the morning of the crime, Abe De Wit, testified that he saw two people, a large black man and a white woman, sitting in a green car parked near the spot where the body was found. It looked like they were in a physical struggle. After a while, he saw the black man, who was wearing a red jacket, get out and walk to the passenger side of the car and open the door. It looked as if he were about to pull the passenger out of the car. However, when the black man noticed the cyclist, who had stopped to watch, he ran back to the driver's side.

The police picked up Andy the next day. He maintained that he was innocent of murdering the woman. Yeah, he knew the deceased, but he had nothing to do with her death. He wasn't even near the crime scene on the day of the alleged offense. To help back up his claims of innocence, he volunteered to participate in a lineup and consented to a search of his family's apartment without insisting on a search warrant.

He thought he had nothing to hide. That he drove a green car, he never denied.

During the lineup, the cyclist identified Andy as the man he'd seen that day. And the search of his apartment had produced a red jacket fitting the description given by the cyclist.

No DNA tests were conducted, but the autopsy report stated that hair samples found on the victim's body revealed African-American characteristics.

Hair samples were often used as evidence in court cases to establish a link between the crime and a perpetrator. But it was still a severely flawed science. The Justice Department and FBI had admitted as much when they officially confessed that almost every examiner in their elite forensic unit had exaggerated forensic evidence.

Out of 28 examiners in the FBI's unit, 26 had distorted forensic results to favor prosecutors in more than 250 out of 268 cases, including 32 defendants who received the death penalty, 14 of whom were executed or died in prison.

This despicable practice had been going on for almost 20 years. If the consequences of their testimony had not been not so dire, it would have been laughable.

She had been following several such cases in progress; six of the defendants had already been exonerated. It was one of the world's biggest legal scandals in decades, and almost no one outside the profession had even heard about it.

The fact that a hair sample was being used as evidence, without even having the decency to go through the motions of DNA testing ,was reason enough to reopen Andy's case, even if there was no other evidence which could be used in his favor.

But that wasn't the only suspicious point about the case.

At the trial, the prosecution's case rested not only on the testimony of the cyclist but also on that of a snitch — a jailhouse informant — who had supposedly overheard Andy's confession, for which the source would receive certain privileges, sometimes even early parole. In Regan's opinion, it was an unacceptable and unsound practice, but most judges wouldn't have batted an eye.

The informant in Andy's case had spent a couple of days in the same cell with Andy and claimed that Andy had bragged about being the killer. Of course, the fact that he had a longstanding "working relationship" with the investigating detective and had testified in multiple cases over the years didn't taint his evidence... not at all.

The jury ignored the contradicting testimony from another man, a witness for the defense who'd been incarcerated with Andy at the time, who stated that Andy had never bragged about the killing and that he'd maintained his innocence the entire six months he'd been awaiting trial.

A red jacket, a green car, a single strand of African American hair, and two witnesses, one of them a Caucasian bicyclist. For the members of the jury, it was a matter of res ipsa loquitur — the facts spoke for themselves. It took them less than two hours to find Andy guilty — 25 years to life. Case closed... next, please.

Regan had been around long enough to learn that evidence, eyewitness testimony, 'facts,' even DNA, didn't tell the whole story. It was just the list of what you knew and had collected at a certain point in time. The whole story was often more complicated and subtle.

Today was Andy's tenth anniversary in prison.

He was a six-foot-two African-American man with 260 pounds of muscle and a GED from the jail system. He'd be lucky if some guard didn't manufacture an excuse to keep him there when his parole was up. The only way he'd be labeled a model citizen was if he was dead.

The bartender floated past her. She turned her head to the side and ignored him. If she made eye-contact with anyone, she was going to cry.

Go home, Miss St. Clair. There's nothing you can do.

She'd put her hopes on Gorman finding more evidence, and now Gorman was out. She wondered if his sudden resignation could have been brought on by a few threats such as a slashed tire or a nasty message. She'd probably never know.

It was clear that someone was paying attention to what she was doing and didn't like it.

She wiped her hands on her napkin and scrubbed at her mouth. She'd put a little lip gloss on in the car before going into the prison. Obviously, it had been wasted.

A man slid onto the bar stool next to her was Blondie from the pool table. Great.

"Hey," he said.

She groaned and put on her anti-pickup-artist armor, sitting up straighter and broadening her shoulders, "Don't bother."

"Don't bother what?"

"Flirting. Trying to pick me up."

"Just collecting a beer, ma'am."

He waved at the bartender and indicated a refill, a Guinness, then headed back toward the pool table. She rolled her eyes at herself. She was paranoid, not without reason, but not behaving in an exemplary manner either.

She should go.

Instead, she recklessly ordered another Guinness. Her stomach was full, but she was still too upset to drive. She carried the beer to a back table so she didn't feel like the entire room was watching her back and stared into space, her mind returning to Jamie Gibbons.

The first time they'd met — at a cheap diner, the most expensive place that Jamie Gibbons would agree to — the woman had leaned across the table and said, "Judge, how is it possible that my husband could be convicted if the prosecutor withheld crucial evidence from the court? Isn't that illegal? Don't they have to make all the evidence known?"

"They do," Regan told her. She held out her hand, and the other woman belatedly shook it. The waitress, dressed in a grease-stained polo shirt and slacks, brought them menus and took their drink orders — two coffees, no cream.

"You must think I'm crazy, making things up," Jamie said.

Regan was taking a sip of coffee. She waved her hand.

Jamie Gibbons took out an old writing pad and paged through it. "I have four pieces of evidence that never appeared at the trial. First, there was another person, Frederick B. Schnatterbeck, who came forward and told the police he saw the perpetrator but was never asked to identify him in a police line-up. Nor was he asked to testify. In fact, they never even took a statement from him."

She leaned forward, raising her eyebrows. Her hair had been pulled back in a bun, but strands of it were getting loose, making her look just a little bit overexcited.

"Go on," Regan said.

She took a sip of coffee. "You're skeptical. That's all right. I'm looking for someone who has a fair amount of skepticism. With the emphasis on fair. To continue, second point: When the police came to our apartment, they did find a red jacket, but it wasn't Andy's. It wasn't even his size; it was too small. It had been left by a friend of his a few days before the crime."

"What was the friend's name?" Regan asked.

"Michael Liu. Who is, I might add, about five-foot-two and weighs about a hundred pounds dripping wet."

Up went the eyebrows again, wide eyes and long lashes turned unrelentingly on Regan.

"Third point, the car: We had a green car at the time, but it was broken down. The engine wouldn't start, and the transmission was ruined. Andy was waiting for a friend to find a cheap new one to put in. You see where I'm going with this? That car had been out of commission for a couple of weeks at the time of the murder. There's no way it could have been the same car. Which someone trying to frame Andy for the murder might not have known."

Another long, steady look. Regan nodded and sipped numbly at her coffee.

"Fourth point:" Jamie continued, "they never found the murder weapon. Why was that? They said that Andy must have thrown the knife over the side of the bridge. If you ask me, they haven't even searched for it."

The implications were horrifying. If true, more than one person had to be involved. Jamie placed her fists forcefully on the table, one on either side of the notebook, rattling the ice in the glasses.

"Is that enough for you? Or are you going to say what everyone else has been saying, and tell me there's no reason to bother with the case, that I should just move on with my life? Or are you going to help me, Judge?"

Regan was still too stunned to answer.

Jamie continued, "Your father was a good man. I voted for him a couple of times." Her voice rose toward the end of the sentence, ending almost in a question.

Regan took a deep breath and put her coffee cup down. Jamie Gibbons didn't look crazy or overexcited anymore. She looked like what she was, a woman putting on bravado in the face of despair. Regan's heart went out to the woman sitting across from her.

She reached a hand out across the table, and Jamie clasped it. The skin was dry, chapped, and cold.

"Yes, Mrs. Gibbons, I will help you."

Jamie stared at her like she was waiting for a "but" at the end of the sentence.

After a moment, the waitress came up to them and said, "May I take your lunch order?"

A fat tear started rolling down Jamie's nose.

"We'll need a minute," Regan said as a smile stretched her face.

I felt so proud of myself back then.

At the time, in her mind Andy Gibbons was already free.

But of course, that hadn't happened. It was now January, and she'd been working on this for three months. Now she was being shooed away, probably for making things worse.

Regan's eyes focused once again as she returned from that diner to the bar at the sound of the break of another game of pool. She sighed and looked down into the glass. The beer was gone. Either she made a break for it now, or she'd be here all night.

Beer never solved anything, but a few more hours in her personal law library might.

Chapter 3 - Looking for a good time

Regan reached into her jacket and pulled out her wallet, then laid a twenty on the bar. After a second she added another ten, then slid off the stool as she tucked the wallet back into her pocket.

Three guys were coming into the bar, their breath steaming neon for a second from the beer signs — three kids really, 25 at the most. One in a Giants jersey, one in a plaid flannel shirt, and the third in a denim jacket. None of them were dressed warmly enough, all of them there to get drunk and listen to horrible music.

The bouncer at the door still slumped casually on his stool said, "Hey boys, let's see some IDs."

"You know who we are Dave," the kid in the jersey said and tried to walk past him.

The bouncer grabbed the youngster's shirt. "And I know how to toss all three of you out of here in about two seconds," Dave said. "Show me your IDs or you don't get a stamp, and then Brett cards you every time you want a drink."

The kid in the plaid flannel had already dragged his ID out and flashed it, shoving a clenched fist into the bouncer's face.

"Good boy," Dave said, and stamped the fist. The kid showed a grin that went all the way up to his gums and pushed past the other two on the way to the bar.

He elbowed Regan as he passed by. She'd stepped to the side as he'd approached, so he had to stick out his elbow to do it. The reek of cheap whiskey followed in his wake.

"Jack and Coke," he said, tapping an ATM card on the bar.

The other two had collected their hand stamps and joined their friend. The guy in the plaid, waiting while the bartender made his drink, glanced over at Regan.

"What's your problem?"

She shrugged and turned toward the door.

A strong hand grabbed her shoulder; she tried to shrug it off. Instead, it switched to her arm and pulled her around in a rough circle. All three of the guys were staring at her like jackals, sizing up her clothes, hair, face, and chest. Probably calculating the contents of her wallet.

"Excuse me gentlemen," she said. The kid in the jersey jerked his head toward the one in the blue jean jacket, who broke off from the other two and circled behind her stopping between her and the door.

They'd done this before.

"Hey." The guy in the plaid had collected his drink and sipped at it, grabbing the glass from the top edges and slurping at it from behind his long fingers. "So you're looking for a good time, huh?"

Out of the corner of her eye, she noticed Blondie taking a little bit too long to line up his pool shot.

"No, I'm not looking for a good time," she said clearly and loudly. "Take your hands off me."

The kid in the jersey smirked at his friend over her shoulder. Something warm pressed against her butt.

She couldn't believe it. Her free arm jerked backward. An elbow to the ribs would do the guy some good. Unfortunately, her elbow only hit the guy's forearm. He'd been ready for her.

"Get your hands off me!" she shouted.

"Gentlemen," a voice said in a way that made it clear that if they didn't start acting as if they were, there would be trouble.

"Back off," the kid in the plaid snarled. "We got her first."

It was Blondie. He'd left his pool cue back at the pool table and had his hands up, palms out. He tsk'd at them and walked up to the guy standing behind Regan. "We don't get to take home women without asking first, especially when we're drunk. Isn't that right? I'm sure someone had a discussion with you about it. Women aren't the same as $20 bills that you find on the street — even pretty ones."

The hand withdrew from her ass.

She picked up a foot and jammed it against the guy's shin, scraping her flats down the front of his leg.

"Fuck!" he shouted.

A fist slammed into the back of her head, and she tumbled forward, seeing stars. The guy in the jersey grabbed her and swung her around so that a bar stool slammed into her gut. She whipped forward and just missed hitting her head on the bar.

"You jackasses get away from that woman!" the bouncer roared. The bartender had his cell phone in hand and was talking into it.

She grabbed onto the bar stool and tried to hang on, but the bar stool followed her as she fell over backward. Landing on the floor with the metal frame of the bar stool on top of her, she tried to push it off, but the guy in the plaid put a foot on one of the struts and pinned it — and her — down.

One of the rungs shoved into her gut. She was going to puke in a second.

"Ted," the guy in plaid said. "You get Dave. Me and Casey got this other guy."

"Should be fun."

The bar stool lifted off her. The next second it swung toward Blondie.

She didn't hang around to see if it hit. Instead, she rolled toward the end of the bar, where the bartender helped pull her off her back. She tried to stand up, but he waved at her to stay down. She crouched next to an aluminum shelf full of pint glasses.

"Cops are on the way," he said.

"Good."

She heard glass shatter and crouched down lower. Blondie tsk'd again and someone shouted in rage. The music droned on for a few more seconds, then cut out.

The sound of a fist hitting meat echoed through the room. The bartender snorted through his nose.

Then came the sound of a body hitting the floor.

Regan stood up.

The bouncer was reaching over the bar for a towel, one hand over a bloody nose and his two fat eyebrows pinched together in the middle. The three kids were all laid out on the floor, the guy in the jersey near the door and the other two on top of each other in front of the bar. Glass and booze had splattered on the floor next to a two-top table.

Blondie flexed his fingers. The skin on them was beet red. "Ice?" The bartender asked.

It was all over. She could hardly believe it.

The bartender wrapped a scoopful of ice in a towel and passed it over with his eyebrows up. Blondie nodded and held the towel against his fist while the bartender poured him a Guinness.

"You all right?" Blondie asked her.

She touched the back of her head to check for blood, but her hand came back dry. She felt a little nauseated but otherwise okay. There wasn't even a bump. "I think so."

Now that the rush of panic was clearing out of her system, the rest of her emotions were catching up. She felt her nostrils flare; she blinked quickly and swallowed a couple of times, trying to keep her eyes and throat clear. Her body tightened up and began to shake.

"Shit," she said.

"Freaking out?"

She nodded.

"Come on back and have a seat with me for a minute. It'll pass. Or I can drive you home."

She shook her head. She didn't want to show him where she lived. She'd be fine. She just needed to sit for a few minutes. "I'll take some coffee."

The door opened, and a young couple came in the door chatting with each other. The bouncer, Dave, cleared his throat, and the two of them froze in the doorway, suddenly aware of the three bodies on the floor. A cop siren whooped behind them, flashing lights turning into the parking lot.

The two of them turned around and went back outside. The door closed, and their shadows crossed the window by the Guinness sign.

The bartender said, "Be a minute," and bustled around behind the bar, setting up the coffee machine.

Blondie led her to the small two-top behind the pool table. The pool cue lay on top of the pool table. A few solids had been left behind; the stripes were all sunk.

She dragged her fingers along the baize.

"You play?" he asked.

"Used to."

He passed her the cue. It evidently belonged to the bar's set and was the straightest one of the bunch — not actually straight, but the straightest.

She leaned over the table, lined up the six with a corner pocket, and slid the pool cue through her fingers a couple of times. She hit the cue ball with a satisfying 'thunk', and it flicked the six into the pocket, then bounced off the bumper toward the center of the table.

She let out a long breath that she hadn't known she was holding. The feel of a pool cue in her hands, the calculations of which balls to hit and how… Admit it, the feel of having a cute guy watching her play — it all seemed familiar.

The seven sat near the middle of the table, the clear shot invalidated by the eight ball sitting between it and the corner pocket. She walked around the table slowly, lining up shots mentally. She'd never been Minnesota Fats, but her talents had paid for quite a few beers and baskets of fries all through college.

She leaned over the table and shot the seven into a corner pocket so that the cue ball rolled back and clicked off the eight. The eight ball rolled toward the side pocket, but not fast enough, stopping a couple of inches short.

She clucked her tongue at herself, then sank the eight. Blondie squatted at the end of the table and started racking.

She leaned the cue against the rack and stretched, feeling her back pop several times as she twisted and reached. She yawned gratefully. She hadn't really relaxed since she'd talked to Andy Gibbons. "What's your name?" she asked.

"Jake. Jake Westley."

"You're not from here," she said. It was something about his accent, but more of a give-away was the fact that he didn't have a pool cue with him.

"That's right, ma'am." He lifted the rack with delicate, yet casual attention.

"So what brings you here?"

It was an empty series of statements, not the best small talk she'd ever perpetrated. She didn't have the heart to flirt today, or enough brain cells left for witty banter.

The door opened and a pair of police officers came through, both of them looking equally competent and resigned to the stupidity of the three kids lying on the floor, two now conscious. The kid in the plaid shirt was still out cold, for which she was grateful. The bouncer sat on a bar stool in full view of the three kids, a Louisville Slugger sitting across his knees and his arms across his chest.

"Trouble," Jake said.

"What kind of trouble?" She handed him the pool cue. He chalked it, swung the cue ball back and forth across the table twice, then set it in place and lined up the shot.

The break was a good one, with three balls going down. The officers, who had started to help the kids up, both looked up at the same time. Jake waved the tips of two fingers at them. They didn't smile or otherwise act as though they knew him. The bouncer said something, and the officers went back to talking to the two conscious kids, each of whom was bigger and taller than either of the officers. One of the officers called something in over a cell phone — probably an ambulance.

Jake started picking off stripes, going in order. He had one eye on the officers by the door, one eye on her, and still had his full attention on the pool game. How he managed to do it, she had no idea.

If it could even be called a game. He sank the stripes without hesitation and started working on the solids. While he focused on the table, she took the opportunity to check him out better. The beer must be kicking in.

To say that he was a handsome-looking guy was an understatement. He was hunky and broad through the shoulders and had good, strong looking hands. A light dusting of blond hairs covered his chin and cheeks, and a little cleft dented his chin. Long eyelashes half-hid the twinkle in the pretty blue eyes that never seemed to catch her own, yet always seemed to be half looking at her.

She caught herself trying to think of a logical reason to stand on the same side of the table as him that wouldn't make it look like she was checking out his butt.

She cleared her throat. "What kind of trouble?" she repeated.

"The kind I get paid to clear up," he said. "Which makes it the good kind."

She hummed under her breath. "Oh?"

"Private investigator." Two more balls sank, one off the other, leaving the cue ball set up for his next shot.

"That's handy," she said. "Divorce cases and serving papers, right?"

"A couple of parental kidnappings." He shrugged. "It pays the bills."

The bartender walked over to them with a pair of coffee cups and a bowl of creamers balanced on one forearm. He put them on the two-top and rolled his eyes toward the officers. "They'll be over to talk to you in a few minutes. After the idiots are hauled off. Again."

"They cause trouble here often?" Jake asked.

"Only on my shift," the bartender said dryly, then retreated across the room. The members of the band had arrived and were standing awkwardly near the bar with their hands in their pockets. Two of them were dressed in solid black. The third had on a frilly white shirt underneath a black jacket and looked like something out of an episode of The Addams' Family.

She sipped the coffee, then slid onto the tall chair. She wasn't going to get much table time tonight; she could already tell.

Jake finished knocking the balls in, then sat down next to her, peeking up at her while he sipped his coffee. Every time someone moved in the front of the room his eyes flickered toward them for the briefest second. She wondered if he was even aware of doing it.

He might not have a flat-top haircut, and he might be trying to hold himself in a casual slouch, but she could tell he had military training somewhere in his background.

Maybe it was because he had just saved her from those punks. Impulsively, she asked, "What would you think about doing something more interesting?" Then she literally bit her tongue. She had no idea who this guy was, let alone if he was competent.

"Yeah? Like what?"

"Research, mostly. Investigative research into a murder case — a convicted man who's innocent."

He leaned back, looking out of a window at the parking lot. The still flashing lights on the police car were being joined by those of an ambulance with its siren off, as well as another patrol unit. He watched another pair of officers enter the building, holding the door open for the paramedics with their stretcher. They lifted it over the curb and rolled it in.

With the arrival of the other officers, one of the latecomers broke off from the others and walked toward the two of them. He pulled off his hat and ran a hand through his curly black hair.

"Officer Rodriguez," he said. "I'm told the two of you were involved in the fight that happened earlier."

"Yes, Officer," Jake said.

"Would you mind if I asked you a few questions."

"Not at all. My name is Jake Westley." He stood smartly in front of the officer, heels together. He offered a hand to shake, then pulled out his wallet and handed over his ID.

"Mm-hmm," said the officer, tilting it under the light and flipping it over to check the back. He passed it back. "Thank you."

Regan had already pulled out her wallet and presented her ID, standing next to Jake as she handed it over. The officer squinted first at the piece of plastic, then at her. He didn't give the ID as close a scrutiny has he had Jake's, but he looked at her closer.

"Huh," he said. "You're —"

"Yes," she said. "I'm Regan St. Clair, Judge St. Clair's daughter." Now she held out her hand, and the man shook it. He was still half-squinting at her. She suppressed a chuckle.

He handed back the ID and took out a small, top-bound notebook. "Why don't you tell me what happened?"

She swallowed and looked back at the three men. The one in plaid had been taken out on the stretcher; the other two were talking to the officers, glancing back at her and Jake as they did so. Probably worried that their stories wouldn't fly.

"Those two men and their friend in plaid entered the bar at about —" She glanced around the room, trying to remember if she'd seen a clock. "Sometime after seven? I wasn't paying attention to the time. Sorry."

"It's all right."

"They harassed the bouncer at the door. I believe his name is Dave. They wanted to enter without having to show their IDs;

they claimed he knew them well enough. He insisted on seeing their IDs. The one in plaid passed by the bar and elbowed me, going out of his way to do so. He smelled very strongly of whiskey. He ordered a Jack and Coke from the bartender. Then his two friends came up to the bar to order drinks. Either I didn't hear what they ordered, or they weren't able to order, I'm not sure.

"I turned to leave, and one of the three men grabbed me and turned me around, I'm not sure which. The one in plaid told me that..." She couldn't remember the exact wording. "Something about looking for a good time. Even though I hadn't suggested it. I loudly and clearly said that I was not interested. The one in the jersey took my arm, and the one in the blue jean jacket stepped behind me and grabbed my rear. I told them to get their hands off me, but they did not.

"At about that time, the bouncer and the bartender started to respond to the incident, with the bouncer telling them to leave me alone, and the bartender initiating a cell phone call. Jake had been playing pool," she waved a hand toward the empty pool table with the cue lying on top, "and arrived about then, stating that the men were not to harass me."

Officer Rodriguez glanced at Jake, who shrugged.

"At that time, I kicked the man standing behind me, and he hit the back of my head. Then I was swung around by the man in the jersey so that I was now behind the man in plaid. I became off-balance and almost fell into the bar. I grabbed a bar stool but fell over on my back, landing with the stool on top of me. The man in the plaid stepped on top of the stool rungs, pinning me down. He instructed the man in the jersey to 'take care of' the bouncer, and the man in the blue jean jacket to help him 'handle' Jake. Or that might have been the other way around, I can't remember. But it was the man in plaid who was giving instructions."

She swallowed. Her mouth had gone dry, and her knees felt like they might give out any second. It was annoying, being carried away with fear all over again. It was over — she didn't need to be afraid anymore.

Her voice shook. "I..."

"You can sit down, Miss," the officer said.

She tried to sit down as gracefully and steadily as she could. The coffee rippled in the cups. She took a sip of her coffee and cleared her throat.

"The man in plaid took the bar stool off me and swung it toward Jake. I don't know if it hit. I rolled behind the bar, and the bartender helped me up. He told me that he'd called the cops." She swallowed; her mouth had already gone dry. "The police, I mean. I heard a glass smash. The — the music technician, I think — someone turned off the music. I heard what sounded like someone being punched, then falling down. And then I stood up. The three kids were all on the floor. The bartender gave the bouncer a towel for a bloody nose, and a towel full of ice for Jake's hand. And then we walked back here. I'm too shaky to drive."

She blinked until the first few tears had cleared, then took another sip of her coffee. She felt like an idiot. Her entire body was quivering with fear all over again. Her teeth felt like they were going to start to rattle.

The officer took a few more notes, then flipped to a clean page and jotted down something.

The officer looked at Jake. "And you?"

"What she said," Jake replied. "I saw a lady in distress, put down my pool cue, walked over to see if she needed help. She did. I handled it with the minimum amount of force necessary, brought her back here to calm down, and waited for the police to arrive like a good citizen."

"Mmm-hmm." The officer looked back at Regan. "Would you like to press charges?"

Regan looked across the room at the two young men. On the one hand was the temptation to make their lives difficult just because she could. On the other, she just wanted to go home, wrap herself in a quilt, and curl up on her bed while she let the shock out of her system.

The two remaining men looked at her with wide, innocent eyes, as if pleading with her not to complicate their lives the way they'd complicated hers. "Yes, I would like to press charges," she said. A little louder than was necessary. The two young men flinched.

The officer nodded slightly as if he'd had an internal bet going on to see which way she'd go. She'd been wondering, too.

Chapter 4 - Which one was more stubborn

White Plains was an ugly town, even decked out in snow. Give him Chicago or New York or Minneapolis; they looked almost good blanketed in white. White Plains looked like the world's biggest prison complex. He kept expecting to see razor wire along the tops of the fences.

His phone buzzed again on the seat beside him.

The Honorable Judge St. Clair was calling him again, probably to tell him that she wanted to cancel on account of the weather. He let it ring and turned into the parking lot of the Westchester Courthouse. It was just another big, ugly building in an entire town full of them.

She was standing in front of the building behind a row of cement pylons, wrapped up in a long wool coat with her hands in her pockets. Her blonde hair glowed golden against the gray cement and mud-spattered snow on the ground.

Jake pulled up beside her, a white knight on his shining horse — or something like that.

He popped the lock on the car door and started to get out so he could hold the door for her, but she jumped in and slammed the door behind her.

"We still on for breakfast?" he asked.

She set a soft-sided briefcase on the floor and put her seatbelt on. "Yes. And I'm buying."

"Capital. I'm tired of Denny's."

"Head north on the street just outside the parking lot, a right."

"Hi-ho Silver, away!"

Her jaw was clenched. He thought for a second about whether he should turn on the radio but decided against it. She didn't look in the mood to sing along to hits from the 80s.

She gave good directions, giving him plenty of time to change lanes, but otherwise didn't say a word. They ended up in the parking lot of a building that looked like it was supposed to look like a real house but instead looked like a classier version of a Denny's. The second floor had a balcony overlooking the parking lot which had the best view, considering the office blocks in a row on either side of it.

He parked the Corolla at the far end of the lot after asking her whether he could drop her off at the door and having her turn him down. The name of the place was *La Ruche* — The Beehive.

They got out of the car, their breath steaming up in the frigid air. The end of her nose had turned red in the car, and she clutched the briefcase in front of her stomach like a shield.

She had looked both ways before she crossed each row of the parking lot, glancing down between the cars as she walked. Either she hadn't recovered from what happened to her the night before, or something else was making her paranoid.

He guessed it was the latter.

He walked beside her into the restaurant, reaching forward to open the first of the two sets of double doors for her. As he expected, she walked to the second door, opened it, and walked through, trailing one hand on the door to hold it open for him. She wasn't going to wait around for him to open doors for her, but she wasn't going to make a big deal out of it either.

He followed her into the restaurant.

He wasn't sure if he'd take the job from her, even though the money was sure to be excellent. Some things weren't worth scratching the surface on — and some things were like bottomless pits, a drain on time, money, and sanity. But she seemed like a good kid, and it was bound to be more interesting than the other possible jobs he'd been trying to line up.

The maître-d looked up at the two of them with a polite expression on his face. For a cheesy restaurant in White Plains, New York, he almost looked French — a short, dense-looking guy with a thin mustache and a goatee. He didn't look at St. Clair like she was a regular.

The place had wood tables with farmhouse chairs, gray carpet, and fake wood rafters. The big windows were bordered with long black drapes. The ones on the east side of the building had been pulled, even though the sun wasn't coming out anytime soon. About twenty people were scattered across half the room. A few of them glanced up as if they felt Jake staring at the backs of their heads.

He jerked his head toward the empty half of the room. "How about you find us a private table? Tell the server I'll tip extra if we're not disturbed."

The maître-d shrugged, pulled out two menus, and led the two of them toward a table in a corner away from the others, near an emergency exit.

It was good. It gave him a view of the front door, the door of the kitchen, and the little hallway leading to the bathrooms.

Jake pulled one of the wall-side chairs out for her honor, then took her coat and laid it across one of the empty seats. Her coat smelled like some kind of light perfume; the place itself smelled like ham. He sat down and pretended to be skimming the menu.

She was beautiful.

She was like the kind of woman you saw on a billboard, only classier — a senator's wife, maybe. She wore a sapphire blue blouse with a gold chain. Her hair fell in soft gold waves over her face. He could just imagine what it would feel like falling over his. He'd been watching her long legs as they'd walked toward the door. Too bad it was winter. Her legs clearly went on for miles.

He shook his head.

She was still looking down at the menu, clearly not seeing a word on it.

"It's a French place," he said. "Order the eggs Benedict and a fruit salad with some café au lait."

She closed the menu and sighed. "Am I that obvious?"

"Yeah, well, I'm a good observer."

A waitress crossed the gulf to the uninhabited side of the room. The look on her face was priceless. She was completely torn between sucking up to the customers and annoyance that she had to.

He passed her another five and her inner debate resolved in favor of sucking up to the customers. St. Clair scowled at him. Clearly she didn't like the thought of having to bribe people to get what she wanted. She was a judge, though, and the daughter of a judge. She'd probably had good service her entire life without having to pay extra for it and had never noticed.

The girl took their orders, St. Clair repeating the order he'd fed to her. He ordered a steak and eggs plate, big fresh-squeezed orange juice, and cafe au laits for both of them.

When the girl had gone, St. Clair lifted up the briefcase and put it on her lap. She unzipped it, stuck a hand in, then hesitated.

"This is confidential," she said.

"Gimme a dollar," he said.

She blinked at him as if one of them was an idiot, and it wasn't her. Sarcasm made her look even prettier than before.

He had to force himself not to smile as he repeated himself: "Gimme a dollar."

She reached inside her coat, pulled out a wallet, and laid a twenty in front of him. She probably didn't carry anything smaller. He took it, popped open his wallet, and stuck it in. Then he peeled the paper wrapper off the napkin around his silverware, took a pen out of his pocket, and wrote out a receipt.

He slid it across the table to her. She looked at it, then up at him. Then she slid it into her wallet and put it back inside her jacket.

"You're the judge. We now have a contract. Doesn't that make it confidential?"

Regan's face lit up with humor. God, she was beautiful when she smiled like that. She pulled out a manila folder filled with paperwork, some of which looked a little frayed around the edges. She held on to it for a second too long, then handed it over.

He laid it in front of him. "So tell me what's going on."

She waved a hand toward the folder.

"Yeah, I'll read it later," he said. "But here we are at a breakfast joint, and if I have to sit through another half hour of complete silence on your part, I'm gonna think you don't like me."

She rolled her eyes and sniffed a little. Not an arrogant sniff, but the kind women make when they're trying to hide that they've been crying. She pulled a tissue out of the briefcase at her feet, then dabbed delicately at her face.

"I had to call his wife this morning," she said. "She wasn't even upset at me. I told her that I was trying to hire another private investigator. She told me not to bother and hung up on me. I don't think she meant it."

The voice was dangerously close to fraying. The waitress, thankfully, came up with a tray of coffee and orange juice, with a little silver pot full of cream. Nice thought, but they were both going to ignore it. The waitress smiled and left.

He gave her a minute to compose herself. She lifted her cup of coffee and sipped from it, holding it in front of her face more than she needed to, like it was there to conceal her facial expressions. The waitress came back with a small air pot full of coffee and left it with them — good thinking on her part.

She gave another sniff. This one sounded like a sigh in reverse and made her straighten up and stick her chin out. The big-girl panties were on.

"Andrew Gibbons," she said, then curled one side of her lip. She wasn't wearing lipstick, just some shiny lip gloss. It had smeared a little, making her skin look shiny. "Stop me if you've heard this one before."

"Go on."

"April 7th, 2003, a woman named Angela Ligotti is found murdered, stabbed to death."

"Where?"

"Brooklyn. 265 Kent Street. Greenpoint."

"Okay. Near the bridge."

She gave him a quick summary of the case, including all the details that he had been able to research, and a couple that he hadn't: the car being out of commission, the name of the friend who had the red jacket. He kept his trap shut and nodded at regular intervals to show that he was paying attention.

And he was. It was a little test of his, listening to people tell him what he already knew. He liked to see what they left out and what they added — how they embellished things.

She wasn't one of the people who left things out. But what else did he expect — she was a judge. Of course, the case wasn't something that had affected her directly, until Jamie Gibbons had contacted her, so the events weren't things that affected her personally. Nobody was calling her integrity into question. She mentioned that one tire had been slashed out in the parking lot of Green Haven and that she'd changed it. She told him about the message in the dust on her car with the same flat tone of voice she'd used to recite the rest of the details.

The things she added, she pointed at the folder as if to say, "And the basis I have for saying that is right there."

She didn't aggrandize much either. It was like a computer took over her mouth, making her speak in more of a monotone. She slowed down too, like an invisible court reporter was taking down every word, and she didn't want a lot of *um*s and *uh*s in the transcript. She didn't want anybody to miss or misinterpret a word. It was obvious she knew how to recite facts and put them in a logical order.

She didn't try to lead him around by the nose, didn't try to plead Andy Gibbons' innocence. Joe Friday would've had nothing on her.

She wound up the story and shut up. The food had appeared in front of them while she was talking. She picked up her fork and started working her way through her breakfast, first turning her plate to the perfect angle to attack her Eggs Benedict.

He followed suit. He hadn't eaten yet this morning, and he was hungry. The steak wasn't anything to write home about. He lifted the eggs over easy on top of the steak and added some salt and pepper to give it some flavor.

"What do you think?" she asked.

He swallowed. "What do I think? Miss St. Clair, I think you need to tell me what you want outta me. It sounds like a big stinking mess; that's what it sounds like."

"How so?"

"You start digging into the case of a guy who was obviously set up in such a way that it required multiple people to pull it off. You start investigating and get nowhere. Your tires are slashed. Gibbons pulls you off the case, and his wife, who does not strike me as the kind of woman to give up easily — even less than you, if you don't mind my saying — doesn't sound upset. If any part of this does not sound like a big stinking mess, feel free to enlighten me."

She snorted delicately. "Oh, I agree. I just wondered what your interpretation was."

"My interpretation is that if you keep digging, you're going to get in trouble."

"I... have come to realize that." Up came the coffee, right in front of the face. "I have looked at the possibilities and have decided to continue my investigation."

"Even if I don't take the job?"

"I'll find someone."

"Lady, anybody else that you find is going to figure out very quickly what you've gotten them into, and then take the retainer and run."

"So you won't take the job?" The look on her face flipped through three different expressions: first relief, then disgust, then back to a smooth, professional mask.

He shrugged. Something was stopping him from saying no. He didn't want to see her get hurt by trying to do this all on her own. There was also something that screamed at his sense of justice and fairness. It really depended on her, though, whether she was committed enough to see this through.

"As you heard last night, my father is a judge," she said. "We used to live in Brooklyn, a nice brownstone in Clinton Hill. When I was young, about sixteen, suddenly we moved north to White Plains. My parents had been fighting, and I mostly put my fingers in my ears and played a lot of chess, either alone or with my...I guess you could call him my uncle, a family friend." Her lips twisted. "Yes, I was a chess nerd when I was a kid if you hadn't guessed already."

"What rank?"

She shrugged. "It doesn't matter. Not enough to make my living winning chess tournaments for the rest of my life. The point is, I never understood why we had to move. Nobody told me. It was just expected that I would go along with whatever my father wanted, and I did. Now I start to wonder; was he driven out? Did he run into something like this on one of *his* cases and have to make a decision between justice and keeping his family safe?"

"Sounds like it," Jake admitted.

"That's what I think too – a man I've looked up to my entire life, running away with his tail between his legs."

Jake put down his fork and raised his hands. "Whoa. That's too harsh. You said he had a family to think about. You can't blame a guy who can put his family on one side of the scale, his job on the other, and decide in favor of his family. My dad, he was a good guy and all, but he made the opposite decision, and I can tell you that it didn't exactly make anybody's life any easier or better."

"What did your father do?"

"He was an Army sniper. I barely saw him, and when I did, he was either fighting with my mom or making up to her. I lived the romantic life of a full-time babysitter to my younger brother and sister until I joined up."

It was only now that she glanced down to see if he was wearing a wedding ring, which of course he wasn't.

"You were in the military, too."

"That's right."

"What branch?"

"Army, Delta Force. And if you bring up the Chuck Norris movie, I'll kick your ass. I am so tired of hearing about the first time people watched that movie and whether or not Norris is the best martial artist ever."

She nodded. Evidently she couldn't care less about the movie, or Chuck Norris, which was nice.

"It's nice to know that...someone else had trouble escaping their father's legacy."

"It was a good legacy — just not a great one for someone raising kids."

"I know what you mean." She looked at her fingernails and the empty wedding-ring finger. Then she picked up her fork and started picking at her fruit salad. "All right, what I want you to do is track down the second witness and find out what he saw and why he was never asked to testify. The car —"

"License plates, find out what happened to it. Them."

She nodded and stabbed a piece of melon. "I have something difficult to ask you."

"You want to know if I will operate within the boundaries of the law at all times while working for you."

She put her fork down beside her plate and dabbed at her mouth with her napkin while he was talking. She blinked at him as if she were surprised that he'd guessed at something that was written all over her face.

"That sums it up, yes," she said. "*If* I hire you, we need to be very clear about what your boundaries are."

"You can't just let me do my job and trust me to get results? You sound like those politician monkeys dictating the rules of engagement to frontline soldiers from their comfy, cozy offices in D.C."

"I realize that other people have," she paused momentarily, "different values than I do. However, my primary concern here isn't just my sense of ethics, but in obtaining evidence that will hold up in court."

He shook his head. It was the wrong approach, totally naïve. He was already convinced there was never going to be a retrial in this case. The whole thing was going to play out behind the scenes. But of course, she wasn't going to hear that —- not from him. She was going to have to find out for herself.

Sometimes you had to choose between following the law and fighting for justice. Anybody who'd ever read a comic book knew that.

He grinned at her.

"What?"

"Just lay down the rules, lady."

She cleared her throat, reached for the coffee, and saw that it was empty. She made a show of pouring herself another cup, then offering him some more. He waved her off.

"First rule. You are not to take any illegal activities in obtaining evidence or answers to questions."

He shoveled a forkful of steak and eggs into his mouth. The eggs were starting to get cold; they'd been talking so much.

"Second. You are not to probe into matters in such a way that will cause negative repercussions for Mr. Gibbons and his family."

He had to close his eyes for a second so she wouldn't catch him rolling them at her. She'd obviously already stirred things up and caused problems for the guy, or else he wouldn't have told her to back off.

"Third. You and I are associates. We will never have a personal relationship of any kind."

It was getting harder not to crack up with every second. "You must have been burned a couple of times if you have to lay that out when you hire an employee."

"You are not my employee. You're an independent contractor - a freelancer. I'm hiring you on a temporary, independent basis, solely to make use of your experience and skills."

He couldn't help it. He leaned back in his chair so the front two feet rose off the ground. "If I'm not your employee, then you can't tell me how to do my job. Independent contractor means exactly that – independent. That's how it works. You hire me to do something; I get it done."

She blew out a breath in a way that said she used to smoke cigarettes. She didn't smoke now — he would have picked up the scent on her when he took her coat.

"Nevertheless, Mr. Westley, those are my conditions."

"Yeah? And what do I get out of it, besides a sense of righteousness?"

"I will pay you your standard rates."

He dropped his chair back onto the floor. "Sixty bucks an hour plus expenses, including fifty cents a mile if I have to use my car."

She looked up to the ceiling, tilted her head to the side and let her gaze go soft. "Seventy-five an hour, plus expenses," she said.

He chuckled. "That's not how negotiations work, lady. I say what I want, you negotiate downward — not the other way."

"I want your full attention," she said. "You're obviously not getting rich from taking on divorce cases. And I want to make this a difficult job for you to walk away from, especially if someone should decide to put a little pressure on you."

"So what's going to keep *you* from walking away if someone puts a little more pressure on *you*? Or on the Gibbons'?"

She shrugged. "Stubbornness, I suppose."

"That's not going to be enough."

The corner of her lip twisted again. "If you say so, Mr. Westley."

He held out a hand. "Call me Jake. I'll get you some paperwork to sign to cover my ass in case you decide not to pay me, and then we can get started."

She didn't need to know that her father had contacted him last night after the incident at the bar had circulated through enough local law enforcement officers to reach the crusty old retired judge.

Jake had taken the job, of course. Gratis. He owed the elder St. Clair more than a small favor like this. Plus, he was pretty sure the guy wouldn't take no for an answer.

It'll be interesting to see which one of them is more stubborn.

Chapter 5 - If he isn't all of those things

Regan met Jamie Gibbons for an early supper at the same cheap diner she had before, yellow pleather seats, brick walls, and a row of stools at the counter. Every table had its own ketchup, sugar, and salt and pepper set. The diners looked like they were almost all eligible for the senior discount, and more people were reading newspapers than checking their phones.

Jamie wore a coat that was too light and soaking wet thin-soled canvas shoes that surely were split across the bottoms. The waitress led them to a lonely table in the back corner, no bribery required. Jamie ordered the same as she had before, a hot open-face turkey sandwich, soup, and mashed potatoes. Not the most expensive thing on the menu, but not the cheapest either.

Both of them drank their coffee black. The diner was too warm inside until someone opened the door, and then the wind would gust in creating a draft all the way to the back of the building making Regan shiver for a moment. Jamie surely would have walked from her apartment — ten blocks away. She left her coat on and pulled the collar up.

Regan said, "Andy told me to back off his case."

Jamie's fists were closed on themselves with the hot coffee mug sitting between them. The skin was red and chapped. "I know."

"He told me not to waste my time."

"I know."

"But what do *you* want me to do? Really?"

Jamie snorted. "What do *I* want you to do? *I* want you to keep on with the case."

"Then why did you tell me to let go of it on the phone?"

"Because it was the phone."

Regan stared at her. Surely the woman couldn't be that paranoid.

"Andy's giving up because he's putting his bets on getting parole someday. He's not thinking in terms of getting killed in prison or losing his boys to the streets. I love him, but sometimes he doesn't think things through. He's a hot head. He uses his charm instead of his smarts. I want you to keep on with it."

Regan sipped at her coffee. Her heart rate sped up. She'd been prepared to let it all go, aside from laying out a few different plans on how she could help Jamie and the boys get by, in the unlikely event that Jamie would accept the help. She needed a moment to change gears.

"Are you sure?"

"I'm sure. It'll be a hard thing to do, even harder if Andy won't cooperate. And we both know that you're making someone unhappy about this, nosing around the way you have done. I'll understand if you have to walk away from this."

Regan took a deep breath until her lungs wouldn't take any more, and then let it go. "I'm glad to hear that."

"You are?"

"Yes, because I didn't have any intention of letting this go. I'm going to stay with it."

"You are?"

"I hired another detective."

"Hmm."

"A good one this time."

"Where'd you find this one?"

Regan felt her face growing hot and took a preemptory sip of coffee, holding it in front of her face again. She had to stop doing that. She wasn't fooling Jamie, she could tell. A little curl touched the woman's lips.

"He saved me from a group of thugs in a bar fight."

"Better than finding him through a phone book."

They sat and drank coffee until their meals arrived. The waitress came back and refilled their cups.

"I think Andy's getting threatened in prison," Jamie said about halfway through her sandwich. "He doesn't like to tell me things that might worry me. Keeps a positive face on everything, no matter how bad it is."

"Who?"

Jamie shrugged. "It's a feeling I have."

"Do you think it's related to...my investigation?"

There were a dozen ways that Jamie could have answered to spare Regan's feeling of guilt, which she'd been fighting all day. "Probably... and don't ask me if I'm still sure I want to do this. I'm sure."

"I ... all right."

Jamie ate her way through the rest of her sandwich. "And don't throw pity-money at us either. Not until it's hopeless."

"All right."

"And keep safe. Keep that detective around."

Regan smiled at her. She'd already finished her club sandwich, asking them to hold the fries. "He seems like a good character: intelligent, quick, maybe even trustworthy."

"Protective and willing to step up, it seems."

Regan took another sip of coffee and watched a couple of frowning old men scowl at her through the window, then enter the diner, bringing a gust of the wind in with them. She'd stepped on someone's toes and probably did need protection. She just didn't have to like it.

"I hope so," she said. "Because if he isn't all of those things, this isn't going to work."

Chapter 6 - A few words with Mr. De Wit

Of the tasks that the Honorable Regan St. Clair had given him — check out the second witness as well as the jacket and the car, but in a completely legal fashion — Jake decided to ignore all of them.

They weren't bad tasks. But they all rested on the idea of him being some kind of errand-boy who didn't need to get a sense of the situation as a whole. And, while he could see her getting ideas like that, working in the big machine of the legal system the way she did, that wasn't how he played; or how he got results.

Instead, he drove into Brooklyn and started with the location of the crime in Greenpoint next to the Greenpoint Avenue Bridge. Despite some recent redevelopment in the area, it was still not a neighborhood to be in after dark — lots of tags on the walls, corrugated tin, and razor wire along the tops of chain-link fences. With a little more crumbling to the walls, it would have looked like a war zone. Most of the cars parked along both sides of the streets were in good repair, owned by people working at the water treatment plant during the day. The streets at nighttime would tell a different story.

It still felt more comfortable than being in White Plains. This place might be dangerous at night, but that place gave him the creeps.

He parked with his front bumper hanging just over the edge of the yellow strip on the curb. The shots of the murder scene had come from a narrow corridor between two buildings, too narrow to be an alleyway. He ducked under a partially open roll-up door that led to the back of a warehouse, a place for a delivery truck to back into. Beside it there were two trash dumpsters in a niche on one side and a narrow access alley on the other.

He walked down it. Bingo. Just underneath a fire escape was a spot on the wall that looked familiar. Bright security lights and a camera covered the entrance to the access alley.

It wasn't an area that you could see easily. But it was where the body had been found, not where the cyclist had supposedly seen Andrew Gibbons parking the car and murdering the woman.

It was a cold day, plenty of wind. Down in the service alley, it was dark and even colder, although the air was mostly still. It smelled of mold and sewage. The whole area smelled bad, being right next to the Newton River and the water treatment plant.

He jumped up trying to catch the release on the fire escape, but it was out of reach, even for him. The wall back here wasn't tagged much as the other end of the narrow alley was a brick wall. A couple of windows overlooked the alley on the theory that a window looking out at a brick wall was better than no window at all. Having been in some places with no windows, he had to disagree. A man looking out a window at a brick wall was a man who was constantly reminded that he was in a prison of one kind or another.

The windows were all out of reach, in line with the fire escape on the third floor. The HVAC systems buzzed overhead, and the traffic and sirens echoed between the closed in walls. The wind carried the smell of the river. No surprises, the area was just as he expected.

He squatted down. A few pieces of trash had piled up: a fast-food receipt, a wadded-up piece of tissue, and a plastic cup lid of the extremely disposable variety.

You didn't get 'a pile of newspapers' blowing into alleyways. You got trash.

A pile of newspapers in a closed-off alley like this didn't just happen by chance. It was someone's stash — a layer to put on the ground underneath them to keep their cheap sleeping bag or blanket from coming in close contact with the sidewalk or ground. A good pile of newspapers was money in the bank if you were homeless. Not as good as a thick piece of cardboard, but still pretty good and easier to hide, too.

The cement was stained underneath the fire escape, but not with blood or black squares where, say, a layer of mold had built up under some papers. Just a couple of puddled drip marks, black with a center streak of rust, where rain dripped from the black stairs overhead and ran down the center of the alley to a small drain.

He made sure he didn't look directly into the security camera. Unless something went wrong, he'd never need to tell the Honorable Judge St. Clair, Jr. that he'd been here.

He left the service alley and headed back out onto the street. The cyclist had reported seeing the interchange in a green car, no definite make, model, or license plate number, parked eastbound on the street. He'd been riding on McGuinness Boulevard and happened to glance down the side street.

A hell of a place to be out cycling at night. Having a few words with Mr. De Wit might be worthwhile.

Chapter 7 - Interesting

Next up, on his to-do list was Detective Peter Marando, a.k.a. Jake's current favorite example of an officer in charge of scumbaggery. Giving the wife a packet of evidence to prove her husband's guilt had been a nice touch.

He had an apartment in Bed-Stuy that turned out to be on the third floor of a brownstone that was nice but not too nice. The windows in the English basement and the first floor had bars on them, but the stairs were crowded with flowerpots full of dead flowers, the kind that with luck would grow back in the spring.

The front door, for whatever reason, wasn't locked. He stepped into the foyer. It had plaster walls and some fine old wood, three enameled gray mailboxes, and a narrow wood door at the end of the short hallway. Marando's mailbox was labeled for the third floor.

He climbed the stairs which were covered with worn-out red carpet from the Seventies. The railing was sticky but in good condition, with square posts at each end of the carved banisters, and some nicks and dents. It took a lot of abuse to tear up these old places.

The second floor smelled like Indian food while the third floor smelled of cigarette smoke. A TV was playing in the background, people bursting out in laughter on a talk show.

He fished in his wallet and pulled out a picture of his sister. The picture was over a decade old, and she was wearing a t-shirt with a striped necktie, along with so much eyeliner that her eyes looked like a cartoon. It was perfect for flashing at people. You'd believe any stupid behavior out of a kid like that. Even if nowadays she was a soccer mom.

He licked his lips and knocked on the door.

The volume on the TV turned down, and Jake knocked again. Springs creaked, the TV flicked off. A drawer opened but didn't shut.

Heavy footsteps walked toward the door. It moved in its frame a little as a weight leaned against it. "Yeah? What is it?"

Jake held the picture up to the peephole drilled in the antique door. "I'm looking for someone."

He heard a tense click in the background. "I ain't seen her."

"There's a reward."

The pause that followed was longer than he liked.

Finally, the door twitched, and a door guard clicked shut. A couple of rattling locks later, the door opened a crack, and stale barroom-like air assaulted Jake. It smelled like the guy had smoked a couple of packs already this morning. Marando's brown eye bulged out of its socket at him like an accusation of heresy from a terrorist. He was wearing carpet slippers, and he hadn't shaved.

Jake held the picture up to the slit in the doorway. The guy looked at it for a couple of seconds. The eyelids narrowed and shifted back and forth between Jake and the picture. "Nah, I ain't seen her."

"Someone saw her in the area on Tuesday about seven o'clock. She came out of this building."

"This building?"

"Yeah."

The eye lost some of its ugly glare. It was still an ugly eye, though. "Some nosy bastard is feeding you bullshit, my friend. Downstairs is an old black widow. The middle floor is a pack of Pakistanis stinking up the place. And up here it's just me. I can guarantee that nobody had a hooker come through in the last couple of weeks at least — unless the widow's been sneaking them in downstairs."

"She's not a hooker. She's someone's sister."

Marando's eye sought out Jake's for a second, looking amused. "Every hooker is someone's sister. Who are you anyway, her brother?"

"Private investigator," Jake popped a card toward the guy, holding it just out of reach between his forefingers, not moving the photo. He wasn't too disappointed when Marando didn't unbar the door to take it.

Marando laughed on the other side of the door, and the smell of smoke got stronger. "Fun times, tracking down runaways. I bet you're about ready to go back to your divorce cases, aren't you? The romantic life of a P.I."

Jake shrugged.

"I'm just razzing you. Good luck, man," Marando said. "Have fun paying the bills."

"Thanks."

The door closed. Jake tromped down the stairs and, just for the hell of it, knocked on the second-floor door, where he ran through the same story again to a suspicious looking Pakistani woman who nevertheless opened her door to him. The widow on the first floor was out.

Marando hadn't recognized him but had still been waiting for trouble.

Interesting.

Chapter 8 - Going to have to wait

The second witness, Frederick B. Schnatterbeck, still lived in the same building in Greenpoint as he had ten years ago, a Nassau Avenue three-story brick walkup with narrow windows and a seafood restaurant on the first floor, apparently run by hipsters in beards, black glasses, and cable-knit wool caps. The narrow flight of stairs up to the second floor reeked of fish and fry-grease.

An old man in a blue polo shirt, sweat pants, and an oxygen tube opened the door when he knocked. He looked Jake over from his shoes to his face and back again, and said in a voice so old it sounded like an out-of-tune radio, "You here to talk about Andy Gibbons?"

"Yes, sir. I'm a private —"

The old man waved his hand. "Yeah, yeah. Come on in."

He led Jake into his apartment. The ceiling and walls were yellow from old tobacco smoke. The old man trailed a small oxygen machine that bumped off the wood floor and onto the stained, rubber-backed rug. They passed an old TV set built into a big wood cabinet with a single recliner in front of it. The recliner was covered with coarse, short white hair all over the arms and back. No dogs barked. A heavily repainted door in the wall opposite the recliner revealed the corner of a full-sized bed, no coverlet. The sheets and plain blue blanket were neatly tucked in with square corners.

"Call me Fred," the old man said. "You wanna beer or somethin'?"

"I'm all right."

"I'm gonna have a beer." The kitchen had a small dining table, white cabinets, cracked linoleum, and an old refrigerator with flecks of gold in the mint-green paint. At a glimpse, it was full of takeout containers and plastic dishes covered in Saran Wrap. Fred pulled out a bottle of Miller Lite and opened it using a bottle opener screwed into the end of a cabinet. The cap fell into a metal trash can with a *clink*.

An efficient system Jake surmised.

"Andy Gibbons' wife called an' told me she finally got someone to listen to her, and when she did, it was worse than when nobody was listenin' to her. What's your name?"

"Jake Westley, Private Investigator."

"Private Dick, more like it. You need a mustache." He held up his finger under his nose, probably imitating Tom Selleck. Jake chuckled. He'd seen this type of guy a hundred times. Usually, they were stubborn as hell and straight as an arrow – as long as you could put up with them "telling it like it was."

"She's a good woman, a good mamma. She deserves better than what she got, even if that no-good husband of hers don't. Ya know what he was out doin' that night? Either cheatin' on her or doing drugs — or both. She didn't want to hear my theories on what he was up to, though; but it adds up."

He stumped back into the living room and sat in the recliner, hauling on the handle so hard it looked like the chair was going to launch him to the moon. "You pull up a chair from the kitchen. I don't have the back for sittin' in those damn things no more. One day they're gonna find me here in my chair, dead for a month."

Jake took a sniff. Either the stink of fish couldn't make it this far, or the guy never opened his door. "Do you have a dog?"

"Used to. Sparky, he's dead now."

He glanced over to a shelf on the wall opposite the TV and recliner. A big brass vase that looked like a fake antique sat next to a porcelain dog. A couple of old Time-Life books lay flat on the shelf. Everything was covered with a thick layer of yellow dust.

Jake grabbed a chair from the kitchen and sat next to Schnatterbeck. "What makes you think Andy was cheating on his wife or doing drugs?"

"Everybody knew that he wasn't just working his shift at the water treatment plant. I was still playin' a lot of poker back then. We talked a lot after poker games. At least the losers would. We was as bad as a bunch of old wimmen—folk about it. Word got around that he had more money than he should'da, and then suddenly one day he didn't. So I say it was both. First, he started selling drugs. Then he started doing 'em and picked up a lady friend for the side — someone who wouldn't tell him to watch the boys and do the dishes."

"Are you sure?"

"Sure? Hell, I ain't sure whether I'm wearin' my pants on backward most of the time. But whatever he was doing, it took him out of the neighborhood three or four nights a week fer goin' on a couple years."

"Huh."

"Uh-huh." Schnatterbeck smacked his lips together and then drank some more of his beer. "Workin' for someone he shouldn't have."

"Who?"

"No idea. For a long time it was a guy named Aniello Gallo. Then he disappeared, 'round the same time that Andy started staying out late and drivin' his wife nuts."

"Mafia infighting?"

"Who knows? The crime around here, it's strange."

"Strange how?"

Schnatterbeck shrugged.

"So tell me what you saw the night Angela Ligotti was killed."

"This was back when Sparky was still on this side of the big doggy door in the sky, and I was taking him out for his nightly walk."

"Down by the river."

"Hey. The dog liked the smell. We started walking past Kent Street and saw a green sedan, a Lincoln, in the drive of one of the back doors of the water treatment plant. The gate was up and everythin'."

Jake grunted.

"The car backed out and —"

"Wait," Jake said. "The car *backed* out?"

"Did I stutter?"

The door jingled at the bottom of the stairs. Schnatterbeck grimaced. The stairs began to creak.

"In an' out," he complained. "Those kids upstairs, third-floor walkup, they got more energy than sense. I hope they have a couple of kids real soon so they'll move out to the suburbs to 'go find themselves' and maybe 'get some space.'"

The footsteps on the stairs didn't sound like they belonged to either half of a young couple. Jake found himself curling a foot around one leg of the kitchen chair, turning it at an angle.

Schnatterbeck reached into the cloth bag hanging over the arm of his chair. The remote was on the other arm of the chair. After he had finished checking the back, he pulled his hand out and reversed the lever, snapping the chair upright with a clunk.

He took a long look at Jake and the way he was sitting in his chair, then grunted and stood up.

The footsteps stopped, then resumed a few seconds later.

Schnatterbeck waved toward the kitchen.

Jake picked up the chair and soundlessly carried it back to the kitchen, then took a step back out of the way so that he wouldn't be seen from the door. The old man followed.

Neither of them spoke.

The footsteps came up to the landing. Schnatterbeck pulled open the fridge and moved a few of the containers around. The bottles clinked against each other. He slammed the door shut and then opened the bottle. The cap clinked into the trash.

The person crossed the narrow landing and knocked at Schnatterbeck's door.

"Well, shit," Schnatterbeck said under his breath, then louder, "What?"

"You got a delivery," a low voice said.

"I ain't ordered nothin'."

"Maybe someone sent it to you — for Christmas. Don't be a wise-ass. You gotta sign for this. It's my job."

"It's not marked *live animal* or something like that, is it?"

"Nah. Just a regular package."

The voice hadn't identified itself. Jake reached into his back holster and drew his revolver, a Smith & Wesson model 627 with wood grips and eight rounds of .357.

Schnatterbeck started to walk toward the kitchen door, but Jake held him back.

"Hey," the voice said. "What are you doing in there? Hurry up. You gotta sign for this package."

Jake gave Schnatterbeck a push backward and held up a finger to his lips.

The guy beat on the door. "Hey! Come on and take this package!"

"I'm *busy*," Schnatterbeck said. "Just leave it by the door."

"You gotta sign for it!"

"Then take it back with you and leave a slip saying I ain't home. I didn't order nuthin' anyway."

Wood crunched and the front door slammed open.

Jake stayed out of sight.

Schnatterbeck's face was red with rage, and his fists were clenched, but at least he wasn't getting any stupid ideas, like running out into the open.

"Get out here, old man!" the voice shouted.

Jake held up a hand for a second. Schnatterbeck nodded, not loving the order but recognizing the source as competent to give it.

The voice came closer, feet clomping across the rugs on the floor. He was breathing heavily. Not a guy who did a lot of stairs on a regular basis.

Jake hadn't heard a second set of steps on the stairs, but he wasn't ready to discount the possibility. He might have missed the sound under the noise of the bigger man's approach.

The bedroom door hit the wall.

"Old man?" The voice wasn't as loud. He was in the bedroom.

Jake took a step to the side, aiming down the hall. It was clear — no backup on the stairs that he could see.

He pulled back into the kitchen.

The bathroom door crashed on the other side of the wall, and the guy inside cursed.

"Where are you? Did you climb out onto a balcony or somethin'? What? I just want to talk to you."

The bathroom door opened.

The floor creaked. "You're in the kitchen, ain't you? If you're getting a beer, you want to get me one too?"

Neither one of them moved. Another step or two and the guy would be able to see one of them, depending on which way he was looking — maybe both.

Schnatterbeck raised the beer to his mouth as if he were getting ready to take a drink.

The guy took another step forward.

Schnatterbeck threw the beer at him.

End over end it turned, whipping through the air and hitting the guy in the face.

A gunshot went off.

Jake had just planned to scare the guy to get some information out of him. But with Schnatterbeck's action, his plans changed rapidly. He grabbed the front of the intruders' throat in his empty fist and slammed his head into the door frame. Then he put his revolver up to the guy's ear.

The guy's eyes rolled back up into his head.

A Glock 36 fell out of the intruders' hands and landed on the floor. He started making a hacking noise deep in his throat as he slid down the door frame, which was now smeared with blood.

Okay, so he might have hit the guy a little too hard.

Jake guided him down.

Then he took a look toward Schnatterbeck and swore.

The old guy was hanging on to a cabinet door. He had a white face and a hand clutched to his chest above an ugly entry wound.

He hadn't just been shot; he was having a heart attack.

Schnatterbeck slid down and knocked a couple of pans off the shelves behind him. They banged on the floor as his eyes rolled around in their sockets.

Jake kicked the Glock under the little dining room table and then put Schnatterbeck flat on his back on the floor with his feet up. A clean tri-fold towel got turned into a compression bandage under one elbow while he pulled out his cell phone and called 911.

A glance at the invader told him that he was going to be out for a while with a fractured skull at least. That the guy was still breathing was more than he deserved.

The operator answered. Jake snapped out the address and added, "Home invasion, gunshots, the owner got a .45 to the chest. Can't talk now." He put the phone down and leaned his head against Schnatterbeck's chest.

The guy's mouth was opening and closing like a fish like he wasn't getting any air. Jake did a mouth sweep but didn't find anything.

Schnatterbeck sucked in a breath, and then coughed up blood. At least, he didn't hear a sucking sound.

"Lung hit," Jake told the phone. A siren wailed outside, but it was too soon for it to be coming for them.

Whatever Schnatterbeck had intended to say about the car backing out of the water treatment plant would have to wait.

Chapter 9 - Solid facts and data

Regan didn't make it to the Brooklyn Hospital Center until almost 11 pm. She was irritated, tired, and worried.

Irritated - because Jake hadn't followed her instructions and now there were two seriously injured people in the hospital.

Tired - because of a trial she was presiding over — a pair of drug addicts.

Worried - because moving people into danger wasn't as much fun as it was with pieces on a chess board. She'd opened this can of worms without even knowing who her opponent was.

What a fine way to pay Jake back for saving me at the bar.

The court case involved two drug addicts, a pair of siblings who might or might not have had incestuous relations with each other, and a pair of old women — twins.

Family. What was one to do?

The addicts, last name of Tarloff, had broken into a home in Harrison and robbed the two old twin widows, shooting one of them when she tried to call the police. The break-in had clearly been planned ahead of time, using information from a local teenager who had helped them clean out their basement the previous summer.

It was a felony murder and a mess, made worse by the fact that the surviving sister was calling for the death penalty for one of the siblings. "An eye for an eye and a tooth for a tooth," the woman had stated.

The defense lawyer, a mildly cocky young attorney named Nick Sikes, hinted that he planned to argue that his clients were being framed by the siblings' mother for reasons unknown.

It was a headache of a case with an endless list of witnesses for both sides, conflicting testimony, physical evidence that had to be reviewed, and some of it thrown out, and the ever irritating presence of television cameras.

The media had engulfed her every time she'd stepped out of the court. One reporter had even followed her to the women's toilet and had to be forcibly removed — camera operator and all.

During a recess, she checked her messages in the judge's chambers. Aside from her home, it was the only true privacy she had.

Jake had texted her about his progress.

First, he'd trespassed onto private property, the location near the Greenpoint Bridge where the body had been found.

Then he'd met Detective Marando, in person at the man's apartment. An "interesting character," he said.

And finally, he'd spoken with Frederick Schnatterbeck at *his* apartment, where they'd both been attacked by a man named Lance Powell. Schnatterbeck had taken a bullet in a lung *and* had a heart attack, and wasn't expected to survive the night. Jake had taken down the attacker, leaving him critically wounded.

But she shouldn't worry about *him;* Jake was fine.

The rest of the trial had gone smoothly for the day, as smoothly as the tangled skein of lies could go at this point. Everyone involved sensed Regan's fury as she came back into the court.

Jake had broken laws, ignored her instructions, and prematurely revealed himself to at least one of the characters at the heart of the case.

She'd get the rest of the information from him tonight at the Brooklyn Hospital Center, and then she'd fire him.

It was better for everybody's sake.

The drive helped calm her down. The fact that Jake and Schnatterbeck had been attacked had serious implications. Someone did *not* want the case to be investigated, even ten years after the fact, which meant there was clearly something to be found.

She pulled into the parking garage and walked to the main lobby. The lights had been dimmed, and the security guard at a small desk near the entrance looked up at her as she entered. She got directions to Schnatterbeck's room, signed a register, and took the escalator upstairs. The coffee shop was closed. Her caffeine craving and subsequent throbbing headache would just have to wait.

She checked in at the critical care unit, where she had to sign in again, show her ID, and wear a visitor badge. She could visit Schnatterbeck all night long if she wanted to, but she couldn't be in the room with him at the same time as Jake.

She waved to a couple of nurses' aides as she proceeded down the hallway. Someone in a room further down was crying — but otherwise, the rooms were quiet.

The dimly-lit halls were small, low-ceilinged, and seemed vaguely threatening. They reminded her of the emergency room she'd taken her father to last year when they thought he might be having a heart attack. In her father's case, it hadn't been a heart attack, just dehydration and stress. But with the way he refused to change his diet or stop smoking, it was likely that she'd be back in a unit similar to this one in the not too distant future.

Schnatterbeck's room was private with a clean but well-aged linoleum floor, no window, and yellow walls that seemed too bright for the late hour, even though most of the lights were off. Jake was skimming through something on his phone, a flickering glow across his face as he swiped across the screen.

She knocked on the door, and Jake looked up. He glanced over at Schnatterbeck for a moment, touched his lips with a finger, stood up, and cracked his back before crossing the room. He slid his phone into his pocket. "Hey."

She looked him over. His clothes were still spattered with blood; the knees of his khaki pants were soaked in it. He'd washed his face and his arms but had missed the side of his head where dark droplets stuck in his hair — all of which reminded her of problems that she hadn't asked f or.

"How is he doing?"

"He's an old-fashioned bastard — used to be Coast Guard. They say he'll be fine if he takes care of himself."

"If he's anything like my father, he won't," she said. "What about the other guy?"

"He's in Bellevue in serious condition. I, uh, fractured his skull when I smashed him into the door frame in the kitchen."

"Yes, you did," she said.

He snorted under his breath. "And me? I'm fine, no injuries; thanks for asking."

They were still standing in the hallway outside the room. She took a deep, calming breath. "The apartment?"

"The cops should have it secured by now. He didn't have any pets — unless you count the cremated dog in the pot on his shelf."

She made a face. "I think his dog is pretty safe."

"Unless a drug addict comes to the wrong conclusions about the ashes."

She gritted her teeth.

"Sorry. I always get a real black sense of humor after this kind of thing. I'll try to keep it a little more tactful."

"Please do." She looked back into the room. Schnatterbeck was a lump under a blanket and a fringe of gray hair around a bald head. He had the kind of face that spoke volumes about his blood pressure. "Let's find a waiting room."

He started walking slowly down the hallway, hands in the pockets of his bomber jacket.

"Anything on your side?" he asked.

"I've been in court all day with the Tarloff case." At his blank look she added, "felony murder and burglary by a pair of siblings, one male, one female. They claim they weren't there at all and were framed by their mother."

"Is the female pregnant?"

"No, thank God. The media feeding frenzy is bad enough."

His eyes narrowed. "You didn't actually answer the original question, by the way. Is there a reason for that?"

They passed another doorway with the light still on, a nurse bending over the bed.

"Maybe. I requisitioned the prosecutor's files on the Andy Gibbons' case, but I haven't had anything sent over yet, which is unusual. I have a good source over in the Records department."

"They're going to turn up missing," Jake said.

"What makes you say that?"

He shrugged. "Let's grab a coffee."

"The coffee shop is closed."

"We'll ask at the nurses' station. Nurses always know where to get coffee."

***

In a corner of the critical care ward waiting room stuffed with toys, board games, DVDs, and a row of Danielle Steel novels, they found a single-serve automatic coffee maker stocked with coffee and hot cocoa. It was so simple that a three-year-old could have operated it — which meant that when Regan tried to brew her coffee, it splattered all over the place.

Jake cleared his throat, pulled the pod out, stuck it back in, and ran the cycle again — presto, instant coffee.

"You didn't do what I asked you to do," she said.

"Is that why you're in such a foul mood?"

"One of the two reasons."

"The trial being the other?"

"I'm paying you on an hourly basis. Explain to me why you're not following directions and yet making me pay for it."

He stared at her calmly, chewing on the inside of his cheek for a second, sizing her up.

She felt her cheeks start to get hot.

"I'm not doing this to screw you out of your money or flaunt my independence," he said. "I'm doing it because I'm a professional. You've been on the ground for what, four months? And you expect me to be up to speed based on a folder full of unreliable evidence, most of which was compiled by that scumbag, Marando."

"You should have called me beforehand. Contacting Marando was inappropriate."

"Maybe," he admitted. "Nevertheless, I had to look the guy in the eye and size him up. Have you met him yet?"

"Yes, on another case, a long time ago."

"How did he strike you?"

"Don't try to change the subject."

He leaned back in his chair, put his paper cup on the seat next to him and folded his arms across his chest.

"Explain to me why you get to — excuse me. Explain why you would even *want* to micromanage me. Didn't you hire me to get the information that you couldn't get out of people?"

"I get to micromanage you, as you put it, because I'm paying you."

He waited.

She took a gulp of hot coffee, praying it would erase her headache so she could actually think for a minute. "Yes. I hired you to get the information I couldn't. That doesn't mean I don't expect you to follow directions."

"Then I won't charge for those hours."

"Don't be ridiculous."

"If you want someone to follow your orders exactly, get yourself a robot. You're no master detective, and I'm no dumb sidekick."

"None of this tells me why you can't follow directions. Maybe I didn't *want* you to see Marando yet. Maybe I wanted to save you for something more subtle than a frontal assault."

"If you had a plan, you should have said so."

"I don't need to explain my plans to you."

"No? Maybe I would have followed directions if you had."

She finished her coffee, walked over to the coffee machine, and started another cup. She was more careful inserting the pod, making sure it was seated properly. This time it worked, and the cup filled properly. She stared at it for a second.

"Tell me what you learned while I was paying you to not follow directions," she said, not facing him.

"Come on back here and sit down, would ya? I hate talking to a woman's back when she's mad at me. Please."

She roamed back to her seat. Her caffeine headache was easing up a little, but she was still shaking. Two people were almost killed, Jake and Schnatterbeck, three if you counted the bad guy. And it had happened following her part of the plan. For all that she'd yelled at him for talking to Marando.

She sat and let out a long breath. "I'm so tired," she said.

"Go home, go to bed."

She let out a sigh and pulled out her phone. The missed calls and message icons had appeared. She could just imagine what was waiting for her. Everyone would want to hassle her for at least a week. Then the interest would die down for a while unless one of the lawyers sprung a surprise on her. Then it would rise back up again near the end of the trial.

"It never ends. Just when the current class of idiots gets old enough to be too lazy to stir up much trouble, a new batch of idiots comes along and you have to start all over again. The real problem is that even if these kids get put away, it won't bring the victim back, and it won't stop two more kids, or 2,000 more kids from doing something just as stupid. It burns me every time."

"That's why you're doing this, isn't it? To keep yourself from going nuts."

"To *try* to keep myself from going nuts. Otherwise, yes."

"Then think about Andrew Gibbons. Think about what it would be like for him to get out of prison and go home to his family. Think about what it would be like for his kids to have their dad back."

She closed her eyes and remembered Andy's goofy grin, half despairing, half hating himself for daring to put his hopes on her for so long.

"I just wish..." She didn't finish the thought; there was no point.

"So, the place where the body was found, do you still want to hear about it or save it for later?"

"Tell me now. I'm not really going to get any sleep."

He told her about the location where the body of Angela Ligotti, Andy's alleged victim, was found. She'd seen pictures of it, but it hadn't really clicked that the location was that far back from the street. His description was so sharp that she could almost count the number of footsteps between the open roll-up gate and the chill in the shadowed alley

"But how did the body get back there?" she asked. "If it was after dark and the gate was rolled down. Nobody should have been able to access the area."

"That isn't the weirdest part. Schnatterbeck saw a green sedan — he said he thought it was a Lincoln — backing out of the drive."

"Wait," she said.

"That's what I said," Jake grinned.

She knew that he knew what she was going to say. She just couldn't stop herself from saying it. "If the car holding Angela Ligotti's body was backing out of the water treatment complex, then why was the body found inside the water treatment complex?"

"Exactly, they'd have to go right back inside, unless someone else lifted the body back over the fence. It was almost like someone screwed up."

He'd sent her a dozen photographs of the area via his phone. She flipped through them until she saw the one she wanted: a solid cement wall topped with razor wire.

"We don't know if the razor wire was there ten years ago," he pointed out.

She drummed her fingernails on the plastic chair arm. "Why there? Why not leave the body in the street? Why not push the body into the river, for that matter?"

"Dunno. Want me to try to find out?"

She paused for a moment. "Not yet. If there's someone at that plant who's involved, then we don't want to alert them."

"I'm on their security cameras."

"Yes, I know. I'm hoping they didn't get a decent look at your face, by the way."

He grunted.

"And then you spoke to Marando," she said drily, "Anything interesting to report about that encounter?"

He told her about seeing Marando, then summed up with: "I got the impression he's a real slime-ball."

She hadn't seen Marando for a long time, but it had been her impression as well. "Did he strike you as the kind of guy who'd help frame Andy Gibbons?"

"Sure, easy."

"But he isn't exactly living in the lap of luxury, is he?"

"Sometimes a man's got bad habits that eat up anything extra."

"Noted."

Jake continued with the theory he'd heard from Schnatterbeck before the arrival of Lance Powell, the man who'd broken down the door of the apartment — the theory that

Andrew Gibbons was a small-time drug runner and possible adulterer.

It wasn't anything that she hadn't heard before. It was, in fact, part of the "evidence" that Jamie Gibbons had received from Detective Marando and part of the packet that she'd handed over to Jake.

"How valid do you think Schnatterbeck's theory is?" she asked.

"Do I think Andy cheated on his wife? I don't know, but if he did, we might have an alibi for Andy at the time of the murder."

Regan leaned back. "I think Jamie would have had it out of him by now and, at the very least, included it in her packet of evidence. She wants Andy back, and she's not afraid to humiliate herself to do it."

"What do you think it was then?"

Repeatedly, Andy had refused to tell Regan where he had been that night, what he had been doing, or who he'd been with. He'd driven around Brooklyn; he didn't think he'd left the borough, but he wouldn't get more specific than that. He'd denied cheating on his wife, although there had been a couple of times that he could see that someone might think he was. He'd also vigorously denied being involved in any kind of criminal activity.

She had chalked it up to her being a judge. He didn't trust her with the truth, whatever it was. She drank some more of her coffee.

"What about delivering packages on the side? Drugs, money, that kind of thing?"

Jake slurped at his coffee. "Tell me something. Does Andy Gibbons strike you as an ambitious guy or not? Family man, company man, or the kind of guy who has a plan to get rich quick?"

She chewed on a knuckle. Jake was right about her needing him to do the work she couldn't. She'd rather have solid facts and data to extrapolate from and leave the intuition to someone else. One of the reasons she'd hired Jake was that he seemed to be able to size people up at a glance. The fact that he'd been able to bribe the server to give them a private table at *La Ruche* had really impressed her. She'd never thought of trying it, for one thing — and if she had, she wouldn't have been able to tell if the woman was the kind of person to take the money or kick them out and report them to the manager.

"I'm not sure," she said. "Let me tell you about the first time I interviewed him. It stuck in my mind, but I've never been sure how to interpret it."

"Go for it."

Chapter 10 - Young and stupid

The first Saturday in November she'd driven up to Green Haven for the first time. She had been treated with open deference coming through the gate. George Williams, the deputy superintendent, had even taken the time to speak with her in his dismal office before letting her in to visit with Andy. He'd assured her that they would make every effort to assist her, but warned her that Andy Gibbons was a murderer and would, of course, lie to her about his guilt and that she wasn't to believe him. In the right mood he could be charming, but she shouldn't trust him.

Then he started talking about her father and how much he'd respected him. The fact that he was hosting more of her prisoners than her fathers didn't seem to register.

She kept a serious look on her face and nodded all the way through his little lecture.

On the recently painted adobe-colored wall behind him were various certificates, a law degree and his bachelor's degree. He probably still had his good citizenship and perfect attendance awards from elementary school somewhere. Where another man might have pictures of his family on his desk, this guy had a row of small awards, glass paperweights, golden stars, and a statue of a man with an upraised golf club.

She had trouble taking the man seriously.

When he was done speaking, she repeated his talking points back to him, thanked him for his time, shook his hand, tried not to stare at the top of his balding head as she towered over him, and left the office at a measured pace, following one of the guards.

She felt his eyes on her back and wondered for a moment whether she had misjudged him. The first part of his speech, the part about Andrew Gibbons, had been too pat. At least she hadn't given him more than a picture of the arrogant daughter of a popular judge to work with. It was a mask that she used more often than not in court, and it held up under scrutiny.

She was escorted to a private visitor's room, one-half of a glassed-in cell with a pane of safety glass in the middle. She seated herself on an uncomfortable fiberglass chair and folded her hands in her lap.

A large black man in a green uniform and handcuffs was led past her door, brought into the room opposite her, and urged down into the matching fiberglass chair.

She'd seen photographs of Andy Gibbons before, but they didn't do him justice. They showed him slit-eyed or angry, with apparently cold, dead eyes, as if he was heartless. He looked like a small-time criminal with something to prove in every single photograph. Even the ones that had been taken of him by the media before and during his trial had the same message.

In real life he had an innocent-looking face, like a baby's, with fat cheeks, a broad forehead, and wide-open eyes. He saw her and smiled, all the way up to the corners of his eyes. She could hear his footsteps and the rattle of his handcuffs via speakers in the ceiling.

"Judge Judy she is not!" he said after the guard had handcuffed him to the bench beside the pane of glass between them. The guard nudged the chair with his knee. Andy Gibbons gave him a look that flashed back to the photos in the news for a second, then turned away from the guard and started smiling again. "Jamie says you're going to get me back to my boys. Is that right?"

"I'm going to try," she said.

"That's about as good as it can get," he said. "Unless you're Yoda, in which case you just gotta do or do not. But personally, I'm pretty good with a try."

He folded his hands in front of him and then scooted the chair forward. The guard backed out of the room and locked the door behind him, standing with his back to the locked door. She doubted that the room provided any real privacy, but at least she didn't have to try to talk over a row of other prisoners.

She pulled two folders out of her briefcase. One was the evidence put together by Jamie, based on the collection given to her by Marando. The other was a folder of her personal notes.

"That Jamie," he said. "She's really something, isn't she?"

"She is," Regan agreed dryly.

Andy burst into laughter. "She wouldn't let up on you, would she? You think, yeah, I'll just hear her out, get her to shut up. But then she starts talking, and everything you assumed gets cut out from under you, one point at a time. She should have been a lawyer, not a nursing assistant."

The words were almost hostile, but his tone wasn't.

"She didn't take it easy on you either, I take it," she said.

"Oh, no. I was quite the hellion when she met me. Did she tell you about that?"

She shook her head. Andy Gibbons was genuinely charming, but he was wasting their time together. They only had half an hour. He shouldn't be telling her about how he met his wife; he should be answering her questions about the case.

"I was out playing a pickup game near a park. She and her mamma were out for a walk off to the side of the court. I went in for a three-pointer, I mean that shot was looking pretty, but it hit the rim and went flying. It hit her momma, right in the head. I thought she was going to skin me alive."

Regan repressed a smile. "She fell for you after you hit her mother in the head with a basketball?"

"She almost caught it, too. Her momma swayed on her feet and just blinked for a couple of seconds. Then Jamie started cussing me out for a fool. Not a single word of strong language but my ears were blistering, and I was about in tears. The rest of the guys ran off, the cowards. By the time she was done I was down on my knees, literally begging her momma's forgiveness. And her mamma said, and I quote, 'I will only forgive you if you take this girl out on a date. She's so harsh that she can't get anybody to take her around, and I'm beginning to despair. She is 24 years old, and I'm afraid I'm going to die without seeing a single grandbaby.' As you can imagine that about let the wind out of Jamie's sails. She crumpled up with her arms over her chest and stalked off. But her mamma gave me her phone number as I was walking her home."

"Happily ever after," Regan smiled.

Andy gave a wry smile and snorted. "Not exactly."

She flipped open the packet of evidence and riffled through the pages. Andy's eyes skipped back and forth between the papers and her face, and his smile faded a little. He was studying her, sizing her up.

"Tell me what happened," she said.

He leaned back, took in a long breath, and said, "I was framed. I ain't no angel; Jamie'll tell you the same. But I didn't kill that woman."

"All right," she said. "What happened? What *did* you do that night? You haven't really explained yourself."

His cheeks dented in like he was sucking the spit from between his teeth. "I got in a fight with Jamie. I borrowed a friend's car — a brown Accord — and went out driving. Ten years ago, you know how old I was?"

"No."

"Twenty-two. When you're twenty-two, you don't have any sense. You can be a good man and still not have the sense to see what your wife's telling you is... well. You've met Jamie. She has a good head on her shoulders. I couldn't see it then. But every year that she sticks by me and tries to hold it all together for my boys, I appreciate it more and more. Plus, I'm getting older; I have more sense than I did when I was twenty-two. I look back now, and I can see that I was wrong and she was right; I should have listened to her. But back then I just got mad and stormed off. The more right she was, the madder I would get."

"So you just went driving around?"

"Yeah, to calm down. Like I said, young and stupid."

"And nobody saw you."

"In Brooklyn? Could have been a thousand people saw me, but who would remember me, behind the wheel of a brown Accord?"

"You didn't stop for anything."

"No, ma'am. I drove around for about an hour, maybe an hour and a half. Thought up an argument that might work with Jamie, and drove home feeling pretty high and mighty. I lost the argument, but I still wasn't ready to admit it. But by then it was late, and I had to work in the morning. We went to bed, her on the couch. That thing where they tell you not to go to bed mad? My last night with my wife, and I made her sleep on the couch."

"You were arrested the next day."

"Yes ma'am, right there at work. It was humiliating."

She nodded. She had no doubt that he had an entertaining story to tell about being arrested, but they needed to stay on track.

"What was the fight about?"

"I can't see how that's relevant."

"It's a murder investigation. Anything could be relevant."

"That's what my attorney said too. See where it got me."

She frowned and closed the folder full of "evidence" and opened the other one, filled with her notes. Inside was a yellow legal pad with the pages riffled from being turned back and forth so much. The pages were covered with her illegible scrawl, almost more effective than a secret code for keeping prying eyes from finding out her thoughts.

"Mr. Gibbons —"

"Andy. Call me Andy."

She looked at him through the glass. The way he'd said it sounded odd, strained. If his face had shown anything other than an infectious grin, it was gone now.

"Andy," she said. "You may call me Regan if you like."

"Whatever you say, Miss St. Clair."

She shook her head. She didn't like it when people put themselves on an asymmetrical basis with her — it felt like their conversation was based on a falsehood. "Andy, tell me something. Did you kill the woman?"

He looked up at the speakers on either side of the glass wall. "No ma'am, I did not."

"Did you kill someone *else* that evening?"

His head jutted forward, and he blinked at her. Every trace of his grin had disappeared, not so much that it was replaced with hostility as that she had just shocked it off his face. "No! What on earth could possess you to ask a question like that? *Did I kill someone else?* No, I didn't kill someone else. And I wasn't sleeping around either, no matter what that low-life Marando says."

She nodded and noted his responses down on the last page of her notes. While she was still writing, she asked, "One more question. Did you do something that would cause someone you love to be harmed or killed if the truth about that evening came out?"

She glanced up quickly and caught the look on his face. It was a look of raw fear and heartbreak, quickly erased by that same grin. The eyes had changed, though. They were cold and emotionless, just like the photographs.

"Nope," he said. "Just what I told you. I was driving around after a fight with Jamie."

"Right," she said. "May I have the name and address of the friend who loaned you the brown Accord? Somehow, it's one of the pieces of evidence that never made it into your file."

He gave it to her, and she noted that down too, then sneaked another look up at him when he might not be ready for it. But he wasn't about to get caught off guard a second time. His smile had faded, and he showed nothing but interested attention.

They went over the rest of the evidence. It was clear that he'd talked to Jamie about the same points she'd listed off to Regan. His speech was a little less rehearsed, and a little less wild-eyed than the one that Jamie had given her, but it was basically the same. If he knew more than he'd shared with his wife, he nevertheless didn't share it with Regan.

The guard tapped on the window at the five-minute mark, then again when it was time for her to go. She cut off mid-sentence, closed the folder around her notes, and packed everything in her bag.

She stood and started automatically to extend her hand for a handshake. Andy's hand twitched, but remained handcuffed to the bench. He smiled at her again. This time, it was just a thin upturn on one side of his lips.

His eyes were neither smiling nor cold, just resigned. The same look would become familiar over time as their meetings progressed. It would haunt her from their last meeting when he told her that she wasn't doing him any good and just to let it go.

"Thank you for your time, Mr. Gibbon," she said formally. The presence of the guard reminded her that he'd been standing watch over them, and she felt too self-conscious to use his first name anymore.

"Thank you for yours, Miss St. Clair. Tell Jamie I love her and that I miss her and the boys when you see her next."

"I will."

She put on her coat and hefted her briefcase onto her shoulder. The guard unlocked Andy's door, then unlocked his handcuffs from the bench. He stood as the guard pulled the chair out of the way and gave her a nod.

The guard led him past her on the way out. He was taller than she was — a feat that most men couldn't manage when she had heels on. He gave her another grin as he passed her, turning on the charm one last time, and then he was out of sight. She waited a few seconds, then opened the door to her side of the glassed-in room and stepped out.

The guard led Andy down the hallway through a pair of barred security doors and down another hallway. She waited in place until someone came to lead her out of the prison. She didn't have to pass through a long hallway of inmates banging tin cups against the bars or anything ridiculous like that, but she couldn't escape the sense of being stared at, even leered at. The only person in sight was a guard at the high-walled desk where Andy had been led, and he was looking at something below the top of the desk, not paying attention to her.

The other three glass visitors' rooms were empty. She looked inside each of them, all of them identical: two fiberglass chairs, the heavy metal bench with the eye bolt screwed through the top on one side, and speakers.

Their conversation had to be recorded.

The guard returned to escort her out of the prison. She walked after him, keeping her head up and her eyes focused on his back.

She needed to find a way to ensure that Andy and his family wouldn't be hurt if he told the truth.

Chapter 11 - Underground taxi service

"You think he's being threatened to keep quiet?" Jake asked.

Her coffee had gone cold. She tossed it back and made herself another cup, letting it gurgle and hiss through the machine and into the cup. The waiting area had a couple of windows that looked out over the city, orange lights on red brick. If they'd been facing the other direction, they could have looked out at Manhattan and Jersey City, almost an entire continent unto itself. Instead, it was Bed-Stuy all the way to the long black stretch of the Atlantic.

She wasn't one of those people who found the ocean fascinating. The sound of the waves got on her nerves — like listening to someone chew with an open mouth. Give her a nice gentle lake anytime. She sat down and turned her back to the waves.

"I think I wanted to believe that initially," she said. "It would answer a lot of questions. No, strike that from the discussion. Why wouldn't he tell us what he was doing that night? His family is suffering because of it. Is he worried they might suffer even more if he spits out the truth?"

"Here's one. Did he know the victim before she died?"

"He did." She looked at the clock. "That's a story for another day, though. The short version is that they worked together at the water treatment plant. You must have read that in the file."

"I did. But I wondered."

"It's suggestive, isn't it? But suggestion is often just another way of being pointed in the wrong direction."

He shrugged. "Sometimes things aren't so complicated. A guy has an affair with a coworker and doesn't want his wife to find out about it."

"Do you really think that's what happened here?"

"No."

"Why?"

He closed his eyes. "I don't know. I just have the feeling there's more to it than that."

She shook her head. "I don't approach things intuitively. I don't like to go on 'feelings.' I deal with facts." She went quiet for a second or two, "and unanswered questions."

"So what facts do you have?"

"None."

"That's what you hired me for."

"Exactly. I just have the unanswered questions. If Andy killed Angela Ligotti because she was a mistress who didn't want to play along any longer, then the prosecutor did a horrible job of tracking down relevant evidence to back up that theory. During the trial, the motive for the killing was presented as 'an argument' between Andy and the deceased, not an adulterous relationship that turned sour.

"You know what's not in that packet of evidence? Witnesses: witnesses saying they saw Andy with Ms. Ligotti before the crime; witnesses saying that Andy had been seen around her apartment; witnesses of their behavior toward each other at work. And yet from the information in the evidence packet that

Marando threw at Jamie Gibbons, that was the extent of their relationship."

"Let's approach this from a slightly different angle," Jake suggested. "Let's say that Andy murdered Ms. Ligotti because she witnessed a tryst between him and a second woman — or a man. Let's not limit this by gender."

Regan nodded. "If that were the case, the prosecutor still should have been able to pull together some sort of pattern reflecting that — reports of Andy showing up in the same neighborhood on a regular basis or rumors at work. Patterns like that are as identifiable as a fingerprint. There is nothing so secret that someone doesn't know *something* is going on. The human brain simply cannot function on high alert all the time. A pattern of long lunches, early days off from work, off-site meetings, bowling nights — *something* should have shown up."

"But there's nothing?" Jake lifted his eyebrows.

"If there is, I'm not seeing it. And I've looked at his schedule up and down, back and forth, at least the parts of it I was able to obtain ten years later."

"What parts were those?"

"His work records — the time he spent clocked in."

"You got his work records?"

"Gary did." The coffee had disappeared again. She had to cut herself off or she'd be up all night with the entire Tarloff case to face in the morning. She paced across the room. The traffic outside moved in bursts along the streets.

"And you didn't see any patterns?"

She shrugged; she didn't have enough data. "He could have had someone clocking in and out for him — something else neither the prosecution nor the defense bothered to find out. And while he was often spotted driving back and forth to work in his green Lincoln Town Car, I noticed that none of the witnesses ever stated they saw him driving it in the evening. According to various statements, he was always in some other car in the evening.

"The only other information we have comes from Jamie. She says that Andy would go out at nights, never at the same time or even on the same night, and it would only be for an hour or two. If she asked where he was going, he'd answer just like he was a rebellious teenager: 'Where are you going?' 'Out.' 'When are you coming back?' 'Later.' She said she stopped asking. He wouldn't come back smelling like anything worse than cigarette smoke — no alcohol or perfume, or even pot smoke. She said that both of them were young and stupid, and she was too proud to beg him to tell her what was going on. The situation became don't ask, don't tell. Sometimes he'd come back with cash. She said she half-assumed he was out playing poker.

"I asked Andy about it multiple times, coming at it from multiple angles. But he never told me what he'd been doing. Not really. He said that sometimes they would fight, and he would leave the house to cool off. Or he just needed space. Or he was having a beer or playing basketball with friends. I asked him about poker, and he offered to let me teach him how to play."

"That means he's a shark."

She snorted. "His eyes were twinkling like my dad's do when he said that. At any rate, he was so insistent about not having a pattern that it's almost a pattern in itself — deliberate randomness."

She concluded with a feeling of triumph. She'd worked out a lot from the holes in the evidence, a lot more than most detectives could have, even when they weren't scumbags like Marando.

Too bad it added up to a whole bunch of nothing as far as an actual lead went.

"Deliberate randomness, just like the cars," Jake said.

He was giving her a look that said he'd worked out something obvious and wanted her to figure out the next step.

"What about the cars?"

"The question is who might keep a car pool of random, unmarked cars? And why?"

"Ah!" she said. She was disappointed in herself for not seeing it. She shook her head. There was a *reason* she'd hired a private investigator and wasn't doing this all herself. "You're thinking of a crime syndicate, maybe the Mafia?"

"Perhaps, or maybe an early version of an underground taxi service, run off the Internet. It could still be running, too."

She felt herself deflate even further.

A nurse walked by the open door of the waiting room and gave her a significant look. She'd been speaking too loudly. She bit her knuckle again and shut up. The dark blue industrial carpet almost seemed to have a darker circle worn into it for friends and family to pace on. She let her feet follow it mindlessly for a while, trying to calm down. She'd had too much coffee. She felt like she could almost solve the universe on a hypothetical basis if she had another cup.

"I'm going to run to the toilet," she said.

"You go ahead and do that." Jake stood at the window now, staring out at the ocean. "But after that, I'm cutting you off on the caffeine. You're starting to freak-out the staff."

Chapter 12 - I know a guy

The night nurse still stood outside the door with her cart, speaking into a small walkie-talkie that chirped softly when she released the button.

"Rodger dodger," a voice said. "I'll see you later, then." The walkie-talkie beeped again.

The nurse hooked the walkie-talkie over the waistband of her uniform and started pushing the cart down the hallway. Regan turned the other way toward the toilets.

Inside, she had to wave her hand in front of the motion sensor to turn the lights on. Nobody had been inside for at least ten minutes. While she was there, she checked her phone messages. She had 23 of them. The first five were what she expected — pleas from local media for an interview.

The sixth shook her.

A digitized, male voice said, "Hello. I have information about the Gibbons case. Please call the following number." And then it rattled off a ten-digit number.

The message ended.

After staring at her phone for an embarrassing length of time, she saved the message, pulled a pen out of her purse, replayed the message, and wrote the number down on her arm. She was too bewildered to find a scrap of paper from her purse.

The bathroom lights flickered out.

She laughed at herself. She'd been sitting stock-still long enough for the motion sensor to turn itself off. She finished up, pulled her clothes together, switched the light on her cell phone on, and stepped out of the stall.

A dull glow spread through the room and bounced off the mirrors over the sinks.

She walked toward the light sensor by the door to trigger the lights to come on. She found it odd that the expected light was not forthcoming, and a shiver ran through her body. She walked toward the sinks to wash her hands.

In the dim light of her phone, it took her a couple of tries to find one with soap, and then she moved to the hand drier and dried her hands.

When the hand drier clicked off, she turned toward the door and pulled on the handle.

The door was stuck.

She pulled on it twice before she realized her heart had leapt up into her throat. The door wasn't stuck, it was locked.

Something moved in one of the toilet stalls.

Regan's hand slapped the wall, catching part of the light switch on her palm. She groped around and pressed the switch up and down several times, then waved her hand in front of the motion sensor.

The lights remained off.

There should have been an emergency light on in the bathroom, even if the main lights failed.

There wasn't.

She clenched her teeth together and sucked in a hissing breath. She was shaking with fear and rage. *Again.* When she'd repaired the slashed tire on her car, she had been angry. Now she recognized her anger as a cover-up for how terrified she was. She doubted that Jake would hear her if she screamed for help.

She aimed the light on her phone toward the back of the room.

A shadow moved under the door of the last stall.

"Hello?" she called.

The door began to open a crack. Regan watched it in terrified fascination.

"Hello? What do you want?"

A woman in a long black wool coat and sunglasses stepped out. She had her hands in her pockets, which concealed a suspicious bulge that made her coat sink to that side.

"Hello, Regan," she said.

Regan straightened up, putting some steel in her spine. The dim light of her phone quavered. "What do you want?" she repeated.

"You know what we want," the woman said.

"We. Who is we?"

"To some extent, we have to admire you. Even now, when you're being threatened, you're trying to wring every possible bit of information from this encounter. But, of course, we cannot let our admiration for you interfere with our goals and plans."

Regan suddenly realized the woman's mouth wasn't moving.

She smirked a little as Regan flinched in surprise. The voice was not coming from the woman. It sounded as if it was coming from a speaker somewhere in the room, and Regan looked around for the source of the voice.

The woman's heels clicked on the tile floor as she approached. Regan looked back at her again. She had come a few steps closer and then stopped as if waiting for a cue. The bulge in her pocket seemed to protrude even further.

"This is your last warning," the voice said. "This is the last demonstration of what we can do before we start hurting you and your family."

Regan didn't answer. They'd just established the *limits* of what they could do to her, which was locking her in a bathroom with the lights turned off. The fact that they were mentioning her family meant that they knew less about her than they thought they did. It was just her and her father now. And no one who had ever met her father would ever think that he would allow someone to scare him away from something he meant to do.

Except that he'd left Brooklyn. And she'd had to rethink her assumptions about that.

She licked her lips.

"And, if that isn't effective, then we will shift our focus to Andrew Gibbons' family. Helpless, impoverished, exposed to and battered by every storm that passes through life, vulnerable in a way that neither you nor your father will ever be. Easy for one small action to have ramifications that you and your money and connections could never fix. Do you understand?"

She nodded.

"We will not ask you what your decision is at this time. We know that it's easy to say words of bravado and foolishness in the heat of the moment — words that, when tempers have cooled, one might regret."

The woman pulled her right hand out of her pocket. It was holding not a gun, but a cell phone, an old-fashioned flip phone. She walked over to one of the sinks and laid it across the back of the faucet.

Someone knocked at the door, and Regan almost dropped her phone. She fumbled with it as Jake called, "Hey, you drown in there?"

The room flickered, and the lights turned on, blinding her for a second. She dropped her smartphone. It made a cracking sound, and she swore.

"Regan?"

"I'm fine," she called back. The screen was completely shattered. She stuffed it in her pocket.

The woman walked up to Regan and stopped in front of her, both hands in her pockets again. She smelled of cigarettes, perfume, and damp wool.

Regan was tempted to grab her and yell for help from Jake, but she was inert. The woman passed her and took the door handle.

By then it was unlocked — of course.

Jake stood in the doorway with one hand stuffed in his jacket pocket, and his eyes swept over the room. They locked onto the woman's face, studying it quickly and automatically.

"Excuse me," the woman said. Jake stepped out of the way, and she left.

Regan hiccupped. She'd been holding her breath. Quickly, she walked over to the last stall and looked inside.

She didn't see anything out of place — nothing that the woman had dropped or left behind. She unrolled a stream of toilet paper and used it to pick up the flip phone on the back of the sink.

Jake stepped into the bathroom and did another one of those eye-sweeps that seemed to take in more than Regan would ever be able to see. He bent down and picked up a piece of dirt off the floor, crumbled it in his fingers. She half-expected him to say something about it being mud from Suffolk or something Sherlock Holmes-ish like that.

"You were threatened again," he said.

There was no chance of being able to conceal it from him. She was too upset. "No shit, Sherlock."

The flip phone began to ring, and she shuddered. He held out his hand, but she shook her head — her case, her responsibility. She tore off a piece of the toilet paper and used it to open the phone. She held it away from her ear.

"Hello?"

"Hello, Regan?" Jamie Gibbon's voice came through the phone. Regan felt her eyes bulge. She leaned toward Jake, trying to angle the phone so they could both hear it.

"Jamie. Are you and the boys all right?"

"Am I all right? You're the one who called my machine and left a message saying that you were in danger and not to call."

Regan lied. "It turned out to be nothing."

"Don't scare me like that. I took off early from work to check on the boys; I was so worried."

"And they're okay?"

Jamie paused for a couple of seconds. In the background, Regan could hear the sound of Jamie's ancient refrigerator kick on and rattle. "Something did happen, didn't it? And you're trying to keep me from getting worried."

"I was pretty shaken for a few minutes; I have to admit."

Another pause. "Better safe than sorry."

"Agreed."

"Well, I'll get off the phone then. When you get calmed down, tell me what happened."

"I will."

The question that Regan wanted to blurt out — *where did you get this number?* — wouldn't seem to leave her lips. But then Jake wasn't giving her any kind of signal to ask it either, just looking at her with calm blue eyes that had gone a deep blue that somehow wasn't pretty so much as it was a threat. She was glad it wasn't directed at her. The sides of his jaw clenched.

She rolled her shoulders a couple of times. "Jamie, do me a favor. See if you can't get someone from the neighborhood to check up on the boys while you're on your shifts, would you? Or I can get someone."

"Is there something wrong?" The response came quickly like Jamie had been expecting it. With reason, obviously.

Regan wanted to say: *If it weren't for your pride, I would pull you and the boys out of that apartment, move you into my house and put guards over the three of you. I'd make you take a vacation so you could put your feet up and watch daytime TV all day, and put your boys in a real school, away from the gangs. And I'd do 100 other things because you're being threatened. And I'd do it right now.*

But she didn't because she had no idea who else was listening to the call.

"I'm just shaken up," Regan said. "I'm going to check in on Fred Schnatterbeck in a couple of minutes. Is there anything you want me to tell him for you? If he's awake."

"Tell him he's a good man, and I'm sorry that he got mixed up in this."

"Okay. Have a good night, Jamie. I'm sorry I worried you."

"It's all right. You keep working at this. I have faith in you."

Regan smiled. If she weren't careful, her eyes would start beading up. "Thanks. Talk to you later, Jamie."

"Night."

Regan turned off the phone and handed it, toilet paper and all, to Jake. Then she put her back against the wall and slid down to the floor.

They'd taken over her phone number, routed it to a completely different phone, and left a message on Jamie's answering machine that had sounded so much like her that it had fooled Jamie, who was not so easy to fool. They'd *known* Jamie would call and had timed their manipulation of her so exactly that... that...

She put her elbows on her knees and put her hands over her face. She didn't want Jake to see her upset.

The phone beeped. She glanced up; Jake was punching in a number from memory.

The phone in her pocket rang, no ID on the number. She turned the cracked screen toward Jake. He had a pen out and wrote the number down in a notebook. The phone stopped ringing.

"Oh, right." She pushed her coat sleeve back on her arm, showing him the other number.

"What's that?"

"Write it down, would you?"

He did.

"I was checking messages; that's what originally took me so long. One of them was a computer-generated voice that told me to call this number if I wanted more information on the Gibbons case. It was buried in the middle of a bunch of requests for interviews on the Tarloff case."

She dialed into her voicemail and handed the phone over. Jake walked across the room with one finger in his ear, listening to messages while pacing. Regan got back up to her feet, still feeling shaky and light-headed.

Jake glanced up at her, his eyes still dark. "It's gone," he said.

She wasn't surprised. "The message is gone?"

Jake nodded. "You need to get someone with some serious computer skills," he said. "I know a guy…"

Chapter 13 - I'm willing to accept that this is serious

It didn't look like much of a place — a brick three-story building crushed between an apartment building and a Thai restaurant, a bakery across the street, skinny trees coated with ice and trapped in holes in the sidewalk, cars with half a foot of snow still on their roofs. Finding a parking place took him half an hour. A small sign read *Coffee* and *Thumbprint Cafe* underneath. The tree in front had been yarn-bombed, a knitted sheath of colorful yarn had been wrapped around the trunk and stitched shut. In the shadow of the buildings, LED mini lights twinkled around the outside of the yarn and up into the branches.

He spotted a mini security camera wired to the LED lights and had no doubt there was more than one.

He walked in. The air was hot and filled with the sound of laptop fans buzzing. Nobody looked up except a girl in a lambs—wool lined coat near the door. She was wearing earmuffs, fingerless knit gloves, and a nasty expression on her face as the cold air rushed at her through the open door. Jake raised a hand at her and closed the door behind him. She went back to her laptop screen, fingers flying over the keyboard.

Long tables lined the room, each filled with people packed in elbow to elbow at laptops. The bare brick walls were hung with blackboards decorated with pastel chalks announcing the available menu and the specials of the day. Electrical outlets were built into the tables. Instead of family photos, collections of TV stars hung on the walls: actors from Star Trek, Star Wars, Firefly, Xena, and who knew what else. A lot of them were signed. The back of the espresso machine was covered with decals and the quote of the day read, 'With A Warning Label This Big, You Know They Gotta Be Fun!' A printer near the wall spat out sheets of paper. A cooler full of energy drinks hummed contentedly under the sound of fingers hitting keys. Three kids cursed and laughed at the same time as they flinched back from their laptops, then leaned back in.

Jake walked up to the counter, where a blue-haired girl covered in tattoos chewed gum and played a game from behind the counter on a small netbook. One of the perks of the job.

She looked up. "Hey. Whatchoo want? You look like a beer guy, not a coffee guy. We don't serve booze here."

"I need to talk to Alex."

"Alex? He's busy. Doing a raid."

"Tell him it's Jake."

She shrugged. "Okay. But plan to wait for a while." She ducked into a door marked *Employees Only* next to the bathrooms, a Batman logo for men and Wonder Woman for women.

Jake spotted four more cameras, mostly nestled between the posters and picture frames on the wall. A couple of motion sensors covered the till and the *Employees Only* door.

Most of the people here had no idea that this place had started out as a money laundering operation for a group of computer hackers that lived in the basement. Now it was a little more complicated.

The girl came back looking impressed. "The king will see you now. You want an espresso to take down with you?"

"Some regular joe, if you got it."

She poured the dark, hot liquid into a mug and handed it to him. He glanced, amused, as his hand covered a picture of a blond guy in sunglasses making a ridiculous macho pose. "Cream? Sugar?"

"No thanks," he said and edged past a woman with a screen full of evil trolls chopping away at a guy in armor. He pushed open the *'Employees Only'* door, ignored the stairs upward and headed down to the basement.

Jake had met Alex Carr when he was 27 and Alex was 18. Now the kid was 29 years old and nowhere near the top of his game. In his line of work, he was never going to run into the limit of what his body could do on a professional level. He was never going to have to wonder if someone was going to die based on his lack of physical capabilities.

Sometimes Jake was a little jealous of him.

He took the narrow stairs two at a time as he descended, making sure he didn't hit his head on the low ceiling. The security door was open and waiting for him, a pair of large, obvious security cameras in either corner above it.

If the upstairs of the cafe had been decorated in heavy Hipster Geek, the basement was pure Aesthetically Oblivious Hacker. The walls were brick where they weren't lined with bare gray metal shelves. The lighting was 100 percent neon lights in cheap fluorescent light fixtures. Tin air ducts, copper pipes, and wiring ran under the acoustic tiles of the dropped ceiling. The intervening space was filled with noise-absorbing foam and a steel plate to secure it from the cafe above.

He stepped under a vent spewing cold air. The basement was packed with so much computer equipment they had to run the A/C constantly, even in the middle of winter.

Six guys and one woman sat at terminals along a big table in the center of the main room. They all wore noise-canceling headphones and typed at keyboards in front of an array of monitors, at least six big extra-wide ones per person. Another five or six empty chairs sat in front of similar arrays. It had the feel of a room full of Warfighters reading satellite information, trying to determine whether or not to inform the president that the big red button needed to be pushed.

They were all playing the same video game: Wizards, dwarves, swords, elves, you name it.

The finest minds in the country, taking a break from working for the FBI.

Most of the work they were doing was for the FBI these days, Alex had said —*Most* of the work.

Alex was standing at a cooler full of the same brand of energy drinks as Jake had seen upstairs. He was downing a slim can full of something that would probably make Jake's eyes bleed. But, like a poisoner building up a tolerance to arsenic, Alex could down enough of the things to kill a horse at this point and barely blink.

Alex finished his energy drink and dropped the can into a recycling bin beside the cooler. "Let's take this into the quiet room," he said in his impressively deep voice.

He was dressed in gray slacks, a purple dress shirt, and a gray vest; his goatee was trimmed into a devil's point. His hair was getting long enough to turn curly, and he was starting to build up a paunch. He was naturally handsome, but genetics and metabolism would only take you so far. Eventually, the guy was going to have to start working out.

He led Jake through a door covered in eggshell sound-absorbing foam tiles and into a small conference room that, as far as Jake had ever been able to figure out, was completely devoid of electronics other than the battery-powered overhead lights.

He waved Jake over to the long plastic folding table. It was grungy and surrounded by cheap folding chairs. The walls and ceiling were covered with more eggshell padding, and the cement floor was covered with hexagonal rubber high-grip mats. The air temperature was at least twenty degrees cooler than the room outside.

Jake grabbed a seat and slurped his coffee as Alex sat down.

Alex folded his hands in front of him on the table. "You want to hire me."

"Yeah."

"You're working on the Andrew Gibbons murder case, correct?"

"Yeah."

"With the Honorable Regan St. Claire."

"Yeah."

"Whose father has also hired you to keep an eye on her."

"That's about the size of it, Alex."

They both knew there was no way Alex could say no. The senior Judge St. Clair, Regan's father, had done the kid a favor back when he was in college. He'd hacked into a major bank's accounting system and had moved some funds around in a couple of accounts, making it look like the accountant handling the accounts had screwed up and put the money into accounts belonging to him.

The problem, as it turned out, with being a computer genius is that sometimes you get swindled by people who call themselves your friends. Alex hadn't been trying to steal the money for himself; he'd just wanted to show off to a small listserv of fellow computer geeks.

A couple of them, however, weren't just computer experts, they were also masters of social engineering — and female. One wild night later, the money had disappeared out of Alex's accounts before he could transfer it back to the bank, and Alex had almost spent a serious chunk of time in prison.

Fortunately, he'd gotten completely wasted and confessed what had happened to an attractive FBI agent who was lurking in the off-campus bar in downtown Brooklyn where Alex had gone to drown his sorrows. He would have been busted either way — but the agent had felt some sympathy listening to Alex's sob story.

And she'd taken Judge St. Clair aside and spread that sympathy around, making sure the judge understood that Alex would be under supervision while he was on parole. *Close* supervision.

Jake had followed along with the story with updates from his younger brother Sean, who was a fellow computer geek and Alex's roommate at NYU-Tandon. Sean had eventually gone into programming for Lockheed-Martin. He didn't have the nerves to venture too far away from legality, but Alex was another story. If he hadn't been a hacker, he might have made a decent sniper. As far as Jake knew, he hadn't lost his nerve since he'd been scammed by the two female hackers from his listserv. The guy was like a piece of socially inept ice.

"So tell me what you couldn't tell me over the phone."

"Do you have a few minutes?"

Alex raised his eyebrows. They were slightly peaked at the top, completing the slightly devilish air. "I'm open. Talk away."

Jake pulled a USB stick, Regan's busted cell phone, and the flip phone out of his pocket and slid them across the table. Alex pocketed each of them without breaking eye contact and waited, his full attention on Jake.

Alex was a good kid, the only one of the old hacker crowd that Sean was still in touch with.

Jake sketched out the case for him, starting with Jamie Gibbons contacting Regan, and ending with the situation from the previous evening.

Alex drummed his fingers on the table top. His eyes looked straight through Jake.

"I'm going to have to cancel some operations," he said finally. "Not all of them, obviously. The Feebs can't suspect anything. But the Russians —"

Jake raised his hand. "You're talking out loud and saying things I don't need to hear."

"Sorry." Alex leaned back with his fingers laced behind his head. "I have to have a couple of days to wrap up some projects and shift some others onto subcontractors. The rest of the team has been vetted, but not for something like this. I'll get them moved out and make excuses. I should be ready to start with a few minor pieces in two days."

Jake nodded. "I'm willing to accept this is serious. There were too many systems that had to be breached and a lot of timing that had to be handled. Whoever these people are, they have some serious backing."

Alex started twisting the end of his curly goatee.

"We're talking con men meets genius computer hackers meets corrupt cops. What about that situation doesn't sound nuts to you?"

Chapter 14 - Trembling with dread

His name within the organization, Pavo, came from the Italian word for trembling with dread, *pavor*. It had come to mean that he was the one who made his enemies shake with fear, which was not a goal he had originally set out to achieve. Who did, but madmen? But he had grown to appreciate that quality of the fear he had instilled in those who knew him from the Organization. It was not the fear of a hurricane which swept away everything before it without discernment. It was not the fear of a homicidal lunatic who had brought a gun to a school and begun shooting indiscriminately. It was not even the fear of man who had made an unintentional mistake that cost his superiors money or status.

It was the fear of the man who dared betray that to which he had sworn loyalty — and who had finally come to understand the depth of that betrayal.

Although it had not been the original trembling with dread that he wished to remind himself of when he had first entered the Organization, it was a perfectly acceptable one. Traitors *should* find themselves dangling over the pit they created for themselves — sometimes literally.

His office overlooked the Brooklyn Bridge, although he kept his back to it most of the time in order to prevent himself from becoming distracted. The interior walls of the building, designed by a top architect, seemed to ripple across the hardwood floor. A small conversational grouping of comfortable chairs waited to his left, in case a meeting required a slightly less formal setting. His secretary waited in an anteroom, available at the touch of a button.

It was time for one of his associates to arrive. He closed his laptop and pressed the top of the desk so that the laptop disappeared into a concealed recess, literally clearing his desk.

A red light flashed from underneath the black glass. He pressed the intercom button. "Yes?"

"Someone to see you, Pavo," his secretary said.

"Send him in."

The door on the other side of the chairs opened, and his associate entered.

Pavo had seen quite a few men enter through that doorway who had subsequently betrayed him; certain patterns had emerged. The simplest types of betrayers exposed themselves with indications of guilt. They smelled of sour sweat, which often beaded their brows and erupted from their armpits. Their eyes were wide. Their hands shook. Even men who had not yet betrayed him would evince the same signs.

The more sophisticated betrayers would appear more feral, despite the expensive Italian suits and immaculate grooming. Their cleverness would be barely contained within their beastlike skins. Their eyes would slide around the room. They would pace and crack their knuckles, and they would lean forward in their seats as if to pounce upon him the second his back was turned.

He made sure it never was.

His associate was neither of these types.

He was dressed in a pearly gray suit, purple shirt, and gold and silver tie. He held a gray trilby in one hand which he tapped against the leg of his trousers. Without being invited, he crossed the room and extended a hand to Pavo, who stood to receive him. Pavo shook the man's cool, dry hand.

The both sat at the same moment, Pavo in his expensive and comfortable office chair, and his visitor in the expensive but less comfortable visitor's chair that Pavo had arranged for this occasion. Pavo had purchased the chairs to match in appearance at a casual glance, but to greatly vary in their level of comfort to the person seated on them.

Today, he had selected a visitor's chair with a neutral level of comfort. His associate sat upon the very front edge of the chair with a perfection of posture not normally seen in those who were not professional ballet dancers. Pavo had the impression that the man would have seated himself the same way on any chair he was offered in this office. Another office might require a different posture — a habitual slouch, for example, that was not truly a habit.

"Fiducioso," he said. The name meant one who was trusting but had come to mean something as different from its original intention as that of his own.

The man inclined his head. "Pavo."

Fiducioso specialized in betrayal. He had infiltrated over a dozen organizations for Pavo and opened the door to allow them to be destroyed from within. Pavo had never been sure whether or not Fiducioso was a sleeper of some kind, whether private or public. Sometimes when he was facing a particularly knotty problem, he would lay it to rest and research one aspect or another of Fiducioso's background, attempting to discover a material discrepancy between what he had said and what was available to be found. When he returned to the original problem, his thoughts would be clearer on the problem in front of him. The mysteries of Fiducioso were so convoluted as to make any other problem seem straightforward and plain.

If he, Pavo, were ever successfully betrayed, he knew it would have to be by this man.

"Tell me the progress," Pavo said, bringing his hands together in front of him in a steeple. "I want to hear everything."

Fiducioso didn't bother to relate past details. The Honorable Regan St. Clair's ineffectual search for the truth of the Andrew Gibbons case had been doomed from the start. She simply wasn't an experienced enough detective to manage it. Her intentions, her connections within the legal world, her money, and even her intelligence weren't enough to make significant progress.

She had, nevertheless, been warned, as had Andrew Gibbons himself. Pavo was nothing, if not fair, to his enemies.

Pavo also knew of her meeting the detective hired by her father to keep an eye on her. Jake Westley was an excellent judge of people, a quick thinker, and sometimes even inspired. He sometimes followed his instincts into situations that would prove a fatal trap to anyone else. He hadn't been out of the Special Forces for long and had found himself frustrated with the ordinary run-of-the-mill divorce cases that were the bread and butter of many investigators.

He, like Regan, was known to have an excessive amount of pride. Pavo had considered any alliance between the two of them to be a self-correcting problem. They would eat each other alive, offending and counter-offending each other until their association was that of mutually assured destruction.

According to the terse message Fiducioso had left him late the previous evening, the two of them had at least temporarily resolved their egos and had worked together long enough to make some interesting surmises.

Fiducioso had decided to put Pavo's last warning, which was to be abandoned if it was judged unnecessary, into play. Umbra had delivered the message inside the ladies' room and then escaped without being followed.

He hoped he would not have to carry out the threat, but sometimes children needed to be spanked.

"And this morning?" Pavo prompted.

"As you know, she is presiding over the Tarloff case today. She did not contact Westley before the case began this morning; she checked in with her office during recess to see if there were any messages. She had about a dozen from local and national news stations and instructed to have them deleted."

Pavo found himself leaning forward slightly. "In your opinion, will she continue working on the Gibbons case?"

"She reassured Jamie Gibbons that she would."

"She might be lying."

Fiducioso smirked, the most personal expression he'd made so far during the meeting. He had a talent for expressionless faces. "She doesn't lie," he said. "Not on purpose. It would ruin her sense of righteousness, and that would break her. She is uncompromising."

"If she cannot compromise, why is Westley still working for her?"

Fiducioso shrugged. "Perhaps I misjudged her."

"One other matter," Pavo said, "the message that she received offering her more information on the case?"

"Yes?"

"Was that another one of your manipulations?"

Fiducioso shrugged again. "I was not aware of it until this morning, after one of my technicians double-checked her phone records as a matter of routine and then looked deeper. She has not called the number. Westley instructed her to hire a hacker to look into its source. He has been negotiating with a possible candidate this morning. My technician has set up alerts to let us know if such a candidate is selected and what progress they make."

Pavo nodded. If Fiducioso was lying to him, it was not in any details that he was able to verify independently. He still felt the need to remain cautious and reserved.

Fiducioso wrapped up the last few details of his report and waited for instruction, but Pavo dismissed him with a flick of his fingers. Fiducioso stood, took three steps backward, then turned and walked out of the room, putting his trilby back on his head just as he crossed the threshold. As always.

Pavo could never work out whether Fiducioso's little ritual was a gesture of respect or if it represented the reverse.

Within the unbreakable privacy of his mind, Pavo made minute adjustments to his plans. The organization must be served. His associates must be supported until he could be certain they had betrayed him. To do otherwise was madness.

Nevertheless, he made adjustments — just in case.

Chapter 15 - It'll get worse before it gets better

Jake waited for her in the parking lot of the Westchester Courthouse. He parked near her car — a Lexus — but not too close. Once there, he took the risk of taking a walk around the car. It looked like a light dusting of snow had fallen that morning but had since melted, leaving a scattering of clear droplets half-drying on the black surface. He couldn't see any sign the car had been touched since the snow had fallen. The parking lot underneath the car had mostly cleared of snow, except for a pile of dirty, half-melted stuff that the plows had pushed to the far end of the parking lot over the winter. That was unfortunate. He would like to have had an easy way of telling if anyone had stood next to the car any time during the day.

He did a quick check to make sure nothing had been stuck to the bottom of the car but didn't spot anything. The examination didn't make him feel any better. He still felt like he was missing something.

The day had warmed up some, but not enough that he could leave the car off for more than half an hour at a time. He drank cold coffee out of a gas station cup, just fast enough to keep him in a heightened state of alertness.

He'd shifted into surveillance mode somewhere between the hospital and White Plains, and it wasn't the kind of surveillance mode where you're half asleep most of the time either. His subconscious was picking up on something that he didn't like at all.

The fact that his conscious couldn't find it just made him more anxious.

It reminded him of one of the Delta Force missions he'd been on that had gone wrong. They'd stopped the bad guys — no prison time for them, not with five angry operators on the scene — but it had been too late. An eight-year-old kid had died.

Jake shook his head and punished himself with a big gulp of the cold coffee.

If he'd learned anything on that mission, it was he shouldn't ignore his instincts while he was performing what seemed like routine surveillance.

Now was not the time to get lost in thought.

A slow stream of people had been leaving the courthouse all day. TV crews wandered in and out, setting up in front of the main doors, doing a short segment for the news, and packing up again. The vans stayed in the parking lot, taking turns running their engines for heat and waiting for the trial to wind up for the weekend.

Jake resisted the urge to check his cell phone for any updates on the trial. If things got hairy, the local affiliates would pass on their reports to the national news stations. The big cable networks were probably keeping an eye on things, waiting to see whether something big developed.

Until then, they didn't need a reporter on the scene.

Even a multinational corporation based news network had to take its chances. You couldn't be everywhere at once.

He jiggled one foot on the floor of the car. He checked the clock on the dash. Four fifty-five. The trial had to be wrapped up for the day by now. But it might take a while for Regan to come out.

She didn't have a cell phone at the moment. He'd picked her up a couple of disposable phones that morning from Alex, but he hadn't been able to give them to her yet. Alex had gone through her old one after dismissing his crew, saying that he'd just been hired by a gaming company to pull a couple of high security ARG tricks. The crew had groaned, and Alex had promised that Jake and his sponsors would pay them all two days' pay for the short notice, as long as they got out of his hair in the next five minutes.

The groaning changed to a couple of quick high fives and a couple of fascinated glances in Jake's direction.

Jake decided it probably wasn't worth arguing about. Regan wanted the information as soon as possible. She'd already approved Alex's rates, which were embarrassingly higher than Jake's, without a second thought.

Already, Alex had been able to report the number of the cell phone that had sent the message to Regan, a prepaid phone with fake registration. At least Jake was pretty sure they weren't being called by an eighty-year-old woman in a nursing home in Nebraska.

He was also able to establish the cell phone tower that had originally handled the message en route to Regan's phone. It was in Brooklyn, a few blocks away from the hospital.

These people were starting to get under his skin.

Alex said he would keep digging on the mysterious text message and the number they were supposed to call, but it would take a little while. He had to make sure that he didn't alert anyone with what he was doing. So far, what he had done was what the geeks called "gray hat" — not technically illegal, but certainly unethical. Okay, sometimes illegal.

Now he was headed into black hat territory and that meant definitely illegal – the stuff Regan wouldn't want them to be doing. Jake had grinned at the metaphor at first. Computer guys liked to think of themselves as tougher than they really were. Five minutes alone in a room with a Special Forces guy would convince them otherwise.

But now, sitting in a cold car in a cold parking lot glistening with slightly thawed snow, drinking cold coffee and wondering what he'd missed, he had to wonder if it wasn't a good metaphor after all. Black hats and white hats and all kinds of gray hats, fighting with guns with practically an infinite number of bullets that traveled all over the world as fast as a fiber optic cable could carry them. Good geeks, like Alex, were the Special Forces of cyberspace.

To get Andy Gibbons out of prison in one piece would require both kinds of Special Forces.

The busted cell phone sat in his coat pocket. Alex had put a plastic cover over the busted screen, loaded it with a bunch of applications, and declared it fit for at least one more phone call. All she had to do was keep them on the phone for at least a minute, and Alex would be able to narrow the signal down to ten square feet. If they answered the phone at all, chances were good that he could get the original cell phone tower that handled the call. It was their best chance of tracking down at least one of the parties interested in the case.

So why did it feel like he had a bomb in his pocket?

The camera crews had set up at the front doors again, and multiple reporters were waiting by the doors with camera operators hovering over their shoulders. It didn't have the shark tank feel of a major news story, but these people were obviously hungry for whatever story they could get.

Each of the stations would have a reporter in the courtroom, but they couldn't do any reporting until they got outside.

The first trickle of people started to pour out of the courthouse. The reporters seemed to have an instinctual sense of who was fair game and who wasn't. People in street clothes were allowed to pass. Business casual dress — also ignored.

Then a cluster of suits exited the courthouse walking alongside a group of cops and two kids in jailhouse orange, holding their hands in front of their faces. Flashbulbs went off. The sun had gone down, and anyone caught in the glare of the cameras' lights would be blinded.

Jake slipped out of his car, closing the door softly behind him, and started working his way around the outer edge of the walkways toward the front doors. He had a baseball cap on — he'd learned never try to do surveillance without something to shade his eyes and had chosen the Red Sox to protect him today — and used it to keep the camera lights out of his eyes.

Someone was moving around in the shadows on the other side of the building, coming in from the street. It was another guy wearing a baseball cap after sunset. Jake didn't like it.

He tried to parallel the other guy, keeping the defendants and the group of reporters between them. He assumed that he'd been spotted. The two of them worked their way toward the main doors of the courthouse.

The guy kept the brim of his hat down — New York Knicks — and his hands in his pockets. His coat, a leather bomber not too far off from Jake's, wasn't long enough to hold a sawed-off or a rifle, but it was bulky enough to hold a couple of handguns, easy.

The bulge in his jacket pocket might have been a cell phone — might.

Jake paused behind a column and watched the other guy do the same. There was something familiar about him. He couldn't put a name to the guy — not without a clear look at his face — but the way he stood reminded him of someone.

The other guy glanced up at him for a split second. Enough to register that Jake was paralleling his moves, but not enough to ID him.

Jake hung back and shifted his attention to the group of suspects and the media, then reached into his pocket slowly, as if going for a camera or a gun.

The other guy hesitated for a second, and then walked quickly toward the front doors, pulling the brim of his hat down even further.

The automatic doors swept open for the guy. Jake turned and followed him, relaxing his shoulders and putting a friendly smile on his face. He left his hands in the open.

Another group of people in suits was coming toward the doors, this one including an old woman in a wheelchair with an oxygen tube situated below her nose. Jake recognized the defendant and her entourage. Jake's evil twin walked toward them but swerved at the last second, going around toward the bank of elevators.

One of them chimed, the elevator buttons flashing white. The door slid open.

Regan, dressed in a long wool coat and heels, stepped out.

Jake ducked around the group of suits and lost sight of Regan for a split second behind a lawyer. When he caught sight of her again, the guy was pushing past her into the elevator, the doors closing after him.

She turned around and watched the doors close.

Jake reached her. "That guy, who was he?"

She turned back to him, a puzzled look on her face. "I don't know," she said. "You know what was odd? He was dressed just like you."

"Did you see his face?"

"No. He was staring at his feet. He said 'Excuse me,' and pushed past me." She put her hands into her pockets and pulled out a pair of smooth black leather gloves. A slip of paper came out with it.

"What's that?"

She frowned at it, frozen in place. "It wasn't there before ..." She spun around to the elevator door. "He must have put it in my pocket."

Jake took the paper from her, holding it delicately by the edges. She put on her gloves and took it back from him.

It was a sheet of cheap, wide-ruled notebook paper, the kind that you give to kids in elementary school to do assignments. On it were the words *'You won't even know what hit you, bitch'* written in a black pen that left blobs of ink along the letters.

Jake leaned over and pressed the up button on the elevator. Unfortunately, they weren't the kind that showed what floor the elevator was currently on, just up or down arrows.

Another elevator door opened. Nobody came out.

"He'll be gone," she said. "He's more likely to come down the emergency stairs, wherever he got off. If you want to follow him up, I'll wait by the door to the stairs for him. See if I can knock his hat off and get him on the lobby cameras."

Jake shook his head. "That's too dangerous."

The elevator doors closed again.

"Do you want to try to get some fingerprints off it?" she asked, still holding the paper with her gloves.

"I can try," he said. "But we're probably not going to get anything. And I am *not* leaving you alone, in case this guy's more than just another warning."

He pressed the elevator button again, but the doors didn't open; someone else had called the elevator away already. A second later, the third set of doors opened, releasing a crowd of what looked like clerks in semi-formal business attire.

He grabbed the doors and waited for them to clear out. "Come on. I want to check that he's not hanging around your office, doing something to the door."

***

All day long, Regan had been itching to call her father to talk about what was going on. This made her constantly aware that she didn't have a phone, even though she couldn't have had it in the courtroom. At least Gary had guarded her office all day during the trial, except for bringing her lunch during recess. And the door of the chambers was locked — not that much protection from people who could remotely lock and unlock doors.

When the court went into recess at the end of the day, she had gone back into the judge's chambers as fast as she could, disrobed, and stood there in front of the mirror, rubbing her hands up and down her arms, wondering if she was being spied on at the moment. She'd literally felt chilled.

She had gone upstairs, grabbed her coat, said a curt goodnight to Gary, and fled. She wanted to get home as soon as she could, and she didn't want to think about how little safety that would probably give her.

She was starving. Ellen, her regular maid from the maid service, had left a message with Gary that she had made Regan "her special cake" because she was having such a hard trial. It was even on the news. But she didn't really have anything else in the fridge to eat, and she would eat the entire cake if she didn't have something else first.

Right, *La Ruche* it was.

Before she knew it, she was on the elevator with Jake, headed back to her office. The thought that the guy might be targeting her office while Gary was still inside it — or just coming out — made her stomach clench.

Her stomach growled loudly, and Jake glanced across at her. She suppressed a reaction, and he looked away again. Maybe Gary would have a stash of energy bars she could wolf down. Someone less ethical than she was might have raided the break room and stolen an entree out of the freezer.

The lights flickered, and the elevator shuddered.

Jake said, "Easy now."

She had her fists balled up in front of her, raised like she was about to punch someone out. She was overwhelmingly sick and tired of people making threats against her. She'd almost rather have someone act openly against her at this point — although maybe not while she was stuck in an elevator.

She felt like she was being watched. The back of the elevator was a shiny piece of brushed steel, too hazy to serve as a mirror but still reflective enough that she could make out her and Jake's shapes — along with a third shadow over her shoulder.

She jumped slightly, turned around quickly, and saw nothing more than the control panel. She was being irrational.

The elevator's lights fluttered again. She put her thumb over the alarm button. Her nostrils were flaring. This wasn't just unfair, it was unsportsmanlike.

"I'm going to kick someone's ass if this doesn't stop," she said.

"It's okay. They're just trying to scare you."

"They're pissing me off."

"We're almost there."

The elevator continued to rise slowly and jerkily, with intermittent flickering, until it reached the seventh floor. Then the doors opened, and the two of them stepped out.

She waited until the doors were closed, then gave them a vicious back kick with one heel. She'd worn three-inch pumps today so she could tower over practically everyone else in the room, even when she was off the bench.

The end of her heel left a shallow dent at the bottom of one of the doors. *Served it right.* Jake laughed as she swept away from the doors and marched down the gray carpet of the hallway.

The corridor was empty. Lights shone down either side of the long hall running through the top floor of the building, revealing nothing more threatening (or deserving of a deadly heel kick) than a row of doors on either side of the hallway. The walls were hung with black and white pictures of historic White Plains and Westchester County buildings, mostly from the 1800's. Somewhere on the fourth floor was a creepy oil painting of her father that she avoided like the plague.

Jake, now wearing a pair of insulated gloves, checked the handles of doors as they passed. She reached her office door, stopped, and let Jake check the door before she went in.

It pushed open easily.

Part of her expected to see a scene out of a TV show, with papers strewn all over the place, chairs on their sides on the floor, lamps turned over, Gary's collection of action figures stomped into unrecognizable forms on the floor —maybe even Gary's dead body in a puddle of blood.

Instead, everything was perfectly in order. Gary was still in. He glanced up. "Back again?"

"You're still here," she said stupidly.

"Yes, yes," he said, waving his hand toward the door to her inner office. "I know that I appear to be such a model of efficiency that I never have to work past five o'clock to accomplish everything that I do for you, but that's just a pleasant illusion. You should definitely give me a raise."

Jake had done his thing, sizing up the room as soon as he came in. He took a long look at the wood paneled walls, bare of anything other than a few silver-toned floral prints. Then he took a longer look at Gary, taking in the immaculate desk, his dress shirt, neatly trimmed goatee, skull-cropped black hair, and the small row of superhero figurines on the top of the cupboards behind him. What he thought of Gary she couldn't tell.

What Gary thought of him was obvious. His mouth had tightened, and his nostrils held the slightest bit of flare. According to Gary's body language, he considered the man a Philistine.

Jake said, "No one else was by here in the last few minutes, were they?"

"No, why?"

"Nobody leaned on the door or shook the handle, for instance?"

"If someone had, I would have mentioned it the first time you asked me."

Jake turned back to her. "Lock the door behind me. Don't open it unless it's me. If I say 'please,' then it means that I'm being forced to ask you to open the door. In that case, call security."

She wasn't sure whether he was taking too many precautions or not enough. "All right," she agreed.

He disappeared, and she locked the door, kicking the door wedge under the door for whatever added protection it could provide — probably none.

"What's going on? Is that..." another wrinkle of the lips "...that private investigator you're working with? Jake Westley?"

"I received another threat. A man dressed like Jake brushed past me getting on the elevator and left a note in my pocket."

Gary popped up, swiveled on his heels, and popped open one of the cabinets behind him. A row of plastic binders filled half the cabinet — the other half had a first-aid kit, a couple of novels, a water bottle, and a box of plastic baggies. He pulled one out and handed it to her.

"Evidence," he said.

She took the note out of her pocket and dropped it into the open bag. Gary closed the top of the bag. He opened a drawer and pulled out a page of sticky labels. He wrote the date and time on the label, Regan's full name, "threatening note received," and initialed it, then dropped it into a folder in the same drawer.

She leaned forward and saw that the folder wasn't empty, but held several plastic baggies with sheets of paper in them.

"What are those?"

"The other threats you've received this week," Gary said matter—of—factly. "Rog from Forensics goes over them for me on Mondays."

"Every Monday?"

"Usually."

"And there's more than one."

"Let's just say this trial has been a real pain for everyone involved. In other news, various people have been trying to get you via cell phone and have panicked because they can't reach you, so they've been calling here."

She'd told Gary that she'd dropped her cell phone and would have it replaced over the weekend; the less he knew, the better.

"Who called?" she asked.

"The Fourth Estate," he said. "The press, that is. I told them that you weren't interested in interviews today either. However, successful members of the press aren't known for their lack of bull-headed tenacity, so I doubt we're going to see any decrease of that until the trial is over."

"Do you have, or could you get, anything for me to eat?" she asked. "If I have to deal with one more thing tonight on an empty stomach, I'm going to bite someone's head off."

"There are plenty of frozen dinners in the break room that I could appropriate."

"Please don't do that."

He chuckled and bent over, pulling open one of his drawers and holding out a cardboard box full of granola bars. He shook it, and the little plastic-wrapped packages inside slid around.

She grabbed the box, pulled out a couple of bars, unwrapped one with her teeth, and shoved the whole thing in.

A soft knock came at the door. Both of them froze.

"It's me, Jake," a voice said. "You can open the damn door."

Her mouth was as full as a chipmunk's. She opened the door, admitting Jake. He took his hat off and gave Gary a nod.

"Sorry about busting in on you like that." He held out a hand. Gary reached up over the desk and shook it briefly. "I'm Jake Westley, and I'm working with your boss on the Gibbons' case."

"I know," Gary said. "She tells me things."

Jake gave her a look, and she nodded. She was going to get nagged for talking about cases with her confidential secretary, and she was going to have to tell him that sharing info with Gary was not negotiable. Great. This was going to be fun.

Gary said, "Your father called, by the way. He wants you to call him back when you get settled tonight. No rush."

Finally, she was able to swallow. "Thank you, Gary. Jake, are we all clear and safe to go home?"

He shrugged. "I didn't spot the guy. That might mean he's gone already or he's on a different floor waiting for us to leave. Or, he has nothing to do with us at all."

"What about the note?"

"Maybe someone shoved it into your pocket earlier. Come on, you know what lawyers are like about evidence."

She took a deep breath. "I do. I gave the note to Gary to hand over with the rest of my weekly death threats. Is that all right?"

"You have an evidence bag?"

Gary leaned over and produced the baggie, lifting it up into the air and turning it from side to side to show off the neatly-printed tag. Jake leaned over the top of the desk and looked into the drawer. "Five other ones, huh?"

"It's the trial. It'll get worse before it gets better."

"That it will," Jake said. "That it will."

Chapter 16 - This was serious

Regan's house was big, but not the kind of cheap big showy house that Jake often saw in his divorce cases. He'd done so many of them that he could predict how much money he was going to make to the nearest hundred dollars based on the Google street view of the house. The worst ones — ironically the ones that made him the most money — were big and sprawling with a huge custom kitchen, a family room upstairs that looked untouched, matching offices, and a room in the basement with a ratty couch, a big TV, and a console gaming system. The kids always huddled together on the couch in the basement, playing games with dull eyes. They were professionals at ignoring raised voices and slammed doors. They had *no* problem ignoring a private detective.

The place had a stone facade in front and looked more like a small, well-behaved church with a garage than a house. Inside the front door an empty wrought iron coat tree stood in the foyer. She took off her long black wool coat and hung it up, then took off her shoes and put them beside it on the white tile.

She activated the alarm system. "Don't leave without letting me open the door for you. It sets off a silent alarm."

He stifled the comment that it must be hell on a lover trying to sneak out before dawn. She didn't strike him as the type to bring people home with her — friends or lovers. The place felt too private.

The front room had smooth gray furniture that seemed to float over the cream-colored carpet, but the room didn't look lived in. Walls in subtle shades of gray and two ceiling fans with dark brown and silver blades coordinated with the furniture. The rest of the light fixtures all matched. Throw pillows in silver-blue with angular braid patterns on them in silver were carefully arranged on the couch next to the dark wood coffee table that didn't have a single book on it — or a speck of dust. The stone fireplace looked like it had never been lit.

The rest of the house was carefully coordinated as well, including the kitchen. Gray and blue coloring, dark-brown wood, and silver accents — the theme was carried throughout the house. Even the pictures on the wall were devoid of warmth: abstract black and white photographs on silver paper; grape leaves; part of a gargoyle's face from a waterspout; feathers of a bird. The work looked like that of the same photographer as in her office. He didn't see a single picture of her father, let alone any other human face.

She took him into the kitchen and started a pot of coffee, pulled an oozing, wet looking cake out of the fridge, and started to dish him up a piece.

He'd already eaten enough when they'd gone to *La Ruche* — he drove. They left her car untouched in the parking lot. He was going to have to talk to her about not going to the same restaurant every night. There was nothing an intelligent attacker liked better than a routine to make plans around. He held up his hand, "None for me thanks."

"My maid brought it to me this morning," she said. "You should at least try some."

The fact that she had a maid didn't surprise him — but the fact that her maid thought enough of her to bring her cake was interesting. "All right, I will."

She scooped up a piece of cake on a fork and held it out to him, handle first. He opened his mouth, and she reversed the fork and settled the cake nimbly in his mouth.

He bit down on the cake, and she pulled out the fork, turned around, and cut off a fat slice for herself.

He let the cake melt over his tongue. It wasn't really cake; it was some kind of delicate lace held together with some oozing chocolatey stuff that wasn't quite pudding and wasn't quite caramel.

"Ish good," he said.

"Chocolate tres leches."

He grunted and swallowed. She shoved a forkful in her own mouth. Two spots of pink had appeared on her cheeks. "Let's go to the library and get started. I take it you have a lot to tell me about your meeting with Alex. And then, of course, we have to make that call."

"Didn't you just eat?"

"You don't understand what this cake does to me." She must have realized how what she'd just said sounded as her cheeks turned pink again.

It didn't bother her enough to put down the cake, though. She shoved a bite of cake in her mouth and took off through a door on the other side of the kitchen.

He chuckled to himself and put a thin slice of cake onto the plate she'd left out for him. A puddle of what looked like thick chocolate milk leaked around the bottom of the plate. It was probably one of those things you had to eat fast before it went bad.

He went through the door and into the first room he'd seen so far that looked like someone lived in it.

The room that would have been a formal dining room in one of his divorce case houses, Regan had set up as a library. From floor to ceiling it was packed with dark wood bookshelves which went up so high that she had a rolling ladder attached to the bookshelves on either side of the room.

Most of the books were legal cases in cloth-backed file folders. But there were also all kinds of books on philosophy, logic, history, and biographies on the shelves around the window and the opposite wall.

A big dark wooden dining table filled the middle of the room. The first mess he'd seen in the house was there, spread out over the table. About 100 case files looked like they'd fallen from the ceiling and exploded on the table top. Most of the chairs had been pushed away from the table and shoved into the corners. She shoved a space clear on the table, put down the plate, and then began chucking case files into a heap in the middle of the table.

"Don't mind the mess," she said. "Just shove it out of the way and grab a chair. These aren't for my current trial anyway — just some research."

"What?"

"Forensic medicine," she replied.

He elbowed himself a clear spot, then moved the case files out of the way so he wouldn't get crumbs on them.

She ate most of the cake while staring over his shoulder, although her eyes didn't seem focused on the titles behind him.

"What are you thinking?" he said.

"About the elevator."

He'd been thinking about that as well. He pushed the last of his cake away; she took the plate. She was serious about that cake.

"What about my car? Why wouldn't you let me drive it? I assume it wasn't because of some kind of male code of honor or something."

He snorted. But he still couldn't get the feeling out of his gut — that there was something off about her car. "I have a bad feeling about it. I gave it a quick check under the bumper, but..." He shrugged. "With that threat showing up in your pocket and that guy disappearing, I'd rather have it checked before you get back in it. Even if there isn't a bomb —" she winced, "— I want it checked for RFID chips, transmitters, that kind of thing."

She shook her head. "I don't like the idea that someone put a tracker on the car — or a bomb."

"Or a hand delivered threat note in your pocket. Be prepared to think about a lot of ideas that you won't like."

"I'm used to not having to deal with that kind of thing. Gary handles it; it's so rarely something to get excited about. Honestly, it's hard for me to take seriously. I'm more upset about the elevator."

"I'll have the car checked out tomorrow. Until then, do you have something else you can drive; maybe even for a few days?"

"I could get a rental."

"Not a rental. A car from a friend, ideally someone who keeps it locked up in a garage."

"My father is a car nut. If I have to, I can call him. But that will mean handing over most of the information about the case to him and telling him about you."

"Can't you just borrow a car without getting the third degree?"

"You don't know my father."

He left it at that. "So let me start with this morning and my buddy, Alex Carr."

As he expected, she didn't react when he told her she was going to have to make up the other techies' wages. She either didn't understand or didn't care the kind of money it meant when Alex kicked them out and dropped his other projects. The information (or lack thereof) Alex obtained off her old cell phone didn't faze her, and she listened to the instructions for the upcoming phone call without so much as a raised eyebrow.

Afterward she said, "Did you want to come along tomorrow and meet my father? He's quite the character."

He was almost positive she didn't have any idea he was also working for her father — but the three of them in the same room at the same time was not a good idea yet.

He shook his head. "I'm almost positive I'll have too much to do tomorrow as it is — especially after we get off this call."

He pulled a disposable flip phone out of his pocket and set it on the table.

"How do we do this?" she asked.

"First, I text Alex and make sure he's ready." Matching deeds to words, he pulled the first of the two new prepaid phones out of his pocket and typed a message to Alex: *Are you ready?*

Regan raised an eyebrow. "It must be eleven o'clock. Are you sure he's still awake?"

She wanted to know if the computer geek she'd just hired was still awake at eleven pm? Cute. "I was more surprised when he was awake before noon today. These guys are nocturnal creatures."

The phone buzzed. *Ready steady go. Use other phone for call.*

Jake took the other phone out of his pocket and set it on the table between them. Regan swallowed, then pushed her empty plate out of the way.

He got the message. No more cake. This was serious.

Chapter 17 - It's a long story

The next morning following Jake's instructions, Regan took a bus to the airport, then picked a cab out of a row. The cab driver, a middle-aged woman wearing a tweed cap who spoke endlessly about the different roads she either would or would not be taking on the way to Judge St. Clair's house in Harrison, seemed smug about getting such a juicy ride, but otherwise pretty uninterested in Regan or her father.

She pulled up in front of the house with a comment of, "Nice place your dad has there," accepted cash payment, kept the change, and drove off without a backward glance.

Regan walked up the sidewalk to the front door. Her father was already waiting for her with the door open, letting the hot air out of the house — a sin for which she would have received a heavy scolding as a kid.

Charlton Heston's double if ever there was one, he was still dressed in a robe, pajamas, and slippers. He called it an old man's luxury, not having to get dressed on weekends. The sun shone into his face, and he shaded his eyes. From Regan's position on the bottom step, it looked as though he were checking her over after coming home after curfew to see if she was drunk or high.

She stepped onto the step and held out her arms. He grimaced and gave her a brief hug while sniff-checking her hair, then turned away and went into the house.

She laughed to herself and followed him in.

"What do you need a car for?" he asked.

"It's a long story."

"No story, no car."

He led her into the kitchen. The rest of the house had a creepy, unused look. It had always seemed empty after her mother died, but something had changed since the last time she'd seen him. She couldn't quite put her finger on it at the moment.

"No coffee, no story," she said.

It was an old ritual from her high school days. No matter what time she came home — late or otherwise — her father would demand an accounting. The two of them had been such caffeine fiends that drinking another cup of coffee before bed would hardly affect either of them. Regan had to slow down her coffee intake after law school, but her father seemed to be completely immune to the effects of all that acid in his stomach.

"I put on the pot already."

The small dark dinette table had been cleared but for a few crumbs, which her father swept into his hand as they passed. His hair was getting a little too long, the hairs jutting out at angles from having been slept on. She could see pink scalp on top of his head, but only barely. Most of his hair was still thick and iron gray on top.

He poured two cups of strong coffee from the silver pot, then brought the cups to the table and set them down with a pair of bangs.

"Sit," he said.

She sat.

"Talk."

He stayed standing, drinking out of his coffee cup while leaning with one hand on the back of the kitchen chair. She almost smiled; it was such a familiar scene. Only now she wasn't frantically trying to remember whether her curfew had been ten or ten-thirty that night.

"It all started with a letter," she said.

He grunted.

She told him about Jamie Gibbons, then Andy Gibbons, about her final meeting with him, the threat written in the dust of the back of the car, the fight at the bar, and the way Jake had rescued her. She told him about hiring Jake, then having him turn around and disobey her orders, about their discussion at the hospital, the mysterious text message, and being locked in the women's toilet.

"You called the number," her father said.

"I did, the next night."

"What happened?"

She shook her head. "I couldn't keep them on the line long enough. Alex, the computer guy, couldn't trace the call through all the transfers and jumps they made with it."

"An idiot could have predicted that," her father said. "What *information* did you get?"

"They wanted to set up a meeting."

"Where?"

She shook her head. "No, Daddy, I'm not going to tell you where."

His eyes narrowed for a split second then widened again. His knuckles were white on the handle of his mug.

"And the reason for that is because...?"

"Because Jake asked me not to," she said.

"Your private investigator," he grinned.

"He said you would likely follow me or have me followed, and that could throw everything off."

Her father grunted and took a drink of his coffee, even though she was almost positive that his mug was empty. It was interesting to see him and know that he was holding back, that it was even *possible* for her father to hold back. It was also just a little bit embarrassing to know where she'd picked up her habit of hiding behind her coffee cup. It wasn't that she minded following in her father's footsteps. It was just that she didn't want to end up with the same style.

"What do you think of this Jake?" he asked. "Is he someone you can trust? What if you're followed by someone else? What if you're locked in the women's room again? Is he going to be able to swoop in and rescue you? And don't tell me that you don't need to be swooped in and rescued. You might be the queen in this little chess game, but that doesn't make you invulnerable."

She smiled up at him. "That's the longest speech I've heard from you for years."

"I'm worried."

She eyeballed the bottom of her coffee cup. Her father pulled the pot out of its holder and refilled her cup, then took his cup back over to the counter and refilled it with his back turned.

There was no question of either of them adding cream or sugar — no sweetener given and none received.

She took a sip as a delaying tactic — hiding behind the mug. It was a difficult question to answer. It wasn't like she'd known Jake long enough to get a real sense of how his mind worked; and she hated making guesses without enough information.

"He's retired Delta Force," she said. "He doesn't always follow directions, and he probably won't always think things completely through before he acts. But, he seems to make reasonable choices nonetheless. At least they seem reasonable in retrospect, and after I've calmed down. He hasn't pressed me for extra money or tried to talk his way into my pants. Watching him enter a room and examine everything in a second and a half is an interesting experience. And, despite appearances, he errs on the side of caution. Every piece of evidence I have points toward him being trustworthy and protecting me as best he can. Although admittedly I didn't hire him to protect me."

"Long speech on your end too."

She took another drink of her coffee to help cover the fact that her cheeks were getting hot.

"Do you like him?" her father asked.

"Does it matter?" she countered. "And don't tell me the story of how you and Mom met. I've heard it."

He shrugged. "I'm just your father. What do I know?"

"What do you think about him?"

"What do you mean, what do I think about him?"

Her hand tightened on the mug. She forced herself to relax. He was just trying to get under her skin. Just because she was his daughter didn't mean he had any interest in taking things easy on her.

"You should meet him sometime," she said.

"I don't need to meet your private investigator unless you're thinking of marrying him," her father said.

"Daddy!"

"Well?"

He'd shifted the conversation away from what he thought about Jake twice. He'd have to be nuts if he thought that Regan hadn't noticed. But then she'd shifted the conversation away from the same subject as well because she felt it was such an unnecessary topic of conversation.

She sighed. Playing games with her father always led to doubting herself and becoming her own worst enemy. She'd learned to walk away from chess, pool, and poker where he was involved. Maybe someday she'd learn how to walk away from his "friendly" teasing.

"Yes?" he asked. "Are we in high school again, with all the sighing?"

She giggled under her breath. She just couldn't win.

"Oh, Daddy," she said, "*Please* may I borrow the car?"

He was chuckling now, too, "Yes dear, since you asked so politely."

***

Regan backed out of the giant garage in the back yard in a dark blue 1990 Cadillac DeVille, a classic car with more soul to it than all the Hummers on the planet smashed together. She looked uncomfortable in the driver's seat, leaning forward with her eyebrows pinched together. It must feel like driving a tank.

Jake's cell phone rang. He gave the number a glance, then answered it. The Honorable John St. Clair the third said, "If you sleep with my daughter, I will have you neutered."

"Good morning to you, too," he laughed quietly as he started the car engine and switched over to his headset. The old coot definitely had a way of getting his point across without leaving any doubts. Regan was moving around the corner at a fair clip. She'd have to slow down in a moment or two after she realized how heavy of a car she was driving compared to her Lexus. She didn't seem to have noticed him. *Is this the way she normally drives?* He wondered as he heard the tires screech against the pavement.

He put the car into gear and pulled into the street.

The old man chuckled. "She says she trusts you."

"She actually said that?"

"No. But she provided the relevant evidence."

He turned the corner. The Cadillac had already disappeared onto another road. If he wanted to keep visual contact, he was going to have to hustle.

"Sorry sir, but I gotta go. Your daughter obviously wasn't issued a camping permit; she drives like a bat out of hell. She seems to think the speed limit is a suggestion, and traffic lights are only guidelines."

"Who do you think taught her?"

Jake hung up and dropped the phone onto the seat beside him. It was all right for the old man to laugh. He didn't have to worry about Regan getting pulled over and missing the meeting, getting into a wreck, or worse.

Or maybe he did.

He'd asked his friend Alden to drive up from Boston to White Plains this morning to check out the Lexus. Alden had checked cars for Jake before while he was working divorce cases. Sometimes the spouse got a little too enthusiastic with wanting to know where one of Jake's clients was — and a couple of times, the client had been the one to cross the line. Alden had found them every time.

Alden hadn't found a bomb, and he hadn't found a tracking device — at least, not one that generated its own signal.

He'd found over a dozen RFID chips, though — small ones the size of a fingernail, and one the size of a flake of pepper buried in a patch of dirt on the rear license plate. The chips were passive and couldn't transmit; they could only respond to a transceiver signal. But that signal could be transmitted dozens of meters away.

In the end, Alden had taken the car to an automatic car wash and told Jake that securing the car from unwanted tracking was more than he could accomplish. Alden said the car probably hadn't been broken into — but he couldn't be positive. The car had a keyless remote lock and was supposed to be completely safe. But Jake had seen a device that forced the lock to release from hundreds of feet away.

How close was the courtroom to Regan's parked car? And how much better were the devices now? How far could they transmit: hundreds of feet; a quarter of a mile; a mile?

Regan pulled onto the highway and merged the Cadillac as smoothly into traffic as if the car were a trout disappearing into a fast-moving stream.

How long would the Cadillac be safe?

Or had the old Judge's cars been targeted already?

Chapter 18 - Too good of a distraction

Regan knew that Jake was behind her. She couldn't see him in her rear view mirror; she couldn't pull him out of hiding by speeding up or slowing down. Changing lanes accomplished nothing. After half an hour, she decided he must be ahead of her. Stubbornly, she switched routes at Yonkers. If he had lost her, he could call on the prepaid phone lying in the seat beside her.

He didn't call.

He'd specialized in divorce cases after he'd left the Special Forces. Of *course* he had no trouble following her.

It still put her hackles up, not knowing where he was. The only thing that made it bearable was knowing that her father probably hadn't followed her.

She pulled the car into a parking garage in Bed-Stuy and walked to the address they'd been read by a computerized voice over the phone the previous evening. She was a few minutes early.

The address led to an unnamed storefront next to a deli. The Internet had spat out records it had been a coffee shop a couple of months ago but was currently vacant.

It looked vacant. The front window had a couple of typed pages taped to the window — construction plans. The front window held a people watching bar with upside down stools, haphazardly laid across the top, their feet pointing toward the glass. The front door had patches where paint had been half-scraped away and Scotch tape partially peeled back. A tagger had painted the sidewalk in front of the door with what looked like some kind of arcane symbol, a pair of arcs with a key. The paint had been chalked over in places and almost completely scuffed out at the bottom.

A bike rack stood at the other side of the sidewalk, filled completely up. A bench sat next to it with a couple of tipped over bikes chained to the posts and a guy in his twenties dressed too cold for the weather sitting on top of it — long shorts, a brand-name hoodie, and a fisherman's cap. He stared at her disinterestedly, like a cat watching a car drive by the window.

She walked up to the front door of the vacant building and pulled on the handle like she belonged there. If the guy had a problem with her going inside, he didn't say so.

The inside of the building smelled like old grease and wall plaster. The counter where a cash register would go had been covered over with a dirty tarp; the walls had been stripped down to the brick. Half the floor had been pulled up, and a roll of carpet lay in the back of the shop.

"Hello?"

She glanced over her shoulder. The youngish guy was still staring in her direction. When she waved a hand slowly back and forth, his eyes didn't track it. He must be staring at his own reflection now. The shop was dark, shaded by the awning.

She walked toward the back of the shop, stepping around a sheet of broken glass and a hole in the floor leading down to some pipes. The back rooms were just as empty as the front — toilets missing, a sink that had been smashed to bits, linoleum tiles askew on the floor. The storerooms were empty, leaving no clue to give her an idea of what had been stored there. The kitchen was a tiny closet of a room, made bigger by the missing oven and other fixtures. A hole in the ceiling led into darkness.

She called a greeting several times. The only answer she received was the sound of someone stomping on the floor above her, trying to get her to keep it down.

She walked back into the dining room, and the phone in her pocket buzzed.

She pulled it out and stared at it stupidly until it stopped. Then it buzzed once more; a text message had appeared on the cheap screen, green text giving her nothing but another address and a new time less than a half hour away.

She cursed under her breath and pulled out the other phone, the one she was supposed to use to stay in contact with Jake and nobody else.

She flipped it open. The lights on the phone had gone out.

Her stomach lurched.

She pressed and held the power button — no response. She closed the flip and opened it again, tried to restart it again.

She blew air out of her cheeks.

Without her smartphone, she had no way of finding out where the address was. Without her prepaid phone, she couldn't call Jake — he'd already warned her that the second that she used the other phone to contact anyone other than the mysterious caller, it would become an even bigger risk for the caller to meet with them.

She walked back out of the shop and up to the younger guy, still sitting on the bench and staring her way.

"Excuse me," she said. "My phone is dead, and I need to find another address."

"Wrong place, huh?" he said. "If you're looking for Jimmy's Coffee Shop, its plumb closed now. They're supposedly going to put in a taco shop here. But I ain't putting any faith in it until I see it, you know? You get your hopes up for tacos, a lot of the time you get disappointed."

"Right," she said. "So can you help me with this other address?"

"Sure," he reached into the pocket of his hoodie to pull out a new iPhone. "What is it?"

She read the address off to him. He looked it up and squinted at the screen. "Uh...lemme just show you."

He flipped the phone around to show her the screen. She looked at the signage on the corner. Four blocks northeast, take a left, two blocks northwest. "Thanks," she said.

"Anytime, anytime," he said.

She patted her pockets, and he waved a hand at her, shooing her away. "You run into a good taco, send up a prayer for me," he said. "I mean the kind that drips down your chin and gets grease all over your clothes."

She nodded and took off in the correct direction — only taking a look over her shoulder when she reached the end of the block.

She still couldn't spot Jake anywhere.

But instead of feeling frustrated that she couldn't spot him anywhere, all she felt was a cold shiver of fear.

What if she really *had* lost him screwing around in Yonkers, and he couldn't call her because the phone had already been out of business?

***

Jake watched Regan go into the empty storefront. The door was unlocked. The sidewalk in front of the shop had been prominently warchalked — probably an artifact from when the place had been a hipster coffee shop.

Regan quickly disappeared from view in the shadows of the shop. He pulled out his phone and checked it. She hadn't called. Either she was doing all right or pretending so well that it didn't make much difference. He'd expected at least one panicked call from her on the way to Brooklyn with the way that she'd been speeding up and slowing down, changing lanes, and switching routes.

If she wasn't out in five minutes, he was going in after her.

At four minutes and forty-five seconds, she came out of the building with her eyebrows pinched together and a puzzled look on her face. She walked up to the player sitting on the bench on the sidewalk across from the storefront and spoke to him for a couple of seconds. He pulled out his phone and showed it to her.

It was what Jake had expected but hadn't brought up — that the first location was a blind. Someone would be in one of the upstairs apartments across the block, watching for someone to go into the empty storefront — and watching to see if they were followed.

That meant he was being watched too, unless they were working with a bunch of complete incompetents.

If they had been completely incompetent, Alex would have been able to track them down already; therefore, they weren't. He put up two fingers and gave the watchers an ironic wave, then went back to watching Regan.

She had turned away from the guy on the bench and was walking toward the end of the block, not heading back to her car. The next location must be close.

He waited until she was almost at the end of the next block before he started the motor. She should have called him to tell him the next address. She was probably just wrapped up in her pride again, too stubborn to ask for help, determined to do it all on her own.

He pulled out into the street. The guy at the bench looked over his shoulder at him for a second, then turned back to stare at the empty storefront. *He must be waiting to meet someone upstairs in one of the apartments, or he's been kicked out after a fight.*

There were all kinds of reasons for a guy to be sitting on a bench in the middle of the morning staring at a blank storefront. Jake pulled down the street, stopped at the stop sign, and then followed a red Prius down the street.

Regan looked back a couple of times, but he could tell she still wasn't seeing him. The red Prius was just too good of a distraction.

Chapter 19 - The damned thing was locked

Regan turned the corner a block early. After barely pausing at the stop sign, the red Prius kept going straight down the street. Her shoulders relaxed. The tan Buick behind it came to a full stop at the stop sign, then suddenly turned in the opposite direction without throwing on its blinker. It burned rubber halfway down the block, slammed to a stop at the end of the block, and turned again.

She might have lost Jake, but at least she wasn't being followed. She continued walking down the block. Fortunately, she'd had a feeling about getting jerked around by the computerized voice on the other end of that phone call. She'd switched not just to her flats, but to a pair of decent walking shoes her father had purchased for her a couple of years ago while trying to get her to go fishing in Colorado with him. She'd refused the "vacation" and had instead spent her time off on Martha's Vineyard at a Victorian bed and breakfast with her phone locked in the B&B safe. It was a glorious break, binge watching TV series and avoiding her father's insistence that she would "love" gutting trout for him while he caught them, as well as his brutal needling that she needed to produce grandchildren sooner rather than later - retroactively if possible.

They were good shoes. She kept her hands stuffed in her pockets and tried to look like she was wandering in a relaxed and entirely unremarkable way, nothing to see here. Instead, she found herself striding rapidly forward, almost running into other pedestrians on the sidewalk.

People were watching her from storefronts, laundromats, delis, and insurance agencies alike. The skin between her shoulder blades itched. It felt like eyes were crawling all over her.

She wanted to pop the collar on her coat but didn't — it wasn't the Eighties anymore and would just attract more attention.

Trying to stay cool when she was this wound up was harder than it looked. If she'd been in a courtroom, she could have handled it. The whole purpose of her being in the courtroom was to be an obvious representative of the unbiased fairness of the judicial system. It was her job to be *seen*.

Trying to hide in plain sight was self-conscious torture.

She turned another corner and got back onto the correct route, then doubled back with the turn. She didn't trust the roads between the two locations to be straightforward. It was Brooklyn. Most of the time things made sense — but sometimes they didn't.

Finally, she was standing in front of a fire hydrant facing a beauty supply store whose windows were packed with wigs on Styrofoam head stands, bottles of hair gel, shampoo, hair spray, hairbrushes, hairbands, and such.

It was the correct address. She'd just been expecting another empty storefront or a coffee shop.

To the right was a frozen yogurt store, to the left a grocery store prominently advertised ice cream. About a dozen people were walking toward her in a group, crossing the street. Three or four cars — no red Priuses or tan Buicks — were driving down the street in her direction.

She waited until the crowd of people was right behind her before stepping inside the beauty shop.

***

Jake watched the tan Buick tear off toward the northwest and then looked back toward Regan. She covered the rest of the block, turned right, and returned to her original street. After another two blocks, she turned left again, walking three blocks until coming to a stop in front of a beauty shop. She kept her hands stuffed in her pockets and continued to avoid calling him.

A group of about a dozen people — dressed similarly enough and formally enough that he thought they might be coming back from a wedding or a funeral — crossed the street and walked toward Regan.

She wasn't stupid. One second the group of people was walking behind her. The next they were gone and so was she — into the beauty shop.

The fact she had stood in front of the shop before her "disappearing" act and therefore given herself away was an amateur's mistake. It was always better to walk straight into a place than to hesitate outside. The fastest way to get spotted doing something was to look like you had something to hide. If you wanted to be forgotten in Brooklyn, the best way was to act a little self-involved — to swerve around objects at the last minute, moving or otherwise, or wear a headset and mumble to yourself.

Switching cars every once in a while didn't hurt either.

The phone he'd reserved for talking to Alex buzzed in his pocket. After groping around an extra second for the right phone, he attached his headset to the right jack.

"Yeah?"

"You didn't tell her to turn her phone off, did you?"

"No."

Jake glanced around. Not a single empty parking spot was to be found. Fortunately, there was a fire hydrant in front of the beauty shop. He pulled up behind the bumper of the PT Cruiser in front of him, trying to will the thing to pull three feet forward so he could park. If it didn't move in five seconds, he was going to hit the bumper and push it forward.

"I can't track it," Alex reported. "Either she has it completely powered down, or she's dropped it."

"What about the other phone? Still have power?"

The Cruiser inched forward. Jake laid on the horn, and it gave him another six inches. Good enough. Jake eased the car forward, scraping the Cruiser's bumper, and pulled into the space in front of the fire hydrant with maybe an inch to spare.

The driver was screaming out his passenger window. Jake flashed his PI license at the guy and rolled over the hood of his car. He put his hand on his revolver but didn't pull it out — not in the street.

Alex said something that he missed under the outraged screaming. "Say again."

"It still has power. But if we use it —"

"We already have a breakdown of plans. Abandon the plan. Call her on another line."

Alex didn't answer. Jake grabbed the door handle of the beauty shop and pulled.

Locked! The damn thing was locked.

He cursed himself for a fool and tried again.

***

Regan crossed the threshold of the beauty shop and was overwhelmed by the smell of hairspray and face powder. The store was packed from floor to ceiling with boxes, bottles, and packets of hair care products for women of all hair colors and races. A row of blank white heads lined the top of every rack, shelf, and cranny — most of them held wigs, ranging from the realistic to the fantastic.

A single sink and chair lay at the far end of the shop, near the cash register. The chair and sink were stacked with yet more boxes. Posters of women in wigs obviously from the Seventies and Eighties had been stapled to every blank surface of the walls and peeked past the bottles with big hair and knowing smiles.

A small Asian woman sat behind the counter, chewing on the inside of her cheek.

Regan smiled at her and pretended to look at a row of shampoos. She pulled the phone out of her pocket. She was a few minutes early, luckily. She'd been worried that her detour had slowed her down too much. She put the phone back in her pocket and picked up a bottle of conditioner. It was for dyed hair, to preserve the color. She put it back down.

The phone buzzed in her pocket.

She pulled it out, half expecting it to be another text message. But it was a phone call.

She answered it, "Hello?"

The same distorted voice as before.

"Regan St. Clair," it said. "You are in danger. When you have completed this call, calmly put the phone back in your pocket and walk out of the store. A familiar face will be waiting for you."

"Jake," she said. "You must be —"

She had been about to say, *you must be Alex*, but the connection cut off; the phone started humming at her.

She closed the flip cover and put the phone in her pocket. She turned back toward the cash register to say something to the woman sitting there, but she had vanished.

Regan turned toward the door, took one step, and promptly kicked over a pyramid of half-gallon plastic bottles. They crashed onto the floor and rolled everywhere.

Regan looked over her shoulder.

The woman hadn't come back. Regan was torn between picking up the bottles and making a guilty break for it.

A figure came to the door. She couldn't see who it was because of all the papers and posters taped to the door.

The figure grabbed the door handle and pulled.

The door didn't open.

Regan dropped the pair of plastic bottles that she'd picked up and walked forward through the pile of bottles toward the door. The man at the door pulled at the handle again.

Then she realized that the door was locked, not just stuck in the door frame. She could hear the door slamming into the bolt. The bells over the door jingled, the man on the other side was jerking on it so hard.

"Jake!" she shouted.

A bottle rattled on the floor behind her.

She turned around.

Chapter 20 - Following a suspect

He yanked the door handle harder the second time. It had been bolted from the inside, no question. It wasn't just stuck. He heard a crash from the other side of the door that sounded like a hundred plastic balls or bottles had been kicked across the floor and gone rolling.

"Jake!" Regan shouted.

Then she gasped.

"Regan!"

He heard the sound of more bottles being kicked and then a thump.

Jake couldn't take a risk that Regan might be right behind the door. Instead of pulling his gun he aimed a foot at the glass door and kicked.

The safety glass crackled as it shattered inside the frame but his foot didn't smash through. The glass was reinforced with wire. He kicked it again, and it began to fall out in small, rough diamond shapes, tinkling on the sidewalk.

"Hey!" someone shouted from the street.

He kicked again. "Regan!"

The glass was broken enough that he could hear sound from the other side. He could see fragments. Several white and silver plastic bottles had fallen on the other side of the poster covered door. Another one rolled into them, making them bounce back and forth against each other.

"Regan!"

He kicked again, this time aiming higher for the door lock. The door shook in its frame. More of the glass fell out, but he still couldn't get in.

From his earpiece, Alex said, "Calling the police to your location," in a flat, everybody-stay-calm-nobody-panic voice.

"Regan!"

Enough of the glass was gone that he could see the bottoms of her feet in dark brown leather walking shoes being dragged across the floor, knocking against the plastic bottles. The bottom of her *coat* — he could see the bottom of her *coat*. He kicked again.

The metal bar dividing the top of the glass panels from the bottom bent and the wire at the bottom started to come loose. The entire panel of glass was coming out.

"Regan!"

Someone grabbed his shoulder. He spun around.

A small guy who looked about 80 years old backed away from him, raising his hands. "What's going on, son?"

Jake ignored him and turned back to the door and kicked again, aiming for the top of the glass where it was already coming loose. The corner came free and fragments of glass scattered.

He gave it one more kick and it collapsed halfway across the panel, bending inward. He ducked down and slithered through the hole, the glass scraping across the back of his leather jacket but not getting caught.

Inside the beauty shop, a stack of bottles had been spilled across the floor, covering most of it from the front door to halfway up the shop. A couple of the bottles had split open, leaving streaks of creamy white conditioner smeared on the floor.

A pair of trails in the goop pointed toward the back of the room.

There was nowhere for anyone to hide except behind the register...and the back of the shop, blocked off by a thick blue cotton curtain.

Jake pulled his revolver and got out of the direct line of fire. The old guy was sticking his head through the busted pane of glass.

"Do you want me to call the police or maybe an ambulance? What's going on?

"Get away from the glass!" Jake shouted. "They've got guns!"

Hey, better to be safe than sorry. The old guy must have agreed. He pulled his head out of the window, and the shadows across the front panes of glass, curiosity seekers, quickly retreated. How long they'd be able to resist the siren call of gossip material he didn't know. Long enough, he hoped.

He sidled up to the cash register desk and glanced over the side. Nobody was huddled on the floor. No tracks led from behind the register. The clerk must have ditched before it all went down — or was the one responsible for sneaking up on Regan.

A long-handled gripper — for the clerk to reach some of the eerie, old-fashioned wigs lining the shelves closest to the ceiling — hung behind the counter. He grabbed it and extended it slowly toward the curtain.

He gave the curtain a poke. It separated across the center, falling into two pieces.

Nobody fired a weapon toward the movement. If anyone was moving around on the other side of the curtain, he couldn't hear it.

A set of sirens started going off down the street. He didn't have time to screw around.

He could use the backup, but he didn't need any amateurs screwing up his rescue attempt, and he didn't think NYPD would be in any mood to accept orders from a guy who had just broken into a business.

He grabbed the edge of the curtain and pulled it back to where he could reach it, then grabbed it in his hand and ripped the curtain rod out of its niche.

The curtain rod went flying, dragging the two halves of the curtain with it. Bottles rattled against each other as they rolled.

"Regan," he said, "if you can, make a noise."

The sounds from outside were getting louder. Several sirens were approaching now, definitely coming this way. The crowd outside was getting noisier and, therefore, bigger. Any second someone was going to try to be a hero and climb through the busted door.

But rushing could mean getting shot, which could leave him in no fit state to rescue Regan.

He stepped across the doorway, aiming his revolver through it, then over to the other side to give himself a couple of seconds to process what he saw.

The other room was dark, filled bottom to top with white shipping boxes as well as black, round-sided boxes with metal trim, maybe zippers. He'd glimpsed a desk stacked with papers and lit with a green banker's lamp. He didn't see any faces, but there were lots of places to hide. All those boxes created one hell of a maze back there.

He ducked back into the doorway, stepped through and moved toward the desk. Nobody was behind it, cowering or otherwise. He walked around the side of the desk toward the boxes as he swept the room with his gun.

The trails of conditioner disappeared into the shadows cast by the banker's light. They seemed to lead deeper into the building.

He pulled his shirt sleeve over his fingers and used it to turn off the banker's lamp. Now it was dark. He stepped into the aisle of boxes and started walking forward, stopping to cover the rows that had been built into the stacks of boxes. He had to walk sideways to keep his coat from dragging against cardboard and making hissing sounds. He had left the tile of the other room behind; now there was nothing but concrete underfoot.

Behind him, someone was shouting for everyone to stand back even as someone half climbed through the doorway. The figure retreated. Boots crunched on glass.

In front of him was an even thicker darkness than the rest of the storeroom. He found a wall covered in white plastic paneling and followed it to a narrow doorway. His eyes were adjusting a little. He didn't have to flip the light switch on to identify the room as the toilet — his nose told him enough. Beyond that was another door — this time to a set of stairs leading downward.

He knew there should be a door in the back of the building that led to an alley, a place for trucks to bring deliveries. Downstairs would most likely be more storage, a thousand pipes leading in all directions, and maybe a janitor's closet.

He hesitated. Going downstairs felt right, but it had to be a bad hunch. They wouldn't want to get trapped in the basement with Regan. They'd want to take her somewhere where they'd be less likely to be disturbed.

He didn't want to think about what they'd be doing with her.

He had to head out the back door.

Had to - no matter what his guts said. If he hesitated —

The front door smashed inward. "Freeze! It's the police!"

A pair of flashlights shone through the darkness, not aiming at him yet. They were still in the other room, still checking for attackers — or victims.

Jake trotted past the door to the basement, reached the far wall, and had a moment of panic. He'd reached a dead end.

He backed up and found an alley through the boxes that looked slightly wider than the others and went down it. The darkness rose up around him, black wig boxes on all sides towering overhead. The smell of dust and old hair made him want to gag.

Flashlight beams played across the ceiling of the back room. The cops had searched the other room and were following the trail back.

They had to be able to see his footprints in the conditioner.

He kept following the alley. It took him around another corner toward the back of the building, running parallel until it reached the back door.

The overhead lights flashed on.

"Come out with your hands up!" a cop shouted. She was bluffing, though. Nobody could see him from where he was. And now that the lights were on, they might not be able to tell when he opened the door.

He glanced over it checking for the alarm. He found it; it was a brand he knew. He slid his fingers around to find the manual switch under the case and switched the alarm off. Then he slowly leaned on the door.

The light outside was dim. The sun had shifted enough to put the alley in shadow. He grabbed something off one of the boxes beside him, realized it was a handful of hair, and winced. Then he got over himself and shoved it into the hole in the strike plate to keep the lock from clicking when he let go of the door.

He slipped out the door and let it slide softly closed behind him.

Nobody shouted from inside.

The alley led in both directions all the way to the ends of the street. Cars drove by in either direction. A couple of padlocked trash bins were the sole inhabitants of the alleyway.

Another dilemma — go the wrong way and he could lose her forever.

Jake swore. His gut was still telling him that he should have gone downstairs into the basement.

A car drove by the end of the alleyway just as he looked in that direction. He glimpsed a semi-familiar face, a baseball cap, a leather bomber jacket.

It was that bastard from the courthouse.

Jake sprinted toward the end of the alley. The car passed the end of the alley before he did and moved out of sight.

"Jake?" Alex said.

"Yeah -"

"The cops have just been pulled out of the building. No reason was given. Where are you?"

"Following a suspect," Jake snapped.

He pivoted at the end of the alley, swerved to avoid a father jogging with his kid in a stroller, and hit the street just behind the car.

It was a dark blue late model Hyundai. He focused on the license plate, HAA 8268. He repeated it to himself under his breath to lock it in his memory.

The car sped up.

Chapter 21 - This is what it must feel like

Regan opened her eyes and closed them again. A radiator hissed. She could smell mold in the air, which wasn't surprising considering how damp and hot the air was. It was like being closed up in a sauna. She opened her eyes again. The light turned her head into a fishbowl full of pain as well as blinding her. Every joint ached. It was like being sick with the worst kind of flu, or what Gary described having a migraine was like. She knew somehow the second she turned her head she would be overwhelmed with nausea. There was a pressure of acid building up in her stomach and trickling up her throat causing her to swallow repeatedly.

Underneath her cheek was a linoleum floor — at least, that's what it felt like. She wasn't about to open her eyes to check. Even the spaces between her teeth hurt, but she didn't seem to have lost any.

She wasn't sure how to tell if she had any broken bones. She knew that if she was being watched her observers had already determined she was awake. She took a tentative breath. Her ribs hurt so badly she started to hiccup, making everything from her head to the tiny bones in her feet hurt even worse. Thick oozing tears burned down her cheeks. Shame and rage kept her shaking on the floor, even though she knew she should try to get up.

Somewhere nearby a television had been turned on. It was a cable news channel. She could tell because most of the voices were announcer type voices —-serious and restrained but with an arch delivery that hinted at gossip, but didn't necessarily deliver.

She didn't hear any living voice or sounds of evidence that another human being was in the same room with her. An apartment, that's what it felt like. She could hear the sounds of traffic nearby, although the street outside was relatively quiet.

When she had calmed down enough to stop shaking, she forced herself to open her eyes and leave them open until her eyes had adjusted. The pain in her head stayed about the same. It felt like her bones were grinding into needles that ran from the back of her neck into her eyes.

She was staring at a white radiator along a painted plaster wall. The floor under the radiator was black with grime and dirt. The floor wasn't much cleaner. She pulled her arms and legs into a crawling position and rolled onto her forearms and knees.

Her stomach immediately started hitching, bringing up what was left of her last meal. Fortunately, it wasn't much. She spat bloody froth onto the floor and licked her teeth. Most of the blood had come from her mouth. Her tongue burned from having bitten it, and of course she had a couple of loose teeth on the side where the boot had kicked her face.

She'd never been punched in the face before. She'd never been threatened with any real violence. *If this is how battered women feel, I'll skip it.*

Regan spat on the tile again and waited for someone to beat her for it. She was overwhelmed with feelings of shame and rage. Shame — that she had let someone hurt her. It made her feel like a weakling, like it marked her as being someone who deserved being beaten, for having let it happen. And rage — that someone had dared to hurt her when she had no real chance to hurt them back.

She looked up. In front of her was an ancient refrigerator straight out of the Fifties — gold-flecked aqua paint and all. The floor in front of it was just as black as the floor under the refrigerator.

She looked around the room, feeling like an animal, less than human. If someone had been within arm's reach, she would have grabbed and bitten them. Every day all over New York City and State, all over the world, people were having violence inflicted on them, just like this.

They were beaten, abused, raped and traumatized over and over until they *were* animals.

And then they were beaten some more for being less than human.

She climbed to her feet. Behind her was a small dinette tabletop, square with two cheap plastic stacking chairs on either side. Grime was packed into every crevice and crack. Nothing was in good repair. The porcelain sink was scratched and stained; the cabinet doors were cracked and split down the middle, patched up with duct tape. Dishes stood next to the sink in neat stacks, spoons inside of glasses, and mismatched plates in tidy pyramids waiting for suds and elbow grease. Eight glasses and at least that many plates sat on the counter with fresh looking food stuck to them.

She still had her wool coat on. She remembered being grateful for it when they had first started beating her and kicking her. They had swung a baseball bat into her side once, but mostly they had used their fists and feet. Later she hadn't been able to feel much of anything but hurt. She had curled around her soft parts. Let them kick her in the ribs as long as she didn't take another boot to the groin or the solar plexus — as long as she didn't have to think about what would happen if someone kicked her in the throat.

Roll-up blinds had been pulled down in front of the window. She grabbed for the bottom of the blind, but it was behind a layer of plastic to seal the heat inside the apartment. Whoever lived here must be crazy. It was already cooking in here — a real steam bath.

She stepped into the hallway. In front of her was a tiny living room filled with thrift store furniture with stains and tears in the fabric. The scrawl across the bottom of the television screen was unintelligible. Her eyes just couldn't focus sharply enough.

The top of the television and the shelves along the wall were packed with photographs. According to the pictures, the people who lived here were sixty or over, a man and a woman along with two young kids. It was like the generation between them had completely disappeared.

She let go of the door frame and took a step toward the door of the apartment. Her legs weren't broken — thank God — but it felt like someone had torn the muscles in her legs to shreds. One hip didn't seem to want to support her. She reached out and grabbed the recliner next to her. The carpet underfoot was grungy and old but had been vacuumed – perhaps in honor of her arrival.

Blood welled up in her mouth again. She could let herself spit on the tile floor, but she couldn't stand the thought of the couple, or their grandkids, finding a lump of phlegm and blood on the floor. She didn't know where she was, but if she had had to make a bet, it would have been that the couple wasn't involved, and would have no idea what was going on.

She stumbled past a pair of bedrooms with the doors open. One room had a pair of bunk bed and stacks of plastic storage tubs.

The other held all four members of the family, huddled together on the same full-sized bed. The man, woman and two boys in t-shirts and blue jeans all sat motionless with wide terrified eyes.

She froze.

They didn't move, not even a blink of an eye or a twitch. She could hear the sound of the man breathing harshly.

"Sorry," she said.

Nobody moved. Nobody answered.

She continued stumbling forward, found a bathroom, and glanced at her reflection in the mirror. Her face was covered with dried blood. Both eyes were black and swollen. A cut on her cheek had crusted over, matted with hair that had dried into the wound. She reached up and touched her nose, then stifled a whimper. It was broken all right.

The question was whether to wash her face and try to find a cab, or to walk out of the apartment and hope that someone called for help.

She put her hand into her pocket. Both flip phones were gone — her wallet, too. She took another step toward the door. Oh God, she was going to have to get out of the apartment and try to go down the stairs, not knowing whether she was about to be attacked again.

She started to weep. She felt so alone, so useless, so *afraid*. There was a hand-towel hanging from a wood hoop on the wall;

it was white with pink flowers on it. Two damp towels hung on towel bars on the walls. They were both a faded, threadbare tan color.

She pulled a long wad of toilet paper off the roll and held it under the faucet for a second, then used it to dab at her face. It just made things worse. The blood only seemed to smear around, and now she had pills of bloody toilet paper stuck to the cut on her face. She dropped the wad of toilet paper into the small trash can beside the pedestal sink.

"I can't," she told the mirror. "I won't make it out there." The face that reflected back to her told her that she knew she was lying to herself. She could and she would.

A hand touched her softly on the shoulder. In the mirror she saw the old woman standing beside her, her wrinkled hand and short fingernails resting on Regan's shoulder.

"Can we help you?" she asked softly. She was barely five feet tall and so thin she looked like a strong wind could have snapped her in half.

"Oh God," Regan said. Everything that had happened to her during the last few hours — she desperately hoped it hadn't been any longer than that — was bubbling up inside her. She hated showing the woman how vulnerable she was, but it didn't seem like something she could stop. Her world, her whole idea of what was safe and what wasn't, the idea that she couldn't be attacked and beaten — it was gone. She felt like she'd been jerked off her place on the bench and thrown into the worst gutter in Brooklyn. She felt like an invisible shield had been stripped from her.

"Please help me," she said. "Please help me."

The woman put her arms around her. Regan sobbed like a baby onto the woman's shoulder. She was probably smearing her clean clothes with blood, but she couldn't bring herself to stop.

This was what it must feel like to be Jamie Gibbons; only what Jamie Gibbons was going through was worse.

Chapter 22 - Two seconds away from an explosion

"I've got a call from Regan," Alex said in a voice hoarse with forced calm. "I'm patching you in."

The car had escaped a long time ago after a serious chase. Jake was hoofing it back toward his own vehicle, half limping on a sprained ankle. He had just passed the beauty shop where he'd lost Regan. The broken bottom panel of the door had been covered with plywood, but the neon OPEN sign was turned on in the window. He couldn't remember whether it had been on earlier or not.

A woman came out of the shop with a wig box under her arm and looked up and down the street surreptitiously. She had three layers of head scarves, black, gray, and leopard-print, and wore chunky sunglasses. Her camel colored wool coat looked too expensive for the neighborhood. So did her Gucci purse. Her gaze turned toward Jake for a few beats too long and then turned away. She escaped down the street in the opposite direction, lingered at the curb, and was picked up by a black Infiniti sedan.

"Jake?" Her voice cracked over the phone.

"I'm here, Regan."

He heard her lips smack. "I'm at the 67th Precinct on Snyder. Do you know where that is?"

"Yeah, I'm on my way. Are you all right?"

The sounds of the precinct house popped into clarity as she paused: Beeps, the police-band radio droning in the background, voices chattering, the particular rhythm of someone getting read their Miranda rights, a coffee pot slamming onto the heating element.

"No," she said. "They wanted to take me to the hospital, but I wouldn't let them."

"You should let them. I can meet you there."

"No. Come and pick me up. I don't want to..." She broke off. Her voice sounded higher pitched and stuffed up. He'd heard a lot of desperate people's voices — men and women both — turn childlike at their first taste of real terror. Later, with more experience, those voices could turn numb and flat.

When she spoke again, she'd put some iron back in her spine. Good for her.

"I don't want to move out of the police station without talking to you first. I'm not so badly wounded that I'm in any real danger. I'm mostly just sore, possibly have some broken ribs. I need to have my nose set."

"What happened?"

"I'll tell you when you get here," she said with something almost like dignity. Then she hung up.

The line was still open; Alex had stayed on.

"Was she calling from where she said she was calling?" Jake asked. He had stopped in order to talk to Regan. Now he started walking quickly down the block. He was still a few blocks away from his car, and it would take time to get to the police station.

"Correct. Did you manage to follow the suspect?"

"No. He got lucky with the lights. He was driving a dark blue Hyundai sedan, New York license plate HAA 8268, empire yellow. It was the guy who looked like me that I saw at the courthouse."

"The Westchester Courthouse?"

"Tell me you're looking up that license plate while you're talking to me."

"Correct."

"What are you finding?"

"Rest assured that I will tell you as soon as I have something. Please tell me you aren't standing around waiting for the information."

"You're a smart-ass, you know that?"

"Correct. I have to be if I want to keep my geek credentials."

Jake moved into a smooth jog down the street, smiling and giving a friendly no-threat-here jogger's wave to the pedestrians on the sidewalk. He even kept jogging when he was held up at the corner of a block, but ran across as soon as traffic left him a gap. People gave him a second glance. His clothing didn't fit with his actions. But they didn't panic, just took a step or two to get out of his way without seeming to acknowledge his existence.

He passed a guy sitting on a bench who gave him more than a second glance. The guy muttered something about tacos. A dozen yards later, it hit him. It was the same guy that had been sitting outside of the vacant storefront.

He glanced back. The guy was gone. *Shit!*

Jake walked back toward the bench. There were enough people on the sidewalk headed in either direction that he couldn't be sure that the guy had just stood up and walked away naturally. He scanned the cars parked on either side of the street. Nobody was climbing into the ones nearby. The traffic flowing down the street beside him was steady, about 15 or 20 miles an hour. He didn't catch a glimpse of any shop doors slowly closing.

"Jake," Alex said.

"Yeah?"

"No dice on the car. I found out who it belonged to. But they reported it stolen earlier today — carjacking in Queens."

Jake cursed.

"Interestingly, it was someone who was doing rides for an independent car ride company, a new startup. She received a call to pick up a passenger, and when she arrived, someone pulled her out of the car and drove away."

"That's one way to steal a car," Jake said. "Free delivery service. Could you trace the passenger who made the call?"

"Already have. They were picked up by a second car a minute or so later. Said they had no idea that the first driver had been attacked. The second car wasn't registered with the company. The passengers didn't notice. It was the same model car, and the driver looked roughly similar to the picture of the driver in the ad."

"Smooth," Jake said. He gave the street another good look. No suspicious movement. No sense of being watched. It was like the guy had vanished – mist before the sun. Sometimes success depended on being able to walk away and try again later. He started jogging down the street again.

Jake put his not-a-threat face back on. An old lady who'd been glancing at him returned his smile. She was on her phone, nodding and smiling. She followed him with her eyes as he passed her. Then she was out of sight — probably still staring at the back of the friendly looking handsome guy who was jogging in blue jeans and a leather jacket. She was probably telling someone about him, but there was no way to tell whether she was talking to a girlfriend or someone belonging to the same group who'd hurt Regan.

Too bad his paranoia couldn't really make her any safer.

***

The precinct house was a building straight out of White Plains — gray cement and ugly pseudo columns along the walls. He pushed his way through the revolving door and found Regan near the reception desk, pacing back and forth with a heavy limp. She looked like hell. Her long black wool coat had grayish smears on it, including what were clearly shoe prints. Her nose was swollen and crusted around the edges with blood. Her hair had been brushed out and pulled back in a bun with a borrowed hair tie — but still had brown streaks of blood dried in the fibers.

Jake's stomach gave a twist.

He wanted to put his arms around her, hold her, and tell her it was going to be all right, to tell her how beautiful she was to him. He wanted to tell her about all the horrible things he was going to do to the people who had hurt her.

Yeah, right. She would probably slap him.

The officer at the desk kept his eyes down on his paperwork, but his body language said that he knew exactly where Regan was in his waiting room at all times. She wasn't being questioned to find out who had done this to her. She was being pushed back onto the street. Clearly the police had better things to do than listen to a woman battered by her husband or boyfriend or partner or whatever.

"Jake," she was trembling. Two raw, swollen black eyes stared at him. With the swelling, it was hard to tell whether she was terrified or angry.

"Regan."

"Get me out of here."

Angry, he decided. Probably about two seconds away from an explosion. He held out his elbow, offering support. Instead, she grabbed his hand hard and jerked him toward the revolving door, only letting go when the glass threatened to chop his arm off as she strode through.

Chapter 23 - You don't gossip

Jake got her checked into the hospital before calling her father.

By the time his ears finished ringing, Regan had submitted to an overly invasive examination, including a rape kit she didn't think she needed. She refused to submit to a phone call from her father, brought to her by a wide eyed orderly on a cell phone held in his fingertips at arm's length as her father bellowed in rage. She'd picked up the phone and said, "Later Daddy," hung up, and handed it back to the terrified man. She allowed herself to be wheeled in a wheelchair to a private room in a locked ward. Two more nurses had inspected her to get her vitals, offer her supper, and caution her that she shouldn't exert herself for the next 72 hours.

She even seemed calm.

As soon as the nurses left, she threw off her blanket and sheet and swung her legs out of bed. Jake winced. From her ankles to where her legs disappeared under her nightgown, her legs were covered with bruises and small cuts. They'd been cleaned and patched with shiny surfaced liquid bandages, but still looked ugly.

She grabbed the robe that had been left at the end of the bed and threw it on. He turned away until she had it belted, getting a glimpse of more flesh through the flimsy hospital gown's armhole. The bruises and bandages made him feel sick.

"We're going to see Schnatterbeck," Regan announced, her voice hoarse.

He carefully did not offer to push her in a wheelchair or tell her to take it easy.

People took their first taste of violence in different ways. Some curled in on themselves and became cowards — once bitten, twice shy. Other people, like Jake, found themselves attracted to the rush. He still wasn't sure how Regan was taking it. She seemed to be reacting more like a chess player — or a general.

The two of them reached the locked door of the ward, which had a camera and an intercom. The orderly, safely on the other side of the door, refused to let out a patient who hadn't been given permission by a doctor to wander outside the ward.

Regan gave him a look through her two black eyes that seemed to say, *you have 30 seconds to deal with this before I bring out the nuclear warheads*. Jake explained they had a friend in another ward who was in pretty bad condition and they were worried that he wasn't going to make it. After getting Schnatterbeck's name, the orderly called over to the critical ward and let them go through.

He could have been a bastard and kept Regan locked up — for a while anyway. Jake made a mental note of the guy's name, in case he needed to get the guy out of hot water.

Regan walked barefoot through the halls, leading him toward Schnatterbeck's room. They were watched but not stopped by the orderlies and nurses in the hallways. They got some strange looks from a number of visitors, especially near the elevator when a pair of teenagers carrying two bouquets of daisies froze outside the elevator door, refusing to get in the car with the crazy lady with two black eyes and an attitude from hell.

Finally, they were alone.

"What happened?" he asked.

She glared at him. If her eyes could have shot fire, he would have been burnt to a crisp. "I was punished for being sloppy. I deserved this."

"Wait a —"

"I have no idea how to do this. I have no idea how to maintain the kind of security we need in order to survive this. Do you know how lucky I am?"

He did, actually. He'd seen it when things had gone badly in hostage situations. The question was whether she did.

She leaned against the elevator wall and wrapped her arms across her ribs, then winced. She straightened up again. Slouching with a couple of broken ribs was a rotten idea. But she'd learn that fast enough.

"I'm putting my own life in danger. I'm putting other people's lives in danger. I have been thinking in terms of a dirty cop or two. They warned me, and I'm *still* thinking as if it's not that serious. Ha-ha, a bunch of computer nerds have figured out how to hack my phone — big whoop."

So she was figuring out how foolish she'd been. In about a second she was going to realize how stupid *he'd* been. And then the blame was going to start crashing down on him.

He deserved it, though. Unlike her, he knew better. She hadn't even been wearing a wire.

"But we're not playing a game of cops and robbers, are we? It looks like one. There have to be corrupt officers involved. But saying that it's cops and robbers doesn't even scratch the surface."

The elevator stopped, and the doors opened. A couple was waiting to get on; they stepped back as Regan strode out. Jake nodded to them as they got on.

"We're not playing cops and robbers. We're playing chess."

He thought about that. He didn't know if she was right — but being a chess player, she might act smarter if she thought of the situation like that.

It'd be even better if he could convince her not to think of it as a game at all. But maybe that was a bridge too far at the moment. At least, she wasn't melting down into a ball of terror.

"And you're the queen."

"I'm the idiot," she said. "I'm flinging my pieces and myself around like a beginner. I'm not paying attention to good advice from experienced players," she waved a hand in his direction, "and in fact, I haven't even met all my pieces, including the new castle that I picked up. I have no idea how they can move. I have no idea who my pawns are. I'm putting my king in danger — Andy, Jamie, and the boys. Have either you or Alex checked on them? Has anyone called Gary to tell him I'm in the hospital? No. And why not? Because I'm an idiot."

She turned toward the critical ward.

"I promise you that once they release me, we're going to have a council of war. You, me, Alex, Gary, my father, and anyone else that you care to recommend. Jamie Gibbons, if you think it's appropriate."

"Good." He cleared his throat. "Ah, I called Jamie on a pretext. She doesn't know about the beating — at least, she didn't when I called her. She and the boys were all right when I called. I've had Alex put a couple of cameras on her apartment, though."

She nodded. It was illegal and a violation of trust. It was taking steps that were neither strictly ethical nor ones that he'd discussed with her ahead of time. And yet that was her only reaction — a nod. "I am *going* to move her and her kids out of that apartment, whether she likes it or not. She can have her self-respect back when it isn't about to cost her and her boys their lives."

"Schnatterbeck?"

"He knew more than he should, and on top of that, he spoke to you. We have to warn him that it's serious, and we need to find out how he knew so much about what Andy Gibbons was doing in the neighborhood."

"He said his poker buddies told him."

"Uh-huh. Because that's what you do on poker night — gossip." She stopped at the critical ward's front desk and began signing herself in while the orderly lifted her eyebrows and looked back and forth between them.

Jake shrugged.

"My father is a decent poker player," Regan said. "You don't play poker to gossip, especially about strangers' lives. You play poker to smoke cigars, drink good scotch, and create the illusion that you're a bunch of men who think about nothing less manly than fishing, fixing transmissions, old romantic conquests, and how to seduce Lady Luck. You don't *gossip*."

Chapter 24 - It was a promising night

The door of the limousine opened, and Fiducioso entered, lowering himself into the tan leather seat with the grace of a hunting cat. His hat was sprinkled with specks of melting snow; the night had turned cold. With any luck the snow would soon begin increasing its pace, forcing Regan and her associate to stay within the city for the night.

As the door closed, Pavo tapped the glass between them and the driver, and the car accelerated into traffic. They had hesitated for only a moment in the street, barely enough time for the cars behind them to register the hesitation, let alone raise a chorus of horns.

Fiducioso lifted off his hat and put it on his knee. He ran his fingers over his shaved face as though making sure his goatee was orderly.

"Well?" Pavo asked. They didn't have much time, only a few blocks before the driver would pause to let Fiducioso out of the car again.

Fiducioso leaned back in the seat. Clearly he was inclined to take his time making his moves. He wouldn't survive five minutes on one of the chess boards in Central Park. But rapidity of thought was not the only hallmark of intelligence, as Pavo had been forced to learn. No doubt the man was formulating the exact response that would keep Pavo's opinion of him — traitor or otherwise — perfectly balanced.

"If you had intended to scare her away from the case, I think it is safe to say the effort has failed," Fiducioso said. "I expected her to panic and flee back to White Plains and her father's house."

He paused, looking steadily at Pavo, judging his reaction.

"But she has not," Pavo said.

"She has not. She rebounded immediately."

Pavo allowed himself a momentary smile. "She was left at the Longden apartment as instructed?"

"Yes."

"The Longdens delivered the message as instructed — that she had been punished?"

"Yes."

"And?"

"Shortly after that, our cameras and microphones in the apartment went offline."

"Interesting."

The limo stopped at a light. The windows glimmered with half melted flakes of snow. The weather was turning — spring was approaching. It made the struggles of winter that much more vehement. People on the streets walked quickly, holding up black umbrellas, wearing thick coats and scarves, or huddled in corners, starving.

"And so she makes preparations to gather her resources and formulate an attack."

Fiducioso shrugged again. "If you like. She went to the police station and was ignored. Another warning, as instructed. Or some might say, a provocation — which is how I see it."

Pavo would have liked to have seen Regan St. Clair come up against personal violence and systemic apathy for the first time in her life – and on the same day no less — but of course, he had too many drains on his attention as it was. "Your opinions are, of course, your own. What happened afterward?"

"She called her pet detective and had him take her to the hospital where she was harassed with everything we could throw at her, including a rape kit and a call from her father."

The corner of Pavo's mouth twitched.

"And then?"

"And then she went to the critical ward to grill Schnatterbeck."

Pavo had anticipated the possibility of Regan behaving contrary to expectations but had assigned a low probability to her being able to question Schnatterbeck. She would be stubborn, but the hospital staff would be more so and would turn her aside.

If they could or would not...

"And after that?"

The limo paused in the middle of the block, and a green light flashed at the door; the lock disengaged. Fiducioso gave one last shrug. It indicated nothing of regret, pity, or even disgust.

"Your orders have been executed."

Ah. Then the old man was dead. It would not have shamed him to say that he felt a twinge of regret.

"Await my further instructions — the usual channels."

Fiducioso opened the door and slipped into the street. A swirl of snow entered the car as he put his hat back on and closed the door behind him. From the way he walked as the limo pulled away, he might have appeared from anywhere on his way to an appointment or an assassination, so little did it matter to him.

The snow was colder now. It slid past Fiducioso's hat and wool coat, finding its way to the pedestrians with their black umbrellas and the homeless crouched on the streets. Nothing could touch Fiducioso, not during the cold. Even the rain seemed to avoid him as much as possible.

The windshield wipers of the limo swept back and forth, pushing the snow into the corners of the windshield.

It was a promising night.

Chapter 25 - She didn't remember anything

The nurse's aide at the desk said, "You're not allowed to see him."

"Yes, you said that." Regan was finding it increasingly uncomfortable to remain standing. However, if she had accepted all the pain medicine she had been offered, she would have been in a coma. "But I asked what's happening, not whether I can see him. It's obvious there's been a change in his status."

The aide looked back and forth nervously, but every other available authority had vanished or been sucked into the situation in Schnatterbeck's room. The door was closed, and loud, panicked shouts were coming from inside — loud enough they echoed down the hallway and curled around the nurse's station.

The aide had obviously been told not to allow anyone in the room — but there hadn't been time for further instructions.

Jake coughed into his hand. "Regan...we should go. Your lips are turning gray, and your knees are visibly knocking together. You should at least go back and get some pain medicine, a wheelchair, and some slippers."

Her knees were *not* knocking together; that was ridiculous. "I'm fine," she insisted.

He put his hand on her back and drummed his fingers against her robe. "Regan, you look like death warmed over, a resurrected corpse. You're about to *collapse*."

He was either being patronizing or giving her a hint. She clutched the countertop with both hands and repeated her earlier statement in a quavering voice. "I'm *fine*! Stop trying to push me around."

"I'm not trying to push you around. I'm just trying to get you to take care of yourself."

"I can take care of myself! I can make —"

She had only been in one play in high school, one of the background dancers in a musical. Everyone had assumed that the tall, long-legged blonde girl would be a shoe in for a chorus line. Never again would the theater teacher make *that* mistake.

Nevertheless, her performance went off without a hitch. She let her knees go out from under her while still grabbing onto the counter.

"Whoa," she said, then let go.

She fell on the tile floor with a thump. It hurt like hell, but she didn't think she had broken anything that wasn't already broken.

She shouted in pain, then started cursing loudly — almost loudly enough to drown out the sounds still coming from Schnatterbeck's room.

The nurse's aide ran around the desk. "Don't get up, don't get up!" she shouted, pulling Regan's hands away from the floor and holding them in her own. "You might have broken something. We need to get a doctor to look at you!"

Regan exploded in outrage, slapping the girl's hands away and resuming her struggle to get up — a struggle that, horrifyingly, she didn't have to fake. "I'm *fine*!"

"Let's get her a wheelchair," Jake said, in a voice that dripped with resignation: *You've done it again, haven't you?* "Do you have one around?"

"In the supply closet," the aide said. Really, it wasn't fair, bamboozling the girl. She looked like she was in late high school or early college. Experienced enough to know how to respond generally to emergencies, but not experienced enough to look beyond the surface event. She turned away from the two of them and disappeared into a nearby room whose light shone brightly across the dim hallway.

Jake turned and jogged toward Schnatterbeck's room. If his footsteps on the tile made any sound, it was covered by the sound of a long, agonized bellow.

Regan said, "I don't care, go get it *now!*"

"Fine, just stay there on the floor until I get back."

"I *will*."

Jake disappeared around a corner. The nurse's aide pulled a folded wheelchair out of the storage room with a multipart crash. She swore, sighed, and then turned toward Regan.

"Where did he go?" she asked.

"I told him to go back to my room and get my purse," Regan said loudly, mustering all the haughtiness she normally used on the bench against an unruly witness. "Now help me up into that wheelchair."

"You really should stay here until a doctor is able to look at you."

"And how long will that be? Put one of those cushions in it. I'll take responsibility for my own snapped tailbone, thank you very much. This floor is hard and cold, I am in more than a negligible amount of pain, and my friend is having some sort of event no one will tell me about. The least you can do is help me into a wheelchair so I can wait in relative comfort until Jake gets back."

Mentally, she cursed herself. She shouldn't have said his name. For all she knew this girl was one of the players controlled by her opponent. She probably wasn't, but probability hadn't been working in her favor lately either.

The aide took a little more convincing — including the promise of a bribe when Jake returned with her purse — but eventually conceded there was probably no real risk in letting Regan rest in the wheelchair. The thought of being able to get rid of Regan faster might have been a factor. She slipped a wide web belt around Regan's waist and lifted her off the floor and into the chair as easily as a mother might have settled a baby from one hip to the other.

She gasped from pain and surprise and let herself tear up a little. It probably was less than noble of her, but if it helped keep the girl distracted from where Jake had gone off to, so much the better.

Regan gave herself a couple of moments to recover from being transferred. The woman put a seat belt on her and then returned to the storage room. After a few seconds of returning the fallen items to the shelves, the girl returned with a lap blanket which she tucked around Regan's legs covering the ugly bruises.

Regan found herself strangely touched but tried not to show it. Instead, she popped the locks on the wheelchair and began pushing herself down the hallway toward the exit.

"Where are you going?" the aide asked as she walked beside Regan, clearly exasperated. The girl had a face like an angel from a Christmas play, plump-cheeked and dimpled. She looked like the kind of girl that you wanted to take home to your mother.

"I'm in pain and tired of waiting. I'm going back to my room now. I'll have my friend bring you a little something later. It's almost eleven now. I'll have him leave it in an envelope for you if you're not here —" she glanced at the girl's name tag — "Taylor."

The girl shook her head. "You should wait for someone to take you back. It can get confusing in the hallways here. It's easy to get lost, especially when you're hurting and tired."

Again, the girl's concern touched her. It was probably automatic, just part of her job as far as the girl was concerned. Regan grabbed the wheels and started pushing again. She needed to keep the girl distracted for as long as possible.

The girl sighed and said, "Just a moment. I'll see if Rob at the desk can push you. It should be okay if there's nobody at the door for visitors for a few minutes."

She walked back to the desk and made a phone call, putting her hand over the receiver and grimacing when she didn't get the answer she wanted at first. But soon she had talked the orderly at the door into coming to get Regan to take her back to her room.

The orderly came and collected Regan, wheeling her slowly out of the ward. The sounds from Schnatterbeck's room had faded in volume and frequency, the loud bellow completely disappearing.

She thanked Taylor and waited until she was out of sight, then slumped in the chair. It made her ribs feel like they were scything through her skin — but they had started to hurt that badly regardless.

"You're not gonna faint on me, are you?" the orderly asked.

Regan breathed shallow breaths through her mouth. In truth, the corridors had started to swim around her. She turned her head slowly from side to side trying to keep it from feeling like it was going to explode, but with limited success.

"Yeah, I know how it goes," the orderly said. "You get hurt, and your body tells you that it's fine, everything's fine. It's the adrenaline talking. It tells you that you don't hurt as bad as you do, and that you have more energy than you really have. It keeps telling you that until you're all out, until every last reserve has been drained out of you. *Then* it says, 'Oh, by the way, all systems are shutting down in ten seconds.' You need to pass out. You go ahead — no shame in it. You're in the north wing on the third floor. I'll get you home."

Regan blinked; it seemed to take an hour. "How —?"

The orderly pointed over Regan's shoulder at her wristband. "I scanned that when you came in. There's an RFID chip in all the bands. It lets us track patients in case they decide to wander or forgot where they were. You gave us permission on the paperwork when they signed you in."

"Oh," Regan said. Then she let her eyes close. She didn't faint — it wasn't that sudden. But she didn't remember anything else until she woke up the next morning, either.

Chapter 26 - I have already made my decision

The morning dawned rosy and bright with sunshine streaming through the open curtains of her window and onto her face like liquid fire. She raised her forearm to shade her face and heard the sound of a slow clap from the other side of the room.

"The angel awakens," her father said.

She muttered something less than flattering under her breath. Out loud she croaked, "Coffee." Just as the orderly had said, the previous evening had taken more out of her than she had realized.

"What time is it?"

"Almost nine am. I hope you slept well."

"I slept through the nursing checks if that's what you mean."

Jake cleared his throat. Better and better, she had quite the audience for her groggy, dull minded awakening. "You didn't, actually," he said. "You sat up and cursed at the nurses several times."

She frowned. She didn't remember a thing. "Do I have a concussion?"

"Not according to the doctor," her father said, drawing out each syllable like the promise of a lawsuit.

"Temporary memory loss," Jake said. "What's the last thing you remember?"

"Talking to the orderly on the way back from the critical ward," she said promptly.

Jake sighed. The window shades purred, and the room went dark.

Regan blinked and put her arm down. Sometime during the night, she had been fitted with an IV tube on her left arm in addition to the ID bracelet on her right. The blankets were pulled up over her breasts, and she hadn't soiled herself, which was slightly better than she had a right to expect.

Her father was sitting in an easy chair next to the bed watching a cable news show on the television, which was turned down low. He had his legs crossed over each other, and his arms crossed over his chest. His jaw jutted out so severely he looked like a cartoon of Dick Tracy.

Jake stood next to the window, arms also crossed over his chest. She hadn't really paid attention to what he'd been wearing the previous day, other than his leather bomber jacket, blue jeans, and baseball cap, but from the sags in his jeans, she would have wagered that it was the same outfit, including the polo shirt.

"How long until the next staff visit?" she asked.

Jake looked at the wall over the sink. It was a couple of minutes before nine. "You have a couple of minutes, maybe."

"Then we don't have time for a full recap."

Jake looked at her, puffing out his cheeks. "I don't know if this is the greatest place to talk, period."

Her father said, "The doctors have already spoken to me this morning. You will be staying here for several days, possibly several weeks."

She frowned at him. "I can't *stay*. I have a trial."

Jake slipped away from the window and out the door. He had good instincts. For someone who'd never met the man, he was good at ascertaining that the best tactic for handling a disagreement with her father was to flee as far away as possible.

The door closed softly. "It's been postponed," her father said.

"Postponed?" It wasn't possible. She'd never missed a day of a trial in her life. Like anyone else she'd missed other days off work, sure, but never a trial and certainly not a murder trial.

He sniffed and turned toward the window. "Did I stutter?"

She slapped the bedclothes next to her. "Daddy, this is not the time."

"This is the perfect time to try to scare my daughter into staying in the hospital until she's well, and to make her leave some things well enough alone. I want you off the Gibbons case."

Her heart seemed to stop for a second. "No."

"Regan, I am your *father*."

There was no escape.

"Please leave," she said.

"You want me to take you seriously," he said. "I understand."

She turned on her side away from him, being careful not to kink up or pull on her IV tube. The sheets felt brand new, rough fibers scraping against her oversensitive skin.

The door opened, and Jake returned with some coffee in a large paper cup with a plastic lid. She could smell it across the room.

"Tell my daughter to drop the Gibbons case. Maybe you can talk some sense into her head," her father said.

Jake hesitated, his face carefully blank. He took two strides forward past the door to the bathroom, set the coffee cup on a swing table beside the bed, and raised the table so that she could reach the edge of it.

"Sir, with all due respect, I sincerely doubt that."

She closed her eyes. "Jake, please get my father to leave so I can rest."

Jake faced her father with his arms crossed over his chest. "Judge St. Clair, I have to ask you to leave."

"Remember I hired you first! And that was to look after her," her father snapped.

Somehow it didn't surprise her. Her father had his notions of how to protect her. The idea of her possessing her own freedom outside his control or knowledge had always disturbed him, especially after her mother had died.

"Yes, sir," Jake admitted, "but your daughter is an adult. If she asks that you be removed from her room, you have no legal or moral right to stay."

Her father snorted. The smell of coffee became one more reason to desperately desire her father to leave. So she could drink it, and maybe even have breakfast, and, miracle of all miracles, use the bathroom and even take a shower in peace.

He wouldn't go. He would shout at the two of them until she gave in and said he could stay. Her father *never* lost. She knew her father wanted the best for her, but he also wanted to be able to define what was best for her.

"She asked you to leave, sir," Jake said coldly.

Her father snorted. "That's gratitude for you."

She smelled his cologne as he leaned over the bed and kissed her on the head. Then he grunted and made a fast exit toward the door. She heard the door swish open on its hinges. Her father's footsteps echoed down the corridor until the hospital door swished once again shut.

"What was that all about?" Jake asked.

"He hired you."

"Yes. To keep tabs on you while you were working the Gibbons case."

"Did you sabotage any of my work to 'protect' me?"

"He asked me to. I didn't."

She took both hands and dug her fingertips into her forehead, which hurt when she touched it but hurt worse when she stopped. "Why didn't you tell me?"

"It was a condition of my employment. I was supposed to avoid you if possible, and to say nothing about your father if it wasn't."

"You haven't sabotaged anything on the Gibbons case."

"I just said that."

"I have to make sure."

"I swear that I have not sabotaged anything on the Gibbons case."

She took a deep breath. It hurt, but not as bad as it had yesterday. It was the drugs that let her drive her father out of the room. That's what it was. Her second-deep breath drove her to start coughing. She scooted slowly onto her back and then fumbled around with the controls until she was able to raise the head of the bed.

She pulled the table in front of her and picked up the cup of coffee. It was black, bitter, and still burning hot. She smiled at Jake in approval.

He smiled back, and her throat tightened. She could see the tight worry lines at the corners of his eyes. She wanted to tell him she hadn't meant to get hurt, she hadn't meant to make him worry — that it was worse than actually being hurt in the first place.

But she was supposed to be angry with him, wasn't she?

She cleared her throat. "Are you working for him or me now? You can't work for us both. And don't lie to me about it."

He leaned back against the wall. His arms hadn't come uncrossed. "I have a few questions for you first."

She gnawed on her lower lip for a second. It was swollen and split and tasted like blood. She was dying to ask what he'd found out about Schnatterbeck, but this had to be done first. Otherwise, everything else would be tainted. "Ask."

"I repeat. What was that all about?"

"Daddy told me that I was off the Gibbons case."

"Ah." Now he was chewing on his lip too.

"As well as postponing the Tarloff trial, presumably so I could heal. Had he stopped with announcing that he'd arranged that..." She spread her hands. "I might have given in."

"He loves you, you know."

"And he has a terrible way of showing it. Can you imagine how many times I've heard those exact words? And they didn't start at my mother's funeral. Oh no, they started long before that. My mother was a great one for saying them herself."

Jake rubbed one hand across his face. She could hear the scrape of stubble under his palm. "And what are your plans now?"

"I plan to continue to investigate the case."

"And do your plans involve changing your M.O.?"

Suddenly she wasn't comfortable looking at him. The ceiling was flat white, the walls pastel yellow. The light around the edges of the curtains had faded — not because clouds had covered the sun, but because the sun had risen more directly overhead. The nurse hadn't come in to check her vitals yet, but it was well after nine am. The trash was a quarter filled with paper towels. Another of her father's coping techniques was to wash his hands repeatedly while worried. It gave him a chance to blow his nose and dry his eyes without anyone noticing.

"Yes," she said, "I agree with you. We need to build a team, an actual team, to accomplish this. I propose starting with you, Alex, Gary, and…" Her throat tightened. She couldn't say it.

"Your father."

She blinked and swallowed. "I no longer want to include him. His instincts in this matter are unlikely to assist us in resolving the issues surrounding this case."

"Spoken like a lawyer."

"I *do* have a law degree."

He smiled slightly, "I'll try not to hold it against you. Anyone else?"

"Yes, my accountant, Jane."

Jake squinted at her. "Your accountant — what has she got to do with anything?"

Her voice came out in half a squeak. "I find it obvious that the next thing they're going to do to me, if they haven't already, is try to find a way to neutralize me."

"Yeah, by killing you," he responded.

She shook her head. It made the bones in her neck grind together; she stopped. "They can't kill me without triggering a huge investigation. While they might be able to shift the blame onto something related to the Tarloff case, it's more likely that some level of information about Andy Gibbons will come to the surface. Once the media gets hold of something like that — I don't care who they are, it would be a lot of work to cover it up again. It would be far easier and better if they could break me and blackmail me, scare me so badly that I no longer have any interest in fighting them, and in fact, am vulnerable to joining them."

She started to speak again, but he raised a hand. "No, I think I got it. If they have the kind of hold over you that they'd need to blackmail you, they own you. And if they own a judge, that could be useful."

"So I'd like to include my accountant so I can protect myself financially."

"I'd want to research and vet these people first — including Gary."

The way he said Gary's name grated on her nerves, but she ignored it for now. Gary could rub people the wrong way, but he could also work miracles.

"Of course," she said.

Jake tapped two fingers on his palm. "Your father doesn't want you on the Gibbons case."

"He specifically told me to leave it alone — be done with it."

"And yet he hired me to protect you while you were on the Gibbons case. I don't like that. It says that he knows more about the case than he's letting on. He knows it's dangerous."

"He knew that I would dig in my heels if he tried to put me off it."

"Obviously." The two fingers still drummed on his palm.

She drank more of the coffee. It was starting to loosen the knot in her throat and ease her headache — but gradually, in tiny increments. She'd need another cup, at the very least.

He switched palms, still drumming his fingers. "He doesn't want to let you know that what you're doing is dangerous, but he does want you protected. Now the danger is clear, now you've been warned several times, he wants you out of the situation."

"What are you trying to say?"

His palms clapped together, trying to catch a thought. But it slipped away. He rubbed his hands together. "I don't know. There's something. But I can't get at it."

They both needed more information, and more than likely, sleep. "It can wait for a round table with all of us, if you're still working for me, that is, and not my father."

"I have to talk to him before I can decide," he said.

She tried to take a long sip of coffee to hide her discomfort, but she wasn't sitting far enough up in bed for that. Besides, holding a paper cup with a plastic lid in front of her mouth made her feel silly.

It sounded like the two of them were still conspiring, which was exactly what she didn't want.

Her throat tightened again.

"Go ahead," she said. "Talk to him all you want. But once you tell me your decision, I expect you to stick with it."

His hands dropped to his sides; he stood up ramrod straight. All expression, all personality was stripped away from him for a moment. She blinked. He wasn't Jake anymore. He was Captain or Sergeant or some other title Westley for the moment.

"Ma'am, once I make my decision, I will stick with it. I knew this setup would be trouble, and I didn't like it. I am done with it now, one way or another."

She nodded awkwardly, trying not to aggravate the pain in her neck. She would see, that was all — they would both have to see.

Chapter 27 - Poisoned?

Two days later it was Tuesday. Regan was still in no condition to go back to work, but she was at least on her way home. That was the tradeoff Jake had managed to make with the hospital staff to keep Regan from driving them crazy. She could go home where a home nurse would take care of her, but she could not go back to work.

It had snowed four or five inches the previous night, and for a while Jake thought he was going to have to tell her that she wasn't going to be able to go home that morning because of the road conditions. Fortunately, the weather had cleared up, and the main roads had been fine. The plows had been clearing them all night long, and gray ridges of snow had built up along the roadsides and in the ditches — gray ridges sprinkled with tire tracks from vehicles that had gone off the roads the night before. Sometimes the vehicles were still in place. But that morning, traffic was only ten miles an hour under the speed limit

He pulled up to the driveway which had already been cleared by someone with a snow-blower.

Regan said, "It's the boy across the street. He knows I'm good for it."

Jake put the rental car in park and turned off the engine. It ticked loudly, and almost immediately the warm air in the car started to chill. "Stay here," he said. "I want to check it out first."

She reached into her pocket, winced, and pulled out her keys. "Here."

He left the car and checked the house. The fact that it had snowed the night before meant that he was able to see any tracks around the house. These consisted of a couple of squirrels, some birds, and some large, ungainly footprints in the shoveled snow along the driveway and walk to the front door sprinkled with salt crystals. A piece of paper fluttered in the storm door. He pulled it out. It looked like a note from the kid who'd cleared Regan's drive.

Too bad the snow also covered any other signs of intruders who might have been there before the storm.

He tucked the note into his pocket and opened the storm door. The door key was a standard one. He unlocked the deadbolt, put his hand on the handle, and then stopped.

Regan opened her door a crack and shouted out the security code. It was unnecessary. He'd driven down on Sunday afternoon, broken into the house, forged about a dozen signatures, and had a couple of additional security systems installed. He just couldn't remember whether he'd reactivated her current alarm system after he'd reconnected the wires.

A judge shouldn't have such a simplistic security system anyway.

He entered the code for the main alarm system, registered his presence for the two additional alarm systems, and gave a wave in case Alex was watching from one of his hidden cameras aimed toward the front door and living room.

Then he checked the house, going from room to room looking for signs of attempted or successful entry. He didn't see anything, and his gut wasn't screaming at him, which would have to be good enough for now. He didn't want to leave Regan in the car much longer. He should have left the motor running for her, but he didn't want it to mask any suspicious noises.

Finally, he went back to the car and opened Regan's door for her. "I didn't spot anything, but that doesn't mean it's safe."

She looked at him, and her chin twitched. They'd made her promise to wear a neck collar until she could be checked by her local doctor. It kept her chin almost painfully high.

"Do you think we should risk it?"

"My gut says yes."

She held out a hand, and he helped her to her feet, then assisted her back toward the house, his hand under her coat and holding onto the waistband of the pants he'd brought her. They toddled up the sidewalk like a pair of senior citizens. The front step took them an absurdly long time to navigate. She was lucky she didn't have a second story on the house. A basement full of paperwork and legal books, yes, but her bedroom lay on the ground floor.

Inside the doorway, she stopped and said, "Help me with my coat, if you please." She lifted her legs feebly one at a time and scraped off her walking shoes. She didn't bother to try to put them in order beside the coat tree. He helped her off with her coat.

"The bedroom," he said.

"I want to argue with you but I can't. I'm exhausted. What time is the nurse coming with the pain meds?"

"A half hour after we call and tell them we're here."

"You should call them soon."

They navigated the hallway to the bedroom, passing the kitchen and the library — which still had the same papers and books scattered everywhere. The dishes and crumbs had been cleared away, of course. The maid had been contacted and would be by in the morning, with Jake there to talk to her about a few things before she reported to Regan. He'd already checked her out; she was fine. But he needed to warn her that she might be putting herself in danger just by being Regan's housekeeper.

They had enough people in danger already -- they didn't need any more.

Regan's regular bed had been moved to the far side of the room. It was so sparsely furnished this wasn't a problem. She had a dresser with a mirror, a single bedside table with a lamp, and a flat-screen television on the opposite side of the room. Other than a couple of photographs of her as a child on top of the dresser and more of the same elegant, cold art prints on the walls, that was it.

He'd had a hospital bed installed, complete with bed rails and a call button. The call button went straight to Alex's nerve center in the basement of his coffee shop, where it was forwarded to whatever phone Jake happened to be using that day. It also rang in the spare bedroom, where a nurse could be set up, if necessary.

She'd been docile all the way back from the hospital, but tensed up when she saw the bed. "So thoughtful," she murmured.

"I know you hate it," he said, "but that was part of the deal."

"I'm not complaining."

Yeah, he'd noticed. He didn't want to say it out loud, but maybe a little practice in humility would do her some good.

He helped her over to the bed, pulled back the blankets and sheet, seated her, and helped her swing her legs up. "The nurse can help you change later."

"Thank you."

He pulled the blankets up to the stiff piece of plastic under her chin and raised the head of the bed. "You want the TV on?"

"No. I've waited long enough, Jake. Tell me, what happened to Schnatterbeck? Is he —?"

"He's dead," Jake said.

"What happened?"

"You don't want to know."

***

The hospital corridor had smelled like ammonia, so thick that his eyes watered. Either someone had spilled a bottle or was trying to cover up a smell. He made it around the half-lit corner before the nurse's aide called out to him. He could hear Regan coming up with some nonsense cover story about sending him for her purse. She didn't even carry a purse. She kept a wallet and her keys in a pocket — that was all. The nurse's aide seemed to buy it, mostly because Regan was keeping her too distracted to think straight.

He followed the corridor down to Schnatterbeck's room, the door surrounded by various carts and pieces of equipment, including an unlocked nurse's cart, complete with meds.

The door was shut, but the lights were on, shining from a strip under the door. Shadows danced across the bright light. Shouts were coming from behind the door.

"Keep him on the bed!"

"I'm trying, I'm trying!"

Then he heard a sickening thump and a yell that sounded like it came from the bowels of Hell itself.

Jake checked the hallway. Nobody was coming. He tiptoed past the nurse's cart and leaned his head against the door.

There was more shouting, and the smack and thump of something hitting the tile floor – repeatedly.

"Stop him!"

Someone shouted "I'm trying," and then he heard a terrible collective gasp.

Jake grabbed the handle on the door and turned it carefully, making no noise. When he had the latch drawn back, he leaned on the door a tiny fraction of an inch.

Nobody in the room was moving. He heard hoarse, shallow, fast breathing. But that was it.

"Oh my God," someone said. "I..."

A woman's voice snapped, "There will be time to discuss how unbelievable this is later, Thompson. Get one of the pads under his head — right *now*."

A rustling of paper and plastic was heard.

"Should we move him?"

The woman said, "No. I want breathing rate and blood pressure, stat."

"I'm on it," someone else said followed by more rustling.

Jake pressed inward with the door until he could see through the crack. Still no one was moving in the hallway — everyone was in the room except the nurse's aide helping Regan at the desk.

He could see a pair of gnarled white legs, blue veins standing out prominently on them, peeking between the crouched forms of several aides and the white uniform of a nurse. The bed rail was still up. Drops of blood glistened from underneath the bed and along the rail. An IV tube lay on the floor near the bathroom door.

Another thud sounded on the floor. Someone cursed.

"Hold him down."

"I am holding him down."

"He needs a sedative."

"What do you think I've been giving him, espresso?"

Jake slowly pushed open the door further.

"He's...not breathing."

"I still have a heartbeat."

"Oh Lord. Oh, Lord. Make him stop that."

The woman's voice: "Shut up, Thompson."

Jake crept into the room, one slow footstep at a time. Each step brought more of the scene into view. Schnatterbeck lay on the floor in a smear of blood, his back arched stiffly off the floor, his limbs thrashing as if he were electrified. The aides were trying to hold him down, but it was impossible. The man had superhuman strength.

Jake was lucky that the staff all had their backs to him, and they were completely engrossed with trying to keep Schnatterbeck restrained. He had to move quickly, though. More help would certainly be on the way.

Another hard thump came from the floor, followed by the rattle of plastic. Jake leaned to the side just far enough to get a glimpse of Schnatterbeck's head. His face was in a rictus grin, teeth bared, and the wound in his chest was running with blood despite the efforts of a nurse's aide to keep a compress made out of hand towels pressed against it. The nurse herself was trying to administer something in a syringe but was being distracted by Schnatterbeck knocking against her.

Jake pulled his head back and backed out of the door. He closed it so silently it didn't make a sound. Then he went down the hallway, away from Regan, the nurse's station, and the arrival of additional medical staff.

He found a mop bucket in the hallway, the source of the smell of ammonia. A bottle of cleaner had been spilled across the floor. He checked the nearby janitor's closet. It was open. He stepped in for a minute. He was shaking so badly that it was affecting his ability to keep quiet. His nerves were shot. He had to take a minute and get control of himself. He leaned against the wall inside the closet.

Schnatterbeck had either fallen or climbed over the side of the bed rails and then fallen, subsequently smashing his head against the floor so hard that he'd broken his skull. Underneath his head had been an incontinence pad covered with pink sludge. The man was dead. His body just didn't know it yet.

***

Regan waved one hand. She was squinting at him from behind puffy black eyes that had started to turn bright purple. It might be just before noon, but the woman was going to be lights out in a couple of minutes, she was so exhausted. He couldn't believe they'd let her out this soon, even with the promise of a home nurse to check on her every few hours.

"Just tell me," she said.

"He was poisoned — with Strychnine." Jake paused, "It wasn't pretty."

"Poisoned? With strychnine? Aren't there a dozen different tests that you can do to determine the use of strychnine? And doesn't it leave some kind of signs on the body?"

He had a flash of Schnatterbeck's body pulled taut on the floor, muscles in convulsions even though his brains were being pounded flat on the floor. "You bet it leaves signs on the body."

"Why be so overt? To scare me?"

"You think?"

Her eyes closed, the muscles around them relaxing, allowing the bulging bruises around them to smooth a little. "I'm already scared."

"You might try acting like it," he said.

She grunted and rolled over. He pulled out his cell phone and backed out of the room, leaving the door open a crack, and retreated to the kitchen to start up a pot of coffee and call the nurse.

A few minutes later when he walked down the hall to check on her, she had started to snore.

Chapter 28 - The enemy wasn't as clearly defined

The nurse, a competent but loud voiced middle-aged woman with a heavy Asian accent, woke Regan and was checking her vitals and alertness while telling her about her sons in college in an incessant stream of dialog that echoed down the hallway.

He moved into the kitchen, slurping his coffee.

It had been two years since he'd left his unit, honorably discharged after a knee injury during a mission. They had located the hostages they'd been sent for, but had lost one of their own — Steve Luttrell, the youngest member of the team. He'd been twenty-three and left behind a girlfriend and a little boy, Danny, aged two.

The mission had involved a night drop from a Black Hawk helicopter into mountainous terrain and then hiking through a ravine to a tightly-packed stone and clay village clinging to the side of a plateau.

He'd twisted his knee on the drop but had pressed onward with his squad. Then he'd taken a nasty slide in the ravine that hadn't done him any good. But it was securing the village that had done him in.

His squad of eight had moved into the northern side of the village. Another squad had taken the road leading up from the south. West was straight up the side of the cliff, and East was almost straight down. There were about 100 civilians in the small sheep and goat herding community, and just five tangos to deal with — chicken feed for a team of Delta Force operators.

The north and south squads had arrived at the designated location without a hitch. Other than Jake's knee, everyone was in good shape. They had surrounded the building where an operator had inserted himself earlier that day to confirm the location of the hostages. They had secured all likely sniper locations — including the one with the sniper that had brought Steve Luttrell down.

And then the "civilians" had attacked.

Jack's outfit had given a good account of themselves. They'd held the enemy down and killed 20 of them, extracted the hostages, retreated, and were airlifted back to base.

It wasn't until he'd been hefted back into the helicopter that he learned Steve Luttrell was dead — a sniper bullet through the head.

They mourned his death. Steve had been a good kid with a bright future. Jake visited his girlfriend and held his little boy, Danny. There was not much he could say aside from acknowledging that Steve had been a good guy, a brave soldier, and that his buddies were going to miss him.

Everyone told Jake that Steve's death had nothing to do with him. He just couldn't make himself believe it.

The doctors examined Jake's knee, taking X-rays and scans, and finally preformed arthroscopic surgery. The specialist told him he wished he had better news, but the injury meant the end of the line for him in Delta Force.

Jake grieved. He mourned for the operator he used to be, the camaraderie, the adventure, the adrenaline, the feeling of being useful.

Then he let go of Lieutenant Jacob Westley, 1st Special Forces Operational Detachment Delta.

For two years he'd been a private detective. He kept in shape and refused the knee replacement they offered him. So far it had worked.

Being a PI was about as much fun as cleaning toilets – divorce cases was what paid most of his bills. For two years he'd been infiltrating, documenting, and destroying what was left of rich people's marriages. Digging around in the sewer of other people's lives had driven him to the brink of depression.

Getting dragged into this kind of situation was exactly what he had been trained for. Here was a challenge a Delta Force operator could understand and face — a covert group executing threats on civilians. They'd murdered at least one person, Schnatterbeck, and possibly a second, Angela Ligotti. They were making threats against a district judge and using sophisticated intelligence techniques. They had kept an innocent man "hostage" in prison for more than ten years. A single mother and her two teenage boys were in dire straits.

The enemy wasn't as clearly defined as they were back in Iraq, Afghanistan, and Syria, but they were no less ruthless and brutal.

The operator, cold and calculating, was starting to wake up. Two years was nothing but a nap for an operator like he'd been.

Jake wasn't sure he was ready. But it was hard to keep the lid on Lt. Westley when he was so obviously needed.

Chapter 29 - Justice by PowerPoint

Regan's queen-sized bed had been dismantled and leaned up against the wall, and her curtains had been pulled tightly closed. Jake had talked about stapling them to the frames, but Regan had vetoed the idea immediately. Even so they were fastened down with masking tape.

The bedroom was packed with dining room chairs and a card table with three laptops on it, all humming busily. Crowded around the table were Alex Carr, a tall old-fashioned but obviously young computer geek with a curled mustache, Gary, and a stiff-backed Jake with ramrod straight posture. He'd been acting strangely ever since he'd left to start organizing this meeting. It was as if the laid back Jake had been replaced with another version, one that had little or no sense of humor — only the professionalism of his military training.

Jane sat at a small desk brought in from one of the guest rooms downstairs. She didn't have a laptop or a tablet but kept a paper ledger book in front of her. With the way that Alex had been rambling on about new ways to hack into computer systems, Regan was starting to wonder if Jane wasn't the smart one. Paper, at least, could be permanently and beyond recovery, destroyed.

Jamie's boys were downstairs watching TV and playing on the game console that Alex had purchased and set up for them. At first, they had run up and down the stairs every few minutes to grab something from the kitchen or drag their mother downstairs to look at something. Just as they started to glory in their lack of school, they fell into despair at the homeschooling program that Gary had already set up for them. Soon after that came the raging and despairing as they discovered the locks on their electronics that popped up with reminders to get their homework done.

Now they had both completed their assignments — even James who had to be threatened by Jake to get motivated enough to get started — and had settled down enough to join forces to save the universe, one game at a time.

Jamie Gibbons leaned against the wall in the bedroom in between bouts of pacing. Her chair stood empty with several manila folders stacked on it, copies of the information she'd put together. She hadn't liked being given a leave of absence from her job and being pulled out of her apartment. She hadn't liked hearing about what happened to Fred Schnatterbeck. She told Regan she felt trapped in Regan's house, as if she and the boys were imposing, and they could find somewhere else to stay.

Regan told her she was needed to help take care of *her*. The day nurse that Jake hired had, upon deeper investigation, been discovered to have recently paid off her car — two years ahead of schedule.

Jake insisted she go — end of story.

Jamie might be only a nurse's aide, but at least she could be trusted to take a blood pressure reading, administer medication, and see when any medical emergency developed without reporting on what was going on inside the house.

Regan had avoided painkillers that morning so her mind would be sharp for the meeting. It was 12:30 pm and already she was starting to ache and breathe more shallowly. It was time to get started before she lost focus. "All right. Are we ready to start? If the preparation for this meeting takes much longer, I'm going to need another nap."

The three guys at the table looked up. Jane was already looking at her, rolling her pen between her fingers, pulling the metal cap off and snapping it back on. Jamie looked narrowly into Regan's eyes, and she had the feeling that Jamie was gauging her pain level pretty closely.

"Ready," Gary said.

Alex cleared his throat.

"Ready," Gary insisted. She already knew he had an uncanny ability to tell how much stress and discomfort she was in. "We can work on the rest later."

Jake walked over to the television and turned it on. The screen read *'The Andrew Gibbons Case',* Justice by PowerPoint. "Just to make sure we're all on the same page, I'd like everyone to state their roles."

The roles weren't difficult to figure out. Alex clicked his mouse, and the slide changed to that of a bulleted list of their names along with their titles.

"Out loud, please," Jake said.

From her hospital bed, Regan read off the slide, "Regan St. Clair, commander. Subject matter — expert in legal matters."

Jake said, "Jacob J. Westley, operational lead. Regan's in charge of the direction we're going. I'm in charge of getting us there — Capiche?"

Everyone checked off with a "yes" as Jake pointed at them, even Jamie and Gary.

"I am the subject matter expert in security, tactical operations, intelligence gathering, and attack and defense."

He seated himself at his laptop.

Alex said, "Uh, Alex Carr, computer geek." Jake pointed over his shoulder at the TV screen and Alex added, "Subject matter - expert in networks, computer security, and a bunch of other stuff that I am not going to read off the screen." His entry on the list was the longest one and included terms Regan had never heard. "As a reminder, don't call out on any of the phones, not even the house phone, without following the directions that have been taped to the phone."

"I'll remind the boys," Jamie said.

"And no pizza delivery," Jake said. "If they want pizza, they have to go through me first."

Jamie chuckled. For a moment Jake looked blank as if he didn't see the humor. Then he smiled.

Regan felt a pang for the other Jake. She wondered whether she would get him back anytime soon — probably not until after the case had been resolved and Andy exonerated.

Gary was next.

"Gary Titschmarsh." He raised his hands. "It may be an amusing last name, but it's also my aunt's last name. She and her husband adopted my brother and me after my parents went nuts, got divorced, and joined a spiritual commune in California together; then they killed themselves when the founder went bankrupt. So, I call myself a Titschmarsh with pride."

Jake cleared his throat again.

"I am the admin," Gary said. "I have a degree in library science, which means I know everything, can find everything, and can attribute quotations properly with sources. I am a subject matter expert in coordinating everything that needs to happen. I am a ninja of..."

"Gary," Regan murmured. Her ribs were burning and felt like they were being twisted out of alignment by the way she was lying in bed. "Just read the slide."

He put his hands down. "Fine, I'm Gary Titschmarsh, administrative tasks. Subject matter — expert in research and library science."

"Thank you."

Jane said with a perfectly bland facial expression, "Jane Hendricks, the financial genius. I'm the reason Regan can pay all of you. We went to college together and made a blood bargain. I get to play with all the money Regan received from her honorary uncle, Paul Travers - the New York Sewage mogul - when she was twenty-one, and she refuses to spend the insane profits I give her on anything more expensive than her mortgage — and now this case. If you can get me the data, I can find where the money goes."

Jamie's dark eyes were fastened on Regan as she struggled not to adjust the head of her hospital bed, or pull herself up, or scream. She said, "My name is Jamie Gibbons. I'm the person who stirred all this up and who is regretting it more every day."

"Read the slide," Jake said.

"Jamie Gibbons, wife of Andrew Gibbons, the unjustly accused — pursuer of justice and the mother of two sons who need their father back. I specialize in keeping Regan from overdoing it, which reminds me..."

She walked over to Regan's bed, grabbed a part of the sheet and lifted Regan upward so she was bending the right way. Her ribs eased their throbbing, and she let out a breath of relief.

"You want to take a break?" Jamie asked.

Regan shook her head.

"Next slide," Jake said.

Alex clicked the slide. The picture was of a younger Andy Gibbons, smiling a big charming smile, still dressed in street clothes. The background looked like a pub of some kind.

"Andrew Gibbons," Jake said unnecessarily, "approximately twelve years ago."

"Eleven," Jamie said, "I recognize the shirt."

"Next."

The next slide showed a list of bullet points summarizing the case and the title *Marando's "Evidence."*

Jane wasn't as up-to-date on the information as everyone else. She flipped open her register and started taking quick notes.

"Andrew Gibbons was accused of murdering Angela Ligotti on April 7, 2003. The next morning, blood stains were seen on the 200 block of Kent Street by several people but were not reported until after the investigation began into the murder. The body was found that afternoon by a security guard inside a walled parking area for 265 Kent Street, a building associated with a nearby water treatment plant. She had been stabbed to death and was covered with newspapers. While there was some blood at the scene, it was not enough blood to account for the murder happening at that location.

"The investigation was led by Detective Peter Marando. A witness, Abe De Wit, was out bicycling the night of the 7th. He testified he saw two people, a large black man in a red jacket and a Caucasian woman sitting in a green sedan parked on the 200 block. He stopped to watch as the black man opened his door, walked around the car, and opened the passenger door. He bent over and appeared to be about to lift the woman out of the car, but stopped when he saw Mr. De Wit, returned to the driver's side door, and got in the car. Mr. De Wit rode to the place where the car had stopped but did not see anything out of the ordinary at that time. He returned to his apartment in the neighborhood.

"Andrew was pulled in as a suspect by Detective Marando based on an anonymous tip that he was the man with the red jacket. A red jacket was found in Andrew's apartment, and Andrew also admitted to owning a green car, a Lincoln Town Car."

Jake looked over at Jamie to see if she was going to protest or add more details. Still leaning against the wall, she shook her head. Jake was clearly on a roll.

"Andrew was arrested on suspicion of murder and Mr. De Wit picked him out from a lineup of similarly sized men. Several DNA samples on the body of the victim were processed. Among them was a strand of African-American hair.

"While Andrew was in jail, he spent a single night in the same cell as Nate Barstowe, a regular police informant with connections to Detective Marando. The next day Mr. Barstowe reported that Andrew had bragged to him about the murder, saying that he had made advances to the woman, then killed her and dumped the body when she refused him.

"Andrew denied being in the area that night. He stated he was not near the area at the time but was driving around in a friend's car after having had a fight with his wife, Jamie. He was unable to produce any witnesses confirming his location and claimed that he didn't know exactly where he had been driving. He said he had not been drinking. He was given drug and alcohol tests when he was arrested which came up negative for everything except for a small amount of marijuana which he admitted to smoking that night.

"He was convicted and sentenced to 25 years to life. Next slide."

Another bulleted slide came up under the heading *Jamie Gibbons' Evidence*.

"Jamie was given a packet of information by Detective Marando, which we believe now was meant to silence her calls for a more thorough investigation on his part. She was able to go through the information and match up the 'evidence' Marando provided with several holes in the story.

"Jamie came up with four main discrepancies between the evidence provided by Detective Marando and the situation as she knew it.

"First: another witness, Frederick B. Schnatterbeck, came forward and said that he had seen the green Lincoln Town Car backing out of a gated area belonging to the water treatment plant. He gave a statement to an unnamed officer but was not questioned by Detective Marando and was not called by either side as a witness. Jamie tracked him down and questioned him. He stated that the man driving the car had been wearing a red jacket and there had been a passenger in the passenger's seat, slumped down so that only the top of their head was showing."

Jamie had more time to talk to Schnatterbeck, but apparently she hadn't picked up on the significance of the Lincoln backing out of the gate. It was Jake who had put that together.

"Second: the jacket. Jamie identified the actual jacket the police seized as evidence as belonging to a friend of the family, Michael Liu, who is approximately five feet, two inches tall, and who left the jacket at the apartment a few days previously. It is Jamie's opinion, and Regan and I concur, that it would have been impossible for Andrew Gibbons, who is over six feet tall, to wear the jacket.

"Third: the car. The green Lincoln Town Car that Andrew Gibbons owned was out of operation at the time of the murder and was at the home of a friend, Tony Aquilone, who is a mechanic. Again, Mr. Aquilone was not questioned about the car, which he said was *not* in a drivable state — the transmission was out. The car was not searched for evidence of blood, fingerprints, or DNA.

"Fourth: the murder weapon. Jamie says that no search was made for the murder weapon, which the autopsy report stated was probably a knife of about three to three-and-a-half inches long with a blade approximately one-inch-wide, and used by a right-handed attacker positioned directly in front of the victim. The victim had been stabbed several times in the chest area and died of blood loss and shock from the stab wounds, one of which cut the pulmonary artery."

Jake turned toward Jamie again. Her lips were pressed together so tightly that a pale ring formed around them, but she didn't speak.

"Next slide..."

The next slide read, *Additional Evidence*.

"Here are the main points that we have, whether intelligently or otherwise assembled about this case since Regan started looking into it, roughly in order of discovery. Let me stress that in no way was this additional evidence gathered with any kind of system. We need to be better about that.

"First is that Regan was asked by Mr. Gibbons to stop her investigation of the case at the same time the detective she had hired to look into the situation quit without providing her any of the material he had acquired. In fact, one of her tires was slashed outside the prison while she was visiting Mr. Gibbons. Shortly afterward, she was attacked inside a bar where I happened to be."

Jane raised her hand. "Mr. Westley?"

"Jake, please."

"Jake. You just happened to be at the same bar?"

He paused. "It's close to where I live. I went there to relax, have a beer, and play pool."

"But Regan's father hired you."

"Yes. He heard through the LEO grapevine that his daughter had been attacked and hired me later that night."

"You. Not a different private investigator — you. Did he learn about you from the grapevine too?"

"We had met previously through a criminal investigation. You can continue giving me the third degree at a later time. We have a lot of ground to cover today."

"One more question," Jane said.

"Yes?"

"Were Regan's attackers that night in the bar involved in the larger plot?"

"I was unable to find any evidence whatsoever that the three young men who attacked Regan had any ties to anyone involved with the case. They had, in fact, only decided to come to that particular bar at the last moment because another bar they were in the habit of frequenting was closed."

"So you think it was a coincidence that the other bar had closed?"

"I did then. Now, I'm not sure."

"Thank you."

Jane settled back in her seat, putting the cap back on her pen and rolling it between her fingers again.

Jake said, "The points that need to be investigated next are as follows. We need to obtain security camera footage from the parking lot security cameras and prison records related to Andrew Gibbons' behavior — especially any altercations leading to injury, whether inflicted or received by him." He glanced at Jamie. "While the incidents themselves may not have occurred as portrayed, the records will indicate whether there are any patterns. We can also track down the backgrounds of those involved and find out whether they have any connections to other participants in the case."

Jamie nodded looking at Regan. "You know that you're going to get railroaded if you ask for that information through legal channels."

Jake turned toward her as well. It was almost like they'd planned it. "And it will allow our opponents to know where we are in our investigation, as the requests themselves will leave a trail."

"If you're asking me whether I approve of your methods, the answer is that I am extremely uncomfortable with them," Regan said. "We have this saying in the legal profession: 'The poisoned fruit of a poisoned tree.' It means that anything we obtain illegally cannot be used in court, and anything we obtain legally because of suggestions that we've picked up using illegal information also cannot be used in court."

"Do you think," Jake said, "that we are going to be able to obtain justice through the courts in this case?"

"No," Regan said. "However, because our goal is to make sure that Andrew Gibbons gets freed from prison, we have to be careful in our methods. We *cannot* create a situation that makes it more difficult for him to be freed. We all know that justice has failed him. But it would still be better for us to drop the case and let him wait for his normal parole review hearing than it would be to pollute the situation with evidence that can be shown to be tainted."

Gary said dryly, "So does that mean you're going to let us break the law to get your evidence or not?"

If she hadn't known Gary for almost 15 years, she would have hesitated. It was a leading question, the kind of thing that would be absolute death to her career and her freedom if he, or any one of them, were wearing a wire.

"The rules are easy. If in doubt, ask me or Jake; and our rulings are final."

Gary leaned back in his folding chair, then put his hands to his head, puffed out his cheeks, and spread his hands outward like they were pieces of debris. "My head explodes. Regan St. Clair acknowledges that it might be possible, in certain circumstances, to put a toe out of line."

"Oh yes, it's the end of the world," she said.

"Not true. It's only the beginning."

Jake continued. "Additional investigation needs to be done on the location of the murder, specifically where the body was found. While there are cameras covering the area now, at the time of the murder there weren't any. However, there was a camera covering the most likely point of access — the entry gate. Again, we need to obtain records — if they still exist or can be retrieved.

"We need to investigate Angela Ligotti. We need to know whether she was having an affair or any other relationship with Andrew Gibbons, or if she was associated with any other type of suspicious activity."

He began flipping through slides as he talked. The points of evidence became a blur. The tasks implied were both illegal and extensive. She couldn't imagine how they would be able to keep their work from becoming so tainted that it was useless. Her head pounded, caught between the rock of illegality and the hard place of injustice.

Ibuprofen — she needed something to take the edge off the pain — and some caffeine. She felt like she was going into withdrawal.

"We need access to the physical evidence as well: hair and fiber samples, autopsy reports, and the newspapers found over the body at the site.

"We need access to the green Lincoln Town Car the Gibbons owned so we can find out whether any DNA or other evidence remains. We also need to talk to Andy's mechanic friend, Tony Aquilone, to find out: what he knows about the car; who, if anyone, asked about the car; about the brown Honda Civic that he loaned to Andy; what happened to both cars; and probably a few other things.

"We need employment records and anything else we can dig up on Detective Peter Marando, organizations he's involved in, if he has a pattern of using any additional informants, pressuring witnesses. We need his financial records —"

Jane did a fist-pump in the air.

"— to see whether he's been accepting bribes. We also need records on Fred Schnatterbeck, financial as well as anything else we can dig up. Who does he have connections to? Is or was there a standing poker game made up of gossips, as Regan questions? Could that have been a source of money laundering in the area?"

"The cars," Regan murmured, "the internet taxi service."

"I'm getting to that. We need the records on an informal, possibly illegal taxi service operating in the area."

Alex snorted, "Which one?"

"No idea. It might be more than one service involved too. We need to see what kind of operational and financial records they keep; we need to know how many of their cars are tied to criminal activity, including car-jacking. Tony Aquilone might be a resource there."

Jamie looked panicked; Jane was starting to look worried. It was a lot of data to obtain and sort through without leaving a trace they had it. Even Gary was starting to look concerned.

Alex made *come on, come on* gestures with his fingers. "Jake. You made this sound like it was going to be something difficult." He looked around to see the rest of them staring at him. "Er...I mean none of this should be too hard — a little social engineering, a little exploitation of loopholes which I may or may not already have set up in anticipation of this meeting, a bit of three-card-monte while I'm transferring files. I can definitely get you any digitally stored information that's been mentioned so far, and I can even crunch it to some extent if you can tell me what I can weed out."

Regan's jaw dropped.

Alex twirled one end of his mustache nervously between his fingers. "It might even be — fun?"

Jake said, "We need to make another, deeper effort to trace the phone call that Regan received that led her to the beauty shop. We need to track who hacked the hospital systems to lock the door of the women's restroom while Regan was in it and shut down the lights, including the emergency lights. We need to trace who hacked the loudspeakers in the room. We need to go over that bathroom to see whether the female operative who had been waiting in there left any physical evidence in there — fibers, DNA."

"That's a lost cause," Jamie muttered. "A thousand people have been through there by now."

"It's all just data," Alex said.

"Uh-huh. You have a DNA testing lab sitting around? I tried to get the hair they used to put away my husband. You know how much time and money they wanted for just one testing? And time"

Gary said, "Mmm, let me guess. You paid well over a grand, waited at least three months, and got back results that said that it was one hundred percent positive that it was your husband's hair...but didn't supply any specifics."

"How *did* you guess?"

"Next," Jake said, "we need to track down the person who confronted Regan in the courthouse. The courthouse should still have the video surveillance records from that day. We have the note he gave her. We need that fingerprinted and tested for evidence and the paper itself sourced in case it's something unusual. The license plate of the car the person was driving when I saw him on the day Regan was abducted, we need that looked at again, deeper this time, and find out where the *other* car came from that was involved in the carjacking and swap.

"We need to interview people throughout the neighborhood to determine whether they saw Regan, the man outside the empty storefront who spoke to her as she went in and came out, and who was seen near the beauty shop after Regan was abducted."

"The taco guy," Regan said.

"The clerk at the beauty shop also needs to be tracked down and questioned. The ownership of both shops needs to be traced, and both shops need to be searched for physical evidence, especially the basement of the beauty shop. We need to search the financial information related to both locations. Based on the behavior of one of its customers, it's possible the beauty shop is involved in some type of extralegal activity. The officers responding to the call need to be investigated to see whether they have connections to anyone related to the beauty shop or any other evidence of extralegal activities.

"We need to investigate the location where Regan was found, the Longdens apartment, to see whether any physical evidence was left behind. We need to investigate the Longdens themselves and find out why they were selected as the location to dump Regan — are they involved in this somehow? Are they involved with, or being targeted by, the group of people that had Regan kidnapped and beaten? If they are being targeted, we need to find a way to protect them.

"We need to look at the 67th Precinct and find out how Regan's obviously desperate situation was ignored by the officers. At what point or points did the ordinary legal process of someone trying to report a crime break down?

"We need to find out how Schnatterbeck was poisoned. Was a human element directly involved? That is, was he knowingly given strychnine, or was it administered after misdirection sent via digital methods? Was strychnine actually used, or was some refined or artificial chemical equivalent used? Schnatterbeck's apartment needs to be searched for physical evidence, and we need his autopsy report. Schnatterbeck's attacker, Lance Powell, has to be investigated and his autopsy report obtained."

"Autopsy report?" Regan asked.

"He died at approximately the same time as Schnatterbeck," Jake said, "from the damage I did to his skull. Fortunately, no charges have been pressed — probably because someone wants to keep things quiet."

"Then they shouldn't have poisoned Schnatterbeck," Regan said.

"As long as they're willing to settle a malpractice suit out of court, they should be in the clear on that one — an unfortunate mix-up."

Regan grunted in disgust. "Granted, go on."

"The fact that they haven't had you killed is significant. But we don't know what it means. We also need to investigate the day nurse that you hired, and that paid off a significant chunk of debt just after being hired. That might be a good way to find out where the money's coming from."

"In that particular case," Regan said, "I can almost guarantee what you'll find. It'll be my father, trying to find a way in."

He shrugged. "We'll deal with that if it comes up," she said. Through gritted teeth. She didn't have much longer before she would have to ask them all to go.

Jake flipped to a blank slide. "That should give us a start on assessing the danger involved in the case and at least a start on finding the killer. Now for the legal system, I think we can all agree that justice was perverted in this case. We need to find out whether the prosecution and the judge were involved and to what extent the defense was involved."

Regan nodded, even though it made her heart fall. All of this was only *a start*. It was not what she wanted to hear, but not something she could really disagree with either. It was overwhelming.

Jake looked around the room making eye contact with each person, one after the other awaiting comments.

There were none.

"Last but not least," Jake said, "Andy's police dossier has gone missing."

Regan looked at him incredulously, then at Alex. Alex shrugged and then nodded.

Gary drawled, "Why am I not surprised?"

"Wait, what?" Regan asked. "Andy Gibbons' dossier — you mean the case files for the murder?"

Jake nodded but didn't say anything.

She'd slid down in bed again. On top of everything else, bones she didn't know existed inside her face ached and felt like they were coming apart.

"Where is it, do you think?"

Jake said, "Marando. Either he has it, or he knows who does."

"You're asking me whether … you can break the law with regards to getting it back."

No hesitation. "Yes."

Her head felt like a drill bit was at work, going from the inside out. She felt nauseous from the pain.

Now was the test. Either she was going to knowingly allow Jake to start breaking the law, or she wasn't.

She took a deep breath.

"Do it. Send Jane and Gary after them while you and Alex work on the various physical evidence and data trails. Now *please* someone get me some Vicodin and get out of here before I start screaming."

Chapter 30 - The Honorable Judge John St. Clair

Jake waited in the hall. He hadn't heard any screaming from Regan's room, but the few gasps and moans of pain had put his teeth on edge. She shouldn't have pushed herself so hard.

Jamie came out, closing the door behind her and standing between him and it. She was, at least, six inches shorter than he was and looked like she might have weighed 100 pounds less. She was too thin through the face. Her hair had been straightened and pulled back into a bun. If she'd been military, she would have been Army — no nonsense, just pure determination.

"How is she?" he asked, stepping out of her way.

"Vicodin is a wonderful thing," Jamie said. She didn't move. Great. There was some kind of test he would have to pass in order to get past the woman.

"I have to talk to her."

"I just bet you do."

Jake took a deep breath and released it. "What is it, Jamie? Be straight with me."

"You better find a way to let go of some of this macho stuff — at least when you're around her. She wants to be able to rely on you. Instead you're acting like this is World War III and nobody needs to crack a smile ever again."

"So what if I am?" he said defensively.

"Your attitude isn't going to make her follow your directions or trust your judgment. It's just going to make her go behind your back if there's ever a difference of opinion."

Jamie was making him sound like an authoritative father — and Regan, a rebellious teenager. "You're saying this because of how Andy treated you."

She grinned at him. "Nope, I'm saying it because of how I treated Andy. He's no angel, and he'll admit it if you ever ask him. He was always in trouble when he was a kid. He needed someone to take him under his wing when he was a young man, if you know what I mean."

Jake did. He'd been lucky to have several men in his life who'd fit that bill, the Honorable Judge John St. Clair being one of them. He nodded.

"When I got pregnant with Tyrone, I got hard on him. All I could think was that I had to shape him up and make him a better man or Tyrone would get stuck in the same position as Andy — no father, nobody to keep him out of trouble. I thought the only way I could make him shape up was to put a stern face on everything I did.

"I'm not saying that it's my fault that Andy got into trouble. I didn't drive him to it; he drove himself. But then it started to look like it was never going to matter anymore. So I stopped being such a hard ass and let him see what was going on with me. I needed someone to talk to. I told him about all the worry and the times we came up short, the way the boys were driving me nuts, all the dumb things that had me tearing my hair out, and the ways they made me proud.

"That's when he started acting like a man — like he would be a father to those boys if he were ever to find his way out. He said it was a real eye-opener, listening to me and reading my letters, telling him how it really was instead of seeing me glare at him all the time."

Jamie didn't understand. It had been Jake's acting soft, like Regan's friend, that had left her vulnerable. He had to be a professional, not a shoulder to cry on. But that wasn't something Jamie could be expected to understand. He tried not to react. She wasn't trying to derail him, just trying to help in the way she knew how. He'd barely spoken to her before. "Question: Did you give this same speech to Regan?"

"No," Jamie said. "I did talk to her, though, mostly about her father. But I think that my words fell on deaf ears, and I decided not to press it with her. The meds were kicking in."

"I should see her before she falls asleep."

"If she *is* asleep, don't wake her."

"No ma'am."

She started to step out of the way, finally, but then she grabbed him by the shoulder and shook it. Not gently, either. "If only I could shake sense into you. You *do* know how fond that woman is of you, don't you?"

He just looked at her.

"Let me put it a little more clearly. She doesn't need this Mr. Macho shit. She needs some TLC, and you better give it to her. It's not like the whole world can't see the look on your face when she smiles at you."

"I —"

"Words from you are not necessary at this time. Just go in there and be nice to her."

Then she not only stepped completely out of the way but opened the door for him.

Speechlessly, he nodded at her.

Regan lay on her side with the head of the bed laid flat. She was breathing in little gasps and clutching her pillow with one hand and the bed rail with the other. Her face was pale. Even her bruises looked a little washed out. A wireless call signal had been clipped to her bed near the head. She kept glancing at it.

"Hey," he said. Now that he saw her, he didn't know what to say. Seeing her in pain was a kick in the gut. Images of losing her at the beauty shop flashed through his mind: seeing her go through the door, trying to kick the glass in, shuffling through the dark aisles stacked with wig boxes, hesitating at the door to the basement.

"I'll be fine in a minute," she said. Her voice had gone hoarse. "You don't need to call her. I can feel the drugs kicking in. Just leave me alone and I'll be fine."

"You don't need your pillow or to be moved or something?"

She shook her head. It must have hurt; he could see her eyes tighten around the corners. She kept panting.

The dining room chairs had been set against the hall wall to get them out of the way. The card table and the desk had been dragged under the TV. He took a chair and set it beside her bed.

"No really, you don't need to stay," she said. "You have things to do and people to organize."

"It can wait," he said.

He sat next to her, one hand hovering next to the rail. He wasn't sure whether to reach out to her or not.

She sniffed hard and pressed her forehead against the bed rail. "The things that could have happened to Jamie and her boys, to Andy. We have screwed this up at every turn."

"That's why I'm being such a hard-ass now."

"I know," she sniffed again. "Please, may I have a tissue? I'm so tired. I don't know where they are."

He looked around and grabbed one from the tiny nightstand on the other side of the bed. A biography of Lincoln lay next to it.

"You want your book?"

"Maybe later. You know what's dumb? I want to play stupid games on my phone — to take the pain away. Only I don't have a smartphone anymore. I keep telling myself that having a smartphone will put me in danger, that I don't need it. But then I forget, and I almost yell at you for taking mine away."

"It is broken."

"I'm in a shitty mood, and I don't care."

She smiled.

He smiled back. He couldn't help it.

She held out her hand between the bars of the bed rail, and he took it, trying to ignore the bruises and the row of stitches across the back. She'd torn a couple of nails. Jamie had cut them all short and put a bandage over the worst of them so she wouldn't scratch her face. Her skin was cool, not feverish — a good sign. The last thing she needed to be doing now was fighting an infection.

"Let me tell you about my relationship with your father," he said.

"Okay."

"He did help me out in a criminal investigation. But it wasn't when I was a detective. It was when I was a kid."

Her eyes closed, and in a sleepy voice she said, "If this is a story about why I should suddenly trust my father, it's not going to work."

"This is a story about how I'm not going to hold out on you. I'm asking you to trust me as a person, a former Delta Force operator, and a private investigator."

The thought of old Judge St. Clair being treated with anything less than respect — no matter what the circumstances of his leaving Brooklyn — was a burning offense in his guts. But that wasn't what was important here. Confessing to Regan, getting her to trust him instead of going around him, was what mattered. Jamie was right about that at least. Trust was essential. In the Delta Force, you learned how to trust the rest of the team through years of training and over dozens of operations.

Here he didn't have that much time.

"Good. What's the story?"

***

He'd been just a kid. raised in Boston, dragged to Brooklyn as a teenager against his will after his parents had split up. He'd wanted to go with his father — as cold and mean-tempered as the man was, he'd still felt a kind of fascination about his father, the Army sniper. He resented every minute under the control of his office job mother.

He'd fallen in with a bad crowd.

Not an actual gang, per se. His father would have skinned him alive. He stayed in high school, showed up for classes, did the homework, and spent the rest of his evenings running around with a bunch of basketball jocks — the ones who strutted their stuff more intensely than they devoted themselves to basketball.

Basketball was a sport that came easily to Jake. It wasn't the kind of high school where people obsessed about sports. He didn't have to work too hard to get on the varsity team as a power forward. He was quick, made clean shots, and enjoyed blocking other kids' throws, showing up where he was least wanted and shoving himself into the way. He'd come home with bruises and developed a lackadaisical free throw shot that drove opposing teams nuts.

The feeling of skill gave him a thrill. It was like being in the Army — being in a unit with people you trusted. He might not be a sniper like his dad, but at least, he wasn't turning into his mom.

They hung out together. According to the school principal, they could do no wrong. They were just boys being boys – until they stole a car.

It was a joke. The car belonged to the history teacher who was an old dried-up stick of a Hispanic woman with a voice that could drill through cement. They'd just had a test in her class, all flunked, and it was April Fools' Day. They thought it was a good time to teach her a lesson.

Jake, who had half a brain to sign up for Army recruiting and read probably way too many crime novels as a kid, knew how to break into and hotwire a car. But it was his friend Morrison, the point guard, who put him up to it. It was always Morrison with the plans, from how to destroy the opposing team through selected fouls, to how to practically get away with murder.

It was Terrell Wyatt, a small forward, who did the driving.

They stole the car in between school getting out on early release day and the teachers getting done with their in-service. The break-in and hotwiring went smoothly. Morrison kept a lookout. The three of them piled into the thirty-year-old Mercedes and took off.

The plan was to ditch the car in Bed-Stuy and catch a bus home. As far as the plan went, it was an excellent plan. The three of them wore leather gloves and baseball caps. Terrell drove under the speed limit, resisting Morrison's urging to drive faster and more recklessly.

Nobody should have ever known it was them. It was just a stupid joke.

Except they'd been seen by a couple of their classmates who had called the principal's office. The one part of their plan that had fallen down was they had counted on the history teacher being so hated that everyone would look the other way when their three-star basketball players climbed into her car and driven it away.

They were a bunch of stupid kids.

Unfortunately, the history teacher hadn't seen it that way and neither had the cops.

Jake's father lost it. For once Jake was glad that his father was hundreds of miles away. In fact, his father being *only* hundreds of miles away was too close for comfort. In retrospect, he wished he'd waited to pull the stunt until his father was overseas.

His mother stood by him with the same kind of workaholic mindset she brought to her office job. "He's just a kid," she said over and over. "He thought he was just playing a joke."

That's what made him feel bad — making his mom repeat herself to the cops, sounding just a little more defeated every time.

The case was brought before Honorable Judge, John St. Clair — Regan's father.

He could have thrown the book at Jake. Instead, he'd pulled him out of court and into the judge's chambers. It was a green room with old woodwork and radiators, a big table with heavy wood chairs around it and a bench against the wall with a stained seat cushion. A couple of blackboards stood together on the far side of the room; he could smell the chalk. A garment bag was thrown across the table, and a briefcase lay next to it.

The judge pointed at one of the chairs, and Jake sat.

He was terrified for his life. Judge St. Clair had that kind of harsh steely face that looked like it came out of an old Western. If ever anyone looked like a hanging judge, it was old St. Clair.

He'd said, "Your friend Mr. Wyatt has made a complete confession of what happened. He is throwing himself on the mercy of the court. Your friend Mr. Gray has said this is all a mistake, it was just a joke that was played on a mean old woman who deserved it. What's your opinion?"

If ever Jake had felt his life hanging in the balance, it was then, not later with gunfire going off around him in Afghanistan, Iraq, and Syria. That was just life or death — and he'd been trained for that.

He said, "We stole a car."

"That is correct. We pulled up the security tapes in the parking lot; we have you on camera. You were the one who broke into the car and hotwired it, isn't that correct?"

"Yes, sir."

"What is your interpretation of these events?"

Jake's mouth tasted like he'd been chewing tobacco for hours. He wanted to spit. "We were angry at a teacher and thought we would bully her so that she wouldn't flunk anyone ever again. Because she's an old woman that nobody likes, we thought we'd be able to get away with it, but we didn't."

"And how do you feel about that."

"Very bad, sir."

"The way you treated her, or the way you got caught?"

Jake shook his head. "My father's going to kill me."

"You feel bad because you got caught."

As a 17-year-old, Jake had trouble putting what he meant into words. It was still something that didn't come easily to him when it came to how he felt. He could give a speech in front of his debate class without a problem, but then he was only handling facts. What he felt wasn't something he could deliver clearly in 30 seconds or less.

"No sir." He clenched his fists. He felt his face getting hot. The judge was walking back and forth behind his seat. Jake wasn't going to twist around and try to keep up. "My father's an Army sniper. He's going to take one look at me and think that I've picked a damn fine target to take down, a defenseless old woman."

The judge snorted. "I might have to have words with your father at some point."

"Please don't. He'll lose it as it is. I'd let my mom handle it."

"And how do you feel about that?"

"About what?"

"About letting your mom handle it."

Jake pressed his lips together. He'd never thought much of his mom until now. She was reliable, invisible, and boring — completely unshakable.

"I don't like it."

"Do you have a better solution?"

"No sir. All I can see is that I should be sent to prison for stealing a car. We did it. We told ourselves it was a joke, but it wasn't. It was just being mean to an old lady. Even if we never got caught, it was mean."

"I've known a lot of mean men, Jake, people who throw their weight around because they think it's fun to push other people around. You don't want to grow up to be one."

"No sir."

"You're a smart kid, resourceful, a lazy basketball player, and an A+ student with B— grades. Do you know what that tells me?"

"No sir."

"That you don't know what to do with yourself. You're bored. You work just hard enough to keep your mom and dad off your back and to have the girls cheer for you when you're on the court."

Jake chewed on the inside of his cheek. "So what, in your opinion, should I do with myself?"

"Have you ever thought about joining the police force? You handled that break-in pretty smooth for someone that both your friends swear has never broken into a car before."

Jake's skin felt like ice. Of course he'd practiced on other cars before. Was the judge messing with him and Morrison and Terrell ratted him out? "No sir. I want to be in the Army like my dad."

"And what do you think you want to do there? Be a — you said he was a sniper, yes?"

Jake shrugged. From the way his dad had described the missions — and how hard it had been to get into the sniper program — he thought he probably wouldn't cut it as a sniper. That sounded kind of like a shooter guard position anyway.

"Then you may want to think about directing your efforts toward joining the Special Forces. They handle everything from kidnappings to counterterrorism. Someone who could break into a car and hotwire it — those talents can be used toward a greater purpose. Your physical agility could be a real asset, I suppose. You should be doing something useful with your life — not bullying old ladies or turning to more serious crimes."

The judge pulled out the chair sitting across from Jake. Still in his robes, he folded his hands in front of him. "I'd like to see you walk out of here with a purpose in life, son."

"Sir?"

The judge pulled the briefcase over to him, flipped up the latches, and opened it. From inside he took out a leather folder, too big to be a wallet. He flipped through it then, turned it around to Jake.

A pretty girl, maybe fifteen years old, sat at a three-quarter angle to the camera. She was blonde and looked like she'd have to be tortured before she'd crack a smile. She wore a prep-school uniform.

"That's my daughter," the judge said. "What if someone had stolen her car because they'd decided she'd been mean to them? How would you feel about that?"

"Pretty bad, sir."

"She says she's going to study law," the judge said. "She wants to be a judge, just like me. I understand the desire to follow in a parent's footsteps. I admire it when you have a good parent to aspire to. But you also have to be able to forge your own path. A good moral compass will ensure you're on the road you want to be on — and not the road to prison and shaming your father. Imagine how he feels now."

"Hurt, sir."

"That surely is correct." The old judge closed the leather folder, slid it back into his briefcase, and closed the lid.

"What would you do if your daughter did something that made you ashamed of her?" Jake asked. "Sir?"

The old man looked at him with his hanging judge face. Then he smiled. "You sure you don't want to go into law, Mr. Westley?"

"I'm sure I don't, sir, unless that's what they want me to do in the Army."

"Just so. To answer your question, I would like to think I would be there for her, in whatever capacity she needed me, whether it was something I agreed with or not."

Jake tried to swallow, but his mouth was too dry. The judge stood up, slid his briefcase back to the middle of the table, and said, "When the judge stands, Mr. Westley, you're supposed to stand as well. It's a sign of respect for the law."

Jake hopped to his feet, turning around to catch the chair before it tipped over. "Yes sir."

"Let's go back into the courtroom and finish this up."

***

"He gave me a deferred sentence of six months for auto theft and made part of my probation that I had to finish high school with a diploma as well as performing some community service. Part of it was I had to help teach basketball in a low income school in another district, which was..."

Something else that he didn't have words for. Life changing didn't seem to cover it. He shrugged, even though he knew Regan couldn't see it.

"And?" Regan's voice seemed a million miles away, and her grip on his hand was limp. She had to be almost asleep.

"And what?"

"Was he proud?"

"Eventually," Jake said. "Mom had to talk him around."

"Mmm," she said.

He gave her hand another squeeze before letting it go. It flopped over the side of the bed. He pushed it back onto the mattress and under the covers.

Two black eyes, a broken nose, a split lip — she was lucky she hadn't lost any teeth.

"Jake?" she said.

"Yeah?"

"I still don't trust my father. I've known him longer than you have. He'll say whatever it takes to get what he wants. Looking noble while being a bastard is his specialty."

He laughed. "Do you want me to sit here and read to you from your book?"

She breathed deeply for a few breaths. In a second she was going to be out.

"Nnn," she mumbled. "Nice. But you have things to do. And I have to sleep."

The breathing deepened until he was sure she was asleep. Nobody even remotely awake would let themselves snore with little peeping sounds like that.

He turned off the light and went out.

Chapter 31 - Mr. X

Jamie shook Regan's shoulder, "You all right in there, hon?"

Her head hurt, and her mouth was dry as a bone. Her lips were stuck together, and she felt a sticky patch under her cheek. She must have drooled. She felt like she'd been sleeping for a hundred years — Rip Van St. Clair.

"What time is it?"

"Its two o'clock, in the afternoon."

"It can't be two. The meeting was at one and Jake talked —" she stopped to swallow, or at least to try. "Jake talked at least that long."

"That was yesterday."

Regan grunted. No wonder she had to use the toilet so badly.

Jamie had to help her get up and move around, but honestly, she felt better. That was, she felt like she had a hangover combined with the flu from the way her head throbbed and her joints ached. But considering how out of it she'd been the day before, it was an improvement. Now if she could just keep from pushing herself too hard again, she might heal.

She'd never been too good at that though.

The room had been set up for another meeting. They had to navigate around one of the dining room chairs, the one that Jamie had been sitting on. Her muscles were loosening up pretty well. By the time she made it across the room and into the bathroom, she was able to walk on her own, her hand on Jamie's arm. Her head didn't feel any better — and neither did her ribs — but it was something.

She kept her mouth shut the entire time Jamie was changing her bandages and cleaning her stitches. Somehow, it didn't make Jamie stop to compliment her on what a good patient she was being. Maybe it was the way she kept gritting her teeth and leaning away — totally involuntarily — whenever Jamie switched to a new patch of gauze.

But finally it was over. Jamie helped Regan get dressed. She got her bottom half on her own, but maneuvering her clothes over her top half was out of the realm of possibility.

Finally, Jamie gave her a glass of water and some pills. Regan checked, they weren't Vicodin, just ordinary extra-strength Motrin.

She nodded and downed the pills, then drank about half the water. When her stomach begged for more, she finished off the glass. Tears flooded her eyes, and she blinked repeatedly. She must have been completely dried out.

"Are we having another meeting?" she asked.

"Uh-huh. As soon as I give them the go ahead."

Regan looked herself over. She was still standing in front of the sink.

She licked her lips, letting her tongue rest on the tender spot. Yesterday her lip had been split. Today it just looked tender and red. It had healed quickly.

"I don't think I've had all my hell beaten out of me yet sir," she said wryly.

"Excuse me?"

Regan shook her head. Her neck was a little stiff, but not too bad. The first time in days she'd been able to nod or shake her head without feeling like her spine was made out of shattered glass. She would be all right. Then she raised her arms about halfway and stopped. Her ribs made a pretty strong argument for her mortality.

Her face was a mess. The black and purple mask around her eyes was fading to purple and green with speckles of red and blue. She felt like she was some kind of Mardi Gras monster. Her re-set nose was covered with a plastic brace and fresh tape. At least it wasn't bleeding.

"I need something to eat," she said. Now that she had some water in her, hunger was moving in like a gigantic predator ready to pounce. If she didn't eat soon, she'd be knocked flat again.

"I'll bring you some sandwiches and juice." Jamie led her out to her chair. "Now sit here and wait. I'm going to make your bed, and then I want you to lie down in it."

Regan made a growling noise in the back of her throat. She'd just gotten up; she wasn't ready to be waited on hand and foot again. It showed a lack of progress.

"You'll follow directions like a good girl," Jamie said, "unless you want to distract everyone else when you suddenly get too tired to keep up the act."

Regan laughed and spread her hands, "Yes ma'am."

***

Jake looked around the room. Everyone was ready and waiting for him to start the meeting. Regan looked better than she had the previous day; there was more of a normal color in her face underneath the bruising. She looked focused on what was about to happen rather than on concealing her discomfort. Jamie looked more relaxed too, like Regan wasn't a bomb about to go off. Regan must be doing better — not just pretending.

Alex looked ready to bounce out of his seat. Good. That meant he'd found something — hopefully *somethings*, plural. Jake had told him not to contact him via the phones — not yet. The information would be safer to deliver in person than over their personal network.

Jane looked as inscrutable as she had the other times Jake had seen her — sharp as a tack and straight to the point ... no sense of humor whatsoever. If he'd seen a flicker of emotion from her, it was sympathy for Regan and nothing else.

If she was their traitor, then they were probably screwed.

And then there was Gary.

It was highly likely that someone in their midst was providing information to the bad guys. And if Jake were forced to pick one of them at that moment, it would have been Gary — no contest. The man knew everything about Regan — where she was, what car she drove, where she lived, and even had a spare key to her house and the code to her security system. Would he have had access to her cell phone, her computer records, her agenda, even her financial information? No, but everything else the bad guys needed, he had access to.

But he'd been working with Regan for so long Jake would have to actually catch the guy betraying Regan before she would believe it.

Just because Alex hadn't been able to come up with anything in Gary's background didn't mean the guy was clean.

Jake said, "All right, let's start with the low hanging fruit. Alex, what did you manage to dig up on your own?"

Alex cleared his throat before taking over the TV set.

"I was unable to find out who or what triggered Andy to tell Regan to leave the case alone. However, I was able to get access to the video records of the prison's parking lot during her visit."

He clicked his mouse, and the screen changed to a blurred video of someone walking across the well-lit parking lot, a man dressed exactly like Jake.

"If I hadn't seen his doppelganger at the courthouse once already…" Regan murmured.

Jake said, "It appears that the man who delivered the threat to Regan at the courthouse and then disappeared, and may also have been spotted outside the beauty shop after Regan's abduction, is the same person who slashed her tire. Alex?"

Alex clicked his mouse again, and another video ran, this time an image corrected version. The man drove up in a brown Honda Accord, parked, stepped out of the car, slashed Regan's tire, and waited for a moment staring at the back of her car. After a moment, he drew in the dust on the trunk with his finger. Then he got back into the brown Accord and drove away.

"You didn't happen to catch the license plates on that one, and they didn't happen to be the same as those of the brown Accord that Andy was driving that night?" Gary asked.

"License plates and photo picked up by a traffic camera show that the same license plate number was not used," Alex said, clicking again.

Gary sniffed, "Oh well, it was a nice thought while it lasted. I suppose that would have been too easy."

"I propose we label my doppelganger Mr. X," Jake said. "I feel that he is a major suspect in this investigation. What were you able to get from the courthouse security cameras?"

Alex clicked his mouse, and another video played. This time it was of the back of Regan's head as Mr. X approached her. The speed of the video slowed, and they all saw Mr. X slip something into Regan's pocket as he stepped by her into the elevator.

"He exited on the sixth floor," Alex said. The next video began to play, showing Mr. X's back retreating from the elevator. "He entered the men's room on that floor and was subsequently not recorded elsewhere by the cameras."

"What do you think happened?" Regan asked. "Did he change disguises?"

"Not that I can tell," Alex said. "The cameras near the restrooms didn't record anyone else exiting from them until the next morning. He either exited the men's room by another exit, waited inside until the next morning, or there was trickery with the camera footage that I haven't yet found."

"Next," Jake said.

The mug shots of the three men who'd attacked Regan at the bar showed up. Alex said, "Additional research came up clean on these guys — if you consider multiple arrests for DWI and domestic disturbances clean."

"In my opinion, either these guys are uninvolved, or they're involved at such a low level that they wouldn't know much. I doubt they're worth pursuing unless we come up empty everywhere else," Jake said.

"Noted," Regan said.

The pictures of the three thugs disappeared. A picture of Andrew Gibbons came up.

"I was unable to obtain records regarding Andy's behavior in prison," Alex said.

"Couldn't hack in?" Regan asked.

"Err —" Alex looked at Jake while twisting one end of his mustache. Jake gave him a thumbs up. "— that wasn't the problem. I couldn't actually show Regan the records."

Regan's eyebrows rose.

"Let me make a small correction," Alex said. "I found records admitting him to the prison as well as yearly health and dental checkup records. His records *exist*. But there's nothing else in them. He should be having, at least, a semi-annual behavioral review, records of meeting with councilors, records of what classes he has been taking, and hours worked in the kitchen, that kind of thing. But there's nothing like that."

"Noted," Regan said. "Next."

Alex cleared his throat again, then forced himself to let go of the end of his mustache.

The next slide showed the location of the murder, near a chain-link fence, next to a picture of the place where Angela Ligotti's body was found. "Because of the absence of security cameras at the time, I was unable to show Regan much more information regarding either the bloodstain on the sidewalk, the place where the body was found, or where the murder weapon might have been ditched."

"The murder weapon's probably in the river," Jake said, "along with a hundred others. It's probably a lost cause. Next."

A picture of the murdered woman, an olive-skinned Italian woman with reddened eyes, showed up.

Alex said, "I went through Angela Ligotti's criminal, employment, phone, and education records, and did a search for her on social media sites. At the time of her death, she was a nineteen-year-old data entry specialist for the water treatment plant. Her marital status was single. Her parents lived in New Jersey. She was a B student in high school. She had started a college education at Brooklyn College, her father's alma mater, but had not yet declared a major. She was taking classes in the evenings and working full time at the plant.

"She had no pattern of contacting Andrew Gibbons, either by phone or by the Internet. She did not clock in or out at the same times he did. They worked in the same building but not in the same department. I was unable to provide Regan any office scuttlebutt about the two of them having any kind of affair or casual friendship.

"What I was able to find was that Angela Ligotti had a pattern of drug and alcohol abuse, starting with marijuana and OxyContin when she was in high school. Her high school records show she was in counseling for drug and alcohol abuse problems. She was arrested twice for shoplifting in high school. When she moved to Brooklyn, the pattern of drug and alcohol abuse intensified — she was written up for coming to work intoxicated.

"I accessed her financial records and was able to see a pattern of large amounts of money being deposited and withdrawn from about her senior year in high school until about six months before the murder. I handed the records over to Jane."

Jake said, "Jane, any results?"

"Not yet, although I did see the same patterns Alex saw. If she's tied to the drug trade, this would be a stupid way to handle the money on her part. I'll get back to you when I have something more definite to say."

"Thanks. Next."

A stock photo of a vial of blood next to a syringe appeared.

"I have been unable to access the physical evidence," Alex said, "so I have been unable to show any to Regan. The fact of its existence is in the system, however, the chain of evidence has been broken. It was signed in by the Front Street Property Clerk but upon later review was recorded as one of several boxes of evidence that was missing."

"Of course," Jamie said.

"I also am unsurprised," Alex said. "The green Lincoln Town Car owned by the Gibbons and listed specifically under Andrew Gibbons' name on the title was seized by NYPD and has since been sold at auction. I have not yet tracked down the buyer of the car, but only because I didn't put a high priority on it for today's meeting. The information is there — I just didn't happen to have a back door set up for that particular system."

Regan sighed.

"Next," Jake said.

A picture of Detective Marando appeared on the screen. He had his feet up on a desk at a police station, looking arrogant, smug — and about 20 years younger.

"Detective Marando's records are very similar to Andrew Gibbons' records," Alex said. "They exist, but they have been stripped of all possibly useful information. In Marando's case, however, the stripping of information is subtle, as though it had been removed at an earlier date and the culprits had time to, uh, make stuff up to fill in the blanks."

"How do you know it's false then?" Gary asked.

"Nobody consistently gets both an average rating on their yearly review along with a larger than average raise," Alex said. "There were other signs, but I found that one particularly telling."

"Sure," Gary said.

"I began the process of examining Marando more thoroughly from other sources, but once again ran up against time limitations. That is, I obtained the information but didn't have time to do any analysis on it. The financial records have been handed over to Jane."

"Jane?"

"He's subtle, more than Ligotti was, if he's getting paid off," Jane said. "More than that, I can't yet say."

Jake grunted. It shouldn't have surprised him that an accountant wouldn't go out on a limb. He just didn't want her caution to slow them down. "Next."

Fred Schnatterbeck's photo came up, an old one of him in his Coast Guard uniform. Jake blinked. Schnatterbeck must have been forty at most — a handsome devil with arched eyebrows and a lopsided grin. A good guy, the end of his life sadly wasted.

"Fred Schnatterbeck's records were available but not especially remarkable. I was able to advise Regan of the names of the other members of his standing poker game, but haven't had time to research them in any depth. They're all old retired military guys. Financial records have been turned over to Jane. As far as his poisoning goes, it looks like the orders were changed somewhere inside the hospital computer systems, although I can't be sure of that yet. That will take some more research on my part. I don't have access to the autopsy reports at the moment. The system the morgue at the hospital is using hasn't been integrated with the one the rest of the hospital is on. It's all systems from the Eighties, though. It shouldn't be too hard to get in once I have a few minutes.

"One thing to note with Schnatterbeck, however —" He cleared his throat and twisted the end of his mustache again. If Alex didn't lose some of his stress, one side of his mustache was going to be shorter than the other in a couple of days. "According to his will, his next of kin was a nephew who died a few years ago in an accident; he has no other living near relatives. If anyone has any experience in dealing with estates, it might be a good idea to see what we can do to have his estate donated to the Coast Guard rather than eaten up in legal fees."

Gary said, "Unless someone else has that, hand it to me. My brother's an estate lawyer in town."

"Do you trust him?" Alex said.

Gary crossed his arms over his chest. "As a brother, no. As a man who hates to see anyone's estate get eaten up by the state, absolutely."

"Is he vulnerable to blackmail, bribery, or extortion?"

"Not to me. I've tried."

"Would having him work on the case lead anyone back to this investigation?"

"If someone takes a look at it, all they should see is that Regan's cleaning up after the mess she left behind when Schnatterbeck was killed. I should have thought of it myself."

Alex looked at Jake. Jake nodded.

"Sending you the information I have," Alex said, twisting his mustache so hard that Jake could hear the ends rubbing together dryly.

Jake stretched his neck from side to side until it popped. "Next."

A picture of traffic packed along a street, bumper to bumper. "Illegal taxi services in the area ten years ago. This is not the easiest thing to track down. I need more time. It's obvious from the decrease in the number of legitimate taxi cabs operating in the area that something was affecting the taxi industry. I was able to track down one by looking up the license plate of the car Jake chased with Mr. X inside. But that was a current service started in 2012. Trying to track down services from ten years ago will be more difficult."

"Noted. Next."

A picture of the beauty shop appeared. Alex blew air out of his cheeks and leaned back in his chair. "The beauty shop — I've traced the ownership to a series of holding corporations. It's a mess. The information appears to be openly available, but it just *feels* weird. I don't know enough about business ownership to be able to tell you whether I've found anything or not. I think the fact that it's not obvious who actually owns the place means something fishy is going on. But is it some kind of money laundering place for the Mob or just a normal business owner trying to evade taxes? When it comes to business, there's so much lying involved that it's drowning out my ability to follow up on relevant leads. I dumped everything in Jane's lap."

"My pleasure," Jane said. "I love sorting through different layers of financial lies. I feel like this is something I should prioritize. Is that correct?"

Jake looked at Regan; they both nodded. "Yes," he said. "I want priorities on anything having to do with Mr. X and with the beauty shop at this point."

"Agreed," Regan said. "And one other thing too, but you'll get to that I'm sure."

"Okay," Alex said. "Next up is the empty storefront." He showed a picture of the former coffee shop. "I'm in a similar fix with this case. Ownership is a mess, and I've turned it over to Jane."

He clicked to the next slide which was a picture of a group of cops entering the beauty shop. "The police — They were dispatched as normal, arrived at the beauty shop, and followed all procedures correctly as far as I can tell. I'm not an expert though. The cops at the 67th Precinct, however, didn't follow normal procedures. However, I'm not sure whether that's normal for the precinct or not. It could be this was a conspiracy to keep Regan from reporting her attack, incompetence of those on watch, or belligerence against citizens coming to report any attack."

"They sent the team to the beauty shop," Jamie pointed out. "So if they were just ignoring everyone, they would have ignored that call, too. Something happened between one thing and the other."

Alex shrugged. "No idea. It sounds reasonable, but it's over my head at this point."

"I'll take it," Gary said. "I have more experience with sorting out when cops are being obstructive or just idiots."

"Sent," Alex said, clicking a few keys. Another click and Regan's first homecare nurse popped up on the screen. "I have confirmed that the nurse Regan hired was bribed by her father to report on her. Upon being fired, he discontinued payments to her but did not require that the original payments be refunded. At least, her car's paid off now."

"There's that," Regan murmured.

"Moving on to the big stuff now — The phone call and the attack in the —"

The phone in Jake's pocket buzzed. Alex froze in place with eyes wide. The TV screen went blank as Alex jerked the network cable out of the side of his laptop.

Gary blinked, then pulled the network cable out of his own laptop — then leaned over and disconnected Jake's laptop as well. Alex unplugged his laptop and was wrapping up the cord and packing his laptop in his backpack, his eyes blank. It was like he'd just received a hypnotic cue.

Jake pulled the phone out. The caller ID was blocked.

"Hello?"

Alex was already halfway to the door. Jake strode over to him and put his hand on the kid's shoulder. He was shaking.

"It's impossible. It's a secure phone. Only you and I know the number. How the fuck did they..."?

The digitized voice said, "Mr. X is approximately five minutes from the residence of Regan St. Clair. Message repeats. Mr. X is approximately five minutes from the residence of Regan St. Clair."

The phone disconnected.

"We need to evacuate," Jake said, "quickly and calmly. Mr. X may be approaching the house."

"What direction?" Gary said.

"No information."

Jamie had vanished from the room.

Alex stood shaking with Jake's hand still on his shoulder. "They shouldn't have been able to get that number. They shouldn't have been able to get either phone."

Regan was swinging herself out of the hospital bed, walking stiffly toward the bathroom, stepping over the power and network cords with exaggerated care. "Mine buzzed as well."

"I don't know how to keep us safe," Alex said. "I can't give you clean communications. I'm useless."

Jake gripped his shoulder hard until Alex winced and looked at him with the expression of a kicked dog. "Don't panic, even if it's worth panicking about. Shut it down for now. You can panic when you get back to your place."

"It's not safe to go there. It's not safe to go anywhere."

Jake shook his shoulder again. "Panic later. I want you to come with me. Leave your car here. Bring your equipment. Do you have anything else in your car?"

Alex took a series of deep breaths and shook his head. "No, Jake. Never leave materials unattended. Yours truly is good to go. Sorry for the freak-out."

"No worries." He gave Gary a look and pointed toward the back of the house. Gary had already packed his laptop, as well as Jake's, and had the straps over his shoulders. The card table was empty and slightly askew. Gary headed down the hallway; a few seconds later the front door slammed.

Pill bottles rattled in the bathroom. Jane, who had brought a laptop this time, had made her equipment disappear into what looked like a normal woman's handbag. Shouting echoed up from the basement as Jamie rounding up her boys.

Regan came out with a plastic bag full of meds in one hand and a first-aid kit in the other. "Ready."

Jake led her toward the back door. The back yard was fairly large, and they'd leave footprints — but they wouldn't be bunched up at the front door when Mr. X arrived.

"Backdoor, Jamie!" he shouted down the basement stairs. Then he headed for the front door. They wouldn't all fit in the same car.

He still had time to get his car from the street out front — probably.

Chapter 32 - I Know Him

The alley behind Regan's house had a single pair of tire tracks leading down it — Gary's car. He'd picked up Jane, Jamie, and the boys, and driven off with them; no one knew where. None of them had burn phones.

It was probably safer that way.

She and Alex were shivering in the shade behind her neighbor's garden shed.

Jake's car whipped around the corner, the back end sliding through the slush at the end of the alley, and he raced toward them, scattering slush and snow all over both of them.

Alex had already turned away from the car before it approached, protecting his gear.

Jake stopped about twenty feet past them and backed up slowly.

She hobbled into the passenger seat. Alex took the back seat behind her, throwing his laptop bag and her pills into the other seat.

As soon as she had her seat belt fastened, she quickly pulled down the visor to use the attached mirror to watch to see if another car passed the driveway. She thought she saw the tail end of a sedan disappearing — but it might have been just a shadow.

It would be stupid to lie to herself. It was Jake's doppelganger. She felt it in her gut.

Jake waited a few seconds and then put the car into reverse.

He moved slowly at first, accelerating as the car gained some traction. They hit the street and slid.

Regan put one hand on the dashboard and grabbed the strap overhead with the other.

"Hang on," Jake said while shifting gears.

The car, now on the plowed pavement, lurched forward. Jake kept the speed just low enough that the tires didn't shriek.

Ahead of them the street was clear.

"Heads down! *Now!*"

Regan ducked down as they passed the entrance to her street. "Is he —?"

"He's pulling up into your driveway." The car kept rolling forward, picking up speed. "We're good. You can sit up now."

Regan straightened up and saw a car behind them in the rearview. "Jake...are we being followed?"

"No distractions."

She leaned back in her seat and put both hands on the dashboard. Jake put on his blinker.

Still driving too fast, Jake swerved around a corner onto another residential street. It looked like the kind of street that dead ended or went around in circles, but it wasn't. A small turnoff led into a back alley behind a strip mall filled with small shops, a couple of restaurants, and a mail delivery service.

He sped up and swerved down the back alley to the strip mall without hesitation. He must have memorized the streets in her neighborhood. Regan was impressed.

Then he followed the alley onto the main traffic artery, matching speeds with the surrounding traffic. Regan wasn't fooled. She kept her hands on the dash. Jake followed the traffic for another few blocks, gradually slowing down until he was driving under the speed limit.

She could feel the tension radiating off him, yet it still seemed as if he had practiced this a hundred times before.

Alex said, "Jake...?"

"Keep your laptop from flying around and keep your mouth shut kid."

The car swerved down a narrow drive, hit a speed bump, and bounced into the air. By the time they came down they had swerved onto a side street. Jake pulled into someone's driveway next to a big repair van, slammed on the brakes, and turned the engine off.

"Duck."

Down she went, slamming her head against her knees. Pain exploded in her face and ribs. A groan escaped her.

"Sorry Regan," Jake whispered.

The car engine ticked loudly. Jake breathed loudly. A dog barked — loudly.

A car engine purred down a street. Whether it was the street they'd left a second ago or the one they were parked on now, she couldn't tell.

The engine got louder and then passed them.

Jake, his face red, grimaced but didn't sit up. "I shoulda changed the plates."

"Think they saw us?"

"They had to."

But the engine kept purring down the street until all was silent but for the sound of them breathing and the dog which was still barking like he couldn't believe that the three of them hadn't been found: *Here! Here! They're here, you idiots! Here!*

They waited another minute – then two minutes. Regan had pulled her burn phone out of her pocket and stared at the readout on the outside flip cover.

She'd missed one call. And it was 2:03 p.m.

Jake sat up. "Stay down."

He backed out of the driveway, then drove back the way they'd come. He turned deeper into the neighborhood of twisted, speed-killing suburban streets, but headed toward Regan's house.

The car seemed to creep forward with incredible slowness. He had to be driving 15 miles an hour or less.

The blinker went on. The car slowed.

They took a left.

"Anybody?" she said finally. She couldn't take it anymore, the smell of rubber mats, wet snow, and little burps of nausea. Keeping her head down like this was making her feel sick.

"Can't tell yet. We're still a few blocks away from your house."

"I can't stay down here much longer. I'm going to be sick."

"Hold out as long as you can. We can clean the car out later if we have to, but there's no way we can —"

The floor of the car went black and white like it was a moonlit night.

Then a noise and a force hit them and shoved the car to the side. Regan's head slammed against the door handle hard enough that she started heaving spit onto the car floor. She had a vague sense that both Alex and Jake were swearing.

The car jerked again.

She screamed and tried to brace herself. It was no good. She rebounded in the other direction and hit the stick shift on the side of her face. She screamed again.

The seat belt locked in place in mid-jerk, leaving her dangling over her knees. Stars fell over her as the window glass fell in.

Finally, the car came to a stop. A roaring sound like a massive fire in a fireplace filled her ears.

She pulled herself up using the door handle and the panic bar.

Down the block was a ruin. A car she didn't recognize, a Jeep, was parked in her driveway. Coming out of its windows and blast opened doors was an inferno.

Her front door, including the stone wall and all the windows along the front of the house, was shattered. She could see all the way to the back wall of her living room. The sofa was on fire.

Jake cursed and turned the key.

It seemed like a miracle but the engine started. Jake pulled forward, driving around pieces of twisted metal. After he'd passed the worst of it, he accelerated and whipped around another corner.

The bones in her neck ground together. She'd undone whatever healing her body had been able to do.

"Pills," she shouted. A second later a plastic bag appeared beside her shoulder as Alex handed it up.

As she dug out a handful of Motrin, she saw the car that Jake was following — a black sedan.

"He parked it down the street," Jake said. Cold wind blew through the shattered front window. "He brought the bomb in a Jeep and parked the getaway vehicle down the street. It looked just like one of your neighbor's cars and was parked in the same place. The license plates are dirty. I should have wiped them clean."

"Too late now," Regan said.

"My gun's in the glove box. Get it for me."

She opened the glove box and pulled out a revolver. She'd never been a gun person. She pinched it across the barrel and handed it to him hilt first.

Then she dry-swallowed the handful of pills and handed the bottle back to Alex.

"Help yourself," she said.

"Thanks."

Jake sped up, racing after the black sedan. He was right. There was no way to read the plate. It looked like black mud had been sprayed over it.

The sedan swerved around a corner. If the driver thought he was going to get away from Jake like that, he was nuts.

The back of the car skidded around the corner. It was almost shocking they didn't have a flat.

The sedan tried to speed up, but Jake was faster, more aggressive. He was fixed on his prey.

Regan gritted her teeth. The back of the other car seemed to fill their windshield.

Then her head whipped forward as they smashed into the sedan.

The car ahead of them spun and twisted, its tires spinning on ice. Jake had knocked it out of reach.

Not for long. He slammed it again, hitting the back passenger corner.

The car turned sideways.

Jake slammed on the brakes and due to the thick layer of snow and ice, his car slid several feet before coming to a stop.

The sedan skidded sideways down the street, turning until it was facing them. The wheels spun like crazy. Any second the car was going to take off, charge toward them, and smash them head-on.

Jake beat him to it. His car jumped forward and slammed into the sedan, knocking it backward onto a patch of clear asphalt.

It just made things worse.

The driver had already slammed his foot down on the accelerator, and the car launched itself over the curb into a yard, through a bush, and into a plate glass window. The engine was smoking, and the driver slumped unconscious over the steering wheel.

Jake stopped the car in the middle of the street, opened the door, and jumped out.

Regan stayed put.

Jake walked up to the other car, pointing his gun toward the black sedan.

Doors up and down the street were opening, smoke was rising over the neighborhood, and sirens were making her sanity start to shred.

Jake jerked the car door open and threw the driver into the snow. The man rolled free.

Blood splattered onto the snow from what looked like a bad head wound. Jake knelt next to the man, grabbed a handful of snow, and rubbed it over his face.

The snow came back red.

Jake stood up, cursing, and stared down at the man in front of him. Just as the police were starting to arrive, he looked over his shoulder to check on the two of them.

"It's Gray," he shouted. "I know him — Morrison Gray."

Chapter 33 - Play stupid

The sirens accelerated in both pitch and tempo until there was no doubt that they were headed toward the three of them, Morrison Gray, and the wreck of his car.

Jake said, "Play stupid. You have no idea who this guy is, and I don't either."

Regan pressed a hand against her ribs and leaned against the back of his Corolla. She needed to get somewhere she could lie down. "I got it."

"Alex?"

The kid stood next to Regan along the side of Jake's car, biting thoughtfully on his thumbnail. "I can confirm I have no idea what's going on."

"Let me do the talking."

"Done."

The first of the cop cars came around the corner. Regan looked up, worry in her eyes. After what she'd been through lately, Jake didn't think he was going to have to tell her not to trust anybody in the legal system. The guys on the beat might be perfectly reliable — or they might be on someone's payroll. There was no way to tell and no way to control who *anybody* talked to.

When the first pair of cops saw Morrison Gray, they called in an ambulance.

When they saw Regan's purple face, they called another one.

Jake had a hell of a time keeping her away from the paramedics, who thought nothing of strapping someone down to a gurney against their will. But they finally settled for a blood pressure cuff, a stethoscope to the chest, and a promise from Jake that he'd bring her in himself after the cops were done with them.

The cops kept questioning Regan at the same time the paramedics were fussing over her. For a second he wondered whether she was going to lose her cool and say something she shouldn't.

He shouldn't have worried.

The officer confronted Regan as she sat in the back of the ambulance, legs swinging over the side.

"Do you know the man who attacked you?"

"No, officer."

"Have you seen him before?"

"I don't think so. His face is completely unfamiliar."

She winced as the paramedic slipped the stethoscope between the buttons of her blouse.

"Breathe deeply."

She inhaled.

The cop said, "Why did you leave your house before the suspect arrived?"

Regan held her breath.

"Okay," the paramedic said.

Regan said, "We'd been working all morning, and I needed a break."

"Were you injured in the attack?"

"No."

"Where did you get these bruises from?"

"I was mugged last week. It has been a hell of a month, officer."

"You've never seen the suspect before."

"Not to recognize him."

The paramedic tore open the blood pressure cuff and helped Regan off with her coat.

"Why do you think you were attacked?"

She blinked owlishly at the man as the paramedic pumped up the cuff. "You mean the mugging?"

"No, the car bombing."

"No idea, unless it has something to do with one of my past or current cases."

The officer settled back on his heels.

The paramedic listened intently to his stethoscope and watched the dial on the blood-pressure cuff.

Suddenly he deflated the cuff with a hiss of air. "110 over 71."

"Typical," Regan said.

"Keep it that way."

The cop said, "Do you think it is related to the Tarloff Case?"

Regan shrugged. "Who knows? But all this media attention always brings the crazies out of the woodwork."

"He could be involved."

"I could care less, as long as he's off the streets."

But the cop didn't hear a word she said. He was already putting together a story, fitting Morrison into the drama of the Tarloffs and their sordid lives. Who knew? Maybe there was some slight connection. Maybe Morrison had seen Regan on the news or something.

They questioned him and Alex too. It occurred to him that all three of them were highly experienced in fending off unwanted questions — playing with terrorists, the FBI, and lawyers had all rubbed off on them about the same.

Answer the question truthfully, but not honestly. Keep your answers short and sweet.

It took longer than he wanted, but eventually they were done. They were told to make their statements at the station within the next three business days.

***

He found them three motel rooms at a place so cheap and far back from any major highway that it didn't have interior hallways, let alone a swimming pool. At least the rooms had microwaves and cheap coffee makers. Both Regan and Alex were caffeine hounds, and he was almost ready to strangle them before they got their fix.

He chased Alex out of Regan's room so he could get her settled in.

She glared at the bed. "I'm sick of lying in bed."

"You say that now. Just wait until the adrenaline dies down. You'll be asleep in five minutes."

"You're kidding," she said. "I'm not going to sleep all night." Then she yawned.

He checked her over, assessing her condition. She looked tired, with dark circles under her eyes, but her color was good and her stats, as taken by the paramedic, had been normal. Her bruises looked a little better than even that morning.

"You're staring at me," she said.

"Can't help it, you're just so darn pretty."

She rolled her eyes and felt her cheeks burn pink. Then she pressed her hand against her side and winced.

"I need to hear you breathe," he said.

"You do not."

"If those ribs are digging into your lungs you are going to be a sad cookie in the morning."

"A sad cookie, huh?"

He nodded. She sighed and lifted her chin.

He knelt on the floor by her chair. The arm of the chair was in the way, so he got up on his heels and leaned forward, putting his head on her chest.

"Breathe," he said.

"You sound just like the paramedic." She breathed deeply and held it.

On the one hand, he couldn't hear anything bubbling, popping, or snapping in her lungs. On the other hand, it was kind of distracting to have her breast right next to his ear.

Her heartbeat sped up.

"You can let it out. Take several deep breaths."

She breathed in and out for a few long seconds. Honestly, he wanted her to continue so that he could feel her warmth and listen to her heartbeat.

"Are you done yet, Captain Hawkeye?"

"Sounds good," he said, straightening up.

"It hurts to say this, but I do need to lie down soon, and I think I need help."

"As you wish."

He helped her into the toilet and shut the door. A few minutes later he assisted her to the sink, and finally he walked her over to the bed. He had his suspicions that she didn't need as much help as she seemed to, but he kept them to himself.

He hadn't forgotten what Jamie had told him — TLC.

If Regan had been shaken up before, she had to be positively rattled now.

She let him help her to bed. Unfortunately, she was already wearing sweatpants and a pajama shirt from her house.

After she was tucked in but sitting up on a stack of pillows with another Styrofoam cup of coffee in her hands — she reassured him that it wouldn't keep her awake *at all* — he gave

Gary's home number a call from the phone in the room. Nobody picked up, and Jake didn't leave a message.

Just as Jake was about to go looking for him, Alex gave a knock and Jake let him in. He was carrying a pair of large paper bags.

"Paid in cash," he said before Jake could ask.

They smelled heavenly — hot meatball subs from the combination gas station and deli down the street.

They all ate quickly; they were hungrier than they had realized.

Regan finished first, wiped her hands and mouth on an already greasy paper napkin, and adjusted the stack of pillows behind her.

"I don't get these people," she said. "Tell me what they could possibly be thinking. One second they're technologically savvy and seem to be everywhere. The next they're a single guy, seemingly without backup, trying to bomb the front of the house. It doesn't make any sense."

"Agreed," Alex said.

They both looked at him.

Jake finished his sandwich, chewing thoughtfully. "We know they can penetrate our security at will."

"And the hospital's," Alex said.

Regan looked at him.

"It's kind of a big deal. Hospitals get sued for millions of dollars. They protect their assets more than most companies or governments."

Jake said, "The question in my mind is, who warned us? If they sent Morrison after us, why warn us? If they didn't send Morrison, how did they know?"

"They can obviously get past Mr. Gray's security as well as our own," Alex pointed out. "Although I suspect that our security was tighter than his."

"Do you think there are two separate groups?" Regan said. "The one attacking us, and the one warning us?"

Jake raised his hand. "Not necessarily. I've worked with splinter cells in terrorist groups that warned us. Not because they wanted to help us, but because they had a personal grudge against another part of the group. This whole situation reminds me more than a little of those guys."

"Do you think that's what's happening here?"

"There's no way to tell for sure, at least not yet. But it does lean that way."

"Can we, I don't know, use the situation somehow?"

"Not without knowing more than we do at present," Jake said.

"So where does that leave us?"

He looked at Alex. The two of them had briefly discussed the possibility of changing tactics a couple of weeks ago before Regan had been abducted and beaten, but at the time had decided it was more effort than it was worth.

Now the situation had changed — more than once.

Regan leaned back against the pillows and closed her eyes. More than the bruises and broken nose, her face looked battered, almost defeated. Alex was so tense even sitting in a motel chair that he looked hardly better.

Jake remembered the last time he'd seen himself in the mirror — while helping Regan. If he was honest with himself, he had to admit that he looked almost irrational with anger and frustration. He could easily become a man who was tearing himself apart with a sense of failure.

Looking directly at Jake, Regan asked, "You're going to tell me that it's time to quit, aren't you?"

Jake said, "That's one option. But first, let me make a suggestion..."

Chapter 34 - I'll send you a Christmas card

The Thumbprint Cafe was exactly what Regan had expected from Jake's description: a hipster/geek coffee shop in Brooklyn. Whether it was the perfect cover or just Alex's opinion of a perfect coffee shop was immaterial; the two things were one and the same.

She really shouldn't be feeling so jumpy. It was just a coffee shop.

Regan winced away from a chain of swinging bells that jingled as the door hit them. The faint smell of coffee on the street turned into a full bore blast of the stuff. She walked up to the counter and ordered a double espresso from a girl with teal hair who took one look at her and pressed something underneath the cash register.

Regan hoped it was a signal for Alex and not a signal to the bad guys.

In a room full of sweatshirts, headphones, and sloppy tennis shoes, Regan stood out like a sore thumb in her black wool coat and dress flats. Fortunately, the rest of the coffee shop patrons were so involved in their laptops, tablets, and phones they were completely oblivious to her presence. Only a young couple in matching hand knitted bobble hats glanced up when she came in, looking up with eyes that really only had attention for each other.

Regan paid in cash and swallowed repeatedly as she waited for the barista to work her way slowly through her rituals behind the counter at the fancy Italian machine. She felt like someone had drawn a red *X* between her shoulder blades.

The machine screamed, and Regan took a step away from the counter. The teal haired barista looked at her over the top of the white espresso cups lined up on top of the showy brass machine. One eyebrow twitched.

Regan flushed. Even the girl could tell she was overreacting.

But the girl didn't live in a world where people would attack her because she was doing her job — or because she was standing up for what she believed in. Or maybe she did, and like Jake had become so acclimatized to secrets and violence she was able to inhibit her natural reactions.

She did work for a computer hacker after all.

The girl yelled, "Cappuccino, Frank."

One of the patrons straightened up from his laptop and stuck a hand in his pocket. Regan stepped away from the counter even further, almost backing into the two-top table behind her.

Bang! Bang! Bang!

Regan quickly ducked, her body shivering involuntarily. She almost threw her arms up in front of her face.

The banging sound stopped.

Regan checked the other patrons. Some of them were looking at her. She scanned the windows. On the sidewalk, people navigated around each other easily, calmly, with faces reflecting nothing more serious than annoyance with the chilly weather, the necessity of going to work, or to do some unpleasant task.

Another *bang* came from behind the counter. The barista was just knocking the coffee grounds out of the filter.

She stood up. The hipster dude in black skinny jeans was standing over her with the large cappuccino cup in front of his face and his hand held out to her.

"Hey lady, are you all right? Do you need help?"

She was panting. She took a deep breath to try to override the urge to hit the front door of the coffee shop and run as fast as she could down the street, pedestrians and traffic be damned.

"No," she said. She shivered. Suddenly the room felt like ice. She was panting for air again, gasping. Tears had started running down her face. Her throat felt like it was on fire.

Her knees felt loose like she was going to faint.

She grabbed onto the bar to steady herself.

"Lady..."

A hand tapped her shoulder. "Regan, it's Alex."

Frank, the hipster, said, "Hey, Alex? Your friend's been beaten up."

"Yes, I know. She was mugged recently. She isn't taking it well."

"Oh. I know how that goes."

Alex's hand tapped her shoulder again. "I've got your espresso. Do you think you can make it downstairs?"

"Yes," Regan said, even though she wanted to moan *no*.

The basement of the coffee shop was just as much a fantasy world as the upstairs — a secret lair, computer hacker style. A bench full of computers lined the center of the room, massive monitors surrounding each station like something out of a spy movie. A small espresso machine and a — she forced herself not to roll her eyes — name brand convenience store style refrigerator full of energy drinks sat against the far wall. A coat rack with an Inverness cape and a deerstalker hat stood just inside the heavy steel door.

Alex probably could have been far less conspicuous and far more effective by keeping his profile lower and more mobile.

But then again, it was impossible for Regan herself to imagine what it would be like to be cut off from her source of inspiration — her courtroom. The room itself had been done in dark-stained wood, with heavy carpet that muffled the footfalls of the lawyers as they paced back in front of the witnesses and the jury box. The walls seemed to absorb sound so that Regan's words stood out when she spoke from the bench, yet the noises from the seats at the back of the room were muffled. And she would have felt positively naked without her chambers off to the side to allow her to talk to people without the stenographer right in front of her — and her robe. She always felt a little stronger when she was wearing it, a little more - *right*.

There was something about playing dress-up and let's pretend that adults apparently never got over. Jake in his bomber jacket, blue jeans, and baseball cap. He was some handsome, devil may care hero out of the movies.

He played it well.

She was still shivering inside her coat. Alex led her through a side door and into a room whose interior was completely covered with eggshell foam.

He closed the door, and the room went so silent that her ears started to ring.

"Thank you for coming. This is as secure as we're going to be able to get," Alex said. "I could probably give you the details of how this works, but I doubt that it would make you feel any better or more secure. But you may speak freely here."

The two of them hadn't spoken directly much. Mostly Jake had supervised communications between them. She sat in a folding chair in front of a cheap plastic buffet table. The fluorescent lights overhead were bare and too bright. The room felt more like a torture chamber or a room for shady cops to question suspects in a noir movie.

"All right," she said.

"I'll cut to the chase," he said. "I'm afraid I have to walk away from this job, Ms. St. Clair. I didn't sign up to be car bombed nor have my systems broken in to. I understand that you're in a difficult situation, but..." he shrugged.

She felt numb. "I'm sorry you feel that way. Is it a matter of money?"

"In part. I'm losing out on a couple of big opportunities, but I owed Jake a favor. He called it in. I'm more worried about disappointing Jake...but he says he understands."

"I can —"

Alex drummed his blunt fingernails on the plastic table, and she cut herself off. "I know that you can come up with a good deal of cash, Ms. St. Clair. I've talked to Jane about the kind of money that you have invested."

"She told you that."

"She didn't mean to. I just ... suggested to her that I was looking for something profitable to do with a windfall, and she said enough for me to guess. When you hack into computers for a living, you end up learning a few ways to get information out of people without them knowing. Social engineering saves time, and we computer geeks are all about the shortcuts."

"I see."

"I've already told Jake that I intend to get out. He offered to pass along my intentions to you himself, but I wanted you to see where I was coming from."

"Literally," Regan said. The man was coming from — a basement.

"Exactly, I have a business to maintain. Two businesses, if you count the coffee shop. I have employees, people who depend on me for their living. You might be able to pay me enough to make it worth my time, but you can't give me the security I need to make life stable for the people who depend on me. What if someone bombs the coffee shop next? You might think I'm as casual about other people's lives as if it was some kind of video game with a reset button, but I'm not."

"Have you ever been involved in violence before?" Regan asked.

He had left his hands clasped together on the table throughout his speech. Now he raised his arm and started twirling the end of his mustache.

"Honestly, other than the normal bullying that a nerd gets via the educational system, no. I've certainly never been car bombed before or been in a car chase. I've never even broken a bone or had a black eye."

"You didn't find it exciting?"

She'd meant to keep her voice light, but it came out rough, wrong, angry, and far too loud.

There was no echo.

Alex leaned back a little in his chair and then straightened up. "No, not in the slightest. Honestly, it gives me acid reflux. If I want a sense of danger and excitement, then I'll hack into someone's computer. I won't mess around with the real world." He looked upward. "Why do you think I have a legitimate business upstairs? Why do I work mostly with the FBI and other white hat organizations?"

"I'd say because you have a sense of justice."

He gave her half a smile and started twisting his mustache again. "I'm not one of the good guys, Ms. St. Clair. I'm afraid, and I want protection. And the white hats are, in the end, stronger than the black hats. Being legit keeps me *safe*."

She raised a hand. All of this sounded unreal, like fake dialog. It was as much as she could take.

"I understand," she said.

"Do you?"

"I didn't come to throw money at you," Regan said. "I've already had a talk with Jake too, about possible security measures we could take, about other people we could hire to put more layers between the bad guys and us. I work for the white hats. In a way, I *am* the white hats, but I'm just one person. It's too big for us Alex."

She chewed on the inside of her cheek.

"I didn't come to bribe you. I came to tell you that it's off."

"Oh," he said leaning back again. "I'm sorry."

"We've packaged up the information we have and sent it to someone in the FBI that Jake knows. It's out of our hands now. Jake's going to look a little deeper into the guy who bombed the house to see if he can find anything, but that's it. We're done."

He blinked stupidly at her. Jake must not have warned him. Not about this.

"I came here because I wanted to tell you in person. Also, I did want to see where you're coming from, what kind of person you are."

Alex gave her half a smile, still twisting his mustache. "I'm a computer geek. WYSIWYG — what you see is what you get — the super—secret underground lair, the high tech equipment bolted onto thrift store furniture, the low tech conference room, even the fridge full of energy drinks so nobody has to sleep. I know it's not much. It's not a wife and kids and a house in the suburbs."

"Not everybody wants that."

"That's true."

They looked at each other. Regan saw sympathy, maybe even pity, in the softness of his expression.

"I'm sorry," Alex said again. "I'm sorry this isn't working out for you. I know how much you wanted to be the one to get Mr. Gibbons out of prison."

"I'll just be happy if he gets out at all. Despite what you might have seen, it's not all about me. It's about Andy."

"How is Jamie taking it?"

Regan looked down. Alex had left her tiny espresso cup in front of her. She picked it up and downed it, barely tasting it. Then she put it down and pushed it away from her. "Poorly. She feels like I've betrayed her and the boys."

"Is she still...?"

"Staying with me? No. There's a cousin upstate she's moved in with. I'm sending the cousin money discreetly, of course. To help with bills while Jamie gets back on her feet. I..."

She spread her hands. She'd done her best, but hell hath no fury like a mother whose children have been put in danger. She couldn't blame Jamie for the cruel things she had said to Regan when the two of them had met in Regan's kitchen, still smelling of ash and chemicals from the fire department. She couldn't blame Jamie, but it had still hurt.

"What about the others?" Alex asked.

"Gary and Jane are back to normal – as normal as the two of them get, anyway."

"That's good."

"I'll give them both an extra week's vacation next summer — after this is over."

"That's nice."

She stood up, pushing her chair backward. Alex stood up too and held out his hand. She shook it. His grip was firmer than she'd been expecting, the skin soft but not delicate.

"It's not so bad. I've worked with the FBI before. They're all right," he said.

"I know," she said. "This just isn't how I saw things working out."

"Hmmm," he said. "Well, take care."

"Take care," she repeated. "See you sometime."

"I'll send you a Christmas card."

The pointless exchange of pleasantries had to stop. She grabbed the doorknob and turned it.

For a split second, the round handle spun uselessly, and she had the image of some awful thing happening — another bomb, a SWAT team, an evil criminal mastermind attacking her out of nowhere — but then she realized there was a silicon cover over the doorknob. She gripped harder.

The doorknob turned, and she let herself out.

Chapter 35 - You're quitting too

Morrison Gray's apartment building in White Plains wasn't much to look at, although with its dull gray walls and stingy windows it definitely fit into the background of prison-like cement buildings. It looked more like an office building than someplace where people lived. In fact, it looked almost abandoned.

He shouldn't have bothered dressing in a delivery coverall. He walked right in and up the stairs with his box under one arm. He could have taken the elevator, but Morrison's apartment was only on the second floor, so he didn't bother. Stairs were simpler. While he was climbing, he put on his latex gloves.

The carpets were cheap but clean; the hallway almost completely quiet. He passed a couple of apartment that had TVs or radios on low volume. Apparently it wasn't the kind of place that allowed dogs or kids.

He stopped at Morrison's apartment door, conspicuous for its absence of yellow police tape, gave the hallway a quick look, and knocked. Then he knocked again. No response, which was ideal. He put the box down and pulled out a small stack of sticky notes and a pen. He tucked the pen between his pinky and ring fingers so he could be pretending to write if he were spotted, and stuck the top note to the door: *Sorry I missed you. Have left your package at the front desk.* It only needed to be signed — and then, only if he were caught.

Between thumb and forefinger, he had a bump key, the modern form of a skeleton key. It was the same brand as the locks in the apartment complex. In his other hand he had a screwdriver. He slid the key into the deadbolt as silently as possible, then rapped it with the butt end of the screwdriver, using the same pattern he had used while knocking.

He got lucky. It worked the first time. He twisted the bump key, and the deadbolt opened. Fortunately, there wasn't a second lock.

He opened the door, pushed the box in front of him through the doorway with one foot, peeled the sticky note off the door, and went in.

The front entrance was almost aggressively single guy normal, with framed posters of the Rangers logo and a 2012 group shot of the team signed by at least five different players. A *'GO AWAY'* mat sat in front of the door with a couple of pairs of hiking boots and a pair of what looked like workout sneakers off to one side. Inside was a leather couch with its back to the door and a wide-screen TV in front of it.

Off the main room were the kitchen, a pocket-sized closet, a bathroom, and two bedrooms, doors closed.

He wasn't sure how much time he had.

Morrison Gray wasn't married and didn't pay child support. He worked — and the coincidence had Jake creeped-out — as a private investigator who had retired as a detective from NYPD in Brooklyn about the same time Jake had left the Unit. Before that Morrison had worked in Boston as a police detective until about five years ago.

He'd made the change after Andy Gibbons and after old man St. Clair. It had to be a coincidence he was in White Plains now. It had to be.

Jake walked over to the short hallway holding the bathroom and the two bedrooms. Left or right, it didn't make much difference, but the left-hand door had a black smear on the paint — not dried blood, more like newspaper ink. He took that one.

The door scraped across the stiff beige carpet. It was thicker somehow, like an extra thick layer of carpet padding had been laid down. The room was dark; the drapes not just closed but sealed over. Jake floundered for the light switch.

It was bad.

It was a cop kind of room; the kind of room they would set up when they were working on a case. There were file cabinets everywhere, a computer desk with three wide-screen monitors, manila folders scattered haphazardly on every open surface, loose photographs over the printer, knee-high stacks of badly folded newspapers next to the printer, and a trash can full with balled up sheets of printer paper, and cut out sections of newsprint.

The walls were covered with pictures of Regan — pictures from newspapers, pictures on computer paper, high school yearbook photos.

There were photos taken with a telephoto lens: Regan hunched over books in her library; Regan sitting up in bed, dressed in pajamas and reading a book; Regan in the shower.

It was a lot to take in all at once.

His skin crawled. Rage was a fraction of an inch below the surface.

Jake forced himself to ignore the pictures and scanned over the top of the desk. There was some specific plan to this, a reason, a method. Morrison had been a point guard. He might wing it if stuff got random, but he would never have gone in without a plan — his own plan.

Morrison Gray would not have car bombed Regan's house without a plan.

Nothing called attention to itself on the desk. No sticky notes were on the monitor or lying out over the keyboard, and there was nothing with bright pink highlighter marks on it.

He shook the mouse. The three monitors woke up presenting him with the standard lock screen message asking for a password.

Granted, Alex was the real hacker, but Jake was no slacker. Also, he'd known Morrison Gray since high school. He knew the guy's favorite passwords from 20 years ago, his mother's maiden name, the first girl he dated, the first dog that died — everything.

He typed in Morrison's old password from their first computer class, *sex4life*.

It worked. The man was a pervert.

The screens brightened. Jake instinctively turned around. The bedroom door was open; he got up and closed it.

The walls and the back of the door weren't as bad as Alex's silent room, but they were still covered with thick wallpaper that felt almost like corduroy fabric. The fan on the computer was loud, a thick white noise. Between the wallpaper and the noisy fan, a lot of sound could be made in this room without alerting anyone else in the complex.

He sat back down in the beat up office chair and faced the monitors again.

The desktop backgrounds on the system were pictures of Regan, of course. Regan, sitting on the bench in a courtroom, dressed in black robes with her blonde hair falling over her shoulders. A print of the scales of justice filled the background behind the picture.

It almost seemed like the guy hadn't intended to attack Regan. More like he had the hots for her.

There were only a couple of icons on the desktop, one for the trash and another one, a text file, marked *Emergency File*.

Jake wasn't sure if it was an emergency, but stuff had *emerged*. Close enough.

Nevertheless, it was too obviously a trap. He right clicked the file and opened it with Morrison's word processing program. Lines of command text appeared.

It was a batch file that, if Jake had double clicked the file, would have reformatted the hard drive. Nice. He left the file open, opened the Word processor menu, and looked for the most recent files. The last one that Morrison had used was one called RSC02132016.

Regan St. Clair, February 13, 2016.

He clicked to open the file and looked around the room again while the file loaded. The back of the door, at least, wasn't covered with photographs pinned to the wall with pushpins.

As he turned around, he spotted an area of the wall behind him that was less dense with photographs than the rest of the room. Behind it was a print of some kind.

He got up and pulled one of the pictures off, Regan walking through the snow with her long black jacket. It was a recent picture taken in the daylight, outside on a gray day. She was looking over her shoulder; there was a gray wall behind her. She was probably in White Plains —.

No. There were no windows behind her. It was nothing but a flat gray wall, stained with black streaks where the water had run off from above.

She wasn't in White Plains when the picture had been taken. She was at Green Haven.

He flipped over to the back of the photo, but there was nothing written on the back of the stiff inkjet print.

On the other hand, what was behind the photo was interesting.

It was a map. The pinhole lined up with a pink splotch marked *Green Haven*.

Morrison had been there, at least once, at the same time she had. Maybe he'd been the one to slash the tire of her car.

Maybe he'd been the one to beat her.

Some of the photos pinned to the map marked sites that he wasn't surprised to see: where Regan lived; the courthouse; *La Ruche;* her father's house; Jamie Gibbons' old apartment in Brooklyn; the 67th Precinct; the Brooklyn Hospital.

Other things that he would have expected to be marked weren't: the location of the murder or where the body was found; Detective Marando's apartment; the vacant coffee shop where Regan had first tried to meet with the mysterious caller; Alex's coffee shop.

But a few of the points marked places that confused him. Why mark *his* apartment in Brooklyn? Why mark a bookstore near Alex's coffee shop, a few blocks over, with a question mark?

Why mark the beauty shop where Regan had been abducted with an X?

He was wasting time. He turned back to Morrison's computer.

The file had opened. It was a checklist — bullet points covering a page and a half. The first two items were:

- *Verify Mitsubishi was not disturbed overnight*
- *Verify gloves, hairnet, sunglasses, and DNA swabs are in gym bag*

Jake almost hit the print button, but leaned over to check the printer to make sure it was on. There was already a copy of the list in the print tray.

He downloaded the file and about a hundred others starting with the RSC file name to a thumb drive, deleted the system logs, packed up, and got out.

***

Regan flipped the paper over, trying to read some kind of sense from the blank backside of the page. "I don't understand."

Jake sat back in the chair, balancing on the balls of his feet. It had been a real pain putting the information together without Alex's help. What he wanted was a real workout at the gym and a night off to get the pinched feel out from between his shoulder blades. "The guy wasn't working for someone else. He was working on his own."

"He was working on his own?"

"You're working with an incredibly sophisticated criminal organization, and you leave yourself a memo to buy a new pocket knife so you can slash your victim's tires and ditch the knife off the side of the road fifty miles later. And all you have to protect it with is a batch file set up to reformat your hard drive."

"It would have fooled me," Regan said.

"It would have fooled me too if I hadn't known what to look for. And, if I hadn't known Morrison, I wouldn't have been able to guess my way in. My point is, the people we've been up against so far haven't been this clumsy. This is amateur work."

"So what do you think he is — some kind of stalker?"

"Yeah..."

The restaurant was busy that night for some reason, loads of couples everywhere. But they needed to be seen together, and it needed to be somewhere the people watching them couldn't miss.

"Ugh," she said. "Like...a sex stalker?"

"Not really." He'd read through enough of Morrison's files to know that wasn't exactly the case, but she didn't need to know that.

She screwed up her face and ate more of her soup. There was some kind of special going on she'd ordered, saying at least the kitchen wouldn't be able to screw it up. He'd shrugged and let her order. His head was too full of the details he'd read from Morrison's files for him to care much.

"You don't think he was working with the other group," Regan said.

"I can't be positive, but it looks like you were his private personal obsession."

"Why?"

Jake shoved a forkful of rare steak in his mouth, which had come with some kind of peppercorn and cream sauce.

"Bad luck?" he mumbled. He swallowed. "He started out as a member of the Boston police force. Later he transferred over to NYPD as a detective."

"Andy," she said. "He was there when Andy got arrested."

"No, Andy's arrest was earlier than that. This was only five years ago. Then two years ago he took an early retirement and became a private detective."

"Hmm," she said.

"That's right, hmm. I did more research when I came back. He'd been investigating a homicide in the Bronx that led upstate to a smuggling route through Canada for drugs and guns. Drugs came in, guns went out, and over —"

"— The Arctic Circle into Russia," Regan said. "I remember that — the Lynch case. He was one of the drivers and was involved in a hit and run. It was tricky. His lawyer was involved in some shady negotiations with the prosecution to get the accused a *longer* sentence, among other things. I held them both in contempt of court."

"You brought enough attention to the matter that it was picked up in the New York papers. A couple of people made connections that tied the driver to the smuggling case. That's when the driver started to talk, and the whole organization started to fall, including the dirty cops who were in on the whole thing — and that included Morrison."

"Why would an NYPD detective be involved in a smuggling ring?"

"To help cover up the bodies."

"Like Marando."

"That's what it looks like."

"So Morrison Gray is obsessed with me because ..."

"If you hadn't dug deeper in the Lynch case, he never would have been asked to resign."

"You didn't say he'd been asked to resign."

"Did I need to?"

"The timing adds up?" she asked, a little surprised.

Jake nodded. "The timing adds up."

"He wasn't charged with anything."

"Hmmm," Jake said.

"Yes," Regan said, "hmmm. It still seems kind of flimsy, like a cover-up for something deeper."

The tables all had candles on them, tiny flickering tea lights. It was very romantic. Across the table Regan's face looked soft and thoughtful, just a couple of wrinkles between her eyebrows as she refused to believe the story he was feeding her.

He knew, however, she wouldn't appreciate being dragged further down into the truth. As far as he could tell, Morrison was working alone, but he was a sick, sick man. He had to deflect her.

He shoved another bite of steak in his mouth and mumbled, "You're like a terrier, you know that? You're always digging."

Her eyelids fluttered as she looked toward the ceiling. "Thanks."

"It is what it is. You came out into the open and broke your routines because of Andy Gibbons. Morrison, who was looking for something like that, took advantage of what was going on to up his game. You were being an interfering bitch again — therefore, you needed to be gotten rid of."

Regan drew back in her chair, pushing herself away from the table with both hands. "You think he was going to murder me?"

Internally he cursed himself while outwardly trying to keep his face blank. "It was a possibility," he admitted. "Personally, I think he was too sloppy to accomplish much."

"He managed to car bomb my house."

"Which failed," Jake pointed out.

"I have an insurance agent and an accountant who would beg to differ."

"You know what I mean."

She breathed deeply through her nose and pushed the last of her soup away. "All right," she said.

Jake felt himself relax a little. She wasn't going to push it. Really, she didn't need to know.

"So about Alex...," he said.

"Alex." She picked up her steak knife and was about to start cutting into the meat. She hesitated. "He's out. What are we going to *do*, Jake? If nothing else, this just proved that we must have a computer guy in order to pull this off. You don't happen to have two world-class hackers who owe you favors, do you?"

He didn't. He shook his head. It was obvious what was going to have to go down here. But it was better she talked this out on her own. No need for him to butt in.

"Then we'll have to find someone else," Regan said.

He waited, keeping his face blank.

Her eyes narrowed. "Jake, we *have* to find someone else. Didn't you hear me?"

"I heard you."

"What are you trying to say?"

Again, he waited. This time he didn't meet her eyes but focused on the plate in front of him, cutting off another bite of steak.

She inhaled sharply.

"You're quitting too," she said.

"I'm going to help you clean up what's left," Jake said, "with Morrison Gray. I used to know him, and I feel a little bit responsible for him. But yeah, with regards to Andy, I have to get out of this."

"You can't leave me to do this by myself."

He held back a response. He watched her steadily, waiting for her to break. This had to be rough on her, he knew.

Her eyes looked like steel. The blue had gone right out, leaving them looking like the color of a storm. Two spots of color had formed in her cheeks, and her lips twitched into a snarl. She was a goddess about to call lightning down out of the sky to split his head in half.

"You don't want me to do this at all," she spat. "That's why you're quitting. You know that whoever is behind this will get to whatever detective I hire after this and bribe them or damage them somehow so that they won't actually help me. They'll run me around in circles. You know I'll figure that out sooner or later and give up."

He nodded.

"They've contacted you, haven't they?"

He shrugged. He'd received a call from an unknown number on one of the burn phones, but he hadn't checked the message that had been left behind. Without Alex backing him up, it was a waste of time.

"They've bribed you."

Now it was his turn to be angry. He threw his knife and fork onto the plate into the juices from the steak. "If you can even *think* something like that..." He shook his head. "Lady, I'm done with this, just done with it. It's not like Andy's a shining example of a good citizen anyway."

"What did you just say?"

"I said he was a crook, a small-time crook. You and I both know it. Jamie and the boys are better off without him."

She pushed her chair back and stood up. "You said you were done with this. That makes two of us, then."

For a moment, the whole room seemed to be staring at them. Then Regan signaled for their server and went with the girl over to the hostess station where the two of them had words together, words that involved Regan's shoulders shaking, either with tears or fury. With Regan, there probably wouldn't be too much difference between the two. A credit card changed hands.

The server gave Jake the nastiest look he'd received in a while, and that was counting both Morrison's face after he'd crashed as well as Marando's unpleasant face in general. He was probably banned from the restaurant for life now — not that he had a huge fondness for French food.

He picked his fork and knife back up and calmly finished eating his steak. He felt the stares rolling up and down his back, crawling over his skin. He reminded himself this was the way things had to go.

He didn't bother eating the asparagus on the side. In return, the server didn't bother bringing him dessert. He finished up, wiped his lips with the napkin, and laid it across his plate.

Then he stood up, took his coat from across the back of his chair, and put it on with as much dignity as he could, surrounded by a restaurant of couples eating their pepper steak across a romantic candle flame. Most of the tables held a rose or two as well.

It wasn't until he passed the maître-d and seen her offended look, he realized something both completely obvious and completely irrelevant.

It was Valentine's Day.

Chapter 36 - Forget I said anything

Pavo sat at his desk and tapped his fingers together, breathing warming puffs of air on his fingertips. He'd been told the gesture seemed both intimidating and pretentious, which was an acceptable interpretation. The underlying truth was it was something he did when he was nervous — or if not exactly nervous, then at least prickly with a subconscious hunch that something was wrong.

Fiducioso sat in his usual seat across from Pavo's desk. His hair was slightly untidy, as though he had run his fingers, rather than a comb, through it while riding the elevator up to the penthouse. A five o'clock shadow dusted the man's cheeks.

"So that's that," Fiducioso said. "The team has been split up, and they've all gone home. Westley said a couple of unforgivable things to Regan at *La Ruche,* and Regan stormed out on him. She's proud enough — that should be the end of it."

"And if it isn't?"

Fiducioso leaned forward. His eyes were showing more whites than normal. "Do you honestly, genuinely think they're going to pick the case up again?"

As Pavo considered his answer — which would depend less on honesty than on how it might influence his associate — the light outside the enormous windows shifted from late afternoon to early evening. The shadow of another building fell across his window; the indoor lights slowly but automatically brightened. Pavo's penthouse was an integrated machine, far superior to Alex Carr's underground hacker lair with its pitiful attempts at maintaining security. The layers of Alex's electronic protection had been no more than a flimsy negligee of discretion, no more difficult to bypass than the protections of the FBI — at best.

"I do not know what they will do," Pavo said finally. "They are not the most predictable of opponents. They don't do what they're expected to do, whether it would be in their best interests or otherwise. That's why so much attention is being paid to them. They are reckless and could cause unpredictable repercussions, including some strongly negative ones for the director who controls the area."

It had been a delicate balancing act between loyalty to the Organization and - other concerns.

Fiducioso looked steadily over Pavo's shoulder, obviously trying to resist the temptation to make a sarcastic — and disrespectful — remark. "Which could cause problems for everybody," he said lamely.

Pavo resisted the urge to twist around and look out the window. "You will continue to monitor their communications?"

"I will," Fiducioso agreed. "You're paying me well enough."

"Let me know if that is ever not the case."

"Certainly." Fiducioso started to rise, then hesitated.

"Yes?" Pavo asked.

"What did you want done with Morrison Gray?"

"Eliminate him," Pavo said.

Fiducioso paused, "Really?"

"I was sent some materials recently that have made me reconsider my position. The man's very existence is pollution upon the earth. And I don't care for the way he seemed to be able to put things together – by himself. It was odd that Morison appeared outside the beauty parlor when he did. Almost as if he knew something more than he should have."

Fiducioso twisted the side of his cheek, almost as if he were going to bite the inside of it. "Very well, consider it done."

In what he thought was a normal tone of voice, Pavo inquired, "Do you think someone has talked?"

"No threats necessary, Pavo," Fiducioso said with a grimace. "If someone talked, then I'll find out who, and when, and to whom. If you don't look good to the higher ups, then I don't look good — and I have ambitions."

"I continue to keep that in mind in all matters dealing with you, Fiducioso. Keep it quiet. I don't want to bring more attention to Morrison Gray and his mysterious information than necessary for a variety of reasons."

Fiducioso straightened up, taking his hat off his knee and slapping it casually, almost arrogantly, onto his head. Sometimes Pavo had to wonder who was in control of the relationship between the two of them.

Pavo said, "You aren't disappointed they have given up, are you?"

Fiducioso shook his head, but there was a hint of doubt in the man's eyes. "It's better this way. We were never going to bend any of them far enough they would work with us, rather than against us. They aren't bendable people. They were going to break one way or another."

"Her father bent."

"Only a little and he got back at us in the end, didn't he, raising his daughter the way he did? He was, and still is, stubborn and proud."

It wasn't like Fiducioso to speak so openly about anything, let alone Judge St. Clair, the Elder.

"What is it?" Pavo asked. "Something is gnawing at you. Tell me. I may be able to help you — if it doesn't cost me too much."

It wasn't the most generous of statements, but Fiducioso would hardly have accepted a gushing magnanimity on his part.

"It's nothing," Fiducioso said.

Pavo raised an eyebrow.

Fiducioso took a deep breath and lowered himself back onto the chair, taking the trilby off his head and lowering it onto his knee again, this time more gently. Today he was wearing a dark gray suit with a powder blue shirt underneath, a luxuriant silk tie with a purple and blue tiled pattern on it, a tessellation of angels. A matching handkerchief with the same but much subtler pattern was in his breast pocket.

Pavo caught a glimpse of a pair of horns and a barbed tail. Some of the angels weren't as innocent as the others.

"I don't mean to suggest that you're not doing your job," Fiducioso said, "but you are having the rest of the team watched, correct?"

"That is so," Pavo said.

"The *whole* team, including Gary."

Pavo tilted his head to the side. "What have you heard?"

"Nothing, and that's the problem. He's gone quiet."

"Quiet?"

"He's normally screwing around in Regan's files, doing his own research into her cases, being a nosy busybody. He justifies it by claiming it's for Regan's own good, so he can anticipate what she needs from him. 'A good secretary is required to be an excellent spy.' is his motto."

"So?"

"He's not spying. He's catching up on celebrity gossip pages and chatting up Hendricks on the phone."

"Hendricks?"

"Jane. She's the accounting wizard."

Pavo clucked his tongue. Of all of them, she was the one he most regretted not swaying over. "Could she be a romantic interest?"

"I thought he was gay."

"Find out. Be sure this time."

Fiducioso nodded.

It sparked a thought. "And Jake and Regan..." Pavo asked.

"What about them?"

"Is there a romantic interest there?"

Fiducioso wrinkled his nose. "Definitely not. That blow-up at the French restaurant would have killed anything that was developing."

"Hmmm," Pavo said.

"Never in a million years. I'll bet a contact name on it."

Pavo's eyebrow rose again.

"A name — what level?"

"A board member."

"Impossible." Fiducioso was suggesting he not only knew the name of one of the highest levels of the Organization, but that he'd be willing to exchange it over a silly wager. He'd certainly never done anything like it before.

Fiducioso shrugged. He had settled and seemed much calmer, like a jungle cat that had stopped to smooth its fur after a hunter had ruffled it. "I have my little ways, as you know. Forget I said anything."

"As you wish," Pavo said.

But he didn't.

Chapter 37 - It was what'd both expected

Without the money from Regan hitting his bank account on a regular basis, it was time for Jake to pick up some extra work.

Fortunately, even though the Gibbons case hadn't been, and might never be resolved, he'd still picked up the extra reputation from working for her — and for her father. Word got around.

The first benefit was that he suddenly had more divorce cases than he could handle. And, because of the influx of cash from Regan recently, his bank account was fat enough that he could afford to hire some help to do the boring parts of the job: the stakeouts and photo shoots — dull stuff. If he never had to sit for six hours in a cold car in February again, it would still be too soon. He was a man of action, not a man of patience, although he could pull off a hefty dose of it if he had to.

He pulled in some old friends, retired SEALs, who could use an extra payday here and there, and a guy named Gorman, an ex-cop-turned-private-detective who'd once bailed on Regan the way he had now.

He had more sympathy for the guy now, of course.

The only case he picked up that called for half his attention was an elder abuse case. Frankly, he didn't trust the SEALs not to bust in and beat the holy crap out of the man's second wife and her sister. He'd step in if things got too serious, of course, but he'd been able to catch a few minutes alone with the guy to discuss matters, and the old coot was willing to take another pounding if it meant that Jake could get incriminating photos.

Don't get mad. Don't get even. Get the bastards some jail time, and watch the holier than thou attitude that's been sustaining them for years get stripped away. See the ugly lying bastards exposed before their friends, families, churches, and jobs for the abusers they were.

For that he was willing to wait out in the cold. It took three days, but finally Jake had the evidence. The old man had a black eye and a couple of broken ribs, and the cops had the two suspects under arrest.

After making his report and calling the old coot's daughter, who had hired him, and listening to her cuss him out for not preventing the beating the two had given her father, he pulled into a coffee shop that looked like it was frequented by more men the old coot's age than his own.

He was shivering. He decided to sit in the car for a few minutes before going inside.

It had taken everything he had not to bust in and break up the fight, and turn the tables more than a little. The cops hadn't taken it kindly either when he'd told them he'd waited a few minutes after the fight started before calling them.

He didn't tell them it was so the old man's bruises would have a chance to develop and show up better in the pictures he was taking. He didn't have to. One of the officers had a grandmother who'd been abused in a nursing home by a "boyfriend" of ninety-two years of age and knew just how important evidence could be. It was like child abuse. Nobody really wanted to know it was going on. Just sweep it under the rug.

He unkinked his fingers from the steering wheel, turned off the engine, and got out. He needed a serious drink, but that would have to wait.

As predicted, the coffee shop was filled with old men hunched over stained white coffee mugs so thick and heavy that a blow to the back of the head with one might kill a man. He let the waitress escort him to a small two-top table and hand him a plastic menu. The place also sold breakfasts — big, hot, and chock full of cholesterol.

He ordered a black coffee and a plate of what should have been called the Kitchen Sink. The waitress evaluated his apparent levels of unruliness, and then took a second look at him. Her eyes softened, and she returned with his black coffee in about two heartbeats.

He leaned forward over the table. Someday, he was going to look just like the rest of the old men. Hunched over and filled with regrets.

A shadow crossed over the table.

He looked up and saw *her* — Regan.

"Hey," she said.

"Hey."

She slid into the booth. The waitress bustled over to the table quickly, holding a pot of hot coffee. From the righteous look in her eye, she was prepared to toss the pot into Regan's lap if necessary — if she were the one who had made Jake look so miserable.

In a way, she was.

He missed her – a lot.

Nevertheless, Jake raised a hand and waved at the waitress. She must be able to read minds. She brought over a menu and a second cup. Regan looked up at her and gave her a smile — not a winning smile, not even a friendly, polite smile, but a smile thanking the woman for taking care of the guy looking at her.

The waitress poured the cup of coffee with a much better attitude. She was obviously still keeping an eye on the two of them, though.

"So what brings you to my neck of the woods?" Jake asked.

Regan frowned at him. "Your car. I saw it as I was driving past. I circled back around to see if it was you."

"It was," he said. "What do you want?"

"To say I'm sorry."

He raised an eyebrow and finally gave her more than a quick glance. Her face had healed up pretty well, just a slight grayish cast around her eyes underneath the makeup. Her nose looked a little crooked, but just a little. Again, the artistry of makeup covered a lot. She was stunningly beautiful. Her breath whistled a little when she breathed.

"For what?"

"You were right. We needed to get out."

He shook his head. "You know what I did today?"

"Divorce case?"

"Normally, you'd be right. But I have people for that now. Movin' on up in the world, you might say, thanks to some kind words from your father."

"Mmm," Regan said.

"This was an elder abuse case. The old guy was being abused by his second wife and her sister. He talked me into doing something stupid. We set up a trap."

Regan sipped her coffee. Her eyes looked pained.

"I would wait outside his room with the camera, and he would provoke the other two into really laying into him. Doing something that couldn't be explained away."

"Did it work?"

"Oh, it worked. The old guy got a black eye and some broken ribs. And I watched it happen while I got the pictures I needed before I called the cops. It was hell."

She nodded. "Is he okay?"

"He's all right. A tough old bird — overjoyed he didn't lose any more teeth, actually. I gather they haven't been feeding him well or brushing his teeth."

"That's horrible."

He waved a hand and drank more of his coffee. The waitress appeared with a plate of food and a slice of pie that neither of them had ordered.

"Pie?" she said.

Regan smiled up at her again, a face full of mingled horror and thanks. "Hot, with ice cream?" The waitress nodded and walked away, after slipping Jake his Kitchen Sink.

"Don't you even care what kind it is?" Jake asked.

"No. It's pie."

He rolled his eyes and dug into the pile of hash browns, eggs, and about 110 different types of meat.

Regan said carefully, "I'm glad I saw you."

"Oh?"

"I ... look. Now that you're not working for me, there's a favor I'd like to ask you."

"What? Name it."

"I'd like to," she said. Then stopped. Her cheeks were turning red under the heavy layer of makeup she'd had to put on. She put her hands in her lap and grabbed the ends of her wool coat under the table, pulling on them until her coat was taut around the back of her neck.

"You'd like to what?"

"I'd like to take you out to..." now her face was beet red, "... I don't know ... a movie or something sometime."

He half expected her to burst out laughing and tell him she'd been joking. Instead, she rolled her lips into her mouth and scraped the lipstick off them with her teeth.

"You mean a date?"

She barely nodded. Her face was completely blazing now.

"I..." His throat tightened up.

The waitress slid the small plate of pie in front of Regan. It was hot enough to steam — the scoop of ice cream was sliding off the top, it was melting so fast. "Anything else?" she asked. She was turned so that Regan couldn't see her face.

Regan shook her head.

The waitress winked at Jake. "Just let me know if there's anything I can do." She swept away.

Regan grabbed a roll of silverware off the table, unwrapped it, and dug into the pie. She winced at the first bite of cherry red pie; it was too hot to eat.

He'd had enough of a break that he could swallow again. He took a deep breath and said, "I think I'd like that. Just don't take me back to that French place. I don't think they care for me much there."

"Sorry," she said.

"Honestly, I didn't care for the place all that much anyway."

Regan stuffed her mouth full of pie. She looked happier.

But it didn't last more than a moment. Suddenly she looked up and over his shoulder out one of the big plate-glass windows. Her eyes widened.

He twisted and looked over his shoulder.

A woman was standing outside the window, looking at them. She looked familiar. Tall, dark hair, dressed in a long coat that looked almost like Regan's. But bulkier, almost as if —

He slid out of the booth as casually as he could. The last time he'd seen the woman, it had been walking past Regan out of the bathroom controlled by the bad guys.

It wasn't the kind of place where he could sneak out the back. To get to the back, he'd have to maneuver behind the entire staff counter, past waitresses, and through the kitchen past cooks. And he was already in full view of the woman.

The back would be watched.

Regan slid out of the booth too, but headed toward the waitress at the register, pulling her billfold out of her coat as she did so. Good. The staff wouldn't interfere, thinking they were skipping out on their bill.

He looked back over his shoulder at Regan. Her face was calm, but her eyes were wide, skimming across the rest of the diner to see if anyone else inside was acting strangely. She was learning.

He mouthed the words, *'stay inside.'* She nodded. He paused at the doorway and mimed turning the deadbolt of the lock. Then he stepped outside.

When he looked back, the woman was gone.

The wind was cold and seemed to slice across the front of the building. He caught a glimpse of a black Ford Explorer with dealer plates and an unreadable paper temporary plate taped to the inside of the tinted glass of the SUV's back window.

They were being warned: *You're still being watched.*

That was all right.

It was what they'd both expected.

Chapter 38 - It's called plausible deniability

They were meeting in a back bedroom of the house of one of Jake's friends, one of the retired Navy SEALs he'd hired when his business had expanded recently. A raucous party, attended by about twenty people, was going on in the living room The houses had been swept for bugs that morning and again just before the three of them had arrived. Jake and Alex had just swept the room in which they were now. The little room contained two folding chairs, a dresser, a bed made with almost painful exactness, and pictures of women, cars, and guns.

"With luck," Jake said, "our subterfuge has blown enough smoke up the bad guys' skirts to keep them off our backs for a while."

They hadn't had any more assaults or threats since they'd gone underground. It had even been kind of fun, playacting all that drama, especially the part where he got asked out on a date by a hot blonde.

But other parts of it weren't so nice.

Gary, Jane, and Jamie hadn't been invited for obvious, as well as non-obvious, reasons. They still hadn't found out who'd been leaking information to the bad guys. Alex was still shattered by the way his phone system had been hacked.

The official reason for the party was to celebrate Jake's official launch of Westley PI LLC, a private detective agency.

Instead of working on his own and meeting clients in coffee shops, he now had an actual office, two rooms in a strip mall that used to belong to a private masseuse. The office now consisted of a front room filled with a couple of desks and filing cabinets, and a back meeting room with a boardroom table, comfortable chairs, and a projection screen so Jake could blow up pictures of wandering spouses to life size.

They didn't have long before they would have to go back out to the party and start circulating again, in case their enemies were watching via telephoto lenses through the imperfectly closed curtains or maybe even someone on their payroll attending the party.

Jake was there because it was his business.

Regan was there because she was helping bankroll the place — as a favor to Jake.

Alex was there because he was Jake's friend, and because Jake had hired him as Westley PI's IT specialist.

Regan sat on the side of the bed with the two men facing her. Jake leaned toward her, his hands clasped in front of him. Alex leaned back with his arms crossed over his chest.

Jake said, "Give her the rundown on how the new phones are going to work."

Alex cleared his throat. "The information will be encrypted well beyond the ability of the FBI to handle, and we'll be on our own private cell phone virtual network. They won't even know we're making a call. We are the only three people who can phone each other on these phones. No one else can phone us, and we can phone no one else. I'm working on getting us satellite phones, which would make them even harder to trace. But for now, this will be safe enough."

"So stay out of sight when I'm using the secure phone, and keep the phone itself concealed?" she asked.

"Correct," Alex said.

"There's also a blind email drop that you can log into. Never send any emails from it. Just use the password and the code generator fob to log in, write your email, and leave it in the drafts folder."

Alex said, "If you need someone to check the email drop, send an empty text to yourself. I have an automatic forwarder set up on our private network. If one of us needs you to check your email, you'll get a blank text from yourself on the secure phone."

"Nice," she said.

"That's it for communications," Jake said. "Regan, stay away from Alex and vice versa. I'll handle any deliveries of materials between the two of you. As much as possible, both of you stay away from the office and especially from this apartment. Regan and I are 'dating,' so I'll have plenty of opportunities to drop physical materials off with her. Alex is my employee, so ditto. Regan, don't scan anything. If it needs to be uploaded, save it for an exchange with me. You don't know how to keep information from being read off a scanner, fax machine, or printer — it's too dangerous."

"Got it," Regan said.

"But you'll be able to view scanned information via the email drop. Just don't forward it to yourself. If you want a copy on your public systems, let Alex or me know, and we'll work out a way to make it look like a natural development. The actual case that we're going to bring to get Andrew Gibbons out will have to be delivered on hardcopy."

"It's going to be almost as hard to hide the evidence of how we — I, that is — found this information without…" She trailed off.

"We'll worry about that when we get closer."

"What information do we have?" she asked.

Alex and Jake looked at each other. Alex tightened his arms across his chest and started chewing the end of his mustache.

"Before we get into that," Jake said, "I have to say something important. You need to talk to your father."

"About what?"

"You need to patch things up with him."

She blinked several times, trying to keep her face calm. "I fail to see what relevance this has to our activities."

"When we come up with the evidence to get Andy exonerated, he's going to know exactly what we've been up to. And I am worried he might unknowingly, out of concern for you do something that could blow us sky high. It's best he knows."

She gritted her teeth and tried to swallow past the lump in her throat. Jake might not be right — but he wasn't wrong. Her father would want to know exactly where she had gotten her information. And if she didn't give him an explanation he liked, he was going to raise hell — *loudly*.

But that didn't mean she needed to tell him what was going on. Just that she needed to come up with a convincing lie.

"I don't trust him with a full disclosure," she said. "He's going to stick his nose in where it's not wanted, no matter what we do. He'll want to be involved constantly."

Jake shook his head. "He won't get full disclosure. That's not what I'm talking about. You need to make things up with your father."

She felt herself leaning so far backward on the bed she started to slide off. She sat up straight again. "No."

"No?"

"He lied to me for years about being a crooked judge. Everything he taught me to stand for, he didn't."

"He did it to protect you."

"That's irrelevant. He presented himself as being above reproach, and he wasn't."

Jake opened his mouth.

Alex raised a hand toward him, cutting him off.

Even Jake looked surprised.

"Regan, what I'm about to say isn't something that I tell many people. For various reasons, not least of which is the FBI has told me not to, but I think it's important you know.

"I know your father."

Regan threw up her hands. "What is this, the John St. Clair fan club?"

"Well yes," Alex said, blinking at her in surprise. "If I hadn't been a fan of your father, I probably would have ditched this job when Gray bombed us."

"Don't tell me you're on his side too."

"Hmmm." Alex twiddled the end of his mustache. "I'm not sure if I would go that far. Right or wrong, your father has never been an especially gentle or sensitive person. But he has been more than honorable toward me, in such a way that I feel he would be a net asset in this case."

Regan sorted through the speech. "Wait, he kept you out of prison, too."

"Yes."

She sighed. "You're saying he's not just the hard ass that he comes across as. There's a decent human being under all that bluster if you know where to find it."

"Exactly."

Regan blew air out of her cheeks. "I'll think about it."

"Thank you. I believe the effort to be difficult but worthwhile."

She nodded at him before looking back at Jake.

He still looked annoyed that his hero, John St. Clair, wasn't on top of the same pedestal for her that he was for him. But he hadn't grown up with the man. He was just going to have to cope.

On the other hand, she was scared to piss him off.

She didn't know how Jake felt, but his attempts to be nice to her and the change in his eyes when he looked at her had not gone unnoticed. She wanted to be honest and tell him that she had feelings for him, not that she'd be good at saying the words. She was horrible at that kind of thing.

And telling him might make him uncomfortable. He might drop the whole thing, which would leave Andy out in the cold.

She couldn't risk it.

She reminded herself he couldn't read her mind, no matter how much his trained gaze could take in. If she could keep it off her face, she could keep him from finding out for a while, at least — hopefully long enough to get Andy out of prison.

Then they could talk about things.

She raised her eyebrows, still keeping her gaze off Jake. "Now that we've covered that bit of trivia, what information do we actually have?"

"Marando," Jake said.

"What about him?"

"He's not just scum, he's a broker of scum. The word in the neighborhood is if you need something nasty done to someone, from a mild threat to a baseball bat to the kneecaps to murder, he's the guy you want to talk to."

"Murder?"

"He doesn't do murders. He's no assassin. He just arranges things."

"Does he have connections to the Mafia, by any chance?"

"Oh yeah, he's useful. Doesn't talk. Stays bought."

"How did you find out about the connection to the Mafia?" Regan asked.

"Easy. I had Alex find it."

Alex gave half a bow from his folding chair.

"Alex, tell the nice lady how you found out about Marando's connections to the Mafia. It's clever."

Alex cleared his throat. "Uh... not really. I happen to have worked with the FBI tracking down several high level Mafioso at one point. I flipped through my files on the off chance that Marando was connected with any of their lieutenants or assassins. It turns out he had several connections — records of phone calls between them, that is — over open lines, if you can believe that." He clucked his tongue. "I only have the numbers, though. This was before the FBI had enough servers to record everything that looked suspicious."

"You have phone tapping records?" Regan asked.

"Don't worry," Alex said. "They're not legal."

"I fail to see how that's supposed to make me worry less."

"I didn't pull them, the FBI did." At Regan's expression, he twirled the end of his mustache. "Regan, the FBI and I have so much dirt on each other now that if they tried to take me down, they'd lose more to the Chinese than they ever gained from me. And they know that I'd be crucified, probably literally, by a couple of darknets if they let out what I've been doing for them. There's a kind of safety you buy for yourself when you let people have the power to blackmail you, as long as you can blackmail them back."

Regan shook her head. When she'd opened the door for the team to work extralegal, she'd opened the door far wider than she'd imagined. Oh well, it was too late to go back now.

"Noted," she said still worried. But how does this all help Andy get out of jail?"

"Now that we have some information, it's time to pay Marando a visit. That prosecutor..."

"Laura Provost."

"She's involved somehow. What we need to do is find out who hired Marando to make sure Andy got framed for the murder, and how deeply Provost was involved."

"You just said that Marando stayed bought."

"He hasn't been in the company of three retired SEALs and a Delta Force operator lately."

Regan closed her eyes. "No torture."

"Okay," Jake replied, "whatever you like."

Alex said, "Incidentally...I thought you should know. Morrison Gray had a heart attack yesterday. Apparently he was on some medication for high blood pressure that nobody told the police about. I suspect it might be somewhat stressful, being arrested after your obsession survives a car bomb that you carefully arranged."

Regan shuddered. "Please tell me you and Jake had nothing to do with it."

Jake threw his hands in the air. "I plead not guilty your honor."

She looked at Alex.

He cleared his throat. "Same here Regan — I mean your honor. I had nothing to do with it."

"A cover up, do you think?" Regan asked.

Alex shrugged. "I checked with his pharmacist. If it's a cover up, it's been going on for almost 15 years."

Regan nodded.

They weren't telling her something; she knew it.

"Jake, how are you going to neutralize Marando?"

"You don't want to know."

"If you're not going to torture him, why not tell me?"

Jake stared at her for a moment, as if the answer were perfectly obvious. "Regan, plausible deniability, remember? You're a judge. Whatever happens, we can't afford to have you kicked off the bench."

Regan opened her mouth to say something.

An image of Jamie and her two kids looking terrified in Gary's car came back to haunt her.

She closed it.

Chapter 39 - Have they now become our problem?

It was windy and cold, maybe fifteen or twenty degrees Fahrenheit out. The air was thick and wet, the clouds low and dark. The snow was supposed to start coming down at five in the morning. But in Jake's opinion, it was going to start a lot sooner — say in an hour or two.

Just after midnight.

The two former SEALs and Jake, all wearing black clothes, black masks, and voice digitizers, held Marando over the edge of the roof, one for each leg, in case Marando got excited and started to kick.

"I'd like to point out here that screaming is not in your best interest." Jake's digitized voice warned him.

"I have powerful friends!" Marando said, raising his voice a little in case he wasn't heard over the sound of the wind.

The SEALs gave Marando a shake, and his jacket scraped against the brick.

Jake said, "I have friends too, you know."

When Marando refused to open his apartment door earlier, a pair of bolt cutters had been shoved into the gap and quickly snapped the door chain before Marando could close it.

The masked men were on top of Marando before he could get a shot off with his Colt. The man had hesitated; he was a cop. The four of them had never been cops. They knew that to reach for one's weapon was to fire it. No doubt. No hesitation.

They knew it was better not to un-holster a weapon in the first place than to hesitate.

A gag in the mouth, a quick search of the apartment, and then they carried him up the stairs to the roof.

"You'll never get away with this," Marando said. "You can't assault a police officer and get away with it. The entire NYPD will be hunting you bastards down."

Jake crouched on the edge of the building next to Marado, looking down at the bottom of the guy's chin. He could look out over a big part of Brooklyn from this angle. He might even thank them later.

Jake was done playing nice.

"Yeah, okay, I accept that," Jake said. "The thing is, I'm in a short term kind of mood, and you aren't cooperating."

"I'm not going to tell you anything."

"Are you sure about that? It's a long way down."

Doug, who had been standing against the wall on the other side of his buddies and watching the distance with a pair of high powered binoculars said, "You know, I think I see someone on a rooftop out there by the river with binoculars watching us." He waved a hand.

"So?" Marando gasped.

"So you've been seen talking to us," Jake said, "maybe by someone who you don't want seeing us."

No response from below. Jake glanced down to make sure Marando hadn't passed out from all the blood going to his head. He'd hate to have wasted this performance.

But Marando was glaring up at him, the black holes of his upturned nostrils flaring.

"You want I should spit?" Chuck, one of the two SEALs on the legs, gave Marando another shake.

"That's disgusting," the other SEAL Graham said. "Try to have a little class."

"I do try," Chuck said. "But mostly I fail."

"Here's what I suggest," Jake said. "You give me the information I want."

"What information?" Marando panted.

A snowflake swirled past Jake's face. "Where are the dossiers you removed from the police archives?"

"What dossiers? I have no idea what you're talking about."

Chuck let his leg slip an inch and Marando yelped.

"In that case," Jake said, "I think we're done here. Too bad we can't leave you alive — since you're not cooperative."

"We really should get out of here," Doug said.

Chuck let go of Marando's leg again, this time holding both hands up in exasperation. "I'm out."

Graham, the biggest and strongest of them was still holding on.

"What do you think, Number Two?" Jake asked.

Graham said, "I think he's getting heavy."

Marando choked. "Please. Don't do it. I'll talk. Please."

Graham grunted, and Marando's leg slipped downward.

"Jesus Mary Joseph," Marando sobbed.

Jake jerked his head toward Chuck, who grabbed Marando's free leg again.

"Okay Marando, Jake said. "I'm in a hurry. The dossiers, where are they?"

"But they'll know," Marando wailed.

"If anyone asks, tell them I made you an offer you couldn't refuse — in more ways than one."

A gust of air brought a burst of snow like needles on Jake's skin.

"It's getting cold out," Graham noted.

"Yeah," Chuck added, "cold and slippery."

Marando gurgled in the back of his throat and pressed both hands against his face. "All right, all right," he said. "Jesus. Pull me up. I'll tell you."

"No, I don't think so," Jake said. "You tell us first. Then we pull you up. And my friends here don't take their guns off the side of your head until your story checks out."

"All right, all right…" The wind moaned through the trees. Marando shivered. "Whose dossier do you want?"

Jake leaned over to him. "Don't fuck with me, Marando. *All* of them."

***

Jake sent Doug and Chuck to retrieve the dossiers. They were hidden behind the toilet. They had to break tiles to get at the hiding spot; everything had been sealed up behind the wall. Doug had been doing contracting work when Jake hired him. The sound of the wall being busted open was limited to soft thumps and a couple of *chinks* as a tile split.

He and Graham brought Marando into the living room and forced him to sit on the couch. Graham was holding his pistol to Marando's head with the steadiness of a marble statue.

"They're here all right," Doug called softly.

In a couple of seconds, Chuck came out with one of the files.

It was thick and packed in a freezer bag, and it belonged to someone who wasn't Andrew Gibbons.

Chuck went back into the bathroom, but he soon returned.

The more files Doug and Chuck brought out of the bathroom, the angrier Jake got.

"Last one," Chuck said.

"Marando," Jake breathed. "You piece of shit."

Fifteen files in thirty or so freezer bags stuffed inside the drywall. It made a stack of paperwork as big as the body of a small child.

Marando sneered. Away from the rooftop and the icy cold, he was working himself up to have an attitude.

He was about to see how well that worked with this crew.

"Who do you work for? Jake asked.

Marando bared his teeth. "I can't tell you."

"Sounds like he's being uncooperative again," Chuck said.

"It's time for another flying lesson," Chuck said. "Final exam."

They dragged him out onto the roof just as easily as they had the first time despite Marando's struggles. Chuck and Graham started swinging the guy back and forth over the side, head first.

Jake was tempted to let them launch the bastard straight off the building. Hell, they might even be able to get enough distance on the guy to drive him headfirst into the wall of the building on the other side of the alley.

But no, he was pretty sure Regan would count that as torture.

"One...two..."

Marando wet himself. Graham grunted in disgust. In a second he and Chuck had switched their hold on him so he was head down, marinating himself in his own freezing cold piss.

The man sobbed. "I don't know who hired me. Please, Jesus."

It quickly became clear that Marando was telling the truth. He identified the man as soft spoken — not a local accent — wearing a suit and tie, a fedora, with dark glasses, a mustache, and a goatee. He hadn't given his name, and Marando hadn't asked for it. The prosecutor had already been leaning on him pretty hard to shift the blame to Gibbons.

A few minutes later, they pulled Marando back onto the roof where he collapsed like a bag of potatoes onto the snow.

Jake looked down at the bastard. He couldn't say he felt sorry for him, but he did want to keep anything ugly from coming back to haunt Regan.

And if this useless piece of shit died, it probably would. She was a good person — not like him.

"Marando, get out of Brooklyn and do it quickly — without telling your bosses — for your own good. We'll be back in a week, and you *will* be gone."

The snow was coming down more heavily now. It swirled into the man's face. He didn't even blink.

"I have one last piece of advice for you concerning your health, Marando. If you come within a mile of any of the people in these police dossiers, you will see us again. And we won't be in such a jovial mood. Capiche?"

Marando blinked slowly, then rolled onto his side and curled up into a ball in the snow.

Jake took that as a *yes*.

***

Jack was still shaking with fury when they got into the car. "He collected them like scalps, like notches on the grip of his gun."

Doug said, "Bastards like that are everywhere: Iraq, Afghanistan, here. Scum is scum."

"Just drive, okay?"

Doug put the car in gear.

Jake pulled the file out of the freezer bag and started to read by the dome light. The file showed that Laura Provost had known about Schnatterbeck, the second witness to the crime, but had chosen to withhold the evidence from the defense attorney, along with the rest of the key pieces of evidence that Jamie Gibbons had pointed out.

"At least the defense attorney looks clean," Jake muttered. He turned off the overhead light and closed the file.

"You think he's gonna talk?" Doug asked. "Marando, that is?"

"If he tries, he's going to have even more fun on his hands," Jake said. "Alex is monitoring his communications. If anything starts going wrong, he's going to end up calling the district attorney and confessing that he collects child pornography, and that he is trying to sell police dossiers to the accused who are awaiting trial."

"He does that?" Chuck asked.

"Au contraire," Graham said. "If I understand Jake's plan, all that evidence would be on Marando's computer and social media accounts. And I would be disappointed if our friend Alex has not already assembled a recording of Detective Marando's voice that says a few sentences he would otherwise never utter."

"Got it in one," Jake said.

"That's not very nice," Chuck replied.

They laughed.

Now he just had to figure out how to get the evidence legalized so it could be used to free Andy. Maybe it could come from a disgruntled clerk handing evidence over anonymously to the non-local judge who had been investigating the case? A paid stool pigeon "overhearing" Morrison confess that he'd found the information himself and held it back, to gain leverage over Regan?

The possibilities were endless — as long as Regan didn't find out how the information had been obtained.

The dossiers would give them what they needed for a breakthrough in Andy's case, but it also created fourteen new problems.

Regan wasn't going to just drop them, of that Jake was sure. And he didn't think he was going to either.

Chapter 40 - This was the nice meeting

The blame had been shifted onto Andrew Gibbons, but who it was shifted *from* was also a mystery. Marando had said, "When you're told to make sure someone else takes the blame for a murder, unless you have a death wish, you stop looking for the real killer."

He'd given Jake a look when he'd said that. It was a look that hinted Jake must have a death wish. Jake had let it go. Usually the reason for a cover up was the truth was so obvious it would be perfectly clear what had happened unless there *was* a cover-up.

Next up on Jake's list was the cyclist, Abe De Wit.

Jake didn't take the other guys with him that time. Except for Graham, they lacked subtlety. And he had Graham working on a divorce case in which both parties needed to be shaken up a little, for the sake of their kids.

So he handled it himself.

Abe De Wit worked at the water treatment plant in Greenpoint, the same place that Andrew Gibbons and Angela Ligotti worked ten years ago. The plant had seen massive changes over the years, transforming from an eyesore to a tourist destination. Eight big silver "digester eggs" rose from the complex, looking like a modern art sculpture or giant eggs from an alien invasion. But the place definitely smelled better than it had ten years ago.

Jake waited in the parking lot for De Wit to get off his shift. He worked the 10:00 pm to 6:00 am shift at the plant as an engineer.

A smart guy with a college degree still doing shift work at the age of sixty; what's wrong with that picture? Jake wondered.

He'd switched out his normal attire for a big fur trimmed black parka and was wearing the world's ugliest pair of wrap—around sunglasses. They looked like something out of a sci-fi movie and would be completely distracting. The parka was so warm he was tempted to unzip it.

The sky was just starting to brighten up. Sunrise was half an hour away, maybe a little bit more.

A bunch of people came out of the plant at the same time, streaming toward their cars. A cloud of hot breath exploded with them, fogging the air above the doors. It disbursed as the group fanned out toward their cars.

De Wit was tall with a high domed bald head and a loping stride that made him look more like a failed basketball player than an engineer.

Jake waited until De Wit was almost to his car before stepping out of the car, hands in his pockets. He'd already swept the cars nearby for bugs.

This should be quick and clean.

De Wit froze in the aisle between cars, a briefcase swinging from his hand.

He squinted. "Do I know you?"

Jake said, "The Andrew Gibbons murder case. Remember that?"

De Wit's shoulders tightened. He didn't answer but pulled his briefcase up in front of him like a shield.

Jake said, "You testified you witnessed a black man in a green car with the victim, Angela Ligotti. Only there wouldn't have been a way for you to be able to identify her from the back, in the dark."

"Oh God," De Wit said. "That was years ago. Can't we just forget about it?"

"Tell that to Mr. Gibbons. He's still in prison. Tell it to his wife and kids who are barely able to keep body and soul together."

"Who *are* you?"

"An interested party — and depending on your answers in the next few minutes, I could be a good friend or your worst nightmare."

"I have a number to call in case anyone ever came looking for me. Why don't I just give you that number and you can do with it what you will, and leave me out of it."

"I already have the number. He says he is more than happy for you to talk to me without him present."

De Wit moaned.

Jake balled his fists up inside his jacket pockets. "Your keys, Mr. De Wit, hand them over."

De Wit shook his head. Both hands stayed gripped on his briefcase.

"We'll just take a short drive around the area, Mr. De Wit. When you've told me what I want to know, you can drop me off and I'll disappear."

"You don't know what they'll do to me," De Wit said. "I'll lose my job, for one thing, and that's nothing. They'll kill my family and me."

Jake'd had about enough of De Witt. He grabbed the briefcase, ripped it out of the man's hands, dropped it, and kicked it under the nearest car.

Then he grabbed the guy's lapels. "Yeah, what else are you going to lose today, Mr. De Wit? You have already lost your honesty and my respect, and I'm about to lose my patience."

De Wit shook his head again. Jake would have to turn the heat up a little.

"You know they have to be watching us," Jake said. "They're probably watching us right now."

"Y-yes," De Wit said.

"And you're moving your lips. I'd say that is a bad sign for you and everyone you've ever loved. You see, for all they know you could be telling me anything. Couldn't you?"

De Wit shook his head again. He was still more scared of the bad guys than of Jake. "I'll scream."

"All right," Jake said.

Keeping his left hand on De Wit's lapel, he put his right hand in his own bulging parka pocket.

"I have a gun with a silencer in my right pocket. It's aimed at your knee right now. If you're going to scream, I'm going to give you a good reason first."

"You're bluffing."

Jake pulled his 9 mm Sig Sauer P938 out of the parka and showed it to De Wit. It even had a silencer on it.

De Wit started shaking.

"Are we taking a ride or am I shooting you in the knee?" Jake asked. He'd hate for the guy to forget what he was supposed to be doing.

"Taking a ride."

"Excellent choice. Now get behind the wheel and follow my instructions."

De Wit swallowed and nodded.

Jake got in the passenger seat, shoved the barrel of the pistol into his ribs, and told him to drive out of the parking lot – slowly — and take a left turn. Five minutes later they pulled up in a little side alley and parked on the side of the street.

"Okay, De Wit. My blood sugar is low. I haven't had anything to eat for more than 12 hours, I haven't slept in 36, and some schmuck has already made my day more difficult than it had to be. I need answers, and you're going to provide them without any delays. You understand?"

"Ye...yes...Sir," De Wit stuttered.

"Your testimony against Andrew Gibbons ten years ago was false. What you told the court you saw happened — didn't happen."

"N...n...no... it was..."

"Listen, you piece of shit. Your lies have put an innocent man in jail for the past ten years. I know you lied, you know you lied, and Marando told me you lied."

De Wit's eyes almost popped out his head when he heard Marando's name. "I am... I am sorry. Yes, that's true."

Jake had to exercise utter self—control not to strangle the man. "Why did you do it?"

"I don't know. It felt like I had to."

"Why you? Not for your good looks."

De Wit slumped forward with both arms over the top of the steering wheel. "I got an anonymous letter. I knew it was an order from the same people who hired me to deliver packages – as a freelance bicycle courier on my nights off."

Jake nestled the gun into the man's ear. "Delivering what?"

"I...I...I... was d...d...distributing drugs. P...please don't shoot me."

"I'll think about it," Jake said. "Although I'm about ready to make this look like a nice clean carjacking so your family doesn't have to suffer your miserable filth anymore."

"Please."

"Here's what you're going to do. You're going to drive up to White Plains to the Courthouse, and when you get there, you're going to ask for Judge Regan St. Clair, old Judge John St. Clair's daughter. Got that?"

"White Plains Courthouse, Judge St Clair."

"I am going to follow you and see that you do it. Inside that building are a few people I know very well. They will phone me and keep me up to date with what you are doing while you're inside. When you get to Judge St. Clair, you're going to tell her you just can't live with your conscience anymore and want to make a confession about what really happened to Angela Ligotti. If she asks you why you chose her to confess to, you'll tell her it's because she is the daughter of the man who is one of the few judges you respect."

Jake paused to make sure De Wit was listening.

De Wit's head bobbled like one of those dolls you put on the dashboard. "Yes sir." But he couldn't just leave it alone. "But aren't they going to arrest me if I tell the judge what really happened?"

"Perjury is a serious crime De Wit, and in this case the consequences of your perjury had caused a lot of harm and suffering. I don't know what they'll do. I suggest you tell them the truth. Tell them what Marando did and offer to testify against him. That might help — but frankly I don't give a shit."

De Wit nodded.

"When you make your confession to the Judge you will be asked if you are making your statement voluntarily and out of your own free will. You will also be asked if you want an attorney present. What are you going to answer?"

"Ah ..."

Jake pressed harder.

"I... I'm making it of my own free will." De Wit broke down and started sobbing. "Oh my God! What have I done? I'm an old man now. I can't take this anymore."

Jake lifted the gun away from De Wit's neck. "Good enough, De Wit. You can say that."

"I just want this to be over. They never leave me alone."

"Man up and get this off your conscience, and maybe you can get some peace in your life for once," Jake said.

It might even be the truth.

Chapter 41 - Confessing

Jake had made De Wit park conveniently close to where he'd stashed his Corolla. Success in life was all about planning ahead, being prepared, and covering your ass — three apparently lost talents that were finally coming back to him.

He switched back into his bomber jacket and baseball cap, got into his car, and pulled out into the street. De Wit was just starting to put his car into drive. He must have sat there shivering, trying to work up the courage to do *something* — *anything*.

Fortunately, he'd worked up the courage to do the right thing — what Jake wanted him to do.

He was an easy tail, barely looking into his rear view mirror, turning on his signal every time he so much as changed lanes.

He *knew* he was being followed and still didn't spot Jake. He must be looking for the weird guy in the parka and shades, not the Brooklynite that followed him all the way out of the city.

The heavy clouds over the city cleared up, and White Plains was bathed in sunshine. It didn't make the place any prettier.

De Wit drove to the courthouse, following the directions on his smartphone, which he kept mounted on the dash. Not once did he raise the phone to his ear to call someone; not once did he send a text. Jake realized he must have scared the crap out of him.

Jake kept up the escort duty until De Wit reached the courthouse. He parked along the street and waited long enough to see De Wit leave his car and enter the building. It took him ten minutes, five of which were with the engine running and both hands white knuckled on the steering wheel. But finally, he got it done.

Jake made a couple of loops around the area to see whether anyone had followed them. As far as he could tell, nobody had.

He parked a couple of miles away from the courthouse and took a bus back. Across the street from the courthouse were several restaurants with big windows. He settled into the one that looked like it would have the best coffee and waited for De Wit to come back out.

If it was the best coffee that White Plains had to offer, no wonder the place was so ugly and depressing. No wonder Regan was addicted to that French place. At least they had wine.

***

It was Thursday, and the Tarloff case was scheduled to resume the following Wednesday. Regan had been "taking it easy" as long as she could. She had heard Gary answer the phone and give her status to several people several times already and could recite the answer by heart:

Regan's looking much better, and no, it's not just the makeup. I think she'll be fine for the trial next week as long as she continues to take it easy. She's trying to get caught up on some paperwork right now. I'll send her home if she looks like she needs it. Of course, she'll listen to me; I'm her secretary. Bye.

On the last call, the speech changed: "Uh-huh. She's doing fine; I can hear the keyboard clicking from the other room. She had some soup, a bagel, and some Ibuprofen. No, not a lot of Ibuprofen, just two capsules. No, I checked her desk before she came in this morning. She doesn't have a secret stash. I know because I looked deep into her eyes about five minutes ago, and she's fine. Really she's fine, so stop worrying. And *yes,* I will call you if she goes home or if I decide she's had enough. Will you give it up already? If you're so worried about her, call her yourself. She has her own line, you know. Do you want me to patch you through? Do you?"

He hung up the phone and laughed. Then he called through the open door into her office, "Regan?"

"Yes?"

"Jake called."

She smiled. "Did he leave a message?"

"He's worried about you, that's all."

"Okay."

She went back to work, which mostly consisted of deleting emails asking if she was all right. Gary had sent out a group email covering the topic already, asking everyone to excuse Regan for not replying individually. He was a life saver.

Gary's phone rang, and he picked it up. Instead of the standard speech, he said, "I'll tell her. Hold on a second."

"Regan?" he called. His voice sounded strained all of a sudden.

"Yes?"

"There's a man downstairs who wants to see you."

"Who?"

Gary paused, "De Wit."

She lowered her hands from the keyboard and put them flat on her desk on either side of it.

"De Wit. Abe De Wit?"

"Sounds like it."

"Have them send him up."

"Do you want him searched for weapons?"

Her heart was already rattling in her chest. Leave it to Gary to make her even more nervous. "No, but stall him if it looks like he's carrying anything."

"Remember, there are metal detectors around the doors now."

"I remember."

Gary went back on the line and told security to escort the man to Regan's office.

She turned off the monitor on her computer and rummaged around in a desk drawer. She had a recorder around here somewhere. If only she could find it.

Gary knocked on her door.

"Come in."

He brought in a tape recorder and a glass of water. When he'd set them down on her desk, he doled out another Ibuprofen from the bottle he kept in his pocket.

"Are you ready for this? Do you want me to stay in here with you?"

She bit her lip. "No, I'm not ready. Go next door and see if Gardner has time to come in here for a minute."

Gary nodded. He returned a moment later with Bart Gardner, another one of the district judges. He was about Regan's age and was known to keep a jar of chocolate truffles and pictures of his six kids on his desk.

He sat down across from her. "What's up?"

"A confession I hope."

"Ah." He leaned back.

She heard Gary moving papers around on his desk, something he only did when he was nervous.

A knock came on the outer door. "Security with a visitor," a voice said.

"Come in."

The door opened, and Gary chatted pleasantly with the security guard. The knock on her inner door, even though she was expecting it, startled her.

"Mr. De Wit," Gary said and let the man in.

De Wit was tall and angular, with a large sloped forehead under his balding dishwater blond hair, and had small dark blue eyes. He gave Gardner a startled look.

"This is Judge Gardner," Regan said, "a colleague of mine. Have a seat."

De Wit held a leather cabbie's cap in front of his stomach with both hands. He sat in the vacant chair on the other side of the desk, leaning slightly away from Gardner. His eyes were just a little too wide, but the pupils looked fine. He wasn't high, although it was clear he was terrified.

He glanced at Gardner, then the recorder sitting on top of the desk.

"You know why I'm here," he said.

"Yes."

She didn't, but she'd learned over the years that when a defendant or witness was about to spill their guts on the basis she already knew something, the correct response was always 'yes.'

"I want to confess."

She held up a finger, turned on the recorder, announced the date and time, and stated that the conversation was being recorded. "State your name, please."

"Abraham De Wit. I go by Abe."

"Bart?"

"The Barton Gardner, district court judge, here as a witness."

"Please proceed."

He did. While she kept an iron grip on her facial expression and he stared at the top of her desk, he told her what he had really seen the night of Angela Ligotti's murder.

He had been out bicycling — it was his day off, and he was often up nights anyway, even when he didn't have to be. A green sedan had driven up to the curb, and a black man had climbed out and started to pull a limp and unmoving passenger out of the front seat.

De Wit had stopped, dismounted, and walked his bicycle behind the chain link fence at the corner of the vacant lot. Then he laid the bicycle down on the ground and crouched behind some junk. A few homeless people in the lot at the time may have seen him, but he thought they were mostly sleeping.

He said he couldn't help himself; he had to watch.

The man, who was wearing a red jacket, dragged a woman out of the car, left her on the sidewalk, then drove off.

De Wit waited half an hour, almost falling asleep. Then he heard a noise from across the street that sounded like a piece of metal being dropped on the sidewalk, startling him awake. He fled the scene and locked himself in his apartment.

Then, a few days later, a girl who worked at the plant contacted him. Not someone he knew, but someone from the day shift. She waited in the parking lot for him, handed him a piece of paper and walked away.

On the paper, which unfortunately De Wit had destroyed, was a note telling him he'd been seen at the scene of the crime, and asking him to contact the police as a good citizen. The note told him the writer had also seen the murder and described what happened — but it wasn't the same scene De Wit had actually seen. It also gave the names of both Andrew Gibbons and Angela Ligotti.

The writer of the note claimed to be an old woman whose health prevented her from going through a court trial and said she'd be grateful if De Wit did what needed to be done. She was sure there was a reward, but only if he acted promptly.

De Wit took the hint, went to the nearest precinct house, and fed the story the note gave him — not the real one, but the one that ended up in his court testimony — to the police.

Later, he received a bonus in his paycheck for an award he'd been nominated for but hadn't received — $5,000 after taxes.

"Looking at that check was one of the most terrifying things I've done in my life," he said. "It's been ten years, and I still have the same nightmare. I'm watching the man in the red jacket drag someone out of a car. Only this time it's me."

Regan nodded. "And the reason you came to me now?"

"I... I've had some bad news at the doctors. I'll feel better for having this off my conscience. And I thought... your father was known throughout Brooklyn as the man to see when you wanted to get something off your chest. If you came to him in good faith, he wouldn't throw the book at you. I was hoping —"

She raised a hand.

"I have to take this to the D.A.," she said. "It will be up to the D.A.'s office what kind of action will have to be taken. But I suspect they will go lightly on you. You've done the right thing. You shouldn't be punished for it."

Chapter 42 - Licorice cats and bees in the snow

Jake exhausted the possibilities of the diner across the street from the courthouse about ten times over, from reading the newspaper to ordering breakfast to reading the health inspection certificate on the wall. It didn't, he noticed, have a "best of" community award on the wall anywhere in sight — so modest. He hated surveilling a place from a restaurant. He always had to look like he was doing something, even if it was just killing time.

His phone rang just as he saw De Wit walk out of the courthouse and into the parking lot.

"Hello? Regan, what's up?"

"Jake. I just had the strangest...you won't believe it."

"Try me."

"Are you busy?"

He checked his watch. It was a little after one. "I just sat down for a late lunch."

"Good. You're not driving. You're sitting down."

"I'm sitting down. Regan, what's going *on*?"

"De Wit. He came in and confessed."

"De Wit's the murderer?"

She barked with a single laugh. "No, I'm sorry. I'm not being clear. He came in and admitted that he had perjured himself in his testimony at Andy's trial."

"Holy shit," Jake said. "So what is he saying happened now?"

Regan told him the story that De Wit had related to her. It was, as far as Jake could tell, the truth.

"Did you...get an official statement from him?"

"Yes. As well as recorded the original statement he made to me on audio with a second witness in the room, another judge."

"Excellent."

"It's a miracle, Jake, a miracle."

Jake grinned. He was glad she thought so.

Regan paused, and he started to wonder if she was already putting things together. *I'd better head that train of thought off at the pass.*

He started to change the subject. "So —"

But she was speaking too. "Jake —"

"You go first."

"We, ah, you remember that thing I asked you last week?"

His eyebrows rose. De Wit's car pulled out of the parking lot. He suppressed the urge to follow it, and instead kept his eyes open for anyone tailing the guy.

"Jake?"

"Sorry, double duty lunch. Watching a client's ex drive off from someplace they shouldn't be."

"Do you need to go?"

"Nah, I got what I needed. But you were asking if I remembered what you asked me last week. Of course, I do."

"I thought of something."

"You did?"

"...how do you feel about a weekend getaway? The workmen are coming to do more repairs on the house tomorrow, and they're going to be there all weekend, so I... I'd rather not be there. There's a B&B at Martha's Vineyard that I know..."

He frowned. Martha's Vineyard was a tourist trap for rich people who didn't know how to have a good time. Okay, Regan was, a) rich and, b) hadn't had a lot of experience having a good time lately, but still...

"I have a better idea," he said. "A weekend getaway, yes. At Martha's Vineyard, no."

"Where then?"

"Trust me," he said. "I've got this."

***

The morning was clear and bright. A fresh dusting of snow had drifted down through a layer of fog the previous night. Now it sparkled on every available surface: roofs, tree branches, the tops of fences, electrical lines, mailboxes, and garbage cans. Now and then, as Jake sat parked in front of Regan's house, a pile of snow would fall off a branch as a bird landed on it and explode on the ground in a white puffball.

It almost made her house look like it hadn't been bombed.

At least the final repairs would be done by the time he brought her back on Tuesday afternoon.

A snowstorm was scheduled to roll into the area on Wednesday morning, but they would be back in White Plains by then, or earlier if things didn't go well.

He wanted to give her a day or two off to relax, but he was going to have to tell her about the other dossiers he'd recovered from Marando's apartment.

She'd probably weasel the truth about De Wit out of him too. Then there would be hell to pay.

Regan had told him she'd call him when she was up and dressed. Instead, the front door of her house opened, and she emerged carrying one medium sized bag over her shoulder and hefting a large rolling bag out of the door and onto the front step.

He cursed, jumped out of the car, and jogged through the unmarked snow to grab her bags.

"Good morning," she said pleasantly, checking to make sure the door was locked.

"You're not supposed to be lifting more than ten pounds."

"They're just being overly cautious."

"Right."

He threw the strap of the smaller bag over his shoulder and hefted the rolling bag to carry it down the steps. At the bottom of the steps, he decided that a little snow wasn't going to hurt anything and let it roll. It felt like she'd packed it with bricks.

"What's in here?"

"Research materials — you said not to expect a decent Wi-Fi connection."

"Did you bring your whole library? This weekend is supposed to be R&R, not work."

He brought the bags to the back of the car and popped the trunk.

She hissed through her teeth. He'd brought copies of all the dossiers with him. The originals were locked up in a safe deposit box in Brooklyn with scanned copies racing through the electrons in Alex's computers.

He'd stuffed them all in black plastic garbage bags, taped them down with duct tape, then dumped them in two oversized sacks he normally used for groceries. From the perspective of someone who didn't know what to expect, he could see they might look like bundles of coke or something.

"What is all that?" she asked.

"Research materials," he grinned.

She arched an eyebrow at him. She'd taken the trouble to cover her bruises with makeup this morning, and was looking like a movie star from the Forties — a blonde Katherine Hepburn maybe. He appreciated the effort, even if she was trying to look more healed up than she actually was.

He said, "Despite appearances, I do actually have some work to get done and not just on the Gibbons case."

"So much for R&R, then," she said as she climbed into the car. He had to stop himself from opening the door for her. She'd probably think that was going *too* far.

***

It was five hours to Malletts Bay in Vermont, and she didn't criticize his driving once — mostly because she had her nose buried in a file. He stopped once for coffee and once at a fast-food joint, and she barely looked up.

At the start of the journey she asked, "How far is it?" and he told her. She didn't react; she barely even looked up to check the time on the dashboard.

He flipped through radio stations and wondered if this was all a big mistake. She'd gone so long without having any fun that she didn't have a clue how to relax now. Well, he didn't want to start an argument. She'd relax eventually.

He flipped through stations, chasing rock and roll around the dial as each station fuzzed out. The further north they went, the fewer options they had until he finally turned the radio off.

Regan grunted and turned her head. The manila folder she had in her hands slid onto the floor, scattering pages.

Her eyes were closed, and her head had tilted against the window. The blonde hair, which she had pulled back against the back of her neck, was coming out of its elastic band. A soft piece of hair had fallen over her face and was stuck to the side of her mouth.

He gave a soft sniff and took a second to brush the hair away from her mouth, back onto her neck.

***

The little cottage looked like something out of a fairytale: gray cottage with white trim and a red door, eight inches of snow on the roof, a tree next to the house, and the icy bay peeking around from the other side.

He let the car roll gently to a stop and turned off the engine. To wake or not to wake, that was the question.

Fortunately, he didn't have to answer it. Regan smacked her lips and came awake like someone had punched a button. She brushed her hands across her legs, then looked down and spotted the dropped file. She bent forward and picked it up, then stuffed the wrappers around her feet into her paper coffee cup.

Then she straightened up and opened the door, holding her long wool coat away from the door as she got out.

Jake's heart sank. She hadn't even looked at the place.

Then she stopped with one hand on top of the car door.

"Oh," she breathed and looked around her. A puff of air gusted from her mouth, rising over her head and disappearing into the sky.

She turned back and forth, looking over the cute little houses covered with snow as thick as frosting, the deep blue sky that stretched out over Lake Champlain, the ice of the lake stretching further than the eye could see.

"How did we get here?" she asked. "Where are we?"

A honking sound came from behind the house. *Geese*, she thought. She looked at him and said, "Is this the place?"

When he nodded, she tossed the file onto the passenger seat, slammed the door, and took off through the snowy yard in her shoes and disappeared. A second later he heard her call, "There are stairs! They go all the way down to the ice!"

He laughed.

***

Regan spent the rest of the day fighting the urge to fling her paperwork to the wind. The inside of the little cottage was kooky, completely covered with wood paneling. The low attic was open to the main room with beams showing where the old ceiling had been. The beams were stacked with snowshoes, ancient wood skis, slim leather ice skates that had to be from another century twice over, fishing rods — even a tattered birch bark canoe.

The fireplace had an iron rod to hang a kettle from and a miniature train sat on the mantle. The TV was an ancient vacuum tube type box that must have weighed two hundred pounds, and was built into a wood stand. The couch was pointed toward the fireplace, though; the TV was an afterthought at best.

It belonged to the family of one of the retired SEALs Jake had hired. It had two bedrooms, a single bathroom, kitchen, living room, tiny pantry, and a storeroom by the back door that was literally packed from floor to ceiling with matching white cardboard document boxes.

The kitchen was already stocked with food in both the pantry and the freezer, and someone had left fresh milk and bread in the fridge along with fresh coffee beans on the counter.

She had switched off her regular phone that morning when she got into the car — Gary could reach Jake if need be. She went outside, walking on the ice or the streets until her legs were cold and wet and she could barely feel her feet.

When she finally came back in, Jake handed her a mug of hot cocoa and tucked her onto the couch with a blanket.

He already had a fire going, and the wood burned steadily in the brick fireplace. It lulled her into a half slumber for a few minutes as she sipped the cocoa.

She snapped awake as Jake brought her a bowl of hot soup and set it on the end table next to her.

"Hang on," she said. "I'll come out to the kitchen, and we can eat."

He disappeared through the open doorway of the kitchen. He'd tucked a towel into the back pocket of his jeans. "Stay put. We're going to sit in front of the fire and relax for a little bit. If you think you can handle that."

She rolled her eyes.

He returned with a bowl of soup and a basket full of oyster crackers and retreated again. She glanced toward the kitchen. Glasses and silverware chimed from the other room. She stuck a pinky into the bowl.

The soup was chicken chowder, not too heavy and perfectly seasoned with lots of garlic.

Jake returned with a pair of wineglasses, a bottle of Riesling, spoons, and napkins.

"All out of crusty bread," he said.

"Did you make this?"

He grinned at her. "It's not your maid's magic cake, but it's all right. I made it while you were on your walk. Try some. Tell me if you like it."

She made a show of pulling the bowl off the end table, putting it on the napkin, and slurping from it. "It's good."

"Good. This is supposed to be a vacation."

"A working vacation," she corrected.

"Yeah, well, from what I gather it's still more of a vacation than you've let yourself have in years."

She slurped from her soup.

The bottle of wine was open, and he poured them both half a glass, reaching across her to set it on the end table.

"Excuse me," he said.

He settled onto the couch next to her and leaned back to watch the fire. Outside the windows it had already gone dark — sooner than she expected.

As she sipped the wine, her thoughts drifted to Jake. She'd never been good at dating or having a lover or any of that. She'd tried — but it had always ended up that she was spending too much time at work, that she didn't like what her lovers were interested in, or they were more interested in her father or helping out their friends with legal favors than they were in her. They told her they admired her brains, but as soon as she acted like anything other than a dumb blonde, they found her inconvenient.

And so she'd just given up on the idea.

What would it be like with Jake? she wondered and then blushed at the thought.

He wouldn't tell her she was spending too much time at work. He'd be able to keep up. He'd probably get overprotective for a while, and if she acted like a dumb blonde, he'd growl at her. She smiled.

"I don't know if I can handle working on the case tonight," she said, putting the bowl on the side table.

His eyebrows pricked up. "Not feeling well?"

"No, I feel better than I have since the beauty shop. I feel relaxed." She could feel another blush coming on. "I mean...-"

Jake studied her face, looking it over carefully. "It's a vacation. That's how you're supposed to feel."

Even if Jake didn't have to deal with his feelings, she did. She'd never been that great at lying to herself. Her hands were shaking, but she reached over and took Jake's face in them. The sides of his cheeks were covered with stubble.

Jake moved closer to her, guiding her hands to fold around his neck while he pulled her closer and placed his lips on hers.

She let out a soft groan of pleasure. Putting her hands against his chest, she pushed him back slightly so she could look into his eyes. What she saw there made her heart leap up into her throat.

**

The sky was starting to get lighter. Not daylight yet, not for a while, but the orange haze on the clouds was starting to fade as the streetlights went out.

The house was chilly. Outside he could hear a truck rolling along the streets — either a snowplow or a garbage pickup.

He lay next to Regan in the full sized bed in the room he'd mentally labeled as 'hers' when he first checked out Doug's aunt's vacation home. She was spooned up against his side with her head on his shoulder, limp as a doll.

He curled a tendril of hair around his finger and let it slide through.

That girl from Judge John St. Clair's wallet many years ago had always held a certain kind of magic for him. But not in his wildest dreams could he ever have imagined how much magic until that first kiss last night. He smiled.

His arm was killing him. Carefully, he started rolling it out from under Regan's neck. She snorted and grabbed his chest.

He froze and listened to her breathe for another minute. She was out, dead out. He tried to move his arm again.

She pulled him tighter against her.

He whispered, "Regan, I gotta move my arm."

"Sorry," she mumbled. "All the cats are picking the lottery."

He chuckled. "Are they?"

"That's why black cats are made out of licorice."

"I see." He tucked his arm up under his pillow and pulled her close. "What do they have to say about Jake?"

"Jake?" She sighed. "Oh, the snow is full of bees."

He chuckled again and settled down to get more sleep. She rolled against him. He pulled the quilt up over her chin.

"I hope you stay," he said.

"Bees," she insisted.

He fell asleep again.

***

Regan woke up cuddled against Jake's chest. The sky had brightened into daylight, and Jake made adorable little snoring noises against the top of her head.

Phee. Phee.

She got up carefully and made a beeline for the kitchen — and coffee. She wasn't sure what Jake had for breakfast usually, but there was bacon and eggs in the fridge, and she probably wouldn't humiliate herself too badly. She was no cook. French toast was about as complex as she could handle.

Outside the kitchen window, she could see the icy surface of the lake.

Would it be awkward once he woke up?

It hadn't been last night. It was incredible: the tenderness, his touch, his voice, his gentleness…

The coffee began to drip into the carafe. No espresso here, just some strong black coffee. She waited until the first two cups' worth had run through, and then poured it into two old stained mugs. She never could wait for the whole thing to brew.

***

The side of the bed dipped, and a hand stroked his hair. "Jake?"

He stirred, trying to pull himself upward out of a deep sleep. It must be some emergency. He sat up.

A cup of coffee approached his chest, handle first. He took it.

"You don't take cream, do you?"

He blinked.

Regan sat on the side of the bed dressed in his shirt, her hair pulled back from her face. She had a cup of coffee in her hand and a stack of notes on the bed next to him.

Oh God. It was over. She'd gone all professional on him.

"Hang on a minute. I'll get dressed."

He started to put the coffee on the nightstand, but she pushed his arm out of the way and slid up under the covers next to him with her back against the headboard.

He backed up carefully until he was next to her against the headboard, their arms touching and her legs over his.

He leaned over and kissed her on the cheek. "Thank you."

"I hope it's drinkable," she smiled.

"I'm talking about last night. I...I...don't..."

"Then don't." She took the cup out of his hand and placed it on the table next to her and pulled him over to her.

An hour later they poured the cold coffee down the sink, started a fresh brew and made breakfast.

***

There was just one problem.

He hadn't told her about the dossiers- - or how he had gotten them.

"Regan..." He couldn't put it off any longer.

Her eyes widened in panic. "What? Oh, God. You have a girlfriend? A wife?" he shook his head.

"No, nothing like that," he laughed. Her eyes relaxed. "No, listen. The papers I have in the trunk of the car. I got them from Marando. We pushed him pretty hard."

She closed her eyes. The arm against his side seemed to stiffen. "You pushed him."

"We didn't torture him. We just dangled him over the roof of his building a little. He has no idea who we are. We made sure of that."

"You dangled him over the roof of a building! Are you sure he wouldn't know who you are?"

"Yeah, we dangled him, and yes, as sure as I can be."

"The timing — when he hears Andy's getting out of prison — he'll guess."

"Maybe," Jake admitted, "but what we have to discuss now is what to do about the rest of the dossiers."

"How many of them *are* there?"

"Marando had fourteen in addition to Andy's."

She breathed out, "Fourteen!"

"Fourteen innocent people, every one of them in prison, and Marando helped put them all there."

She glanced at him out of the corner of her eye.

"Marando's still alive, right?"

"Yes, as far as I know. We left him in good condition – just a little wet in the trousers."

She sighed, slumped back in the chair, then finished her coffee. "You weren't kidding about having work to do. I need a chance to go over those files. No. We need to focus on Andy and our strategy for getting the D.A.'s office to take our request to have him exonerated seriously. I'll read the rest of the files later."

"But you want to do something about it?"

"Of course, I do. But we have to take things one at a time, and we have to plan better..." She glared at him. "We can't just rush into these things, Jake. Someone's going to get hurt."

He laughed.

Someday he had to tell her about talking in her sleep, licorice cats and bees in the snow.

But for right now — it was just for him.

Chapter 43 - She sketched out her plan

She watched the snow falling outside her bedroom window, soft and gentle but incessant. It was already stacked an inch deep on the branches of the trees.

It had been a magnificent weekend, but it couldn't last forever. Jake had driven her home last night so she could spend a night in her own bed and get ready for the resumption of the Tarloff case.

Tomorrow she would have to take up the case again, but today she had to decide whether to confront Provost and try to get Andy freed or go after the real murderer first.

Regan laid the pieces of the case in front of her on the bed like a jigsaw puzzle.

If only she could focus. She was reliving the weekend with Jake.

She'd been putting off rereading her materials, and instead watched the snow fall in the back yard and thought about Jake.

A couple of White Plains detectives had come over to the house and questioned her this morning. No, she'd told them, she had no idea that Morrison Gray was obsessed with her. She'd had several friends over to cheer her up while she was recovering from her mugging, and they'd left the house on a sudden impulse to watch a movie.

She said it with a completely straight face while pressing her ribs. They did ache, but they also helped focus her attention away from the fact she'd been lying through her teeth.

Lying — it got easier, or at least more comfortable. Which in and of itself made her more uncomfortable.

They had enough information to confront Laura Provost in the DA's office back in Brooklyn. They had the original Gibbons file, with all the information the DA's office had collected — and then hidden. It was obvious evidence had been altered and repressed.

Marando's testimony would be the key, and he would have to do it too. They owned that corrupt son of a bitch.

De Wit's confession made a good corroboration.

But if they brought the file to Provost now, their chance of catching the actual murderer would vanish.

On the one hand Regan wanted to help the living, and Andy wasn't getting any younger. Plus, the only way Jamie was going to forgive her for putting her boys in danger — if she ever did — was if Regan got her husband out of prison.

On the other hand, Angela Ligotti had been *murdered*. And, but for a few exceptions, Regan had never been able to see any justice in that.

She picked up the secure phone and called Alex. She'd received an empty text message half an hour ago, making the phone buzz. The encoded email drop had instructed her to call and let Alex and Jake know what she wanted to do — keep digging, or take what they had to Provost.

They were waiting for her to call and give them direction on what she wanted.

Alex said, "Hello Regan."

Jake cut straight to the chase: "Do we take it to Provost or keep digging for her murderer?"

She took a deep breath.

She'd expected Jake to go all protective of her. She hadn't expected the irrational need *she* felt to keep him safe from all possible harm to come up within her.

Like a coward she said, "It's time to move on. We take it to Provost and stop stirring up the hornet's nest."

***

Jake tossed the phone onto the computer bench and stood up to stretch. Alex rolled his shoulders, slipped his headset off, unplugged it from the phone, and coiled the cord up neatly before dropping the secure phone into his pocket.

Jake pointed toward the quiet room. Alex nodded but walked over to the cooler to pick up an energy drink before following him. The kid had been awake almost the entire weekend, trying to find more information on the murderer to give to Regan before she made her decision, but no dice.

Jake sat down and leaned back in the chair, putting his hands behind his head.

He wanted to spend the rest of the day thinking about Regan. Remembering...

But of course with his feelings for Regan came responsibilities.

Alex popped the lid on the slim can of whatever nerve wracking semi poison he was drinking, closed the door behind him, and sat down across from Jake. Most people wouldn't have noticed — but Jake had worked with the kid enough times to recognize he was dejected.

"I didn't want to discuss this with Regan," Jake said. "She has enough on her plate with Provost, but I want to keep looking for the murderer."

Alex took a deep breath and let it out. When he looked up, his shoulders looked more relaxed, and his eyes had regained a little life to them. "You know this is a bad idea."

"I'll tell her later."

"It's your ass, not mine," Alex replied shaking his head.

"Agreed."

He sipped the energy drink, grimaced, and then drank half the can in a long gulp. "If that's the case, I'm in. I don't *even* want to have the murderer connect me to this — unless he's already in prison."

"Then let's get back to work."

***

Jake sat up in bed and looked around his room. The place was Spartan, not because he wanted it so plain, but because he never had the time to go shopping for what normal people put on their walls. He had a few photographs in frames, mostly pictures of his family or other people in the Delta Force. The bookshelf that divided his bed from the rest of the studio apartment was filled with nonfiction books and a few knickknacks; that was it.

He could have sworn he'd heard a knock at his door and took his handgun out of the bed stand. But the sound wasn't repeated, so he put it back.

It was late morning already. He'd spent more than a few hours in Alex's basement doing additional research on different hypothetical murderers.

It wasn't like a mystery novel where you met all the possible suspects by page fifty, and the great detective got to send the sidekick out to do all the leg work. He couldn't skip eight hours of research by flipping the page.

He swung his legs over the side of the bed, climbed to his feet, and ignored the pain in his knee. It always felt worst first thing in the morning or sometimes in the middle of the night.

The rest of the apartment — white walls and cabinets, a wood floor, a sagging brown sofa that really should have been accessorized by a big hairy dog, and a small door toward the toilet and closet — was empty. No threats there.

The coffee was waiting for him, preprogrammed to run first thing in the morning. Usually, that was enough to wake him up, but today he'd overslept.

His secure phone rang.

It was Regan. Today was her meeting with Provost.

"Jake," she said coldly. "Tell me you didn't kill Marando."

He leaned against the sink. "What?"

"Tell me."

"I didn't kill Marando. What happened?"

"It's on the news. He was found dead in his apartment. It's reported as a suicide."

Jake swore. Without Marando, they would only have De Wit's confession to back up their story. They *needed* to be able to put pressure on Marando in person, otherwise there was no way they could use the dossiers he'd collected. As Regan would say, it was 'poison fruit from the poison tree.'

"It wasn't suicide," he said. "That guy was a weasel, and they never kill themselves."

"You didn't do anything to make him kill himself?"

"No!" He clenched the phone too hard; it dug into his hand. "We scared him, all right, but that's as far as it went."

"Then he was killed, probably by the bad guys."

He poured himself a cup of coffee. "Regan, you have to back out of this meeting with Provost. It's too dangerous. What if…"

What if the killers made Marando talk? What if he told them more than he knew he knew? Jake had seen it before. Some people were sharp enough to put together a puzzle from one corner and a middle piece, with the rest of it missing.

"I'm not backing out," Regan said. "It's now or never. In fact, if I intend to scare Provost, now is the perfect time. Listen."

She sketched out her plan.

Jake had to admit it was a good one — except for the part where it required Regan to lie to the woman's face.

She wasn't all that good with lies.

Chapter 44 - And then they would all be safe

The homicide bureau of the Brooklyn D.A.'s office looked like something out of a movie, one of those places where old mysterious artifacts — or in this case paperwork — went to die.

There were cardboard boxes, filing cabinets, cheap shelves bolted to the walls, wire shelves that ran almost to the ceiling, all of it stacked with paper, plastic binders, file folders, manila envelopes, brown accordion files stuffed to bursting, and more.

Welcome to the Information Age – just not necessarily the Well Organized Age.

A copier was running, fan humming, and bright light flashing from somewhere deep inside a pile of brown accordion folders that spanned several desks. The woman at the copier, wearing a cardigan and reading glasses on a chain, looked up.

"Laura Provost's office?" Regan inquired.

The woman looked toward another clerk slumped in front of a computer terminal. He nodded. The woman looked back at Regan and pointed toward a door half hidden by the cheap shelving.

The door was open a crack. Regan and Provost had met several times before at conferences. The woman had always struck her as some kind of predatory bird. She'd insulted Regan's father in front of her and then watched to see Regan's reaction.

Regan considered her a power hungry ladder climber, a trait which would have made it easy for the bad guys to pull her into their orbit.

She knocked.

"Hello? Are you officially in?"

"Come in."

Regan ducked in and closed the door behind her. It was like entering another world. The office was filled with oak bookshelves packed with gold trimmed books, awards, and ass kissing, hand shaking, gold framed photographs on the shelves.

Provost rose from her desk and extended a hand. She was a thin faced woman of about medium height with brassy colored dyed hair, wide spaced eyes, and a hatchet for a nose. In general, she made herself taller with a range of impressively tall and narrow footwear. She had been known to use her heels to spike an instep or two.

"Thank you for seeing me on such short notice," Regan said.

"It's not a problem."

Regan smiled. It would be – shortly.

"What's this about?" Provost asked.

"As I'm sure you've heard by now, last week I had a visit in White Plains from a man named Abe De Wit regarding the Gibbons' case."

Laura's eyebrows went up.

"Oh?"

"He had a tale to tell — he'd been anonymously bribed to change his story at the trial."

"I don't remember him," Provost said.

Both of them sat at the same time. Now the desk was between them.

"It's been ten years," Regan agreed.

"Why didn't he come here? It's closer."

"Apparently he remembered my father fondly from his childhood."

Provost snorted.

Regan suppressed a brief urge to punch her. "At any rate, I've been interested in the case for a while, and when I heard what he had to say, I dug a little deeper and contacted a friend of mine in the FBI."

Provost was good she had to admit. The woman's gaze barely changed.

"I was able to obtain this." She slid a manila folder out of her briefcase and set it on the desk.

"What is it?"

"A copy of a dossier found in Detective Peter Marando's apartment."

Provost stood up, knocking her rolling chair back. She looked like she was about to peck Regan in the face, she was staring at her so intently. "Detective Marando was murdered last night."

"I heard that on the news this morning," Regan said, "except they implied it was a suicide. However, I would tend to agree with your assessment. You see, prior to his death he was being investigated by the FBI. He was apparently working with several different competing drug cartels in the area. I wouldn't be surprised if you discover he was murdered when information leaked to the wrong people."

Provost pressed her knuckles into the blotter on her desk.

"But that's not what I came to discuss. I found something interesting in the file I received from my friend. The file contains information that isn't in the public version."

"What do you mean the public version? There's only one version of a case file."

"Oh, I assure you this one's different." She flicked open the cover of the manila folder and turned several pages. Provost's eyes twitched, trying to follow the movement while keeping an eye on Regan's face at the same time.

Regan reached the photograph of the crime scene. It showed something that had surprised her, Jake, and Alex when they'd seen it: a photograph of Fred Schnatterbeck.

"Recognize him?" Regan asked.

Provost didn't look down. "No."

"Fred Schnatterbeck. He died recently of an overdose of strychnine, a mix up at a hospital he was in after being attacked during a break in. He was a witness to the case who had some very interesting information to present to the court — information that might have cleared suspicion from Andrew Gibbons."

She flipped the photograph over.

"And look — a signed statement from Mr. Schnatterbeck. You might want to read it."

Provost's nostrils flared.

"Strangely enough, Mr. Schnatterbeck's evidence was not provided to the defense, and Mr. Schnatterbeck was not called upon to testify in court."

Regan flipped through the pages of the statement until she reached a page that held a black and white copy of a sticky note.

It read, *Hold from public file — Provost.*

"I'll just leave this here for you to read, Laura." Regan stood up, holding her briefcase in front of her. "I'm sure you're very busy today."

She turned to go.

"Wait," Provost said.

Regan stopped with her hand on the doorknob. "Yes?"

"What are you going to do with this?"

"This is merely a courtesy call, Laura. I'm going to bring the file to light so I can get Andy out of prison. It's been ten years, you see, and he has two boys who are growing up too quickly without him. He needs to be home as soon as possible."

"Who gave this to you?"

Regan tensed. "I told you, a friend in the FBI."

"That's not possible."

"Oh?"

She didn't think Provost was about to say the FBI couldn't have had the files — because they'd been stolen by a gang of masked men several days ago.

"What if... if... I took up the case?"

Regan turned around. The woman was leaning over her desk, practically standing on tiptoe.

"I don't know," Regan said. "Would that help Andy get out any sooner than taking it to the media?"

Provost snarled. "You know it would."

"Then that might be beneficial — all around. I have one hesitation, though."

"What?"

"According to my friend, there were other cases in which Marando looked to be involved — fourteen of them at least, he said."

Provost's face shuddered. Her teeth were bared now.

"I would expect a similar level of cooperation from you, and all the other, hmmm, let's call them *surviving* personnel involved with those cases," Regan said. "The FBI itself might only be interested in certain aspects of those cases, but my friend and I have broader interests of justice on our parts."

Provost's face seemed frozen in an agony of hate and fear.

"I... don't know...who I'm working for," Provost said. "But they will find you."

Regan brushed her hair back from her face. She'd deliberately worn it down today and left the makeup off her cheek. Provost blinked at the swollen bruise.

"Go on, go running to the bad guys and tell them you've been found out," Regan said. "I'm sure that will go well for you. Just like Marando."

***

A few minutes later, it was over.

She leaned against the carpeted elevator wall, headed back to the parking garage. The smell of perfume mingled with the stink of fear was still in her nostrils.

It hadn't been much of a lie — Alex worked *with* the FBI but wasn't an agent. And it had been Jake who had found the file, not Alex.

But it had come out of her mouth as smoothly as if it had been the truth.

Everything had gone by so quickly.

But it would be over soon.

And then they would all be safe.

Chapter 45 - Abandoned

Admittedly, Jake knew the theory of disguise better than he knew the practicalities. What he had done to his hair and face wouldn't have fooled someone in the theater. A professional makeup artist would have raised one eyebrow and given a little snort at the transparency of his disguise, but most people wouldn't look twice.

There was a reason he wore the same clothes most of the time: bomber jacket, jeans, hiking boots, and a baseball cap. Most people recognized him more by his outfit than by his actual features.

For example, today he probably could have walked right past Regan, and she wouldn't have recognized him. He was wearing a suit.

He'd also brushed some dark hair color into his hair and parted it differently, abandoned the cap, and changed into some dress shoes that he didn't like and would give him blisters after more than three or four hours on his feet. A titanium watch, a pair of sunglasses, and a briefcase completed the outfit.

He was a new man.

He knocked on the door of the Ligotti residence, a small white clapboard house in Bensonhurst with cement for a yard.

An old woman opened the door, tiny and Italian. She was wearing an apron and brought a waft of garlic and tomatoes with her that flooded Jake's mouth, nearly causing him to drool.

"Yeah?"

He swallowed quickly. "Ma'am, do you have a minute? I've come to ask some questions about your granddaughter, Angela Ligotti."

"Angie," the old woman said, shaking her head. "I knew that girl was going to be trouble from the day she was born. I told Mike and Tina, you better use the whip on that girl, or she's going to wind up pregnant or dead or both. Let me see some ID."

Jake blinked then took out his private investigator's license and showed it to her.

She gave him a look, switching back and forth from the ID. "You're not dressed like a private investigator. You're dressed like you're a government man — FBI or something, I don't know."

He grinned at her and leaned forward. His disguise was so good it couldn't even hold up for an old Italian grandmother. "I'm in disguise, ma'am."

She grunted and handed the ID back. "Then you better come in." She pushed open the screen door. Jake stamped his shoes on the rug in front of the door but didn't take them off.

She led him to a tiny living room with two recliners and a small couch. The walls looked like they'd been plastered with thick, minty fresh toothpaste. However, the air smelled like someone had quit smoking recently, but not so recently the shag rug had given up the butt ghost yet.

He handed her his card, the one that matched the detective license. He didn't want to have to complicate things. Plus, the number went straight to Alex.

"Angie," the old woman said, waving toward a cluster of photographs on the wall behind the entryway, "my granddaughter."

Pictures of Angela Ligotti in a cap and gown, in a prom dress, as a little kid, wearing a yellow dinosaur pool float, hair in pigtails — about a dozen photos in all. She was a cute kid.

"My name is Olympia," the old woman said, "Ollie for short." She sat on one corner of the couch next to an end table with a stained cork coaster that sat exactly at the end of her arm. A basket of knitting sat under the end table.

"Mr. Dovolis —" The name from the investigator's license had been changed, more to protect the old woman than anything else. "— I have wondered for years whether her murderer had been brought to justice. You'll be working for Mr. Gibbons, won't you?"

He opened his mouth and closed it.

She nodded and pushed herself backward on the couch until her feet dangled off the floor. "I thought so. Nevertheless, it's a good thing you're doing, even if it isn't for my granddaughter. Ask your questions."

Jake cleared his throat. "Ah...can you tell me whether your granddaughter Angela was having an affair with Mr. Gibbons?"

"Can't," the old woman said. "I didn't keep track of her every waking hour. All I can say is that he wasn't the guy she was going around with at nights. Tina won't let me leave out the pictures of the two of them where they're together. But I have a photo album with him in it."

"Him?"

But Ollie had already hopped off the couch and headed for a shelf full of books beside the fireplace. She pulled off a photo album and handed it to him. "Sit. Either chair's fine. They won't be home for hours. Just don't lean your head back — wouldn't want to get hair dye everywhere."

She must think he was a complete clown. He'd come during the day, specifically because he'd thought the old woman would be the member of the family most likely to be deceived by his disguise.

At least she was the one most likely to give him information.

He sat in one of the two recliners, the one nearest him. It felt old and over-used. One of his hips sank lower than the other, and something poked him. He kept his head off the back of the seat.

Ollie grabbed the edge of the photo album and pulled it open at the three-quarters mark. "There."

Angela Ligotti stood next to a large black man in a red leather jacket. It looked like they were in a bar together, the kind of place with dark wood booths and plastic seats. They were both drinking out of beer bottles — neither one of them looking at the camera.

The other pictures on the page had more pictures of Angela, big hair, olive skin, earrings that draped past her shoulders. She had a love of '80s fashion and no sense whatsoever. In about half the photographs, she was completely bombed out of her mind, pupils dilated. In one picture he even spotted a trace of white powder next to her nose.

The big black guy showed up in several pictures, always looking away from the camera, as if the only way to get his photograph was to wait until he wasn't looking.

"Who is he?" Jake asked.

"Nobody knows," Ollie said.

"He's in your photo album," Jake pointed out.

She thumped one heel against the base of the couch. "Nobody looks in this photo album but me. I asked around for any pictures of her when she died. I wanted them for the funeral. People sent me everything they had, which means that a few people sent more than they realized. She never brought him home to meet anybody. She just ran around with him."

Jake skimmed through the pictures again.

From behind, it might be conceivable that Andrew Gibbons was the man she was standing with. But there was something about the man that Jake thought didn't match up.

"Can I take some pictures of these?" he asked. "I'll leave the originals — just some pictures with my phone."

"Sure," Ollie said. "What harm is it gonna do?"

Jake took snapshots on his phone, one picture at a time.

"The first time I saw Andrew Gibbons' picture on the news, I thought, '*Good*'. Then when I saw the pictures I was getting back from her friends, I thought, *that must be the right guy*. Big and black, you know? But things didn't add up in the trial. The red jacket they showed as evidence wasn't the same one he was wearing in the photos. The shape of his head is wrong. You can't see his face in any of the pictures. So, I told myself that I wasn't sure. But I was sure. Whoever that man was, it wasn't Andrew Gibbons."

"You're sure you don't have any pictures of his face?"

She shrugged. "What you see is what you get."

"It's more than I was expecting," Jake admitted. "I'm sorry. I have to ask. Was your granddaughter using drugs?"

"You think?" Ollie asked. Her face had twisted up. Ten years later, and it still got to her. His heart went out toward her. "She was an addict. She stole things from the house. You couldn't leave cash in your purse. All the time when she was younger she was always stealing things, shoplifting. It just got worse and worse. About the only place she didn't steal from was work."

"Strange," Jake said.

"That place — most of her friends worked there. They would go to parties together."

"All right, I have another painful question. Why do you think your granddaughter was killed?"

"She messed up big time," Ollie said promptly. "Right before she died, she was talking like she was about to come into some money. She talked about moving out of her apartment in Greenpoint, not a nice place I might add, and getting a place of her own in East Williamsburg. Then she was dead. I can only think she was killed for screwing something up."

It sounded like what he and Regan had been thinking.

Ollie said, "I just keep thinking she was supposed to move some drugs around but stole them instead. She liked to live like she was in a movie."

***

The car sat across from the Ligotti house under the shade of a dead tree, half parked on a ridge of snow in front of a fire hydrant.

He hadn't been ticketed; it must be his lucky day.

Jake pulled off his suit jacket and tie and tossed them in the back seat. He slid his bomber jacket on and shivered. The lining was cold against the dress shirt. He put his hat back on and slouched a little, relaxing. Wearing a suit made him feel like a member of the Secret Service, standing stiff and tall and wearing an earpiece with a curled wire leading into his jacket.

If he'd been thinking, he would have brought his hiking boots with him — the dress shoes were already killing his feet.

He dialed Alex. "I have some pictures on my phone's drive. I need you to upload and delete them."

"Hey. What's up?"

"We have a possible suspect. The guy looks just like Andrew Gibbons from behind. He habitually wore a red leather jacket, and Ligotti was doing a lot of drugs. Even the grandmother saw it. The guy might be someone she was having an affair with or might be her dealer."

"Hmmm," Alex said.

"I didn't get his face," Jake admitted. "He's either turned away from the camera or holding up his hand in front of the lens. We need to see if there's any other way to identify this guy, any clues in the rest of the photographs."

"I see," Alex said. "Well, keep me updated. I wouldn't want your girlfriend to feel like her friends have abandoned her."

Jake frowned.

"Got it," he said.

"Let her know I'll be thinking of her," Alex added. "Fingers crossed."

"Sure," Jake said.

Alex hung up.

They'd set up a danger word — *Abandoned*.

Alex had been careful not to say Jake's name — or Regan's.

What made it worse was Alex sounding like he was saying goodbye.

Chapter 46 - Staying calm

The murmuring in the courtroom felt like a needle running from the back of her eye deep into her skull. The faces of the people in the audience seemed to leer at her like demented clowns. Her skin hurt from twitching so much.

Her first day back on the Tarloff case and she was having serious thoughts about whether she should have come back or not. During her weekend with Jake, it had been easy to ignore the remaining hurt and soreness, but not back in the courtroom sitting for hours on end. She was reminded of every bump, bruise, and sore muscle a thousand times over, and had to admit she wasn't giving the case her full attention.

Murder cases took time. Fortunately, this case didn't look like it was going to take much of it, relatively speaking. The defendants, who had insisted upon their innocence, were rapidly getting an education in how quickly an alibi could be ripped apart, especially when backed up by good DNA and witness evidence. The defense attorney looked like he wanted to slap his clients. The main question now wasn't whether the defendants were guilty, but whether premeditation could be established.

Finally, it was time for a break.

Regan rose; the rest of the court rose with her. She proceeded out of the room and to her chambers. The courtroom buzzed with chatter as she left the room.

After loading herself up with a significant number of painkillers that she hoped wouldn't be too many, she fished around in her coat pocket for her phone.

She still hadn't replaced the broken screen. Instead, she had put a plastic screen guard over it, so she didn't scratch her face.

There just wasn't enough time.

The usual messages were waiting for her. Everyone who was anyone had called her, in case she was thinking about handing out exclusives.

Even more than the case, everyone wanted to know about the bruises on her face — or, if they were on the ball, about the lunatic who had tried to bomb her house.

She deleted the messages one by one, only listening to each one long enough to make sure it wasn't important.

What she should have done was leave the phone with Gary and have him go through the messages as they came in. But he had enough to deal with. She was making him assemble dossiers on everyone involved in the Tarloff case.

They were dealing with an organization with resources so deeply related that there were no apparent connections between them.

Regan intended to start tracking down the non-apparent connections.

She put her cell phone back in her jacket pocket.

Out of habit, she pulled out the secure phone from her locked briefcase, the hard sided leather one her father had given her when she graduated from law school.

She flipped open the phone.

She had a message, a blank one, from just over an hour ago.

Jake and Alex knew she was in court today. They wouldn't have called unless it was an emergency. Nothing should have happened. They were waiting for Provost to push Andy's exoneration through the system — that was all.

She couldn't check the email account from here; it was too risky. She didn't know enough about what she was doing. She also couldn't stand to wait.

She dialed Jake's secure phone.

No answer. He must be busy somewhere.

She stared at the row of photos of judges on the wall. Her father stared back at her.

She hung up with a sick feeling in her throat and called Alex.

"Regan..." His voice sounded like a croak.

"What is it?"

"Jake's been kidnapped."

She stopped breathing. She'd told him he was exposing himself too much, taking too many risks.

"Kidnapped?" she said.

"They left you a message. Are you ready for it?"

"Do I need to write anything down?"

"No. But I would be sitting if I were you."

She pulled a chair away from the table and sat down. She felt like passing out. "Go."

"'If you want to see Mr. Westley alive again, you will find a way for the Tarloffs to go free.'"

"What?"

"'If you...'"

"I heard you. I just can't — Jake?"

"Yes, he's been kidnapped. They called just over an hour ago. I ran a check on Jake's car; I have a tracking device on it. It hasn't moved since the last time Jake was in it, which was at the Ligotti residence. The last time I talked to him was right after he left the house. He sent several photographs that Ms. Olympia Ligotti let him take from her photo album. The photographs were of a black man that vaguely fit Andrew Gibbons' description, but didn't show his face."

Alex stopped talking as if he'd just realized she wasn't responding.

Regan couldn't force herself to respond. She had to remind herself to keep breathing.

Why was he at the Ligotti house? Because he's still searching for the murderer. Oh, God. Of course he was.

"He habitually wore a red jacket. Regan, are you still there?"

She felt dizzy. "I'm here."

"I'm going through the photographs, trying to see what I can find out about the guy in the red jacket. Can you stall things from your end? How long do you think it's going to take to wrap up the case?"

"I'm not sure. The prosecution's case is almost over. They're being extraordinarily thorough, and so is the defense. But it looks like the defense attorney is about to lose his mind. He may not have much. It could be over soon."

"And — forgive me — *could* you do what they're asking at this point?"

"I could try to find an excuse to declare a mistrial."

"Wouldn't that just be a delaying tactic?"

"It depends, but yes, usually."

"Hmm," Alex said. "If they contact you, what are you going to tell them?"

"I'm going to tell them that I need more time. Isn't there any way you can find him?"

"I'm tracking his phones, but they look like a bust — literally. They're both in a large trash container in an alley next to Angela Ligotti's parents' house."

"Oh, God," Regan said.

"I'm sending someone over there to check on an 'important document' that may have been thrown away. She'll call back if she finds anything…uh…bigger."

"If anything happens to him, I'm going to shoot myself," Regan murmured, more to herself than anyone else.

"Sorry?"

"I'm just reminded that it's hell playing chess with real people."

"Is it? I wouldn't know. I'm a checkers' man. You never know when someone off the board is going to come back, more powerful than before."

"That's nice," Regan said. "But it doesn't work like that in real life. Dead is dead."

"True."

"What are we going to do?" Regan asked.

"I don't know. Uh... try to...uh...stay calm?"

She said goodbye to Alex and hung up. Then she spent the rest of the break sitting at the table, staring at the silent phone and shaking.

Staying calm was good advice. But staying calm wasn't going to be enough.

Chapter 47 - Keep my little girl safe

Regan sat at the dinette table in her father's kitchen with her hands wrapped around a cup of coffee and her teeth chattering. She kept the mug in front of her face and her eyes on the top of the table. The polished wood table was so clean the only fingerprints she could see were the ones she'd put there herself when she'd lowered herself onto her seat. She felt like she was coming down with the flu.

She stuck her tongue between her teeth to keep them from making noise.

Her father stood over her for a moment, then set his coffee mug on a cork coaster on the dinette table. He sat across from her, still dressed in his robe, pajamas, and slippers, even though it was six in the evening.

"You hungry?" he asked.

She shook her head.

"Good." He drank about half of his coffee with a series of loud long gulps. It was piping hot. "Tell me."

"They've kidnapped Jake."

He grunted. "I didn't have anything to do with it if that's what you're wondering."

She raised her eyes to his. He was looking at the table with his coffee cup in front of his mouth. His hand trembled. Fortunately, he'd just drunk half the liquid out of the cup, so it didn't spill.

His skin was thin and papery across the backs of his hands. She could see hazy brown spots on them — the beginning of liver spots maybe. His forearms weren't sticks, but they were thinner than they should have been. His neck had wattles. He was getting old.

Her eyes filled up with tears. "Oh, Daddy, I didn't think you did."

"You've blamed me for a lot of things."

"That's because you did them."

He put his coffee mug down in front of him, completely missing the coaster. "We need to talk this out. Get this out of the way."

"It's not important," Regan said.

"If something gets in the way every time one of us opens our damn mouths, it's important. We can take five minutes and put this to bed so it doesn't get in the way of saving Jake."

It made sense, even though she didn't want it to.

"All right..."

"When you were young, I was ambitious. I didn't just want to be a judge. I wanted to go all the way to the top, to the Supreme Court. I was an arrogant son of a bitch."

He grimaced.

"Your mother always told me that I was too arrogant. She was right. Not that I wanted to listen to her. She would say things that hurt my pride. She told me that I was making the wrong people angry. What hot blooded young male wants to hear that kind of thing from his wife? Making the wrong people angry — wasn't that what I was supposed to be doing?"

A few months ago, she would have agreed with him.

Now she wasn't so sure.

"Then I was handed a lesson. Your mother was involved in a bus wreck, along with about thirty other people. She busted open her head right here —" He ran a wrinkled, gnarled finger along an eyebrow. "— and broke her left arm. If she hadn't left you with a neighbor that day, you would have been with her and possibly injured as well.

"It scared the crap out of me. I told her to stay home after that, and she laughed at me. She asked me who was going to do the shopping and run the errands while I was out saving the world. She got her arm in a cast and completely ignored me.

"I was steamed at her. You can imagine.

"Then I got a letter — no return address on it. It had been hand delivered to our mailbox. It was one of those letters that had been cut out of newspapers and pasted together.

"It said, 'If you want to keep your wife out of bus accidents, get out of town.'"

Her father stopped to wet his throat with the coffee.

"The accident had been in the papers. The threatening letter included a picture of the bus that had been clipped out of one of the papers. But more to the point, it also included a print of my wife on the bus, before her arm was broken. I recognized the dress she was wearing. They had been watching her."

"So you left," Regan said, "and you lied to everyone about the reason why."

"No, that was only the beginning of it," her father said. "There were other threats. They didn't directly attack your mother again. Instead, they threatened attorneys, clerks, defendants, even my secretary.

"I held up until they threatened to hurt you, and then the heart went out of me. I never found out who they were, or why they were so insistent on having me out of the way. I was too beaten down."

"You lied," Regan said. "And even after I was all grown up and Mom died, you didn't tell me the truth. And you went behind my back to have me watched in order to 'protect' me."

She felt numb. She wasn't sure what she felt anymore.

But if they were going to talk things out — and not just have her father tell her his side of the story — then they needed to be said.

"I did," he said. "I didn't think you could handle it."

"Really?"

He cleared his throat. "I'm a proud man. I didn't think I could handle it if you found out...you'd be all over me like white on rice. And I was right."

"That doesn't mean..."

"You have a lot of your mother in you," he said. "I try to tell myself that you look, and act like a softened up version of me, but that's not the whole truth. Your mother would have said the same thing, more politely, of course."

She gritted her teeth. "I'm too much like you to be polite about having someone lie to me."

He leaned forward and put his hand on the back of her head, drawing her forward across the table until their foreheads touched. "I know. Regan, I should have told you. I should have warned you. I was too proud. Even now I don't like to have old trouble raked up and dragged out in the open. I'm at peace with my skeletons, thank you very much."

He let go of her, and she sat back in her chair. A little of her coffee had spilled on the table. She looked around for a napkin but made do with a kitchen sponge on the back of the sink. It left behind a wet streak.

"You still my girl?" her father asked.

She tossed the sponge in the sink. He clucked his tongue, got up, and put the sponge back in its original position.

She sighed. "Yes Daddy, I am."

"Good. And just so you know, I don't want to hear about this ever again."

He hugged her.

And then she was hungry.

After she'd made bacon, eggs, and toast with strawberry jam, her father complaining about the cholesterol even as he lifted almost half a pound of bacon onto his plate, they talked about Jake.

"He knows what he's doing," her father said.

"You can't seriously think I can ignore the threat to him," Regan said.

"Are you sleeping with him?"

"That's none of your business."

But her face felt hot.

"If you aren't, you should and get it over with." Her father snorted.

"Daddy!"

He chuckled into his coffee. He was just yanking her chain.

She straightened her back, wiped her mouth with her napkin, and said, "I like him, Daddy, very much."

"Does he know that?"

"I certainly hope so."

Her father held up his hands and looked toward the ceiling. "Someone has to go first. You're a modern independent woman. It should be you."

She gritted her teeth again. "This isn't helping."

He grinned at her. "We're clearing the air again."

"No, you're pushing my buttons to make me mad, which, by the way, doesn't clear out anything — and it doesn't help me find Jake."

"Didn't you hear me? He can take care of himself."

"So what do I do, just leave him there?"

"Unless you plan to wreck the Tarloff case; yes."

She stopped. The thought of acting to alter the outcome of the case was repugnant. Her stomach had actually lurched.

Her father ticked off on his fingers. "You can't find him on your own. Alex says he can't find him. You're not going to wreck the case, no matter what they threaten. I can see you delaying it if you have to, but justice will be done to the best extent possible."

"Okay."

"You've had the money you needed to quit for years, and you haven't. You're not going to quit now."

"What if I do?"

He lowered his hand. "I've known you since you were old enough to trade cleaning out the cat litter for dollar bills. Your mother could tell you to do it, and you'd just do it. With me, you always made me give you a dollar. But that was because I charged you a dollar every time you didn't get an A on your homework. No matter how much I threatened you, you wouldn't clean a damned thing unless I gave you a dollar first. I know you. Bribery might work — *if* you saw a reason for doing the thing anyway. But threaten you? Your heels dig down to China."

"I wish I could feel that confident about myself."

"Look at it this way," her father said. "At least he's not your child — or your husband. You're in as good a position to resist these people as you ever will be."

"So I should do nothing?"

"I didn't say that. Tell me, do you trust this Alex character?"

Regan blinked and leaned back in her chair, her palms pushing her back from the table hard enough to make the chair rock briefly back on its legs.

"Of course I trust Alex, and so do you. Otherwise, you wouldn't have given him a second chance."

"So he told you."

"So did Jake."

The old man waved his hand. "Never mind that now. Jake said someone was giving away secrets in your group. He thought it was Gary, but he wasn't sure."

"But..." She shook her head. Now was not the time to wonder how her father knew Jake's suspicions or argue with her father about how wrong he must be. "If Alex is the traitor, then we're done — Kaput. He works with the FBI. If he wanted to, he could have me in jail in a heartbeat, the same way he set up Marando for child porn and selling police dossiers as a threat, just in case.

"He *can't* be the traitor. He wouldn't need to kidnap Jake to get what he wants. All he'd have to do is call the FBI."

"Jake doesn't even have to be kidnapped," her father said. "Regan, don't think like a normal person. Think like a chess player. Alex blocks Jake's phone calls and tells you that Jake's been kidnapped. He tells Jake there's a problem with the line, and they need to switch phones. He asks Jake to lie low for a few days."

"Then I wreck the case," Regan said, "Jake comes back, and because we're not complete idiots, all of this comes out. And, Alex is no further ahead than he would be if he just...gave the information to the press."

"Wrong," her father said. "By the time you and Jake would have talked to each other, you would already have compromised your integrity. And, you would be a thousand times easier to control. That's what these people want: Control."

"They told *you* to leave Brooklyn," Regan pointed out. "That's if we assume it's the same people. It might not have been the same group, and maybe they think they have a better chance of turning me than they did you."

"The same people," her father murmured.

"What?"

"I never knew who was threatening me," her father said. "Not for sure. But sometimes I had a suspicion that the notes came from someone I knew."

"Who?"

He shook his head. "I don't want to accuse where I don't have proof. And if he *did* do it, I wouldn't want to warn him by having you confront him over it."

It was someone she knew.

"But *Alex*," Regan said. "What kind of proof do you have there?"

"No proof, just opportunity. What about Gary?"

He was going to give her a migraine. "What about Gary?"

"Could he have done it? Guessed where Jake would investigate next, and then waited for him — abducted him?"

"Either Jake was abducted, or he wasn't. Make up your mind." She raised a hand. "No, no, I see what you're saying. Gary has all the case notes. He could narrow down the next steps and take his chances with which witness Jake would handle first. He finds Jake at the Ligotti residence, waits until he comes out, and then, knocks Jake out with sleeping gas or threatens to hurt me or something. I don't know.

"Gary calls the threat into Alex using Jake's phone before taking Jake to an undisclosed location."

She closed her eyes. If only the whole world would go away.

"What if it's Jane? Or Jamie Gibbons? Or me?"

"Oh, Daddy," she said. "Please stop. I can't take any more."

"You can't trust anyone," he said. "Not even your own pieces. Once corruption gets on the board, it's like playing someone who is constantly cheating. You know it's going on, but you don't necessarily know when, where, or by whom. Turn your back, and the whole board could be changed." He paused. "It gets to you, after a while. You have to be sure you're ready for this."

"I'm not," she said. "But I have to deal with it anyway."

"True," her father said. "All I ask is that you keep my little girl safe."

Chapter 48 - The sound of a lock

Jake dropped the secure phone into his lap; his mind was racing. *Abandoned* — it meant Alex was in trouble. He had made some mistakes in his life, but this one took the cake.

The first thing to do was get back to Brooklyn and the cyber cafe, and find out what had happened to Alex. It might be FBI agents checking up on suspicious activity.

FBI agents would be a relief compared to what Jake was imagining just then. He should never have dragged the kid into this.

He put the key in the ignition and started to turn it just as a shadow fell across the windshield. He looked up.

The car was surrounded by four guys in suits and dark glasses, the same kind of outfit he'd been wearing a couple of minutes ago.

At least he knew for certain now that his disguise had been effective. Looking up at them — and the muzzles of the handguns they pointed at him — was definitely intimidating.

The muzzle of the gun nearest to him tapped on the glass twice.

Jake could take a hint when it was pressed up against his window like that.

He put his hands up.

His door was pulled open. The other doors were still automatically locked from him having just driven.

"Get out of the car," the one nearest to him said.

Jake slid out of the car, not using his hands. It wasn't the first time he'd done that, and it was always harder than it looked.

He stood up. The man behind him shoved Jake's hands onto his head, then patted him down.

Meanwhile, the guy in front of him opened a badge case with a silver medallion on it. He might have been with the cops, the FBI, anybody — or nobody at all.

The guy behind Jake relieved him of his revolver, as well as a knife he kept strapped to his calf, and the small multi-tool that he kept in his pocket. That was annoying.

All three went into a plastic baggie. The guy doing the patting down had put on latex gloves somewhere in the process. He handed the bag over to one of the other men before he stripped off the gloves.

The question was whether to go with these guys or not.

If he was a civilian, say if he were Ollie in the house across the street, he would have advised her to start screaming her head off and make a break for it. She wouldn't escape, but at least she'd call attention to herself.

He wasn't, strictly speaking, a civilian.

He'd been working his ass off to convince these jokers he was one.

And now his bet was paying off.

But, because he didn't want to make it look *too* easy, he tackled the guy in front of him. He slammed him in the stomach, lifted him up, and knocked him onto the hood of the Corolla.

The guy slid backward and off the other side of the hood, onto the sidewalk. His gun went flying.

The guy behind Jake said, "Don't move."

Jake must have been hard of hearing. He ducked under the second guy's gun.

This time, he didn't have a handy car roof to shove him onto. The Corolla's trunk was a narrow strip. You could fit a body inside — but only if it wasn't a six-foot-tall, 300-pound man.

Jake and the second suit bounced off the back of the Corolla. The guy fell backward onto the sedan behind it, which promptly started shrieking.

Car alarms — wonderful inventions.

The guy groaned and rolled off the hood, landing in a pile of half melted snow beside the sedan's tires.

Jake rode the guy down to the ground to make sure the wind was knocked out of him.

A split second was all it took to judge his move successful.

He twisted the gun out of the guy's grasp and whirled around.

The other three men were pointing their revolvers at him. The first one had retrieved his gun and was standing up again. Too bad, Jake had been hoping to get a black eye out of this, at least.

"Drop the gun," the first guy shouted over the car alarm.

"Make me," Jake said.

The first guy nodded toward his friend by the rear passenger door, the shortest of the four. Shorty sidestepped through the crunchy snow toward Jake, still covering him with outstretched locked arms.

Jake waited. What he wanted to do was disarm the guy and use him as a bullet shield. A split second was all he needed.

He forcibly restrained his instincts.

He'd been working for days, if not weeks, to make this happen.

The alarm was still going off, deafeningly loud.

The curtains twitched across the street at the Ligotti house, and he knew Ollie would be watching all this. Yes, she would.

The muzzle of Shorty's gun reached Jake's. Shorty glanced toward Number One, whose eyes widened as he jerked his head toward Jake.

Shorty lowered his arms, put his gun in his pocket, and reached out to take Jake's revolver.

He hated to let the bozo touch it.

So he allowed himself one last moment of struggle. He swung the muzzle across Shorty's face and felt the satisfying crunch of cartilage.

Shorty clapped both hands across his face, but it was all right. Jake had made sure not to hit bone.

Not that these bastards deserved the consideration. But he didn't want them out for too much revenge.

Not before he found out who had sent them.

The guy who'd set the car alarm off kicked his legs over Jake's. He went over, rolled, and slipped on a patch of ice as he came up.

A hand grabbed the back of his neck and swung him, face first, into his own car. His face hit the side of the car, making the world turn dizzy and bright for a second. Then he was dragged to his feet, leaned against the car, and worked over by a pair of fists more enthusiastic than skilled. A couple of punches to the gut, and then the guy started working over Jake's face.

He felt his nose go. Oh well, he probably had it coming.

Hot blood sprayed over his clothes.

The guy hitting him didn't really have a taste for it. He took one more punch to the temple and was shoved into the back seat of his car with a guy on either side of him. The three of them were like the Three Stooges bleeding on upholstery.

Jake leaned against the shoulder of the guy on the passenger side.

It was a good thing he wasn't too attached to his car. It was going to be hell getting all that blood out.

He closed his eyes. Hopefully, they'd think he passed out.

***

Jake kept his eyes to thin slits that let him absorb where the car was going without making it look like he was watching. If anyone had pulled his eyelids up, all they would have spotted was the whites. Jake had the trick of rolling his eyes back up into his head on command.

Unfortunately, they were either on to him or more cautious that he'd hoped, and a fleece jacket was draped over his face and chest after a few blocks. He was reduced to trying to listen for clues — but he was no Sherlock Holmes, able to determine what part of the city he was in based on the sound of the road underneath the Corolla's tires.

They drove for over an hour — maybe an hour and a half.

When they pulled to a stop, he let himself stay limp as the others pulled him out of the car. He couldn't completely pass for being unconscious, but he was hoping they'd think he was at least stunned.

The dried blood under his nose itched. It was hell trying not to pay attention. If he'd even thought about it too hard, he might have flinched.

They dragged him up six stairs that felt too smooth around the edges to be cement, but were too solid to be wood.

A heavy silent door was opened for them, and Jake was dragged inside someplace dark that was almost as cool as the outside air.

His skin prickled. Other people were nearby.

His dress shoes dragged over a bare floor, then a rug, then back onto the floor with barely a thump. Another door was opened, this time a narrower one. The two men holding him under the arms turned sideways to go through, then down some stairs.

Once again, Jake was left completely mystified as to where he was.

On the other hand, it wasn't like he had anything better to do.

There were 22 or 23 stairs. As usual, when he was forced to count higher than the number of his fingers and toes, he lost count.

The air got colder — but not much.

From the bottom of the steps, he was dragged down a short hallway, then into a room. He could tell it was a room because the jacket fell off his face as they tossed him onto a bed.

He bounced, fought the instinct to roll off the bed and leap for an attack, and heard the door closing near his feet.

Then he heard the sound of a chain followed by the click of a lock.

Chapter 49 - Almost family

Pavo's room at the top of the tower overlooked the city. It rose above the petty squabbles that drove the humanity below him. But it also felt exposed.

He stood at the window. His secretary had been sent away, and other than the guards at the elevator door and the trees next to the window, he was the only living soul in the penthouse.

The traffic moved in jerks along the streets below him. At night, the rivers of lights would seem like the pulse of a slow moving heart of an enormous beast.

The city was always a split second away from collapsing on itself, turning into its own cancer.

He didn't have to like what he did.

He only had to be a surgeon performing triage on his patient.

Regarding his latest cancer, he said, "They haven't given up. They've only gone underground."

He knew he couldn't have tracked the computer hacker's byzantine nest of connections and deceptions in time to do any good. So instead he had watched the detective and the judge going through a romance, at the same time plotting against him, to undo his good works — again.

Andrew Gibbons was a thug and a criminal, a man who neglected his family in favor of insignificant thrills while delivering drugs.

He was disposable — as had been the thief Ligotti.

If the Organization was to eliminate the drug trade, it first needed to control the drug trade.

There was a demand. If the Organization did not control the supply, then someone else would.

Sacrifices had to be made. Justice sometimes had to be delayed, misdirected. Pavo had ensured those who received the brunt of the punishment were, at least, in some sense guilty.

He tried to shift the harshest burdens on those who had lost whatever value they had to the world.

Other members of the Organization were not so particular. All in all, they were lucky to fall under his jurisdiction.

The detective had run brashly into the light, attacking Marando with his little band of thugs, then harassing De Wit, and finally intruding into the lives of the Ligotti's, to stir up painful memories of a worthless daughter, memories that had settled years ago.

It was a challenge intended to draw out the Organization.

The man blundered about like a mad elephant — which meant he wasn't blundering at all.

Pavo's fingernails were short and blunt out of habits formed in days long past, and now they dug into his palms.

The endgame was forming.

It would happen quickly, sweeping pieces off the board in a cascade. He would try to save the healthy cells — but the cancerous ones *must* be removed.

First, he would take the hacker, then the detective, then the queen — and finally, checkmate.

There was nothing worse than a betrayal — and this one was almost family.

Chapter 50 - If he didn't answer

The prosecution's last witness left the witness stand after cross examination by the defense lawyer.

The prosecutor, a woman named Robyn Nealy, got up and said. "Your Honor, the State rests."

It was time for the defense to present their side of the story. The defense attorney, Nick Sikes, looked green around the gills. He was sticking through to the bitter end — but it was clear he thought nothing of his clients' chances of success. The suggestion the mother had framed the two siblings had fallen through.

He stood up to call his first witness, his gray suit looking slightly disheveled as if one sleeve had been cut shorter than the other. He had light brown hair with a little bit of a curl to it, and a gentle forgiving smile — one that concealed an apt legal mind most of the time, but today seemed like a premature apology for fainting in the courtroom.

He paused and looked at Regan with a sick question in his eyes.

She kept her face blank and stared him down. If he was in communication with whoever had or was concealing Jake, she would gut him.

He cleared his throat and said, "The defense would like to call Edna Connor."

The guard escorted an old woman in a flowered print dress with a wide collar into the room. It didn't look warm enough to be wearing in the middle of the winter, and Regan wanted to wrap her in a blanket.

Edna leaned on the guard's arm and looked brightly around at the audience, the prosecution, the jury, everyone but Regan, who was probably too far away for the woman to see clearly.

The bailiff swore her in, and she was gently seated in the witness box.

The defense attorney walked over to her and began questioning her. Regan kept half an ear on the proceedings, just to make sure Nick wasn't leading the witness. But he was keeping things clean.

The old woman was a next door neighbor of the Tarloff sisters. On the night of the double murders, she hadn't heard a thing all night from the sisters. In fact, the older of the two sisters, Frances, was supposed to have been out of the house that night. She had gone out to visit an old school friend, leaving the younger of the two sisters (by 20 minutes), Mildred, home by herself. She had thought it was odd when the night nurse had come to check on Mildred and found both of them dead in their beds. Of course, she, Edna, would have known if Frances had come home early.

She had, she affirmed, seen Frances leave earlier that morning. Her front window faced theirs, didn't it?

The courtroom exploded with noise.

This was a big surprise to the prosecution.

Regan couldn't believe that the police hadn't questioned the woman already.

If they were repressing evidence, they were doing a damned poor job of it.

The prosecutor, Robin Nealy, gave Regan a look. Regan knew what Nealy was thinking: *Aren't you going to say something?*

Regan raised an eyebrow and tilted her head toward the witness box. She wanted to hear what Sikes got out of the witness first. Nealy shrugged.

Nick Sikes wrapped up his questioning of the witness, asking no more or less than he needed in order to drive the implication home: his clients might have broken *into* the Tarloff home, but their crimes might not have been as extensive as the prosecution had painted them.

The two old women might have already been dead when they got there.

The jury seemed to be all ears.

Nealy started her cross examination, "Your original testimony to the police was different than what you have stated here in court. Allow me to remind you what your statement, which you signed, says ..."

She read out the statement. It said nothing more than the old woman hadn't heard anything the night of the murder.

Edna said, "Yes, I said that."

"Explain why your statement has changed."

"The police didn't ask me. Mr. Sikes asked me. He said, 'Tell me Edna, was there anything that you were surprised not to hear or see that night?' And I thought about it, and I told him that I was surprised not to hear Frances come in, the way she was found dead in the house and all."

Nealy's jaw clenched visibly.

"And yet you said earlier you saw Mildred leaving the house. Is that correct?"

"Well, I had to run to the toilet about then. I saw the car drive away, though."

"What car?"

"The car belonging to Mildred's school friend's son. He's a tall boy with dark hair. I don't know his name, though."

Nealy looked over at Regan, looking incredulous. *Can you believe this?*

Regan left her face blank again. She hadn't heard anything that had crossed, or even come close to crossing the line.

Nealy said, "Would the Court entertain a request for a brief recess?"

Regan checked the clock, then tapped the gavel on the sound block. "The Court is recessed until 2:00 p.m."

"Thank you," Nealy said.

Nick Sikes strangely didn't look happy or relieved, but his clients did. The attorney himself merely looked numb.

"Counsels for the defense and prosecution meet me in my chambers in ten minutes," Regan said.

"All rise," the bailiff said. She swept toward the door of her chambers, crossed the threshold, and then doubled back on a hunch, looking out over the courtroom.

The bailiff noticed her, but she shook her head and gave him a little wave. She wasn't coming back in. He nodded.

Sikes and his clients had seated themselves again.

He closed the folder in front of him and stared at it for a few seconds, then stood up. The two defendants were chatting to each other at the table, looking utterly unconcerned.

In contrast, the skin on Sikes's face drooped as if he'd aged ten years in the last day. He stumbled against his chair, almost tripping over it.

Then he took two steps toward the aisle and swayed on his feet, grabbing the bar to keep from falling over.

He left the folder, the briefcase, and his jacket behind.

His pants pockets were slim and flat enough that she could tell he didn't have a wallet or phone on him as he made his way down the aisle toward the back door.

Sikes walked like a man who'd just heard about a death in the family.

The jurors filed out of the room. Nealy stood next to a cluster of people across the bar, all of them shooting rapid fire statements at each other. The D.A.'s office would be in chaos right now.

Sikes exited through the doors at the end of the courtroom.

Regan backed into her chambers and closed the door.

She had a bad feeling about Sikes. Something was wrong with him.

She skipped checking her regular phone — the opposing counsels would be in the room in a few minutes — and went straight to her secure phone.

The secure phone had a blank text message on it.

She dialed Alex's number. It rang about a dozen times, no answer.

She hung up.

Jake's number was on her mind. She tried to put the phone away, but it made her throat tighten.

She dialed his number. It was going to hurt even worse to hear the disconnected number message...

"Hello?"

Chapter 51 - Begun his move

The room was fifteen dress shoes by eight dress shoes.

It had cement walls, an electrical outlet for a washer and dryer, and a drain in the floor.

Lifting out the ceiling tiles one by one revealed nothing more interesting than solid flooring, water pipes, and an air conditioning duct.

The bed was an extra-long twin with a thin mattress, pink flannel sheets, and a matching pink plaid coverlet — the kind of blanket set you'd send off with your daughter to college.

Wondering what the bed was doing down here was frankly making him sick.

The light switch worked.

A covered plastic bucket under the bed told him his captors were thoughtful but not the smartest uniforms standing in line.

The water and vent hookups had been removed. He was going to have to be reasonably polite if he wanted water.

He paced until the rush of adrenaline left his body. It was okay. He knew where to get more if he needed it.

He didn't spot any cameras or microphones. As far as his captors were concerned, Jake was now neutralized — taken so far out of the picture that it didn't matter what he did or said, as long as he remained healthy enough to threaten Regan with.

He stayed alert until he felt sleep calling him, and then he lay down on the bed and let himself fall into the light sleep that he'd learned all the way back in boot camp.

He didn't dream. He waited.

The next morning, they brought him a clean bucket, this time with hot soapy water and a washcloth, along with two rolls of gauze for his nose. Two of the men in suits guarded the door while a third brought in the clean bucket and took the dirty one away.

Jake faced the wall with his hands pressed against the cement.

He had to give Regan time.

First, they had to threaten her. Then she would have to think about it for a while.

Either she'd come up blank, or she'd see where he was going with this. She was going to be angry either way.

If she came up blank, she'd call Alex first, then maybe Gary — or her father.

Her father would see where he was going with this.

Alex might too. He was usually a couple of mouse clicks ahead of Jake. He probably wouldn't tell Regan though. If Jake hadn't told her what was going on, then Alex wasn't going to get in the middle of it.

Gary. Who knew with Gary?

The suits finished up with the bucket exchanges. The one with the busted nose was not in attendance, but the other three were the same.

He let them go.

The next time they came back, he was hungry and thirsty, and eyeing the bucket of now cold, somewhat bloody water he'd washed in. Wads of gauze floated on top.

They brought food — a bowl of Chinese takeout and a soda.

This time, the guy with the broken nose was with them. His nostrils flared around the gauze packed in them as he picked up the bucket and put the lid on.

"Your girlfriend must not love you," he said, sneering around the tape on his nose.

Jake didn't answer. He was watching the other two guys. This time, it was the tall one from the driver's seat who was out.

"She doesn't have much time to make a move. And if she doesn't, it's *crrrrick!*" The guy drew his thumb across his throat. It was really quite impressive. "You better hope she changes her mind."

One of the others cleared his throat. The one with the broken nose backed out of the room while the other two covered him. Then the door was closed, chained, and locked.

Another period of waiting.

After giving himself long enough to get truly bored, and then another half hour after that, Jake spent some time teasing the door open one hair at a time, to see how tightly the chain had been attached.

It was sloppy. Even with the door only slightly cracked open, he could see that he had enough slack to put his arm out of the door all the way up to the elbow at least. Plenty of room.

If he hadn't changed his shoes, he would be on easy street. Several helpful items had been glued between the boots and the soles.

It wasn't like he was completely helpless, though.

A single guard sat outside Jake's room, reading a magazine by the light of a lamp on a table.

He looked vaguely Middle Eastern, olive skin, and a prominent nose. He might have been Italian with overgrown locks. He shifted uncomfortably on his folding chair.

A slight whiff of spice came from the corridor. The sounds from above were muffled by the thick floor, but Jake thought he might have heard the sound of someone banging a wooden spoon against a metal pan — as if he were being held below a restaurant.

It was like the beauty shop all over again — a random storefront being used for illegal activities, taken over by the bad guys on what must have been short notice.

Like an online B&B service for criminal activity.

The guard by the door was probably just one of the people who worked at the restaurant, picking up some extra cash.

On the table beside him, Jake saw something metallic and black. Not a gun. A walkie talkie.

The bad guys didn't seem like professionals. Not just the guard by the door, but all of them.

They gave him too many opportunities to attack. They didn't anticipate Jake being a real bastard. They acted like they got their experience from acting school.

Even rookie cops knew better than to leave a guy his *shoes* when you were locking him up.

It hit him — they might not even *be* the bad guys. They might just have been hired from somewhere.

He grimaced.

In a couple of hours, they were going to come at him with a cell phone or a video camera and either beat the crap out of him or tape him being tortured — something melodramatic to send to Regan to convince her to cooperate.

His plan had been to wait until that moment to turn the tables. He'd keep one of them conscious enough to answer questions.

Hopefully he'd be able to get at least the of name of someone out of these guys. With luck, he might be able to find out what their connection to the Gibbons case was.

But if the suits were just another layer of hired help...

It was no good worrying about it beforehand. Either he would find out something or he wouldn't. If they were nothing but hired help, he'd at least be able to get the way they'd been hired out of them.

And then?

Easy come, easy go.

Jake settled back on the bed and ran through scenarios. A question stuck in his mind if the place was a restaurant, why had they brought him takeout?

***

They came for him earlier than he was expecting.

He had a few seconds to snap himself fully awake as the chain rattled and the round padlock was opened, and then the door slammed open.

Two of the suits entered, their handguns held stiffly in front of them, elbows locked.

Whoever had taught them trigger discipline should have been shot. They both had their fingers inside the trigger guard.

The third guy who entered, however, wasn't one of the other two.

Instead, he was a tall, hawk nosed older gentleman in a suit that looked like it cost thousands of dollars.

It was so classy that Jake couldn't tell how classy it was.

Jake sat up. The tall man entered, glancing around the room. His glance took in the bucket they'd left him, the ceiling tiles, the electrical outlet, the bed that wasn't bolted to the floor, and the fact that Jake wasn't handcuffed to it.

He looked into Jake's eyes. For a second the guy looked familiar.

Maybe it was just the sense they were the only two people in the room who knew how bad the setup was. Maybe it was something military in the guy's stance. He was definitely an alpha male.

Jake rose from the bed.

The guy came up close, so close there wasn't more than an inch or two between them.

"You did this," he said.

"Did what?" Jake asked.

The guy swung a backhand directly at Jake's cheek without moving his enormous green eyes away from Jake's.

It wasn't a gentle love tap, either.

Jake waited for a follow-up. When it didn't come, he rubbed his jaw and cheek with his hand.

"Don't insult me," the guy said. "Your games are over. They were always too thin to succeed. At first they were amusing, but now they must come to a stop."

He should *know* this guy.

No rings on either hand, no telltale white skin on his fingers. No watch. Ears never pierced. Eyes normally dilated. Hair gray and thinning, neatly trimmed and brushed back from a sharp widow's peak. Long, thin chin. High cheekbones. His Caucasian skin that had seen the far side of 60.

He should recognize the guy from somewhere: the newspaper; some king of high finance; something.

"You did this," the guy repeated. "Don't bother to deny it. You went behind Regan's back and arranged the whole thing. It was unconscionable."

Jake still didn't have a clue what was going on, but it must have been pretty bad if it bothered *this* guy.

"Well?" the man said.

"You asked for it," Jake said. It seemed like a reasonable statement to be making if he had the slightest idea of what was going on.

"Hah!"

It was like standing in front of Sherlock Holmes. The only reason the guy hadn't figured out why Jake had done what he had done was because he hadn't done it.

He still had no idea what was going on, but it didn't really matter.

Whatever had happened had brought this guy here, within Jake's reach.

Clearly he was some kind of boss.

"There's one thing I don't understand," the guy said.

"Yeah?"

"Why put Regan in danger?"

The guy answered his own question. His eyes widened. Jake could have sworn he mouthed a single word: *Checkmate.*

Jake still had no idea what was going on, but it didn't matter.

The guy took a step backward, but it was already too late — Jake had begun his move.

Chapter 52 - The wall disappeared

"Regan," the digitized voice on the phone said, the same one as it had always been.

She glanced around the chambers. The wide framed paintings and photographs of the pictures of the judges along the walls watched her with bland, expressionless eyes, judging her.

"Who is this? Jake?"

"A friend," the voice said.

She shook her head. If that was supposed to be a hint, she wasn't getting it.

"Mr. Westley is under your enemy's control," the voice said. "If you would like to see him again..."

Regan held the phone at arm's length. She felt like taking the thing and throwing it against the wall.

Not again. Not another threat from yet another direction. "Whatever you want, forget it," she breathed into the phone. "I cannot do this."

"I *am* trying to warn you," the voice said. Even though it was digitized, it still managed to sound puzzled.

"I don't care," Regan said. "Do whatever you have to do. I'm not cooperating. Go to hell."

The phone stayed silent so long she almost thought it had gone dead. She moved her thumb over the disconnect button. The voice cleared its throat. With the distortion, it sounded like a miniature thunderclap. She put the phone back up to her ear.

"Regan, Nick Sikes is wearing a bomb. Get out... now."

"What about Jake?" she asked.

"Get out," the voice said.

"What about *Jake*?"

"Sikes is about to knock on the door. Get out now. I'll call you back later."

"Tell me, or I'll stay right here."

"You should have played checkers instead of chess," the voice said. The phone went dead.

The door to the corridor rattled; during trials she left it locked. The bailiff had keys. "Judge St. Clair?"

She stuffed the phone through her robes and into the pocket of her dress slacks underneath. Stepping back into the courtroom, she caught the eye of the bailiff.

A fist knocked on the door of the chambers — too hard.

"Judge St. Clair? Are you there?"

"Just a moment please," she said. "Is that you Mr. Sikes?"

"Yes."

She leaned further out the door and waved frantically to the bailiff again. The man glanced around the room, taking it in all at once. His eye lingered at the defense table.

The two defendants, dressed in street clothes but with their hands handcuffed behind them, chatted with each other without apparent concern. For a second they looked like a pair of kids, waiting for their parent to come and punish them. A second guard watched over them, as well as making sure they didn't swipe their lawyer's briefcase.

The bailiff hitched up his pants by his belt and started walking slowly toward her. She wondered if it would be faster to sprint across the courtroom and push the man.

The knocking at the door had become a pounding. "Judge St. Clair? Please let me in. I have something important to say."

Another voice spoke.

"No, I'm fine," Sikes said, his voice shaking. Clearly it wasn't true.

The bailiff finally made it up behind the bench and through the door of the chambers. "Yes, your Honor?"

She touched a finger to her lips. "I just received a phone call stating that Mr. Sikes is wearing a bomb."

The bailiff blinked and frowned.

It suddenly occurred to her how Nick was dressed. He was wearing a suit, just a normal suit. He was such a slight man. Not a bulge on him.

"Judge St. Clair!" Nick Sikes shouted from the hallway. "Dear God, open the door before it's too late!"

The world seemed to stop. "The briefcase," she said. "On the —"

The bailiff vanished out the door to the courtroom. *Now* he could move.

Regan followed him. The courtroom was almost empty. The jury hadn't come back yet.

Only a few people remained: several on the other side of the bar; the last witness, Edna, sitting stupidly on the witness stand looking confused; the defendants; and the guard.

Regan hissed through her teeth. Her habit against swearing in the courtroom was too strong to fight, even now.

The bastards were trying to murder the defendants — so much for innocent until proven guilty.

The two defendants broke off talking to each other as the bailiff charged the defense table.

The guard took a step toward the table. Fortunately, she was too late.

The bailiff grabbed the briefcase, grunting as he swung it off the table. It was heavy.

The room was sealed, windowless, safe from outside influences and difficult to evacuate.

"Put it in the chambers," she said.

The bailiff turned around and ran back toward the bench. The door to the chambers was open.

"Everyone get out!" Regan screamed. "Clear the courtroom!"

A shout went up.

Regan ran over to the witness stand and pulled on Edna's wrist, almost lifting her off the chair.

"What are you doing?" Edna shrieked, pulling backward against her seat. There wasn't time. Regan grabbed the woman in a hug and swung her bodily out of her seat.

The door to the chambers slammed with, thank God, the bailiff on their side of the door. He ran behind the bench and crouched down.

Regan pulled the woman onto the floor and bent over her. Those *bastards* — they didn't care whether anyone was innocent or guilty. They didn't even care whether they killed the innocent, in pursuit of the guilty.

The wall of the courtroom disappeared.

Chapter 53 - If not you, then...

Jake's shoulder slammed into the guy's solar plexus and carried him toward the center of the room. They went down near the drain in the center of the floor.

The guy's body at over 60 years was still as hard as a rock. He flipped Jake off him with one hip and rolled free.

Jake bounced to his feet and twisted one of the handguns away from the goons guarding the door.

"Hey!"

Jake slammed the butt of the gun against the other goon's temple. One fewer conscious goon in the room just couldn't be a bad thing.

The old guy chopped him across the back of his neck with something hard. Jake groaned and went down on one knee. His skull throbbed. His eyes bulged, and he could barely see.

Rather than let the guy knock him out, Jake leaned forward and slammed a foot backward blindly. He connected with something that made the guy curse.

Great, now all he had to do was whirl around, grab the weapon out of the old guy's hands, and beat him to death with it — while he felt like simultaneously puking and passing out.

He turned around on his hands and knees. Dizziness made it hard to tell when he was supposed to stop. Jake grabbed the smeary dark shape in front of him and pulled downward. The man dropped to the floor with a yell.

Jake had a gun a second ago, but now it was gone. Too bad, he'd just have to do without.

A kick hit him from behind and almost knocked him on his face. Oh, yeah. He'd left one of the goons behind him.

He kicked out again, sweeping the goon's feet from under him. He heard a smack against the floor and kicked toward that. He was rewarded by a melon like thud.

The old guy was crawling away from him, heading for a red splotch on the floor — the slop bucket. Uh-huh. Just what Jake needed — a face full of *that*.

Jake reached forward and grabbed the first thing he touched - the guy's legs.

The old man twisted and flipped over on his back. One blob reached out for a blob on the floor, then lifted and swung it.

Jake dodged. Metal rang against cement.

He grabbed the swinging shape and twisted it out of the man's hands — a cane.

He held the cane above his head ready to swing.

His eyes ran like waterworks, and his neck felt like someone had set a blow torch to it.

"Move and I'll smash your head in." He could barely tell where the old man's head was among the swimming shapes in front of him.

The old man made a jerking motion. Jake slammed the cane down on what he hoped was a hand or an arm.

Metal went skittering.

The old guy must have found the goon's dropped gun.

"Did you miss the part where I told you not to move?" Jake asked.

"It was a trap," the man said coldly. "There was no attack on Regan. You knew I would be forced to react if she were truly in danger. It was merely a trap."

"Correct," Jake said.

The old guy was going to kick himself when he found out Jake had no clue what was going on and in fact could barely see at all.

"How?" the man asked coldly. "How did you find out?"

Jake raised his eyebrows. "It wasn't too hard," he said, "Regan, her father, chess, and you."

The words had come out of his mouth before he realized he wasn't just pulling nonsense out of thin air. In the back of his head, he'd been putting an idea together — a guess. Not a bad one either.

"Someone in or near the group had to be a traitor," he said, "someone who knew what we were doing before we started doing it, and more than one person, probably."

"Probably," the old man said bitterly. "For all the good it did."

Jake's eyes were starting to clear. The blobs in front of him were starting to resolve into the legs, arms, and head of a pissed off looking old guy in an expensive suit.

"The way you kept using kid gloves on Regan. That beating could have been a lot worse. The easy conclusion was you wanted to have a judge in your pocket." Jake went out on another limb. "It must have been handy."

"It was — for a while."

Aha. Judge St. Clair the Elder. It *had* been the same group. The pieces started to fall into place. "And then you pushed him too far, didn't you?"

The old man sniffed, lifting the blunt square of his chin. "He was weak."

"The business aspect of the relationship went sour, but you didn't want to lose out on the friendship so you covered your tracks."

"The Organization demanded it. If he had known, they would have lost more than a judge."

"Yeah," Jake said. "They would have lost you."

"Oh, I could have been replaced," the old man said bitterly. "I've always known just how much and how little I mean to the Organization. They've never trusted me. How could they? The judge who betrayed them was my best friend."

"And still is." Jake allowed himself to close his eyes for a moment and rolled them behind his eyelids. When he opened them, it was all pretty clear.

Regan had mentioned the man only a couple of times, but Jake remembered him — her almost uncle. The one who had put her through college and who had given her the money Jane Hendricks was in the habit of playing with — Paul Travers.

He'd looked familiar because he was the executive the city had hired to run the sewage system in Brooklyn.

Oh, he lived in Manhattan in a big penthouse, but his specialty was dealing with the human waste flowing through Brooklyn. Apparently he'd taken his mandate from the city further and more literally than anyone had ever intended.

"You used the plant to move drugs," Jake said. "You used employees to do the local deliveries."

"Angela Ligotti was a meaningless piece of trash."

"She had enough meaning to have a grandmother who loved her."

"That reflects more upon the grandmother than the granddaughter."

Jake wasn't willing to argue the point. "What I want to know is why Andrew Gibbons? What did he ever do to you?"

"He informed us that he was done with his duties to the Organization. It would have been admirable if he hadn't taken the first opportunity afterward to try to take the information he had about us to the police, not that they would have done anything about It — not at *that* station.

"Sending him to prison was a mercy. It taught him a lesson in what was important — his family. Family is always important."

"Then why have *Regan* beaten?"

"She also needed to learn a lesson."

Jake shook his head. Jesus, for a smart old guy, the man was a real idiot if he thought that Regan was the kind of woman who could be taught to behave by a fist in the face and boot to the ribs.

"What did you think you were going to teach her — humility?"

The old man smiled. "An interesting question," he said, "from someone who just had her bombed in her own courtroom."

Jake flinched.

The old man's eyes widened.

"You didn't know, did you?"

Jake shook his head.

"You *pumped* me."

"A little."

"If not you, then —"

Chapter 54 - Don't let him in

Daylight shone into her face. Not a good sign. She tried to open her eyes; the lids felt glued together. Trying to sit up got her nowhere. At least she could move her arms. Otherwise, she might have convinced herself she was dead, and this was one last slip of consciousness before she moved on.

She gasped for breath as she came fully awake and detected the scent of Pine cleaner, rubbing alcohol, and latex gloves. She was in another hospital.

Something pressed her arms back down to her chest.

"Nnn," she said.

Fortunately, she had more than a little experience being terrified, injured and in a hospital lately, and she didn't panic.

A hand took hers. She knew it; it was just slightly larger than hers, and the skin was old but smooth.

"Da-ee," she mumbled. Her lips were swollen.

"I'm right here, Regan," he said.

"Hhhhap?"

"A bomb went off in the courtroom."

"Nnn," she said disgustedly. *Not again.*

"Jaaay?" she asked.

Her father's hand squeezed hers. "He's disappeared," her father said. "Alex called me."

"Mmm."

"He said to tell you there was no news."

"Mmm." She smacked her lips, and her father put a straw to them. She sucked at it thirstily. It felt as though the water were being run directly to her eyes. She blinked them open and let the tears run down her cheeks. The room was too bright. They must have given her the good drugs.

She couldn't remember the bailiff's name. She'd worked with him for a year now, and...

"Bob?" she asked.

Her father hesitated long enough she knew the answer.

"Regan..."

She cut him off with an impatient slice of her hand. The IV taped to the back of it stung.

"Ed-d-d," she said. Apparently the name *Edna* was beyond her.

"Everyone else made it," her father said. "Edna Connor, the witness that you pulled out of the witness box, is in Intensive Care."

She nodded. Ah, yes. The grinding in her neck had come back.

She clasped her father's hand harder. "Glaa," she said. *I'm glad you're here.*

"I'm glad too," he said. "Now stay in that bed or I'll strangle you."

"Haaa."

A phone rang. Her father turned around in his chair, then let go of her hand. His shadow moved away from the bed, then drifted ghostlike around the too bright room.

The phone stopped ringing. A few seconds later it started up again.

"Damn thing," her father said.

A door opened, and the phone got louder. Plastic rustled.

"It's in your pants pocket." He grunted. "It's an old one, all right. Not sure how *that* survived."

It was the secure phone.

The phone beeped as he pressed the answer button. "Hello?"

Her father held the flip phone to his ear, frowning at her as if he were about to burst into a cranky old man rant telling the caller to get off his lawn. "Who is this?"

Regan held out a hand. "Daddy please, it's for me."

Her father handed the phone over, and she pressed it against her ear. The hospital room seemed suddenly colder. She pulled the blankets up to her chin.

"Regan," the digitized voice said. "It's me."

The shivering got worse.

She was down to her last two choices for the voice at the other end of the line.

It had to be either Gary or Alex.

The voice at the other end of the line cleared his throat.

"Alex," she said.

"I'd turn off the modulation software, but I'd have to restart the phone to do it."

"It's all right."

"I wanted to tell you something. It's about the person behind the bomber. I've been working for him."

Regan swallowed. The sound seemed to echo back to her from the phone.

"I do a lot of work," Alex said, "for various people and agencies. I had to pick up freelance jobs again after we went underground. I had to keep up appearances, you know like you said.

"This job ... I had a bad feeling about it. But there was no logical reason to turn it down. So I didn't."

Her father wandered across the room, back to his seat by the window. With the sun at his back, she couldn't see his expression. Her eyes were still goofy from being knocked around so much.

"Okay," she said, "so far, so good – go on."

"It was mostly moving data around, secret communications, that kind of stuff. But I was suspicious about it so I did some research."

"And?"

"And it took a while, which was odd because even undercover FBI agents weren't buried as deep as this guy."

"Who is it?"

"You're not going to like it," Alex said.

A knock sounded on the door.

A nurse's aide looked in. "You have a visitor," she said.

"Who is it?"

"He said, 'Tell her it's Gary Titschmarsh and a friend.'"

"Gary?" she said.

Alex heard her and said, "Don't let him in."

Chapter 55 - Who is he?

Jake didn't have time to take Travers to the cops or secure him in the small cement basement room. It would only take five minutes, and Travers would have been on his tail anyway, so he brought the man with him, cane and all.

The guard outside the door had wisely disappeared. In other good news, the pockets of the first goon Jake had knocked out contained Jake's car keys as well as his .45.

Jake climbed the stairs up to the main floor and slowly opened the door.

It was a spice shop, hundreds of types of spices in glass jars all around the small storefront. The smell was enough to make Jake gag. The place was empty. The sign on the door said that the shop was closed due to 'family business.'

He waved Travers to follow him up, tucked the pistol in his pocket, and let them out the back of the building.

Travers led Jake to his car, limping and leaning heavily on the cane. Fortunately, it wasn't far. From there he'd only have to walk far enough to get a cab.

"Thanks," Jake said. "Look, as soon as I deal with whatever is happening with Regan, we're coming after you — both of us. But that doesn't mean you can't have a head start."

Travers gave Jake a sour look. He leaned against the Corolla and set his cane aside. He steepled his fingers together, breathing onto his fingertips like a real old-school type of. "Any head start I have will be invested in making sure my niece is safe."

"It's your prison sentence," Jake said. "Get in."

"As you say," Travers said.

They got in.

After a few minutes, Jake tossed his phone into Travers's lap. The traffic was thick enough that he had to keep both hands on the wheel.

"Call this number," he said and rattled off Alex's number.

"Busy," Travers said.

He gave the man Regan's number.

Also busy.

He started reciting old Judge St. Clair's number, but Travers cut him off. "That one I know."

After a pause, the phone beeped.

Travers said, "Pertinax, it is I, Pavo — Regan's in grave danger." He licked his lips and continued, "And so are you. The Organization has decided that you are no longer to be trusted. I was ordered to indoctrinate your daughter and then decommission you. You know what I mean."

Jake kept his eyes on the road. The traffic had started to open up, and he zipped the Corolla through gaps in the traffic like a kid playing a video game.

Travers put one hand on the dashboard as he continued leaving his message. "I allowed myself to be distracted by the bombing at the courthouse. I had Mr. Westley trapped in a safe house. I rushed to confront him, but he knew nothing of the attack. Therefore, he was not behind it.

"I have an associate, a less than trustworthy one, who is my subordinate. I fear he has come to do what I cannot and therefore replace me. I'm afraid that he is quite willing to kill Regan in order to discredit me. He has already tried once in the courtroom.

"I believe he will seek to rectify his failure. He will be wearing a hat and a long coat, and will be impeccably dressed. He will come bearing gifts and speaking soft words. Kill him on sight.

"Whatever happens, send Regan my love. Pavo out."

Travers took the phone away from his ear, and stared at it for a moment before switching it off. "I should have left him the number I suppose."

"I think he gets the point. His daughter's in danger, and we're on the way."

"Very well."

They crossed the bridge, and traffic slowed to a crawl again.

"Pertinax?" Jake inquired.

"Latin for Stubbornness," Travers said. "I'm Pavo, which is Fear. We all have names."

"Who else?"

"Fiducioso," Travers said. "Faithfulness. An irony if there ever was one."

"Who is he?"

Travers told him, and Jake swerved out onto the shoulder of the parkway and started honking his horn.

Chapter 56 - But her mind was racing

The door of the hospital room swung open. From behind the door, Gary said, "Knock-knock. Who's awake and ready for visitors?"

His voice was thick with artificial cheer.

She couldn't believe it. Not a traitor. Not Gary.

He took one step past the door and stopped.

He was wearing a sharp looking hat and a black trench coat over a suit and had a bouquet of assorted brightly colored flowers in one arm, the kind that looked garish in real life but look almost elegant in a black and white photo after the fact. A contemptuous sneer twisted his lips.

"Hi Gary," she said, lowering the phone into the bedcovers beside her. On the other end, Alex had gone completely silent.

"Mmm-hmmm," he said. "Now tell me to come in." He waggled his eyebrows at her.

"Come in," she said helplessly.

Gary pushed into the room, carrying the flowers over to a side table where he appropriated a squat water jug as a vase.

Behind him came a second person — someone who looked almost exactly like Gary, except he was missing Gary's goatee. He was somehow dressed even more tastefully than Gary.

One hand was in his pocket, next to a small bulge.

"My brother," Gary said, "Lawrence."

"Not Larry?" Regan said.

"Do *not* call him Larry. And these flowers are from me, not him."

Lawrence took off his hat. "Good afternoon, madam," he said. "It is a pleasure to finally make your acquaintance. Believe me, I've been following your career with interest."

Gary, who had gone to the sink to fill the vase with water, hunched his shoulders at the sound of his brother's voice.

"Good afternoon," she said.

Lawrence walked past the end of the bed to her father's chair and extended a hand. "And the Honorable St. Clair," he said. "I've heard so many good things about you."

"Bad things too, I'm sure."

"Nothing worse than you have a slight case of stubbornness."

"That's true," her father said. "And you are?"

"The ever faithful brother of Gary Titschmarsh, Lawrence del Rey, at your service." He made a slight, almost mocking bow.

"My brother was visiting a mutual friend of ours and happened to mention your name," Gary said. "When he heard that you were in the hospital, he decided to come with me to see you."

"Oh? Which friend?"

"Alex Carr," Gary said.

"Oh?" Why hadn't he *said*? She wanted to strangle him.

"A delightful fellow," Lawrence said, "entirely noble."

Her father frowned and mouthed the word *noble* to himself. "Patrician," he said. "Pa... yes, I see. The Organization is still up to its old tricks."

The exchange went over Regan's head.

Still with a pleasant smile on his face, Lawrence said, "Speaking of the Organization, there were certain conditions to your retirement I was sent to remind you of, or have you forgotten?"

"I haven't forgotten."

"That's just as well. I'm not especially fond of reminding people of their obligations — or the consequences of not meeting them."

Regan licked her lips. She had an IV in her hand, and the bed rails were up. If Lawrence was a threat, she wasn't going to be able to do much about it — security might, though. She reached her hand up to scratch her nose and then pressed the worn call button built into the side of the bed.

A discreet light appeared and then turned off again.

"I hope you don't think that the only person I have on staff with IT skills is your friend Alex," Lawrence said, "Miss St. Clair."

She glanced at her phone. The call had been cut off as well.

Gary had moved a step closer to his brother, holding the plastic water pitcher with the flowers as if to carry them closer to the window.

"Don't worry," Lawrence said. "We won't be interrupted. Your detective and the so called head of my division are distracting each other at the moment. The hospital staff has been pulled away on other business, and communications in and out of the room are being rerouted elsewhere. It's important we have our little talk. There are, you see, a few different ways this can go."

Her father's face turned bright red. "You fool. You have no idea what you're doing."

"Daddy," Regan said.

"Don't interrupt me."

Either her father was losing his temper or trying to keep Lawrence's attention on him and away from her — or Gary.

Either way, she didn't like it.

"Daddy. Let me handle this. Please."

"You don't know the kind of games these people play."

"I do, Daddy. They treat people like chess pieces."

Lawrence gave a little bow. "I'm sure my superior would try to tell you that all of this is for the greater good. I just like to play chess."

"Pavo," her father said. "You work for Pavo."

"Indeed."

Her father's eyes softened. He turned his head to the side. If Regan hadn't known better, she would have thought he was trying to hold back tears.

"Talk to Regan a second," her father said. "I need a moment."

Lawrence turned on his heels toward her.

Hell. Now his side was turned toward Gary, not his back.

And Gary had come close — very close — to being able to take a swing at the back of his brother's head.

"Your father has, despite his agreement to do otherwise, knowingly re-involved himself in the business of our Organization. Moreover, he has allowed you to become involved without warning you of the danger."

"Understandable," Regan said, keeping her eyes away from Gary who was just past arm's length away now. "That would have involved talking to me instead of hiding yet another layer of lies."

"Yes, it is understandable but entirely disagreeable to the Organization. It is my sad duty to inform you and your father there will be repercussions to your father's choices."

"What kind of repercussions?"

Lawrence turned around to face his brother, pulling a small, old fashioned pistol out of his pocket

Gary had just started to raise his hands, the pitcher of water almost in front of his face.

Lawrence waved the pistol.

"Don't you think you should put that on the table, over there?"

Gary lowered the pitcher and brought it to the small table beside Regan.

The flowers wobbled.

"Now step over here, beside the elder Judge St. Clair. I hate having you running around behind me. It feels as though someone is reading over my shoulder — or getting ready to stab me in the back."

Gary hesitated. Lawrence gave a jerk of his chin.

When Gary was balanced on the windowsill next to her father, Lawrence said, "The agreement was if your father ever involved himself in the business of the Organization again, he would be destroyed."

"You mean killed."

"That is one of the options. The other is to have his reputation as a judge discredited. Unlike Mr. Westley's efforts with regards to Detective Marando, this does not involve planting false evidence."

Her father still had his head turned away from her.

She wanted to be angry at him for lying to her yet again; for not being the man she thought he was. And yet her heart went out to him.

He must have been driven out of Brooklyn because he refused to do what these people wanted. It had probably started innocently — a few favors here and there and then grown until they had broken her mother's arm and threatened his child. They had probably done worse too, and he just wasn't telling her.

Now it was happening all over again — the bomb in the courtroom. Poor Nick Sikes, he must belong to them too.

"There is," Lawrence said, "a third option."

"And just what would that be?" Regan asked.

"You can take your father's place in the Organization."

She frowned at him. "So you can destroy my reputation instead? So I can be killed?"

"We're not that crude, most of the time," Lawrence said. "It's only when the pieces move against the rules that we have to treat them so roughly."

Gary snorted.

"I take it that you aren't going to provide me with a written contract to review," Regan said.

"I've already had Gary review it," Lawrence said dryly, "years ago."

Gary looked at her with a sick expression on his face. "I'm no lawyer, but I advise against signing – no real benefit."

"Oh, I wouldn't say that," Lawrence said. "I'd say it has made Miss St. Claire the woman she is today, wouldn't you? She is wealthy, well educated, and well placed."

Regan's mouth opened. No sound came out.

If she was wealthy, well educated, and well placed as a judge, it was because of two men — her father and her "Uncle" Paul Travers, the razor sharp man who had taught her how to play chess, and who now ran the water treatment plant in Brooklyn, among other things. She hadn't seen him since Christmas.

If her father had been involved in the Organization, then so had Uncle Paul.

As the saying went, they were thick as thieves and had been since college.

"Who are you people?" she asked. "You're everywhere. You're everyone I know practically. You have your fingers in everything."

Lawrence gave a short informal bow.

"Some of us like to think we're making the world a better place. Others of us just like the game."

"And the rest of us were bullied, blackmailed, or bribed," Gary said.

Regan's heart sank. What could she do? She was surrounded by these people — her father, Gary, Lawrence, just to name the ones in the *room*. For all she knew the nurse could be one too, the janitor, the doctor, and who knew who else! What could she *do*? Nothing. Most of the people involved in this didn't even *want* to be. Some probably didn't even know.

"Regan," her father said. "Don't agree to anything. The worries were never worth the advantages. And that was even after I set aside any sense of justice. I've made my bed. I'll lie in it."

"Is Jane in this too?" she asked.

"No," Gary said.

"Not yet," Lawrence added. "We have a nice little cell forming up here. You, Jake, Gary, Alex, Jane — imagine what we could accomplish with a group like that."

She shuddered — a great deal. They could control and manipulate a great deal. If Jake were here, he'd knock the guy out. But that wouldn't solve anything either.

She couldn't see any way out but to agree to what Lawrence and the Organization wanted. But wasn't that what the Organization wanted her to see? Unified, indivisible, monolithic, powerful, agile, wise, mysterious, untraceable, invisible...

"Who was it," she said, "who tried to set up the meeting with me at the defunct coffee shop?"

Gary looked down.

"I did," Lawrence said.

"You?"

"I was ordered to allow you to punish yourself for not heeding our warning. If you had not been so consumed by curiosity, you would have been in no danger."

"It was a trap? The whole thing from beginning to end was a trap?"

"It was a trap."

She wanted to bare her teeth.

"And the bomb in the courtroom, were you trying to kill me or not?"

"Of course not. By then I had captured Alex and instructed him to contact you. If you hadn't been so stupid, you wouldn't have been hurt."

Since when is trying to save other people's lives being stupid?

"And the reason that Jamie Gibbons contacted me in the first place?"

She could still remember the white puffs of steam outside her window hanging in place. She could still remember the reason she was involved, even if it did seem naive and a million years ago.

It was because I was losing my passion for my job. Because I wasn't sure I was making a difference.

Lawrence shrugged. "We ensured your name was one of the ones recommended to her as possibly being interested in real justice."

"So I'm only involved in this because you arranged it. That's what you're saying. You set this whole thing up."

"More or less, yes."

His words built a cage around her. They cut off every avenue of escape. She kept waiting for him to say it: *checkmate.*

He didn't, though. He kept telling her all the ways he had put her in check. But he hadn't actually told her she now worked for the Organization. He held a threat over her head. But he was still giving her a choice. That meant somewhere, somehow, there was still a way out.

She licked her lips and said, "There isn't coffee in here somewhere, is there?"

But her mind was racing.

Chapter 57 - Now that's a checkmate

Jake hit the outskirts of White Plains beating the heel of his hand against the steering wheel and honking at every car in his path. He knew it was useless. Even racing straight to White Plains at 100 miles per hour, he still would be too late.

A white puff of steam hung over the town. He tried to keep himself from imagining it was Regan's last breath but had mixed success.

"If you hadn't locked me up in that goddamned basement," he told Travers.

"I didn't," Travers said. "It was Fiducioso that arranged it, naturally enough."

"Didn't you suspect him?"

"My suspicions of Fiducioso were so complex as to be meaningless."

"So he followed your orders, but you had no idea what he was up to."

"That is correct."

"And you can *work* like that?"

"It is important to allow one's subordinates a measure of independence. I, myself, rely a great deal on the gap between receiving an order and reporting on how successfully I have implemented it."

"I can see that," Jake muttered.

"But for such an arrangement to endure requires a certain measure of trust, and Fiducioso and I never achieved that."

***

Still holding the dark gray old fashioned pistol, Lawrence said, "I'm afraid that I cannot allow anyone in or out of the room until you have made up your mind — even for coffee."

Of course not — he wanted to keep the pressure on her. He didn't want to give her time to think.

"And if I say I can't make a decision?"

"Then I shall leave it up to your father. Whether or not he is alive in a week will indicate his preference."

"Then I'll cooperate," she said.

Gary blew air out of his cheeks and rubbed his hand across his face.

Her father slumped forward, looking finally like an old man instead of a hero who just happened to have a head of leonine white hair.

She focused on Lawrence's face until the rest of the room seemed to gray out.

"You'll join the organization?" he asked.

"Promises made under duress aren't binding, but I'll cooperate to keep you from destroying my father. *If...*"

Lawrence closed his eyes for a moment and inhaled as if the smell of victory were indeed sweet.

She didn't disturb him.

Gary raised his eyebrows at her. She shook her head.

"That is acceptable."

"I said *if*," Regan said. "There's a condition. Andy Gibbons goes free."

"That's not how duress works," Lawrence said. "I make the threat. You acquiesce, or I carry out the threat. We do not negotiate."

"Nevertheless, Andy's been punished long enough for something he didn't do. Whatever he *did* do to make you people angry, he's paid for it. His sons need him. Or isn't that something you think is important — family?"

She hit a tender spot, she knew. Not that Lawrence gave her any reaction. He was too polished and smooth for that, but Gary winced.

In order to win this game, she had to reverse their positions — put Gary's bastard of a brother in checkmate. She'd deal with Uncle Paul later.

"You don't need to expose the real murderer. You just need to let Andy go," Regan added.

Lawrence hesitated.

He was caught between telling her whatever it would take to get her to agree to join them — and being unable to clear the matter with his superiors because communications had been cut off...and because he would have to go over Uncle Paul's head to do it.

Victory was a phone call away, and yet it was a phone call he would find impossible to explain to his superiors.

He covered it well. "Then we have a tentative arrangement."

"Excellent. As long as it's *tentative*, I'm free to stab you in the back, and contact Uncle Paul to tell him how you've betrayed him."

He grimaced and turned the pistol on her.

"I won't agree to anything else," Regan said, "and neither will my father."

"I won't?"

"He *won't*," Regan insisted.

"I won't."

"If you walk out of here without an agreement with me, then they'll want to know how you lost control over not only my father but me too."

The tip of the pistol began to jitter.

"You could blame it on Uncle Paul — if he were here — except that he would never risk my life, and his superiors would never believe he would. It could only be you, playing chess."

He blinked. The pistol began to shake harder.

"What happens if you lose the game?" she asked. "Are you the next piece that gets sacrificed to the greater good?"

***

Jake pushed past the nurse trying to block the hallway.

"You can't go in there!"

"I'll be damned if you're going to stop me."

Travers stopped at the nurse's station and picked up the phone. "It's dead."

"So is this Lawrence guy."

He grabbed the doorknob. It was locked.

He heard the click of a hammer being cocked.

***

The door jumped in its frame, making Regan jump. Jake bellowed on the other side of the door.

The metal door frame groaned and creaked.

Whatever Lawrence was going to do, he had about two seconds to do it.

He dropped his pistol back into his coat pocket, reached into the opposite pocket, and pulled out a cell phone.

"Unlock the door," he said.

The door opened and slammed against the wall, inches from the back of Lawrence's head.

Jake burst into the room.

In a second he had his gun leveled on Lawrence.

"Put your hands on your head."

Lawrence gave a long look at Regan, sizing her up one last time. Then he did so.

Gary leaned forward and took the pistol out of his brother's pocket and unloaded it, dropping the jingling bullets first into his palm, then reaching across Regan and dumping them into the pitcher full of flowers.

Uncle Paul walked into the room, far more sedately. He had a black eye, and his suit was dirty along one hip. He leaned heavily on a cane she had rarely seen him use before.

"Hello Regan," he said.

"Hello Uncle Paul."

"I'm glad to see you are well."

She blinked back a tear. Even after all this, she was glad to see him, too.

"Regan," Jake said. "Are you all right?"

She pointed at Lawrence. "No. This bastard had me bombed."

Jake edged past Lawrence, the two of them turning to keep facing each other as Jake moved from one side of the bed to the other.

Jake calmly handed the revolver to her father, who trained it on Lawrence with an iron precision.

Then Jake grabbed the front of Lawrence's coat, cocked a fist, and slammed Lawrence in the jaw.

Bone crunched.

Lawrence's hands flew up, and he started to fall back toward Uncle Paul.

Uncle Paul took a step to the side and let him fall.

Lawrence's head landed under the sink. The back of his head knocked against the side of the metal trash can, ringing it like a bell.

Then Jake had his arms around her, watching her face to make sure he wasn't hurting her, pulling her forward when she wrapped her arms around his neck, kissing her.

"Now that's a checkmate," her father said with a smile.

Chapter 58 - Yes

It might not have been Valentine's Day at *La Rouche*, but considering how slowly the wheels of justice might have turned, it wasn't that far past. Regan's heart was almost too full of satisfaction to keep it within her chest.

She'd rented the private room for the night and sent Jake and Alex over early to make sure the place wasn't bugged. It was, but only by the owner's security cameras. She had them take the cameras out for the night — she'd pay for the repairs later.

The room had sedate wallpaper, wall sconces made to look like old fashioned lamps, and wingback chairs upholstered in velvet. It was the kind of place that called for brandy snifters.

Jane dragged tables around for her until they had a large circle decorated with a white tablecloth and set for 15. They set the table with vases of get- well flowers until Regan made them move them to side tables. She wanted to be able to see everyone.

The original group (Regan, Jake, Jane, Gary, and Alex) met first the others, (the retired SEALs, her father, and Uncle Paul), and Jamie and the boys would be there in minutes.

As it turned out, having Jake punch Lawrence's lights out might not have fixed anything, but it had made her feel a thousand times better.

Uncle Paul said he'd kept a lid on things lest his superiors have him removed. And Lawrence's broken jaw and cracked skull would be enough of a reminder, for a while at least, to stop him from going behind his boss's back again – at least until he had enough material to replace him. They should be safe — for now.

The five of them stood just inside the double French doors. A server had just brought a cart full of ice and champagne bottles to them. Jake pulled out a bottle of champagne and opened it. The pop echoed around the room, and Regan and Jane cheered.

Jake filled the glasses and handed them out.

Gary had a pained look on his face and gnawed on a knuckle. Regan wanted to reach out to him — but the wound from finding out he was part of the Organization was still too raw. Things could be mended, but it would take time.

Jane, who had been less than shocked when everything had been explained to her, had an almost smug smile. Regan had come through her latest adventure without spending too much money, after all. And Jane had found out some things about how Uncle Paul had made his money that she had been curious about for years.

Alex clutched his champagne glass in one hand and twirled the end of his mustache with the other. He looked inscrutable. In the game between him and the FBI, she knew where she'd place her bets as to who would win — eventually.

As for Jake...

His eyes were also busy, sizing up the rest of the group. He was still suspicious of Gary, neutral toward Jane, and friendly — almost rueful — toward Alex.

And when he looked at her? She raised her glass to him as she saw the affection in his eyes. Bubbles rose in wavy lines through the golden liquid.

"To us," she said. "I won't say we've come through the fire unscathed. None of us is as pearly white as we were when we started this, except Jane, who has no morals other than 'don't get caught' and was more of a muddy gray in the first place."

Jane grinned.

"We still don't even know who committed the murder. But *our* man is exonerated, and he's coming home."

"To us," Jake said.

"To us." They all raised their glasses and drank.

Alex cleared his throat. "Ah ... actually, with regards to the murderer, I think I've found him. I can't prove it in court, but I think I know who he is."

They were all staring at him. His cheeks turned pink, all the way up to his hairline.

"His name is Ron Earl Taylor," Alex said. "I pulled an ID on him using a reflection of him off a beer bottle in one of the photographs."

Regan gaped at him.

"He works at the water treatment plant, a mid-level manager who's been there since 2002. He looks like Mr. Gibbons, that's all, and wears a red leather coat. I don't have any actual proof, but I think it's him."

"To Alex," Regan said.

"To Alex."

Jake refilled their glasses.

The door cracked open, and someone slipped in.

A big man, black, wearing a bomber jacket and a pair of khaki pants. No hat, no hiking boots.

Andy Gibbons.

He looked at the five of them.

Gary reached over and picked up another glass and handed it over to Jake who filled it from the bottle.

He gave it to Andy with a little salute. Regan cursed herself for a moment — she had no idea whether Andy drank or not.

He took the champagne glass and held it but didn't drink.

He looked like he wasn't sure if he was welcome.

Regan said, "To Andy."

"To Andy," they all raised their glasses and waited for him to join them.

Andy swallowed a couple of times. His hand clutched his champagne glass like he was about to crush it. "I haven't seen her yet," he said. "I'm so nervous, man — you know."

Regan didn't know. She'd never been in love before. She'd never been married before. She'd never let anyone down like that before and had to beg for forgiveness.

It was all still too new. She felt drunk — constantly drunk.

Jake said, "She still wants you. I talked to her once about it — she was trying to give me a hint about Regan, actually. My guess is that it'll be a long road for both of you, but she still wants you."

"I'll drink to that." Andy raised his glass and drained the whole thing.

They all followed suit.

"It's not that I don't appreciate being out of prison," Andy said, "but what about the Organization? You don't know what they can do to you."

"It's a long story," Regan said, "but the short version is the cell that used to control you is under our control now — mostly — for a while."

Andy shook his head. It wasn't easy for her to believe, either.

A server came to the door and peeked in. "You said you wanted to be notified when Mrs. Gibbons and her sons arrived."

"Oh, God," Andy said. "What am I going to do? What am I going to do?"

Jane pulled a chair out for him. "Sit here Andy. Don't worry. We have this."

She and Gary hustled him over to the chair and got him seated. The rest of them stood in front of him waiting.

They heard heels clicking on the floor and the scuff and squeak of sneakers before they saw them. Regan glanced back at Andy. He was grinning from ear to ear.

Jamie came around the corner with her two boys in tow. Both of them were at least as tall as she was, dressed in button-up plaid shirts and khakis. They looked grown up, but not too big for Jamie to handle though.

She wore a nice new teal blue dress with a V-neck. It looked good on her, and she walked as if she knew it. Her pride wouldn't stretch to a new purse though. Jamie looked them over. She knew they were up to something.

Regan said, "Come in Jamie."

The door was opened, but Jamie wasn't about to step over the threshold until she knew what was going on. "What is this news you wanted to celebrate?"

Her face was ready to burst into tears, pulled in half by hope and hurt.

Regan elbowed Jake in the side, and the two of them stepped aside.

"Dad!" Tyrone shouted. He pushed through the door and leaped into his father's arms as he stood up. Andy might weigh three times as much as his son, but he still stumbled backward against his chair as Tyrone hit him.

James hesitated at his mother's shoulder.

Jamie's face went blank for a second, and she shivered like she'd seen a ghost. Her hands opened, and her purse slid off her shoulder. James bent forward and caught it before it hit the floor.

She took a step forward into the room. Her chest was heaving, and her eyes filled with tears.

Andy let his son go.

Gary tapped on Tyrone's shoulder, pulling him to the side.

"Is it you? Is it really you?" Jamie asked.

You don't ask, Regan thought. *The answer's always no.*

Jake had appeared by Regan's side. He took her hand. His calluses rubbed against a hand that rarely did anything more strenuous than bang a gavel.

"It's me," Andy said, voice hoarse, "if you'll still have me."

The look on Jamie's face said *yes, a thousand times yes.*

Regan looked down at Jake's hand, holding hers, at their shoes standing next to each other, and she remembered the night before.

She could almost understand how Jamie felt now — almost.

Yes.

~ The End ~

Thank You

Thank you for taking the time to read my book. Please keep in touch with me at www.jcryanbooks.com and also sign up for special offers and pre-release notifications of upcoming books.

Please Review

If you enjoyed this story, please let others know by leaving an honest review on Amazon. Your review will help to inform others about this book and the series.
Thank you so much for your support, I appreciate it very much.

JC Ryan

Other books by JC Ryan

The Exonerated Series

https://www.amazon.com/gp/product/B01MQJEQ5R

Book 1 - Judgment Call
Amazon USA - http://amzn.com/B01EQ1P0UI
Amazon UK - http://amzn.co.uk/dp/B01EQ1P0UI

Book 2 - Damned if you do, Damned if you don't
Amazon USA - http://amzn.com/B01GGIJMA8
Amazon UK - http://amzn.co.uk/dp/B01GGIJMA8

Book 3 - The End Justifies the Means
Amazon USA - http://amzn.com/B01MRIS56Q
Amazon UK - http://amzn.co.uk/dp/B01MRIS56Q

Please visit my website and my Amazon author page to see my other books.
http://jcryanbooks.com

https://www.amazon.com/author/jcryan

The Rossler Foundation Mysteries Series

http://www.amazon.com/gp/product/B016PWGAKA/

Click the link below to see more details about each of the books.

http://www.amazon.com/gp/product/B016PWGAKA/

The Carter Devereux Series

http://www.amazon.com/gp/product/B01DPUGKH8/

Click the link below to see more details.

http://www.amazon.com/gp/product/B01DPUGKH8/

Made in the USA
Middletown, DE
06 February 2020